THE COLD HOME
WAY

ALSO BY JULIA KELLER

A Killing in the Hills

Bitter River

Summer of the Dead

Last Ragged Breath

Sorrow Road

Fast Falls the Night

Bone on Bone

THE COLD WAY HOME

JULIA KELLER

MINOTAUR BOOKS
NEW YORK

First Published in the United States by Minotaur Books, an imprint of St. Martin's Publishing Group

THE COLD WAY HOME. Copyright © 2019 by Julia Keller. All rights reserved. Printed in the United States of America. For information, address St. Martin's Publishing Group, 120 Broadway, New York, NY 10271.

www.minotaurbooks.com

Designed by Omar Chapa

Library of Congress Cataloging-in-Publication Data

Names: Keller, Julia, author.
Title: The cold way home / Julia Keller.
Description: First edition ǀ New York : Minotaur Books, 2019.
Identifiers: LCCN 2019009083ǀ ISBN 9781250191229 (hardcover) ǀ
    ISBN 9781250191243 (ebook)
Subjects: ǀ GSAFD: Mystery fiction.
Classification: LCC PS3611.E4245 C65 2019 ǀ DDC 813/.6—dc23
LC record available at https://lccn.loc.gov/2019009083

Our books may be purchased in bulk for promotional, educational, or business use. Please contact your local bookseller or the Macmillan Corporate and Premium Sales Department at 1-800-221-7945, extension 5442, or by email at MacmillanSpecialMarkets@macmillan.com.

First Edition: August 2019

10 9 8 7 6 5 4 3 2 1

For Karen and Paul and Meeko

Acknowledgments

There it was, high on a hill overlooking the neighborhood where I spent the first several years of my life: the Huntington State Hospital in Huntington, West Virginia. The ancient, stately behemoth was haunted—or so the stories went.

Later I discovered that it wasn't a regular hospital. It was a public psychiatric facility. Later still I found out the name by which it had been known when it was built in 1897: the Home for Incurables.

The Huntington State Hospital shows up in the pages of *The Lobotomist*, Jack El-Hai's excellent biography of Walter Freeman, the physician who pioneered the barbaric procedure. In the 1950s, when Freeman was touring the country to show off his operation, West Virginia had the highest per capita rate of lobotomies in the nation. The Huntington State Hospital was the site of assembly-line atrocities. The poor and the sick were systematically exploited.

I must thank El-Hai for his superbly researched biography. My story is fictional, but its roots are always reaching toward the aquifer of fact.

I am also deeply grateful to the friends who offered support along the way: Susan Phillips, Marja Mills, Brenda Kilianski, Joseph Hallinan, and Holly Bryant. Kelley Ragland is the best editor in the business. Christina MacDonald is a peerless copyeditor. Lisa Gallagher is as kind as she is wise.

ACKNOWLEDGMENTS

History speaks softly sometimes, but its voice still carries. In 1952, a fire raged through the Huntington State Hospital. Fourteen patients—all female—died. Many were locked behind steel mesh, unreachable by firefighters until it was too late.

Here are some of the victims, their names found in newspaper accounts: Ada Carver, 89; Evangeline Elzy, 15; Joyce Tucker, 20; Lena Wentz, 11.

Remember them.

Grief is an amputation, but hope is incurable hemo-philia: you bleed and bleed and bleed.

—DAVID MITCHELL, *Slade House*

Dire sight it is to see some silken beast long dally with a golden lizard ere she devour. More terrible, to see how feline Fate will sometimes dally with a human soul, and by a nameless magic make it repulse a sane despair with a hope which is but mad . . . Humanity, thou strong thing, I worship thee, not in the laurelled victor, but in this vanquished one.

—HERMAN MELVILLE, *The Encantadas or Enchanted Isles*

THE COLD WAY HOME

Prelude

It was 7:17 P.M. on Thursday, October 24th, and Deputy Steve Brink-sneader was ready to call it a day. More than ready, actually. He had a full shift under his belt and supper waiting on the table at home. He was supposed to be done. He should've been finished more than two hours ago, if you wanted to get technical about it, but there'd been too many reports to write and an obese, unruly prisoner—probably high on something, given that he was twisting and lunging and machine-gunning obscenities—that he had to subdue, in order for his col-league, Deputy Dave Previtt, to squire the man into a cell. He didn't know what the man had done. The man was Dave's prisoner, not his, and there'd been no time to talk about it, because the man had bro-ken free from Dave and he had to render assistance.

And now: this.

The call had come crackling over his radio a minute and a half ago and Steve knew he had to respond, knew he had to attend to it. Duty was duty. When he got the chance later he'd phone his wife, Holly, and explain why he'd be late—again—and hear her sigh, hear her murmur about how food reheated in a microwave never tastes the same as it does in the first full flush of its tangy, flavor-mingling warmth from the oven, which was undoubtedly true, and which she knew that he knew, but she'd say it, anyway.

Damn. Tonight was pot roast night.

Pot roast was his favorite. It tended to give him indigestion—hell, what *didn't,* these days?—but he'd put up with that. Holly sometimes joked about serving Tums as a side dish. Fine, he'd reply. You do that. As long as you don't stop making that pot roast. Which caused her to smile.

Might be hours, now, before he'd be seeing that smile. Or his dinner.

Good Lord—would they ever catch a break around here? What *was* it about this place, anyway? Trouble magnet, he'd heard it called, and he'd have a hard time arguing the opposite. But you could slap that label on a lot of small Appalachian communities, couldn't you? Especially these days, with the opioids and the way they'd burned through town after town—and soul after soul—leaving nothing but graves and anxiousness.

It took a toll on you. It surely did. He'd seen the sorrows of this place break the hearts of the best people he knew—for starters, Bell Elkins and Nick Fogelsong—over and over again. He'd seen it run them right out of town.

But they came back, didn't they?

Yes, they did. Which told you something: Maybe it was bearable, after all.

Steve had parked his county-issued Chevy Blazer in the court-house lot an hour ago. He'd finished his business inside—*You're welcome, Dave,* he'd replied to Deputy Previtt's heartfelt thanks, *but next time, could you please arrest somebody who's under three hundred pounds and is maybe weak from the flu?*—and then made his way back out to the lot. He had just hoisted his broad body up into the driver's seat when the call came in, a smudged bundle of words from the dispatcher over in Blythesburg. If the dispatcher here in Raythune County was swamped, Blythesburg took the spill-over.

Steve had thumbed the button on the side of the small black radio pinned to his shoulder—the radio had the dimensions of a pack of cigarettes—and answered: "Roger that, Sally Ann." Despite the static, he'd gotten the gist.

"That you, Steve? You were off at five, wern-cha?"

"Supposed to be. We're down a deputy, though. Simmons is on vacation."

"Gotcha. Well, maybe this'll be nothing."

He fired up the engine. "Yeah. Maybe."

They both knew better. It was never nothing. Not in Acker's Gap, West Virginia.

He lowered the window so that he could stick out his head and do a quick check of his surroundings, peering left and right, back and front, making sure he had clearance to pull out. Mirrors were fine but mirrors never told you the whole story.

As a matter of habit his gaze rose up and up and up, toward the iron ring of mountains that caged the town. The last of the day's light lingered along the tops of those mountains, a fugitive glow that would be gone before you knew it. Night after night, as it grew fainter and fainter and finally left altogether, that slow withdrawal made him a little bit sad, the same kind of sad he'd felt when he was a kid. It was as if he was losing a living thing—something precious, something unrecoverable—and not just a swipe of dwindling light.

He pulled his head back inside. He yanked the Blazer into gear, and then he swung the big wheel, heading for the location that Sally Ann had given him: the Burger Boss up on Route 12. Report of some kind of trouble.

As he rounded the corner on Main, he spotted Jake Oakes. Jake was crossing at the end of the street, maneuvering his wheelchair with an ease that made it look as if he'd been handling it a long time— which he hadn't. Only a couple of years. But he'd adjusted well. On the outside, at least. Steve didn't know about the inside. He and Jake were friends, yes. But not that kind of friends.

Had he not been responding to a call, Steve would've slowed down, waved, tipped his hat, maybe stopped for a chat. No time for that now. Jake would understand: Duty was duty.

Steve roared right on past him. In another few seconds he would be clear of the downtown area. He flipped on the siren. The sole pleasure of this mission was watching other vehicles pull off to the right and the left to let him plow through.

He knew the Burger Boss well, picturing the place as he drove. It was a saggy-roofed shack with pea-green vinyl siding that was curling away from its flanks in crinkly strips, like skin sloughing off a tired reptile, and a carry-out window through which a sweaty-faced cook passed greasy brown sacks of burgers and fries and white Styrofoam cups of watered-down Coke. A hand-painted wooden sign next to the door read BEST BURGERS IN THE USA, a claim that Steve seriously questioned, even though he'd never actually eaten anything from the fly-misted kitchen, being as how he valued his stomach lining.

Before it was Burger Boss, the building had been a used car dealership, and before that, a place that sold capped tires, and before that, a payday loan place, and before that, the showroom for a kitchen and bathroom fixture supplier, and before that . . . something else. Something that nobody remembered. There was always a string of "before thats" in the buildings around here, Steve reflected as the Blazer's jumbo engine tackled a steep incline. The topic always put him in a sour mood, but hell: He was already in a sour mood. Might as well double down.

When was the last time he'd seen any new construction in these parts? He couldn't say. He honestly couldn't recall, and that depressed him even more. *Jesus,* he thought. The past just hung on and hung on. You couldn't budge it. The past was like a freeloading cousin who'd promised to stay only a week—ten days, tops—but never left. Every time you turned a corner, there it was, grinning at you, wearing the pants it had borrowed from your closet without asking, using your comb and your toothbrush.

Steve felt the first burning *urp* of indigestion stirring in his chest. And he hadn't come anywhere near that pot roast yet.

He made the sharp turn onto Route 12. Yep, just about every place he could think of around here had housed another business before the one currently occupying the spot. Bankruptcies and sudden closings were common. A few months after a place shut down, another business would pop up in the same location. The ghost of the old business haunted the new one for a long, long time. If you peered closely at the front window of a tattoo parlor called Skin U Alive, for instance, you could just make out a line of faded letters that once had read ZODIAC COMIX.

Opening a business in Acker's Gap was, he supposed, like the old joke about second marriages: It represented the triumph of hope over experience.

The sky was getting on toward full dark now, which perversely cheered him up. The people he worked with—other deputy sheriffs, EMTs—typically dreaded the coming of night, when human behavior was unloosed from its daylight moorings and tended to spin off in crazy directions. But Steve Brinksneader liked night better than day. Night hid a lot of the ugliness.

The Burger Boss parking lot was lit up by the hard blue glare of a mercury-vapor bulb clipped high on a pole. A memory flickered in Steve's mind: A couple of kids had OD'ed in this lot a year and a half ago, during a terrible twenty-four-hour period that saw a black wave of overdoses from fentanyl-spiked heroin.

They'd survived. Not everybody was so lucky.

Only two vehicles were parked in the lot right now: a gray, dinged-up Dodge Charger with an absence of glass in the rear window, and the big red EMT truck with RAYTHUNE COUNTY FIRE RESCUE painted on the side in important-looking white letters, its engine grinding and straining like a paper shredder that had been fed a few dozen phone books. The cab was empty now; the EMTs were already inside.

He slid out of the Blazer. He slammed the door shut and took a quick glance around the lot. He didn't see what he'd expected to see, based on the dispatcher's use of the all-too-familiar word "trouble": a couple of drunk or stoned young men in the middle of a brawl, having recently tumbled out of the screen door of the Burger Boss in a bristling, snarling ball of redneck fury, all to impress a scantily clad young woman who admired her manicure while her earnest suitors beat the shit out of each other.

That particular scene, he'd come upon so often that the details were etched on his brain like a woodcut: bloody fists, flying spittle, ripped shirts, the odd tooth.

Not this time. The lot was serene. Whatever was happening, it was happening inside the Burger Boss, and it wasn't the usual frantic mess. He knew that because he didn't hear any noise coming from the interior. No screams, no shouting, no—God forbid—gunshots.

He could relax a bit.

Making his way toward the front door, Steve passed the square EMT truck and sneaked a look inside the cab, hoping for a hint that it was Molly Drucker's unit. Molly lived with Jake. Steve knew and liked all of the EMTs, but Molly was special. As hard as it was to deal with a trauma, it was slightly less awful if he got to say hello to Molly, and was able to feed off her remarkable poise. She knew what she was doing. She put other people—be they victims or law enforcement like him—at ease.

No clues in the cab, so he kept on walking. Once he'd rounded the truck, he saw an old man hunched next to the entrance, sucking forlornly on a cigarette. It was Clem Smith, owner of the Burger Boss. He lifted his shoulders with each mournful pull on the Marlboro.

"Hey there, Steve," Clem said. The words came out of his mouth at the same time the smoke did. Clem was in his late seventies. Tridents of stiff white hair sprouted from his crusty scalp. He wore a dirty gray apron tied over a pair of too-big jeans, a green plaid flannel shirt, and battered black Converse sneakers. "Rest of 'em's already inside. Hated to bother you folks, but didn't have no choice in the matter."

"Okay." In Steve's experience, Clem Smith was never one hundred percent sober. It was a sliding scale, and hard to tell which notch he was on at any given moment. "What's going on?"

Clem scowled. He rubbed hard at his mouth during a brief interval between drags on his cigarette. His skin was so slack that Steve half wondered if he was going to rub his mouth right off one day. "World's goin' straight to hell," the old man mumbled.

"Sure is. So what's the trouble?"

Clem shuddered and tried to straighten up, before wincing and dipping right back down into the crouch required by his wrecked spine. He dropped his cigarette and flattened it, grinding his heel into the gravel, twisting his knobby hips.

"Same thing it always is. Damned junkies. Got one passed out in the bathroom and her boyfriend passed out at a table. They come in here twenty minutes ago and I shoulda thrown 'em out then. I knew what they wanted. Wanted a place to sit down so's they could pump that shit in their damned veins. The girl went in the can and locked the door and wouldn't come out, and Helga needed to pee so she told me to call you folks to get that girl outta there. Normally I let 'em alone, I let 'em do what they want until they move on down the road, but like I said, Helga needed to take a piss. If it'd been Chester—he's my new cook—well, I woulda told him to go out back and be quick about it, but you can't never say that to a woman." He grimaced, causing the wrinkles on either side of his mouth to spread to his ears. "I'm tellin' you, Steve, the world's goin' to hell in a—"

"Yep."

The deputy cut him off, moving past the old man. The EMTs might need a hand in there. Lord knows they had enough experience with overdoses—they carried naloxone as a regular part of their lifesaving arsenal now, along with oxygen masks and defibrillators and all the rest of it—but addicts could be a handful. Just ask Dave Previtt, Steve thought ruefully; if Steve hadn't been there to give his colleague a hand, no telling what kind of mayhem might have ensued. Drugs made people sleepy and compliant, sure—except when they made them furious and defiant. And crazy-strong.

The interior of the Burger Boss was gloomy, a dark-paneled room with a swaybacked ceiling. On the left side was a long countertop, which partially hid the infamous kitchen. In the middle was a clump of grubby wooden tables and chairs. The floor was predictably sticky, and the air was blurry and turgid from the nonstop frying of meat. The smell was the kind that clung to your clothes for weeks, no matter how many times you washed them.

Steve paused to assess the situation with a left-to-right swivel of his big head.

Two employees stood side by side behind the counter, arms dangling, gawking unashamedly. One was a wispy old lady with too much red lipstick and erratic butterscotch-colored hair; Helga Something-or-Other. She'd been around town for years but he had never learned her last name. He nodded. She nodded back, adding a shaky finger-point toward the bathroom door on the other side of the room.

"Got it," Steve said.

The other employee was a very short, very fat middle-aged man whom Steve had never seen before. This, he assumed, was Chester the Cook. The man had tiny gold-rim spectacles that seemed in imminent peril of being swallowed up by the encroaching bloat of his face. He wore a hairnet over his thin lick of gray hair. His large belly flopped over an apron even dirtier than Clem's.

Both seemed to be waiting, with quiet anticipatory relish, for something terrible to happen.

All they need is some popcorn, Steve thought grimly. *People.*

The only customer was sitting at one of the tables. Steve couldn't see his face, because the kid—somehow Steve knew he was young, without observing his face—had passed out, forehead pressed to the tabletop. Steve assumed that the battered Charger with no back window belonged to him.

The kid had a small head and short, curly brown hair. The collar of his denim jacket was pulled up around his neck.

Oh, you're cool, aren't you? Steve thought, unreasonably irked by the sight of that upturned collar. *You're so damned cool, you little punk.* The EMTs, he knew, would have already checked him out. If he'd needed help, they'd be giving it. Instead, they had moved on. Which meant the kid was okay, and he hadn't overdosed—just nodded off. It was the woman in the bathroom they were working on.

So that's where Steve needed to go.

A gurney was stationed just outside the door. Steve swept past it. The bathroom was tiny and gross. No stalls, no mirror. No paper towel dispenser. Just a toilet and a sink, plus a noxious, all-over stink that easily crushed the cheap disinfectant used to thwart it. A light bulb dangled on a chain from the ceiling. It cast a sickly, lurid glow.

Steve felt a mild spike of disappointment. This wasn't Molly and her partner, Ernie Edmonds. It was another EMT unit: Gil Marple and Tommy Kilgore. Both young men looked fit and efficient in what passed for their uniforms: dark blue Dickies work pants, light blue polo shirts, brown Redwing boots, and latex gloves. Feet spread for stability, they stood on either side of the toilet, Gil clutching a blood pressure cuff and Tommy preparing the Narcan nasal spray.

Straddling that toilet was a rag doll of a woman, a skinny, ravaged-looking, barefoot thing in denim cutoffs—they'd been pushed down to her ankles, along with a pair of skimpy panties—and a tiger-striped tank top. She had long bleached hair and dead-white skin. The syringe had dropped to the floor and rolled next to her left toe. Her eyes were closed. The numerous bruises imprinted on her face were as fuzzy and haphazard as passport stamps.

"Could use a hand over here, Steve," Gil called out. He didn't sound panicky, only focused. He had a grip on her arm, but he couldn't do his work that way; if he let go, she'd flop down onto the floor.

The deputy moved forward, pushing in between Gil and Tommy. He grabbed the woman's arm and held her steady. He noticed, too late, that she'd already thrown up on the floor; his boot skidded briefly in the smelly tan mess.

"Okay," Tommy said. "All done." He'd administered the Narcan with a couple of deft sprays in her nostrils. The effect was amazingly quick. The woman's eyes flapped open. She coughed and shivered. She made sticky, gummy sounds with her mouth.

She was, Steve knew from experience, already grieving the fact that they'd interrupted her high. Sure, they'd saved her life—but naloxone plunged addicts into instant withdrawal. Guaranteed to piss them off.

"Motherfuggers," she muttered, right on cue. "Lemme go, you gulldamned—" She interrupted herself to cough again, a long string of phlegm-packed rattles. Each one made her small body quiver.

"I got this," Steve said. The EMTs had done their jobs. Now it was time for him to do his: pick her up, haul her outside, offer to take her to the hospital. She'd refuse—they always did—and she'd continue cursing him while he called Rhonda Lovejoy, the prosecutor, to ask if he should bring her in and charge her with heroin possession or let her go. Sometimes they just let them go. What was the point of putting them in jail?

"Thanks, Steve," Gil said. He wasn't looking at him; he and Tommy were already packing up their equipment, rolling up tubing and replacing vials.

From his stance in front of the toilet Steve leaned over and secured the woman's other arm, preparing to raise her up and off. He'd done this dozens of times before—or was it hundreds?—with addicts drowsing on toilets or floors or chairs or beds or sidewalks, and yet he wasn't rough with her, despite his frustration. And make no mistake, he *was* frustrated; frustration was his default setting these days when he dealt with overdoses. He was damned tired of seeing these young people throw away their lives, causing anguish for their loved ones, causing extra work for him and his colleagues. These selfish, lazy kids had turned beautiful little mountain towns into syringe-littered junk-yards where everything decent had died.

But he wouldn't take it out on her. He'd do his job. And he'd do it professionally.

"What's your name?" he asked her.

"You're a motherfugger."

"Fine, but what's your name?"

Something—habit, maybe—made her answer. "Andrea."

"Okay, Andrea, here we go. One, two, *three*."

He lifted.

"Motherfugger," she repeated, breathing her foul breath in his face, resisting him.

He pulled harder. It was no contest: He was much stronger than she was. On account of his extra effort the woman popped off the toi-let like a cork plucked from a bottle.

And then it gushed out of her, the thick river of pinkish-yellow fluid, the dropped gob of blood and pus and some kind of dangling . . . rope.

Rope?

What the—?

Steve peered in the toilet, and he felt his insides shift and quiver from the shock of it.

"Gil! Gil, Tommy—for Chrissakes—"

He held the swaying woman upright and he watched, aghast but fascinated, as the EMTs plunged their hands into the toilet. They scooped up the tiny white dripping blob. Andrea looked at what had come out of her, her face creased with annoyance and then confusion, and said, "Didn't never know about *that.* Damn." She laughed, a sharp startled cackle.

"Is it breathing?" Steve asked. He was surprised he could speak, surprised that his throat hadn't closed up on him. He'd been in this particular situation before, of course he had, and twice he'd even had to deliver babies when the EMTs didn't get there in time, but in those cases the 911 call had been *on account of* the impending birth, so there wasn't this shock, this peculiar feeling that moved through him in waves, as he stared at the wrinkled mass that was barely bigger than his fist. "Or is it—?"

They didn't answer him because they didn't know. He realized that. He held the woman upright while Gil and Tommy did their jobs, moving quickly but with purpose and skill. Tommy rubbed and prodded the impossibly tiny creature, trying to warm it up, while Gil procured the oxygen mask. The mask was made for an adult and it looked all wrong when Gil fit it over the tiny face, but it was all they had, it would have to do.

There was a moment of indecision—protocol dictated they should just put mother and baby on the gurney without cutting the cord, just stick the kid on the mother's belly and wrap up both of them and let the ER staff deal with it, they'd done it that way before, many times—but Andrea was swaying and cursing and they weren't sure, frankly, what she might do if the baby was within her reach. Steve noted with admiration how Tommy and Gil moved as one unit, reading each other's minds. No words were necessary. Tommy held the baby while Gil grabbed two clamps and a pair of scissors from the kit and *snip,* just like that, he'd cut the cord between the two clamps, and then Gil found a pad in the kit and thrust it up between the woman's legs to catch the gooey effluvia, and then he added a second pad when the first one soaked through in seconds, and then a third.

It's a boy, Steve thought, scanning the tiny white blob. *It's a boy.*

But he still didn't know if it was alive or dead. The baby hadn't twitched. Or cried.

Tommy caught Steve's eye. He nodded toward the woman. "Get her out of here," Tommy said in a low, guttural voice. "She'll be fine." The face he showed Steve was red from the effort of holding back disgust and anger—and something else, too, something Steve couldn't identify right away—while he worked.

"Damn," Andrea said again. She looked down at her spread-apart legs. Steve had one hand fixed around her upper arm, keeping her upright, and with his other hand, he yanked up her panties and her cutoffs, both in the same fist, struggling to get them up and over the thick pads.

"Damn," she said for a third time. A crease of pain hit her. "You motherfuggers. You dirty . . . you dirty . . . you motherfuggers." She was too exhausted to come up with another noun.

"Come on," Steve said, guiding her away from the toilet, catching her when she stumbled. "Let's go."

He made it out of the bathroom, shepherding her. He didn't check, because he didn't care, but he was pretty sure she was leaving a trail of blood and other liquids. His long arm was cupped around her tiny waist. He had to make sure she didn't slip out of his grasp like a greasy eel. And that was a distinct possibility: There was a boneless feel to her, a lack of any supporting sinew or active will to do anything more than just melt away onto the floor. She couldn't have weighed more than ninety pounds, and her body had just been through an ordeal.

That body had an odor—stale and pungent, caused by the heavy sweating one did in the throes of heroin addiction, no matter what the outside temperature was. Her dark hair was a disaster, all furious knots and tangles, and it smelled rancid. Her head only came up to his armpit and so it wasn't as if his nose was all that close to her hair, but still. The stink radiated from her.

"Where's Jess?" Andrea slurred. Her head bobbled and teetered on her thin neck. "Jess. Jess." She spotted the man who was facedown at the table. He didn't move. "*Jess!* Jess—I love you, baby. Love you love you." She tried to lurch her way out of Steve's grip.

It didn't work. He got her through the door and into the parking lot. Clem was sitting on the ground by now, his back still jammed against the building, his knees up, his head in his hands. For all Steve knew, he was asleep. Well, let him rest; the old man had a long night coming up, even though he didn't know it yet. If the baby didn't make it—or even if he did—there would be questions galore. An official inquiry. Talk about trouble.

If the baby didn't make it.

Steve tried to cut the phrase out of his brain, like a bad spot on an apple, but he couldn't.

"Dammit—lemme go," Andrea mumbled, managing to add a little squeak of a scream. "Lemme *go,* you motherfugger." Just before they reached the Blazer she turned her head and rammed her face hard against his shoulder. Steve realized, with the kind of intuition that deputy sheriffs develop early in their careers in order to protect themselves, that she was seconds from taking a bite out of his biceps. He tilted away from her, hoping to keep out of range of the very few teeth left in her head. He still had to hang on to the spindly body, however. This required a delicate balancing act: holding her—but not too close. He'd been bitten once before by an irate suspect, and he didn't relish the shots and the course of antibiotics. *Give me a pit bull any old day,* Steve thought as he seesawed with her. *At least they don't curse you out while they're biting you.*

"Fug you," Andrea fumed. She'd gotten a burst of energy. "Fug you, you fugging fugger. Fug you!"

She fought him, summoning a sudden glut of strength from who knew where, but he managed to push her into the back of the Blazer and lock the door. Given the steel mesh that separated the backseat from the front, she could thrash and curse and scream and claw and pound and slam around the space as much as she liked, and it wouldn't matter. No escape from that backseat. The good news was, she'd more than likely wear herself out doing it.

"You got—you can't do this, motherfugger! Jess—Jess, don't let them—" Before he shut the door, Steve heard her words. After that, he didn't; the specifics were muffled by the thick glass of the Blazer's windows.

He hurried back inside the Burger Boss. The kid at the table hadn't lifted his head. Helga and Chester still stood behind the cash register, watching the carnival. He started to say something to them—a caution about staying back, a word of warning about the seriousness of the situation—but there was no need. They weren't going anywhere.

"Hey, Steve."

It was Gil. He and Tommy were coming out of the bathroom, side by side, moving with haste but not running. Gil kicked the gurney out of their way; they didn't want it. Not for this. Tommy held the newborn but Gil stayed close, glued to his hip, two hands under the bundle in Tommy's arms. Another layer of protection.

"Is he alive?" Steve asked. His voice was husky, strained.

Gil freed up a hand from under the blanket to wave him back, meaning that Steve should guarantee them a clear lane across the dirty concrete floor, around the clump of tables and toward the front door. Nobody was impeding them, but Gil wanted to be sure.

"Yeah," Gil answered.

Steve felt something twist inside him.

Gil, he realized, was still talking; he talked as fast as he and Tommy walked: "She probably thought she just needed to take a shit. So she goes in there and shoots up and—*whammo*—ready or not, here it comes."

As soon as they'd passed, Steve fell into step right behind them. Out in the parking lot, where serious dark now cloaked the world, three sets of boots crunched against the meager gravel. A car growled by on Route 12.

Gil and Tommy had almost reached the truck. In a few seconds they would be on their way to the Raythune County Medical Center, leaving Steve to deal with the . . .

Steve couldn't do it. He couldn't call her "the mother." Not even in his thoughts. Not even after he'd seen the child attached to the woman's body.

While Gil raced around to the driver's side, Tommy cradled the baby in his beefy arms. "Do you friggin' *believe* this?" Tommy said, his voice suffused with awe. He stood in the midst of the blue glaze created by the mercury-vapor light. "A baby in the friggin' Burger Boss." Tommy was a big man, six foot four, 250 pounds, with a blond crew cut and a barrel chest, and as he held the blanket-wrapped newborn securely against that enormous chest of his, Steve saw something he was pretty sure he'd remember forever.

Not just for a few months or a couple of years—forever:

In the glare of blue light, he saw the look in Tommy's eyes. Despite the unthinkable circumstances that surrounded this baby's birth, despite the horror of a woman so lost in her addiction that she didn't know she'd given birth—hell, she didn't even know she was pregnant—and despite the massive load of troubles that clearly lay in wait to pounce upon this tiny boy as he made his way in the world, despite all of that, there was, in Tommy Kilgore's eyes, a rising joy, a bright gleam.

At first Steve didn't understand it, but then—suddenly—he did, he did understand it, he understood it perfectly, even though he'd never be able to explain it to anyone, not even Tommy:

Life.

This was life, and life was a sacred thing, a holy thing, no matter the grisly circumstances out of which it had arisen. Steve was sure that he and Tommy Kilgore—and maybe Gil, too, although he didn't know about Gil, because he hadn't had a chance to look into Gil's eyes, the way he'd accidentally looked into Tommy's—were feeling the same thing: an awe, a reverence that moved through their bodies in an upward thrust of warmth and hope, like a sunrise in the blood.

No telling how the kid would end up. The odds were lousy. His mother—Steve finally broke down and let the word form in his brain, but only because he had to, only because it was biological fact—was a drug addict. His father—well, who knew? Maybe the kid at the table—Jess was the name, right?—was the father. Maybe not. Chances were, the mother didn't know, either. The kid had so many strikes against him, right from the get-go, that you might as well stop counting. Because you'd be counting a long, long time.

He'd been born, God help him, in a toilet in the Burger Boss. He'd been born in a toilet in the Burger Boss in a bleak town in a state swamped by its troubles.

But it didn't matter.

Because this was life.

Steve slapped the side of the EMT truck as it shot forward, the big tires spitting forth small sprays of gravel and dirt as it spun out of the lot and plunged headlong toward the hospital, twenty-seven miles away across three hills. The slap was Steve's way of saying: Godspeed. And: good luck.

He was aware of a lump in his throat, and he realized that the lump was the only thing that kept him from embarrassing himself by getting visibly emotional. He swallowed. Swallowing hurt, because of that damned lump, but still—he was glad it was there, wasn't he? Otherwise he'd be bawling, most likely.

He heard a series of muted thumps. He turned. It was the woman in the back of the Blazer, pitching a fit, pounding at the window with her tiny fists, her face screwed up like a dirty dishrag as she yelled at him. She didn't consider the glass. She thought he was ignoring her. So she started head-butting the window. Anything to get his attention.

He turned away. He didn't want to look at her right now.

He had to get hold of himself. He had to call for backup, for another deputy to come retrieve the man inside the Burger Boss. He had to notify Sheriff Harrison. He had to contact the prosecutor. He had to start making notes for his report, which meant he had to take statements from Clem and Helga and the cook, and he had to . . .

He didn't have to do anything.

It came to him just like that: *I don't have to do a damned thing right now. I can take this time.*

For the next few seconds all he was required to do was stand here and feel the wonder of it, feel the enormity of what had just occurred. The sacred profundity of it. The holiness. Something was shifting inside him. He felt . . . different.

It was the child. It was that fragile breathing creature coiled in the dirty porcelain cradle that had changed him, that had changed this parking lot and this town and this night, and such a change just might, he thought, in the fullness of time and the mysteries therein, change everything.

Chapter One

"Somebody brought coffee, right?"

By way of replying to her, Nick Fogelsong set the cardboard carrier in the middle of the round wooden table at which Belfa Elkins sat. Four large cups of take-out coffee, their warmth sealed in by brown plastic lids, were rooted snugly in the slots.

Outside the small office, the streets of Acker's Gap slid seamlessly from twilight to darkness. No streetlights fought back. As of a few months ago, the bulbs of burnt-out streetlights were no longer replaced. At issue wasn't simply the cost of the bulbs; it was also the salary of the city worker whose job it was to switch them out. That city worker, Carter Shively, had retired earlier in the year. Like the bulbs, he wasn't replaced.

With a pop and a hiss, the last remaining streetlight had gone out two Tuesdays ago. Night was now a hard, blunt dark.

It was just past 7:30 P.M.

"Excellent," Bell said. She made a show of silent counting, pointing a finger at Nick, and at Jake Oakes, who had come through the door shortly after him, bumping his wheelchair across the threshold, and then at herself. She seemed perplexed by the total. "I see four cups. So who gets the extra?"

"Gimme a break." Nick sat down next to her and offered her a *Really?* squint. Her love of coffee was legendary. She didn't keep a pot in the office in a doomed attempt to cut down on her consumption. "You gotta ask?"

"Just testing you." Bell grinned, reaching forward with both hands so that she could twist two cups at once out of their little square pens. "Hi, Jake."

"Hey." Jake nudged his wheelchair as far up under the table as it would go. He was frowning. "Risked my damned life crossing the street just now. A county Blazer was headed somewhere in a hurry. Couldn't tell for sure, but looked like it mighta been Steve. Anybody know what's going on?"

"Nope," Nick replied, "but give it ten minutes or thereabouts and it'll be old news. You know this town." He levered a cup out of the carrier and handed it to Jake, who nodded his gratitude, and secured his own. Then Nick leaned back in his chair, tucking a thumb in his belt. He'd unbuttoned his jacket but didn't take it off. Jake didn't take his off, either, and Bell was still wearing her coat as well. The office was equipped with a space heater, "but not so's you'd take any notice of it," Bell had remarked wryly a few days ago, when she pointed out that her favorite beverage had turned into iced coffee right under her nose. She didn't like iced coffee.

It was, she had realized at the time with the kind of surprise endemic to preoccupied people, almost November.

"So why'd you send up the bat signal?" Nick asked. "Thought we'd said our good-byes this afternoon. Now we're right back here."

Here was a storefront a block away from the Raythune County Courthouse. The compact establishment was wedged between the Raythune County Public Library and a nail salon named Razzle-Dazzle. It featured a single room, twice as long as it was wide, with a small bathroom in the back. In former lives it had been an insurance company office, a bookstore that specialized in used paperback mysteries, a dentist's office, and sometime in the 1920s—or so Bell had been told by one of the elderly townspeople—a ladies' hat shop.

It wasn't any of those things now. It was a far more unlikely enterprise: a detective agency.

The straightforward name of the business—INVESTIGATIONS— had been stenciled in small black block letters in the lower right-hand corner of the plate-glass window by Nick's cousin, Lulu Truscott, who had an artistic flair. Below the name was a phone number. Below that, a Web site address. Below that, the street address.

"Might have a new case," Bell said.

"'Might'?" Jake's voice was skeptical, but not aggressively so. He was simply curious about the conditional nature of the news.

"Depends on the particulars," she answered. "Got a call about an hour ago from a woman named Maggie Folsom. Works in the cafeteria at the grade school. She's on her way over. Her daughter hasn't been home in three days. She wants to hire us to find her."

Nick used a thumbnail to scratch his left cheek. "I know Maggie Folsom. The only daughter she's got is Dixie Sue. They live in a trailer over in Swanville. And Dixie Sue must be eighteen or nineteen by now. If she doesn't want to come home—that's her choice. She's an adult. She can do as she pleases."

"Ordinarily I'd agree with you," Bell said, "but according to the mother, we could be looking at an abduction situation. Running away might have started out as Dixie Sue's idea, but maybe it didn't end up that way." A meaningful pause. "There's a boyfriend involved."

"This guy have a name?" Nick asked.

"No—well, yes, of course he does. But Maggie doesn't know it. She's never met him. Only found out about him when she called some of Dixie Sue's friends to check on her. Apparently her daughter was keeping some secrets. And she hasn't shown up for work, either. She runs the front counter of a florist shop in Swanville."

"Still sounds like an ordinary domestic dispute to me," Nick said, making no attempt to hide his disgruntlement. "I don't have the patience anymore for family dramas. Wish people would just work it out their own damned selves. Quit bothering the rest of the world."

Jake leaned forward in his wheelchair. "Well, Nick, what *you* call family dramas—I call job security." He took a sip of his coffee. He made a cringing motion with his shoulders. "Where'd you get this crap, anyway? That rusty barrel out behind the Jiffy Lube where they store the used oil? Or maybe you scraped it off the bottom of your boot and mixed it with a little hot water? This can't be from the diner."

"JP's closes early now. You know that," Nick replied gruffly. "Had to go on out to the Highway Haven."

"Tastes fine to me," Bell said, before Nick could formulate an additional retort alluding to beggars and choosers. She finished off her first cup to drive the point home. She stowed the empty next to the closed laptop on the table.

Nick, though, had stopped paying attention to their debate over the merits of his gift. "If it's kidnapping," he said, "then Maggie Folsom should be talking to the sheriff, not us."

"Granted." Bell uncapped the second cup. Sipped, smiled, gave the requisite *Ahhhhh*. "But that's the problem. She knows Dixie Sue might very well have gone off with the boyfriend voluntarily. She's worried, though. There's been no communication at all from the girl. Maggie doesn't want to bother Sheriff Harrison unless she has to. Which is decent of her. Not everybody's so thoughtful."

"Or," Nick countered, "she knows the sheriff would tell her there's nothing to be done. Adults are in charge of themselves."

Jake gave him a thoughtful look. "You got some kind of beef with this Folsom woman? You sound a little testy."

"Just don't like wasting time," Nick snapped back. He cast an eye toward his wristwatch.

"Late for something?" Bell asked.

"No." Emphatically.

She let a minute go by, hoping that the tension—and Nick's bad mood—would dissipate. She took another drink from her second coffee, allowing herself a quick glimpse around the wood-paneled room. She hadn't quite gotten used to it yet, even though they'd officially been in business over a year now—and even though there was precious little to get used to: a table and chairs, a mini-fridge, a black metal filing cabinet shoved against the wall. On top of the filing cabinet, a printer. In the corner, one extremely ineffective space heater.

The circuit of her gaze ended at the big glass window, which reflected the images of the three people sitting around the table.

Here we are, Bell thought ruefully. *In all our glory.*

She allowed herself a few seconds to contemplate the images, starting with herself: She was a fifty-four-year-old woman with a thin face, narrow shoulders, and straight, medium-length hair that she wore tucked behind her ears. The skin beneath her gray eyes was slightly darker than it was elsewhere on her face. Her hair was brownish-blond. For most of her adult life she'd looked younger than her actual age; that gap had now officially closed. She'd caught up with herself. Little wonder: Her life over the past few years had not been easy. A lot of people ended up wearing their histories on their faces. She was one of them.

She moved on to her colleagues.

Jake had just turned thirty. He had a lean, handsome face with somewhat delicate features—large brown eyes, high cheekbones, noticeable eyelashes—that he'd recently decided to complicate with the furry scraggle of a beard. The tough-guy look was offset, though, by the butternut-colored hair that tumbled to his shoulders in a soft wave. "You look like Jesus in one of those paintings on the Sunday school wall," Nick had teased him the other day, the first time he'd deigned to comment upon Jake's appearance. "Far as I know, though," Nick went on, "you ain't the Savior. You drink too much beer for that." Jake's reply had involved the cheerful brandishing of an upraised middle digit, a gesture at which Nick couldn't take offense because, frankly, he'd been known to employ it himself on more than one occasion.

Nick was sixty-eight. His body was large but solid, and his face was seamed and leathery. He had a crew cut and a square chin. His deep-set hazel eyes looked out at the world with a definite wariness and a default attitude of mild suspicion, the inevitable result of having spent multiple decades in law enforcement. His broad forehead was scored with horizontal lines. Somebody had once told him, in Bell's hearing, that he looked a little like the retired NFL star Howie Long. That pleased him. And then the guy added, "Or maybe Howie Long's dad." That didn't.

Nick was sending a quick text. Like a lot of older people, he typed with a single index finger, not with both thumbs moving in an ambidextrous blur.

Bell was about to get back to business when she was struck by a thought. She'd had this particular insight before, to be sure, but somehow the force of it was intensified now, as she studied the visual echo of the three of them, sitting at a spindly table in a small, lighted office surrounded by the darkness of a disintegrating town. She couldn't help but think of this place as a lighthouse jutting from a rocky cliff, while just beyond it, an ocean slapped and clawed at the hapless ship trying to make landfall. All that stood between a desperate crew and certain disaster was this: the faint but steady source of light.

Nick, she knew, would've instantly made fun of her if she'd shared the metaphor. *What's all this crap about a lighthouse?* he'd ask. *Bunch of nonsense.* She didn't care. She'd think it, anyway. She'd gotten used to his cynicism, just as she had Jake's irreverence. They made a good team, the three of them.

These men were the closest thing Bell had to a family, now that her sister had passed away. She had her daughter, yes—but Carla was twenty-five and lived in Charleston, more than an hour's drive away. Carla was busy with her work at an environmental lobbying firm. She came back to Acker's Gap from time to time, but she wasn't a regular feature of Bell's life anymore. For that, she had Nick and Jake.

They took the cases that the Raythune County Sheriff's Department was too busy to handle. Sheriff Harrison was smart, and she was honest, and she worked very hard, but she lacked the time, the budget, and the personnel to fight the drug dealers who had set up shop in these mountain valleys over the past decade. Drugs—and the fact that the dealers didn't give them away for free—had kicked up an avalanche of other crimes, ancillary crimes: homicide, burglary, home invasion, grand theft auto. The county was overwhelmed.

And so Bell had rented the small office on Main. At first, she'd only been looking for a way to keep busy while she waited for the chance to get her law license reinstated. She had one more year to go before she could apply. A felony conviction—for a crime committed when she was ten years old, a crime that many thought was justified—and her time in a minimum-security prison had triggered mandatory disbarment.

If she wanted to stay in Acker's Gap—and she did, for reasons that were not entirely clear to her but that she hoped might become so eventually—she needed a place to go every day where she had work to do. Good work. Fulfilling work. A detective agency would play to her strengths.

The same was true for Nick and Jake. They didn't need a way to make a living. They needed a way to make a life—a means of feeling useful again. Nick, the former sheriff, had his pension. Jake, a former deputy sheriff, had the settlement he'd received from the county for being critically injured on the job. Bell, for her part, was the former county prosecutor.

That's a lot of damned formers all in one spot, she had groused to herself in the beginning. But it was the truest way to describe them. No use pretending otherwise.

Rhonda Lovejoy, Raythune County prosecutor, had made it official by hiring them as special consultants on a case-by-case basis. So far they'd tracked down a fair number of bail jumpers and cornered more than a few suspects in hit-skip accidents. Gradually, they had started picking up their own cases, small ones and large ones: Background checks for employees at the fast-food chains up on the interstate. Consultations on security procedures for retail stores in the mall over in Blythesburg.

And tracking down missing loved ones, when the sheriff's department couldn't spare a deputy. These cases typically involved a grandparent with dementia who'd wandered off when nobody was looking, or a runaway teenager. Once, they had located a hunting dog who'd become disoriented in a storm and separated from his owner, a giant of a man named Jefferson Ferris. When they returned the German short-haired pointer, Bell had been astonished to see the six-foot-six, 310-pound Ferris drop to his knees and sob like a baby, his wet cheek pushed up against the dog's quivering flank as he embraced him.

Ferris and his dog had reminded Bell of a lesson she'd learned early on: People get to choose what they love. Nobody else has anything to say about it; nobody else can judge.

"Just hope Maggie Folsom doesn't try to tell us how to do our jobs," Nick muttered. "You know how people are. Reminds me of that old sign you see on the wall of every car repair shop that ever was. The charge is twenty-five bucks an hour. But it's fifty if you stick around to watch—and make suggestions." He put a big hand on top of his bristly scalp, rubbing it vigorously as if he had an itch, which he didn't. He was just restless. "We're not committed, right? You didn't officially take the case?"

"Of course not," Bell answered quickly. "That was our agreement. Nobody takes a job without getting the okay from the other two. Checks and balances." She let her gaze rove back toward the window. Beyond their reflections was a solid wall of darkness. The lack of streetlights had taken a toll on Acker's Gap. In mountain towns the darkness was the serious kind, solid and seamless. Too much darkness, she knew, could affect your dreams, your ambitions, hemming them in like a stockade fence.

She put the lid on her coffee cup to preserve its heat. And she put the lid on that kind of thinking, too, to preserve something else: the fragile scrap of hope that enabled her to keep fighting.

She started to say something else to Nick. It was going to be a wisecrack, something to nudge him out of his sour mood. Something clever. Something silly, even. Something to make him laugh, or at least grunt appreciatively. Before she could do that, though, the office door swung open, letting in a surly punch of cold air.

Long after this night, Bell would remember the odd, unruly feeling that overtook her just then. *This is where it starts,* she thought. She didn't know what the phrase meant in this context or where it had come from or why—but suddenly it was there, filling her mind, followed by another: *It's beginning.*

Chapter Two

Maggie Folsom took a tentative step into the room. She closed the door carefully behind her. That didn't work—the wood was too warped to fit neatly in the frame—and so she tried again, jamming the handle harder to get it to shut and stay that way. She looked at the three of them apprehensively, as if fearing she might have been too rough with it.

Bell waved her over. Maggie nodded, her chin tilting up slightly as she did so.

She was a tiny woman, barely five feet tall, and thin. Her small stature was misleading, Bell realized; you glanced at her and assumed she must be young, but her face, a pale oval pinched with worry, corrected the record. She was old and tired. The lined face was topped by a windswept mound of artificially blond hair. Gray had made inroads at her temples; she was plainly overdue for her next appointment at the Kut 'N' Kurl, the only hair salon left within a twenty-mile radius. She wore a belted tan trench coat and clutched a large black purse that aspired to be mistaken for leather.

She seemed to be holding herself together purely with nervous energy, a sort of furled, binding pulse. She was like so many women Bell had observed over the years in small mountain towns; they wore themselves to a frazzle trying to live up to other people's expectations of what women ought to be doing—which was, more often than not, taking care of others, be it a husband, a parent, a child, or all three, while holding down an outside job. Or two.

"Hi," Bell said, and Maggie gave her a wan, wince-like smile in response.

Nick fetched the extra chair from the corner. Maggie looked at him, then looked at the chair, and remained standing. He shrugged and sat back down.

"I brought this," Maggie said. She plunged a hand into the big purse and fished out a thin envelope. It had been used before—the paper was crinkled and the original address had been X'ed out—and she had wound a rubber band around it several times, to make sure the flap stayed closed. She handed it to Bell.

"What's this?"

"Money. For you to start looking."

"I didn't say anything about payment."

Maggie's reply had a belligerent ring: "Don't need charity."

"Didn't offer any." Bell handed back the envelope. "We'll talk about that later. We don't even know if we can help you yet. First, I'd like to introduce my associates. I figure you might know everybody here already, but we like to do things by the book." She peered at Maggie. "You sure you won't have a seat?"

"I'm sure."

Bell didn't react. To each her own. She tapped Jake's forearm. "This is Jake Oakes."

"Ma'am." Jake dipped his head. Maggie gave him another one of her worried smiles.

"And this," Bell said, "is Nick Fogelsong."

The smile vanished.

"How are you, Maggie?" Nick asked quietly.

"Fine." She didn't make eye contact with him. "Sure hope you folks can help me find Dixie Sue. I got a bad feeling."

"Has she gone off like this before?" Jake inquired. "Without telling you, I mean?"

Maggie shrugged. "We do argue. I won't lie to you. Sometimes it gets—it gets real rough between us." Maggie checked out the floor. She didn't raise her gaze until she was ready to begin speaking again.

"I'm just gonna say it, okay? Dixie Sue is kinda slow. She's a nice girl and she tries real hard—but she's slow. And she's got stars in her eyes, too. She ain't practical. The right kind of person—especially if it's a man—can turn her around so's she don't know which end's up. Yeah, she might be nineteen—but she don't have good sense. Thing is, she's a pretty girl. She's—" Maggie faltered. "—she's what you might call well-developed." She moved her hand in the vague direction of her breasts. Her embarrassment was clear. "Some people get the wrong idea. Men, I mean."

A few seconds of silence went by.

"So that's why you want us to find her," Jake said gently. "You think she might've gotten in over her head. With a man who manipulated her—and even if she's realized that by now and wants to come home, she can't."

"That's it," Maggie said, a gush of relief in her voice. Somebody understood. "She's got a boyfriend. Maybe she wanted to go with him at first—but if she changed her mind, it'd be too late. She ain't smart. She wouldn't know how to get out of a bad situation."

Bell opened the laptop. She made notes, her fingertips systematically grazing the keys. "I want you to tell me about your last interaction with your daughter. What she said, what you said. Try to be as specific as possible."

Maggie spoke for a few minutes. It was a familiar story: Dixie Sue declared that she'd be staying out late that night; Maggie said no. Dixie Sue fought her on it. Harsh words were exchanged. "She was mad and she cursed at me," Maggie murmured, with a hitch in her voice that Bell realized came from shame. "Past coupla years, she's picked up some bad words. I mean *real* bad."

Bell looked up from the keyboard. "I raised a teenage girl myself. Cursing's just a phase. She'll grow out of it."

There was gratitude on Maggie's face. Bell understood. Her remark had implied that Dixie Sue was still alive, that she'd get the chance to grow out of something. That she had a future.

"Anyway," Maggie went on, "next morning, she was gone. No note, no nothing. She must've waited till I fell asleep and then sneaked out."

"You've tried her cell, right?" Jake asked.

Maggie nodded grimly. "Just rings and rings."

"Well, don't worry about that," he said quickly. "Thing is, young people watch cop shows, too. They know about pinging cell towers to find somebody's location. She probably turned it off." He rolled the wheels of his chair back and forth a quarter inch or so, while he pondered. "Tell us about the boyfriend. You didn't know him?"

Maggie looked stricken. "Thought I did. But the boy she'd been dating—I called him when I saw that Dixie Sue was gone, and it turns out they'd broken up. She never told me. Matt hasn't seen her in weeks."

Bell asked, "You think he's telling the truth?"

"Yeah. He's a real good boy. Always liked him."

"Okay," Bell said. "I'll need his contact information so we can double-check, but that'll do for now. You brought some photos, right? Like I asked?"

Maggie opened the big purse. She pulled out a manila folder with several dozen photos and spread them across the table. "I've got more on my phone, but I kept these displayed around the trailer. Took 'em out of their frames. They're a lot better than the digital ones."

Bell picked them up one by one and studied them, trying to get a better sense of Dixie Sue Folsom. The photos showed a plumpish young woman with a distractingly voluptuous figure. Her mascara had been applied with such a heavy hand that her lashes looked like twin tarantulas. A brazen shade of red lipstick turned her mouth into something borderline pornographic. Her long, straight, black hair was so thick and shiny that it appeared almost blue, and she enjoyed swinging it around in a circle until, in a moment captured by the camera, it spun away from her head almost horizontally. She wasn't shy: Most of the poses were saucy and provocative, and involved a pouty expression, finger on chin. In one, she was blowing a kiss.

Amy Winehouse, Bell thought, answering her internal question about which celebrity this woman reminded her of. *Not a happy ending there.* When she finished with each photo, she passed it over to Jake. Jake passed it to Nick, who took a quick look and then flipped it back onto the pile.

"She's a good girl," Maggie murmured, as if the nature of the photos—the fact that Dixie Sue was leaning forward in many of them, pushing out her rear end—might make them less inclined to search for her. "She just gets carried away. She wants to get on that singing show on TV. People tell her she's got a beautiful body and she's grateful to them, and so she thinks she has to—" Maggie paused. "I tell her over and over again that she has a lot more to offer than just that. But she's like her daddy. She got his good looks. All that black hair. But he wasn't what you'd call smart, either. So people—well, they take advantage."

"Where is he now?" Jake asked, a second before Bell could ask the same thing.

"Died five years ago. Front-loader turned over on him and crushed him. He was working on that bridge over in Muth County. The land was too hilly for that kind of equipment. Everybody said so. But Carl wasn't in no position to turn down work. After he passed, Dixie Sue just kinda—kinda went a little wild. Like nothing mattered anymore. She loved her daddy. That's for sure."

Bell gathered the photos, squaring up the edges. "Can I keep these?"

Maggie nodded. "I'd thank you to be careful with 'em, though. They're all I got. I mean, the cell ones are okay, but they're—they're not the same. Somehow people look different in them. You know? Like they know they were taken real quick and they can be deleted real quick and so they don't rightly matter. Whereas these—" She swept a hand toward the stack. "—these here are *real,* somehow. Took time to make 'em. You gotta work at it. And have some patience while you wait to get 'em developed."

Bell knew what she meant, and she was sure that Nick knew what she meant, too. Jake—and Dixie Sue herself—probably wouldn't have a clue.

Maggie changed her grip on the handle of the big purse, working her hands back and forth across the strap. Her anxiety was palpable.

"So you'll do it?" she asked. "You'll find my girl?"

Bell looked at Jake, and then at Nick. Nick shrugged. Jake nodded.

"We'll do our best," Bell declared.

"Thank the Lord." Relief made Maggie's sentence sound like a sigh. "And about the money, I don't have much but I'll give you all that I—"

"Let's hold off on that for now," Bell said, interrupting her. She stood up. "We'll be in touch." She had just spotted the glimmer of what might be tears in Maggie Folsom's eyes and wanted to hustle her away before it got serious. She didn't like dealing with emotions— neither her own nor anyone else's.

"One more thing," Maggie said. "Got something that might help. This morning I told my friend Willie Sykes about what's going on. He lives in the next trailer over. Turns out his cousin hunts in those woods out behind Briney Hollow. It might be nothin', but Willie's cousin told him that he mighta seen a couple of people out there the other day. Running in the woods. Just a flash in the corner of his eye—like maybe they heard him coming and took off. It was out near that old hospital. The one that burned down a long time ago. Well-wood."

Nick sat up straighter in his chair. Despite himself, he was in-trigued by the clue. "A lot of the young people hang out there," he said. "Don't understand it myself. Not much left. The roof's long gone and the walls are whittled down to mostly nothing—but it's still a place they go."

Maggie's voice rose half a notch. She had a reason to hope. "That's what Willie's cousin said, too. Do you want me to maybe go out there and—?"

"We've got this," Bell said.

Chapter Three

The door had barely closed behind Maggie Folsom before Jake Oakes went into Full Checklist Mode.

"I'll contact dispatchers in all the surrounding counties," he declared. "See if there's been any incident reports filed. Probably ought to wait till morning to call the civilians—the friends and cousins and coworkers and such. You know how it is—lots of folks around here are in bed by eight o'clock."

A two-part clicking sound. Somebody was getting a text.

"Not mine," Bell said. She felt the need to so stipulate because Carla often texted her.

"That's me." Nick dug his cell out of his jean pocket. He squinted at the screen, scanning the text. It was a long one. "Okay," he finally said. "Here's what I was waiting for. I texted Bob Childers a few minutes ago. Teaches civics at the high school. Dixie Sue never graduated, but except for having Hollywood on her mind and thinking she'll be the next Miley Cyrus, she's basically a good kid—Maggie had that part right. Bob kept in fairly close touch with her, he says here. He's been encouraging her to try for her GED. He knows some of her friends, too. Made some calls for me. Apparently Dixie Sue's been hanging out with a guy named—" He squinted even harder, moving the cell further away from his eyes. "—named Travis Matson. Bob's lost track of him lately, but says the kid's a real waste of space.

Big-time loser. Makes any kind of promise to get what he wants. Lies, cheats, and steals. Despite all that, though, he's catnip to the ladies."

Bell laughed. "You don't get it, Nick. Pretty clear you've never been a teenage girl. He's catnip to the ladies *because* he lies, cheats, and steals." She shook her head. "Is it just me, or are all the sexy, inappropriate boyfriends in the world named Travis?"

"Only the ones who aren't named Jake," Jake said.

Nick groaned. "You wish."

"Hey," Bell said. She took advantage of the lighter moment and put a hand on Nick's sleeve. "What's going on?"

"What do you mean?"

"Come on. You were a grouch when you got here tonight. Did I interrupt something when I called? And what's with the tension between you and Maggie Folsom?"

"Oh, for Christ's sake," he replied brusquely. "Yeah, I know Maggie. Or knew her. It was a long time ago. Back when Mary Sue taught at the elementary school. I'd run into Maggie sometimes when I stopped over there to pick her up."

Mary Sue was Nick's wife—soon to be ex-wife. Shortly after they retired to Florida three years ago, Mary Sue had begun a relationship with another man. The mental illness that had plagued her for years had finally loosened its grip, but her recovery came at a price. She told Nick that he would never see her as anything but a patient. Someone weak, someone dependent on him. She wanted a fresh start, she said. So she filed for divorce. Nick had moved back to Acker's Gap a year and a half ago, renting an apartment on the road to Blythesburg.

"So you know her from way back when," Bell said. "And?"

"And what?"

"Well, she didn't seem any happier to see you than you did her. What's the deal?"

Nick stood up abruptly, wincing from the pain in his back. "Nothing. Just don't have much to say to her, now that Mary Sue's not in the picture anymore."

Bell wished she had the nerve to utter out loud what she was thinking: *Oh, Nick. Mary Sue's still in the picture and always will be. You don't just walk away from forty years of marriage. Part of you is always back there, always with her.*

She knew the truth of that from her own divorce a dozen years ago. She could go many months, even an entire year, without talking to Sam Elkins, who lived in Washington, D.C.—but he was still there, just over the horizon of her thoughts.

"So that's it," she said instead. "That's your story."

"Yeah."

Jake had remained quiet throughout their exchange but now he spoke up. "Need to get home. Gotta make supper for Malik. My neighbor came over to play cards with him so I could join you all here."

"I thought Molly had the night off," Bell said.

"She thought so, too. She was called in. There were a bunch of other calls stacking up. They needed her." Molly Drucker was the EMT with whom Jake lived. Malik was her younger brother. He'd been born with profound physical and cognitive disabilities. He and Jake had a bond, and the makeshift family was a splendid success. Bell had been to Jake's house—now Jake's and Molly's house—many times, and she always left with a lightness in her heart from having witnessed the everyday, ordinary joy that the three of them shared.

"Sure." Bell stood up. "I'll go to Briney Hollow in the morning. I could do with some exercise. And even though I haven't been out in those woods for maybe twenty years—I know that place like the back of my hand."

"Want some company?" Nick asked.

She gave him a look. "You hurt your back, remember? That uneven terrain's not what you need."

Nick frowned. He didn't like being almost seventy years old. Didn't want to give the fact any room in his life.

"Fine," he muttered. "But text me when you're heading out tomorrow. You won't have any cell service at Wellwood. It's in the middle of nowhere."

Bell nodded. "Will do." She made a flipping motion with her hand as if she was shooing away a couple of flies. "You two get out of here. I'll lock up."

Nick wasn't quite ready to go yet. "Got a question. Is it Carla?"

"What do you mean?"

"The reason you want us to take the case—is it because of Carla? You know what it's like to worry about a daughter. You identify with Maggie Folsom."

"I'll think it over and let you know, Dr. Freud." Bell rolled her eyes.

Still he lingered. "What's your instinct?"

"You said *a* question. As in one." But she knew what he meant. He was asking if she thought Dixie Sue Folsom was alive or dead. She needed to answer.

"I don't know," she said. "But there are a lot of bad things that can happen to a young woman out in the world."

"And you?" Nick inquired, looking at Jake. "What do you think?"

Jake shrugged. "I'm with Bell. Don't have a sense of things yet. But Maggie Folsom's right to be concerned."

Nick buttoned the top button of his jacket, finishing the row. Keeping his voice casual—he knew how sensitive Jake was about his independence—he asked, "Need a lift?"

Jake shook his head. "Brought my van." He let Nick hold open the door for him, the only sort of help he'd accept from anybody.

They had departed before it dawned on Bell: Nick hadn't answered her second question. About whether she'd interrupted something with her call to him tonight—which plainly she had.

You've got a secret, Nick Fogelsong, she thought. *And I don't care how busy we are—I'm going to find out what you're hiding.*

An hour later Bell was still working. The office had grown even colder. She was finishing up the paperwork for a case involving a church secretary suspected of dipping into the collection plate, an investigation that had mandated some delicate queries among the woman's neighbors as to any large purchases or fancy vacations.

When her cell trilled, it startled her. She almost knocked over the second coffee, the one she'd been drinking slowly, to make it last. The caller ID told her that it was Rhonda Lovejoy.

She closed the laptop and sat back in her chair. "Hi, Rhonda."

Instead of a return greeting, Bell heard a sigh, one freighted with sorrow.

"Hey," Bell said. "What's going on?"

"It's just—I can't—" What came next surprised her even more. Rhonda was crying. Softly, discreetly, but she was crying, all the same. "Sometimes it's just too much. The things that happen around here. I mean, sure, bad things happen everywhere, but it's like we never get a break. You know?"

"I know." Bell paused. "Do you want to talk about it? I could come over to your house and—"

"Mack's asleep. He just got back from a sales trip. I don't want to wake him. But thanks for offering."

Mack Gettinger was Rhonda's husband. He was seventeen years older than she was—it was a second marriage for him—but it had proven to be a good match.

Bell listened as her friend acquired and then slowly relinquished a deep breath. She could imagine her round face, bright pink now on account of the tears, with a dash of smeared mascara adjacent to an eyelid.

When Rhonda next spoke, her voice was normal again. She had regained her composure, just like that. Bell had mastered the same trick—the quicksilver emotional recovery. It was necessary for anyone who held a public position. You didn't get the luxury of a long, luxurious wallow in whatever grief had waylaid you. "Steve Brinksneader just called," Rhonda said. "He filed his report at the courthouse but wanted to make sure I knew what was going on. Couple of addicts stopped by the Burger Boss tonight." Her voice was clipped now, almost matter-of-fact. "EMTs Narcanned the woman in the bathroom. Her name's Andrea Krieger. And guess what? She'd given birth in the toilet."

"Oh, my God."

"Yeah. The mother's in custody. So's the man who was with her."

"And the baby?"

"Doing okay, believe it or not. I just got a call from the ER nurse. He's holding his own. They moved him to Evening Street,"

Rhonda said, naming the special clinic set up for babies born to drug-addicted mothers. "I just needed to tell somebody. I know it'll be all over town by morning, but for now—I just had to say it out loud. Let it sink in. Before I have to start thinking like a prosecutor again, thinking about charges I'm going to file and what's best for the child and—everything else." She sighed. "Well, I should let you go. I know you've got your own work to do. You're looking for Dixie Sue Folsom, right?"

"Lord. News sure spreads fast in this town."

"I've known Maggie and Dixie Sue forever. They go to my church."

"Everybody goes to your church."

"Well, they ought to. Be a different world if they did. Anyway, I'm the one who told Maggie to call you in the first place. Any sign of the girl?"

"Nothing yet. The law says she's an adult, so you know the drill—we have to tread lightly. If she doesn't want to come home, we can't force the issue. But Maggie's convinced that something's happened to her."

"Drugs in the picture?"

"Doesn't look like it. Just an inappropriate boyfriend."

A brief chuckle. "Ah, romance," Rhonda said wistfully. "I hope that's all it is. Couple of randy young folks—what I wouldn't give to have *that* kind of problem for a change."

"There was an unofficial sighting in the woods behind Briney Hollow. Out near the spot where Wellwood Hospital used to be. I'm heading out there in the morning to check it out."

No response.

"Rhonda?" Bell asked. "Still there?"

"Just watch yourself, okay? When you're beating the bushes and turning over rocks in that godforsaken stretch? Something happens to you—that's it. I'm done. I can't take any more bad news. I swear—I think I'm about to lose my mind sometimes. It's the terrible things that *have* happened—like finding a newborn baby in a *toilet,* for God's sake—and the terrible things that are probably just around the corner. Sometimes it feels like it's all the same thing. What *is* and what will be—all the same. I'm pretty ragged here. So be careful out in those woods."

"I'll be fine. You and I grew up in these parts. We know our way around. Not much we haven't seen before."

"Don't say that. You're tempting fate."

"Come on, Rhonda." Bell made her voice sound playful. "Fate doesn't need to be tempted. Around here, it shows up whenever it damned well pleases. Does whatever it wants. Which is always something bad. And in a strange way, that's good."

"Good?"

"Yeah. Good. It means you can relax. No surprises. Expect the worst—and you're never disappointed."

Chapter Four

Bell emerged from the dense woods and stopped. She had reached a small clearing. Behind her was a living cross-stitch of brown and gold and olive and russet—fall colors, the colors of doomed things intent on flinging off a last vivid hue before sinking into pure earth. Overhead, the sky was flat and drab. A cold wind wouldn't stop bothering the few leaves left on the trees; at first the rattling sound had unnerved her, because it sounded as if someone was coming up behind her, but then she'd gotten used to it. She hardly heard it anymore.

She had been walking for about twenty minutes. She had maintained a slightly stooped posture all that time, her boots crackling across the underbrush, her head bent at an angle in order to avoid the chronic menace of low-hanging branches.

With the clearing before her now she stood fully upright—doing it slowly, testing the resistance as she would a creaky hinge. She was aware of an answering twinge in her lower back. *You're not the only one who's feeling the years, Nick Fogelsong*, she thought ruefully.

She checked her cell. *Damn.* He was right: no bars. She'd be out of touch until she returned to the road.

Finding her way to Wellwood had been relatively easy. That surprised her. So many years had gone by. Despite her assurances to Nick the night before, she'd expected the woods behind Briney Hollow to be so dramatically altered as to constitute a foreign landscape. But that's not what happened.

The memories had kicked in right away. She seemed to know instinctively where she needed to go, at least in a general way, moving through the thicket of stripped-down trees and shredded leaves and slowly disintegrating logs and stubborn weeds and mean-tempered sticker bushes. Certainly things had changed. But the bedrock elements—the creek, the slant of certain hills, the field of boulders that had been shoved here and then left behind when an iceberg pushed through the region tens of thousands of years ago, carving out the mountain valleys—had remained. The infrastructure was intact.

Faint voices from her past had whispered to her, reminding her to follow the twisting creek in the opposite direction of its choppy flow. And then to head north at the fork, where a smaller stream broke off from the larger. At one point she'd stumbled into a shallow ditch that was hidden by a cluster of crunchy brown leaves, and worried at first that she'd sprained her ankle, but she managed to walk it off.

You could walk off anything, any pain. If you had the grit.

These were her woods, hers and Shirley's. She and her sister had played here when they were kids. Well—*she* had played here, and Shirley had watched; Shirley was six years older. These woods weren't exactly close to their trailer on Comer Creek, but they weren't that far away, either. And they were the best woods around, so this was a frequent destination.

More often than not, after a fitful, rambling, zigzag journey that covered several miles and included multiple stops for Bell to shinny up a tree or snatch crawdads out of the creek, they'd ended up at this clearing, site of the ruins of the old hospital. Predictably, there were rumors that it was haunted, that the souls of the people who'd died here still stalked these woods, searching for children whose bodies they could inhabit.

Ghosts gotta have bodies so's they can walk around. That's what Chick Means, a kid who lived in a trailer across the way from theirs, told her when she was six years old. *Everybody knows that. A ghost don't have no body. It's gotta go out and find itself one. Then it's gotta gnaw out your insides so's it can move in and take over.* The explanation had frightened Bell so badly that she'd stayed out of the woods for a solid week.

But then she came back. She always came back. The woods were too much fun, too wild and mysterious and compelling, for her to stay away for long. But after that she made Shirley come with her every time. Just in case.

She'd risk the chance of a ghost nabbing her body—and then scooping out her insides with a slotted spoon and taking over the controls—for the opportunity to scramble up into trees, branch by branch, and jump down, using the soft carpet of leaves and the spongy ground to cushion her fall. She even had a favorite tree: the one right next to the fork in the stream. It was gnarled and gray, and thick across the middle, and it had a creepy-looking canopy of spiky branches that curled at the ends just like a monster's claws, and so naturally it was called the Monster Tree. Bell had loved to climb up its scaly sides, grab a twisted branch with both hands and swing on it, her feet dangling, yelling *Watch me!* at Shirley.

Staying in motion helped. It helped her forget what their lives were really like.

And then, one day, she and Shirley had stopped coming. Things happened to them. Big, terrible things, after which nothing was ever the same. They never came back to the woods again.

Until today. She was alone this time, and she was on the job, but it still felt special. This was a sort of reunion, she realized. A reunion between her and the woods. Both had changed—but not as much as she would've guessed.

Just past the clotted garden of gray boulders and up a familiar hill she had found it again: the site of the old hospital. She hooked her thumbs under the straps of her backpack and examined the space. She indulged in a deep breath, long and slow, specifically to break the rhythm of the hasty, shallow respiration she'd been forced to maintain during her crash and blunder through the dry woods.

The clearing was a revelation. A world that had been crowded and dark and slightly sinister—the overgrown trees blocked out major portions of the sky—was suddenly open, airy, free.

She waited for the sinister feeling to go away, too, as had the trees and the nettles and the murk.

It didn't.

Chapter Five

"Dixie Sue!" she called out, just in case the young woman was hiding nearby. "Hey—Dixie Sue!"

Nothing.

In the center of the clearing were the charred remnants of what had been an enormous stone structure. The roof had gone AWOL a long time ago. The top edges of the four walls were dramatically jagged. In some spots the wall soared until it was five or six times as tall as Bell herself, while in others, it plummeted until it was not much higher than ground level, a mere stub of stone, like a rotten tooth that had snapped off at the gum line. The entirety was black with filth and ancient soot, and crusted with random blooms of greasy-looking moss.

This was—or once had been—Wellwood. The old hospital had stood here for—how long was it, exactly? Wellwood, she knew, was built in 1919. It burned in 1963. Or was it 1964?

So: forty-four years. Or maybe forty-five.

Back in high school, Bell had written a term paper on the history of Raythune County. It was an assignment from the teacher—because God knows a sixteen-year-old Bell would never have picked the hideously boring topic herself—and that was how she'd learned about Wellwood.

Named for Joshua James Wellwood, a coal company executive who had donated the land in the early 1900s, the hospital was built to house the unfortunate souls who suffered from debilitating psychiatric illnesses—"incurables," they were called back then, a word that had startled Bell the first time she came across it. From his obscenely large fortune, J. J. Wellwood had begrudgingly given back a pittance to the citizens of Raythune County, the men and women who risked their lives and sacrificed their health in order to ransack the coal from the vast dark tunnels, in the form of this facility. He died in 1928 at age thirty-seven, as his epic appetites in three areas—sex, alcohol, and food, in order of importance—took a predictable toll. In her term paper, Bell had been forced to bend to the delicate sensibilities of that history teacher of hers, a snippy old prude named Harriet Bledsoe, and refer to the reason for his demise as "natural causes."

Well, fine: Bell hadn't been sure how to spell "syphilis," anyway. She was okay with leaving it out.

In the early 1960s, a fire purportedly caused by a lightning strike raced through the structure and left it in need of expensive repairs. The hospital was closed for good. The few remaining patients had already been transferred to other institutions. The place was padlocked shut, the windows covered with plywood. Its director, Dr. Emmett Trexler, left town and never returned.

That was what Bell had learned in her research. The rest she knew from personal experience, from roaming through these woods and wandering around the site. Over the decades the high stone walls had been pummeled by sledgehammers and clawed at by mattocks, as scavengers pried loose and swiped the stones. The walkways were overrun by ravenous vegetation. Anything valuable was taken; everything else was left to rot. Wellwood sank down into a daze of benign devastation.

And yet in one of those West Virginia history books she consulted, Bell had seen a striking photo from the hospital's heyday: the enormous front door had a beautiful copper inlay of a rising sun—an incongruous touch of elegance for a public hospital. The door had disappeared years ago, of course, wrenched off and carted away by vandals. Gone, too, were the stately rows of leaded windows, and the metal frames of the dozens and dozens of patient beds, among the few items that had survived the fire.

"Dixie Sue?" she called again.

No answer. Just a rippling series of faint crackles as the wind worried the few leaves still clinging to the trees back in the woods.

She walked the length of the front wall, counting her steps the way she'd done as a little girl. The rhyme she'd made up at the time came back to her: *One, two, three, four, Who's that knocking at the door? Five, six, seven, eight, Monster! Monster! at the gate.* She'd chanted it out loud while she marched. Shirley had made fun of her: *You're going to scare yourself silly, Belfa. You'll have nightmares tonight. Cut it out.*

She stopped at a part of the wall that was broken off low enough for her to peer over. Flung across the enormous rectangle of muddy black ground—the space where the four floors of the hospital once had risen in symmetrical precision—were massive heaps of garbage, some new, some decades old. Bell spotted used syringes, orange Cheetos wrappers, wadded-up paper sacks and crumpled cups printed with the logos of McDonald's and KFC, sodden clumps of dirty clothes, an old mop, a rusty tricycle, a headless doll, a ripped canvas tent, stacks of crushed beer cans, two TV sets with busted screens, a bent golf club, at least five waterlogged mattresses, squiggly transparent piles of used condoms. Excavating the layers of garbage, she thought, would be a job for an archeologist.

An archeologist with a very strong stomach.

"Dixie Sue!"

Still nothing.

Bell liberated the water bottle from the mesh pouch that hung off her backpack and treated herself to three long gulps.

She tried again: "Hey, Dixie Sue!"

She recapped the bottle and wedged it back in the pouch. She stood still, listening intently.

The quiet, she realized, was a little freaky. Back in the woods, she'd been surrounded by small but constant sounds: the thump and thrash of her boots as she marched along, ducking at tree branches; the agitated chitter of squirrels; the trickle of birdsong. Here, the noise simply . . . *ended*. It was as if the sounds were unwilling to cross the threshold that separated the sweeping generosity of the woods from this sere, pinched-off clearing.

The whole world stopped right here.

"Dixie Sue!" Louder than before.

Her voice was instantly swallowed up by the silence, like a pebble dropped into a bottomless well. Had she really spoken, or just dreamed that she had? She couldn't have said for sure.

"Dixie Sue?" Bell called out, for what she'd decided would be the final time.

No answer. The young woman wasn't here.

Still, Bell had to be thorough, had to make sure she'd missed no clues that Dixie Sue had visited recently, so that she could report as much to Maggie Folsom. Which meant traipsing across the space where the hospital's interior used to be.

Sifting through Garbage Gulch, in other words.

Maybe I should've let Nick come along, after all, she reflected. *Wouldn't chivalry demand that he do the honors and wade through the used condoms?*

She stepped over the wall.

Chapter Six

Bell kicked at the garbage.

Gross, she thought. *Dixie Sue—why aren't you home with your mama, girl? The two of you can work it out, okay?* She had already decided that if she did come across Dixie Sue and Travis, here or anywhere else, she wouldn't deliver a lecture. That wasn't her job. Her job was to find the young woman and take her home. Maggie Folsom could handle all the how-could-yous.

She had been looking down too long. Her neck ached. She needed some relief. Lifting her eyes to the sky, she spotted the brief, frantic glitter of a black wing. The bird was big enough to be a crow. She waited to hear, trailing in its wake, the familiar raucous complaint, the avian equivalent of an angry letter to the editor, but there was nothing. No sound.

Maybe she was mistaken. Maybe it hadn't been a crow, after all.

Or maybe even crows were intimidated by this place, or were simply repulsed by the squalor, the blight, left behind by creatures who couldn't fly but who ravaged the earth as if they were somehow superior to all other creatures who relied upon it, too. Maybe the crows, upset but dignified, kept their own counsel when they crossed the hospital grounds.

And maybe I'm being ridiculous. Bell hiked the backpack higher on her shoulder; it kept sliding down. She really ought to adjust the strap.

She called out, "Dixie Sue?" one more time, for good measure, despite her earlier pledge to herself, and she added, "Travis?" just in case.

Nothing.

And then she smelled it.

Bell was just inside the perimeter, a foot or so beyond the place where she'd stepped over the ruined wall. The odor was vivid, unmistakable. It had separated itself from the other smells breathed out by these woods, by any woods—the rotting scent of decay as organic matter slowly unwound—and by the sickly-sweet smell of the newer garbage, wafting by on a scallop of wind.

She knew. She knew *before* she knew, actually; she knew what it was before she had spotted any objective fact to prove it. This was a visceral feeling, a primitive sort of knowing that lived well below the level of conscious thought.

Later she would wonder—when she finally had time for such reflection, which definitely wasn't right now—how the human body realized that it was in the presence of death. The death of a fellow human being.

The intellect was not involved. Somehow the reality entered through the skin, through the senses:

Death was close. Death was *here*.

She turned around, looked down, and verified her dread.

Tucked against the inside of the broken wall, in the center of a heaped-up mound of leaves and sticks and thistles, a ragged vertical slit had been opened slightly by the wind, revealing an object that resembled a pale hand. Acutely conscious of the need not to contaminate a potential crime scene, but also aware that she had to be sure before raising an alarm, Bell reached for a long crooked branch that she spotted on the ground nearby.

She used it to push away—gently, delicately—the dry brown hash of dirt and sticks and grass and crumbled masonry that had fetched up against the wall, uncovering the rest of what lay beneath.

The hand was attached to a body. The body was facedown on the cold autumn ground. It appeared to be—Bell's guess was based on the long black hair and the narrow shoulders—female.

In the middle of the back of the head was a gash lined with crusted blood. The wound was so deep that brain matter was visible at the bottom of the steep V-shaped chasm.

Bell stumbled backward, catching herself just in time to keep from tripping into a pile of trash. Her hand was trembling so badly that she dropped the stick. Her breakfast rose in her throat. Thoughts came in a frantic tumble:

I've got to get back to the hard road. There's no cell service out here—and I have to notify the sheriff. I have to go. I have to run.

She had found Dixie Sue Folsom.

Chapter Seven

The front door opened and closed. It wasn't a loud sound—a mild click and rasp as the handle turned, a muted creak of the hinge, then another click of closure—but it was a familiar one. It was a sound that Jake felt as much as heard; his heart seemed to shift its rhythm for a few seconds.

Because it was her. It was Molly.

Before the shooting that left him in a wheelchair, he hadn't minded silence. He lived alone, after an early marriage had ended in divorce. He'd enjoyed being in a quiet house, a place where all the sounds were made by him. All the messes, too. He liked having no one to answer to—just himself. He could come home after a long day's or night's work as a deputy sheriff and yank his brown shirttails out of his brown pants, kick off his boots, grab a Rolling Rock, rear back in the recliner. Bask in the silence.

After his injury, though, when he didn't have his work anymore, the silence changed. It felt weaponized. He feared it. He would never trust it. He knew better than to turn his back on it.

Which was one of the reasons he'd asked Molly and Malik to move in. Yes, he loved Molly, no question about it, but he also realized he needed to counter that silence. Fight back against it. He still had periods of solitude, especially on mornings such as this one, when Malik went to a workshop run by Goodwill and Molly wasn't yet home from the overnight shift. But he could appreciate the solitude—even savor it—because he knew it would end soon.

"In here," he called out.

He'd pulled his chair up to the kitchen table, his favorite place to wait for her when she came home from work. The kitchen window faced east and was filled with late-morning sunlight. He had started another pot of coffee a few minutes ago. The heavy smell quickly insinuated itself throughout the space, an area so tiny that there was barely room for the refrigerator, stove, sink, and the small green metal table in the middle. It wasn't a space designed for a man in a wheelchair.

"Hey, there," Molly said. "Thought I'd never get out of there. Ton of reports to write. First we save lives—and then they punish us with the paperwork."

She stood in the threshold linking the living room to the kitchen. He changed the angle of his chair so that he could look at her straight on, not sideways, and his heart jumped. The breath caught in his chest. Like always.

She was an African-American woman of average height and medium build. Her skin was a rich, lustrous black that seemed to capture the light and hold it. Her hands—they were what Jake had first noticed about her, years ago when they frequently ended up at the same accident scenes as deputy sheriff and EMT, before he'd found the courage to ask her out—were large and strong, the nails cut short and square to accommodate the work she did. She wore her black springy hair pushed back from her high forehead; a blue bandana kept it there. Her dark eyes crackled with energy, despite how fatigued he knew she must be.

Jake smiled. *God,* he thought, *I love this woman.*

Each time he saw her after they'd been apart for any length of time, he realized anew the depth and complexity of what he felt for her. He cherished her for her steadfastness, for the quality of her character, which manifested itself in her devotion to her younger brother, Malik, and in how she did her job as an EMT. But he was also passionately attracted to her—most definitely so. Their lovemaking was a continual surprise to him, an ever-renewing source of joy. It was a marvel. It was a sort of thrilling, golden release that, in the deep well of his despair after he'd been shot, he never thought he'd be able to share with anyone, ever again.

"Hey," Jake replied. "Bus came right on time for Malik. He did good this morning, by the way. Brushed his teeth without me having to ask."

"He's getting better about that. Remembering, I mean. All on his own."

That wasn't true, and she knew it. The truth was, it was always hit or miss with Malik. A crap shoot. Sometimes he brushed his teeth with no prompting; other times, when they reminded him, he pitched a furious fit, flinging the toothbrush into the toilet, grabbing the tooth-paste tube and squirting the striped goo all over the bathroom. His frustration erupted randomly. Jake now bought toothbrushes in giant multi-packs.

But if Molly wanted to see progress where there wasn't any prog-ress, that was fine with him. He'd go along with it. Sometimes he thought that that was the real secret of life: pretending things were getting bet-ter even if they weren't. Living as if there really might be something better around the corner.

Well, why not?

"Made coffee," he said, unnecessarily.

She grinned and made an *Mm-mmm* sound. "That's how I found my way home. The smell."

"I know you might want to just crash—but if you're up for it, I could go for a talk."

Sometimes, after working the overnight, Molly came home and went right to bed. She didn't even shower first, much as she yearned to rinse off the night. That was how Jake knew it had been a long, difficult shift. Other times, she was still relatively fresh, and ready to chat. Their conversations, she had once told him, were how she first realized she loved him. *Not my handsome face?* he'd teased her. *Not my muscles and my fancy deputy sheriff's hat?* She answered him seriously: *Nope. It was how you talked about the people who live around here. Like they matter.* He wasn't sure he understood, but it pleased him. Because it came from her.

"I'm fine," Molly said. "Not too many runs. Just the usual. Lotsa calls that shouldn't have been calls in the first place—earaches, toothaches, crying babies. If you don't have insurance, you call the squad." Stepping into the kitchen, she repeated the *Mm-mmm* sound. "Coffee—my favorite thing in the world."

"Wow," Jake said, pretending umbrage. "Guess that puts me in *my* place, right?"

Instead of bantering with him, she leaned over, took his face between her hands, and gave him a slow, deep kiss on the mouth. Jake instantly felt the melting sensation that her touch always induced in him. She tasted like the Juicy Fruit gum she chewed to keep herself alert during long nights on duty.

"Okay," he said, when he was able to talk again. "I guess you're kind of partial to me, after all."

She laughed. She was at the coffeepot now, filling her mug. The countertop had been lowered to accommodate Jake in his wheelchair. They were still paying off the contractor who had done it. "Ready for more?" she asked, holding up the pot.

"I'm good."

"Tommy and Gil had a helluva run." She sat down next to him. "They found a baby in the toilet of the Burger Boss. Some addict had given birth right there."

"Jesus."

"Yeah."

"Makes you wonder."

"Sure does." She drank her coffee, closing her eyes as she savored it.

"Did the kid live?"

"Last I heard, he was doing okay." She shrugged. "You never know, though. Gonna be a lot of problems later. Addicted mother and all."

"Jesus," Jake repeated. He didn't want to picture it, but he did: a newborn nestled in a dirty toilet bowl in a public bathroom. The miracle of birth—reduced to that. "I delivered a couple of babies myself when I was on the job," he went on. "One was in the backseat of a car. The other was in the lady's living room. Squad was held up so I did the honors."

"You never told me that. I've heard about the time you did CPR on the old man and the time you put the splint on that woman's broken leg while she cursed at you and all the rest of your medical adventures—but not delivering babies."

"One of the moms named the baby Jake in my honor."

"Really."

"Yeah—but when the dad finally sobered up and came to the hospital a few hours later, he made her change it to his own name. Didn't want another man's name on his kid, he said."

"Well," Molly said, grinning as she pushed at his shoulder, "glory is fleeting."

"Damn straight."

This was what he loved, and he knew that she loved it, too: just *this*. Being together, trading news of their days, reveling in the amazing luck of having found another person in this strange, cold world who cared about you and looked out for you, and whom you wanted, at the end or the beginning of every day, to tell your story to.

"So," Molly said. "You've got a new case, right? A runaway. How's it going?"

He had texted her when he'd left the office last night. Just a few details about Maggie Folsom's visit and the search for her daughter. Molly liked to keep up with his work. She'd seen what having work again—real work, work he cared about—had done for him.

"Yeah," he said. "I have a ton of calls to make this morning to deputies in other counties. Checking to see if she's been picked up anywhere. Nick and I split up the list. Bell's hiking through the woods by Briney Hollow. Had a report of a sighting out there." He took a drink of his coffee. "Not bad, if I do say so myself."

She nodded, her mind elsewhere. "With everything else people have to deal with around here—keeping the rent paid and food on the table—you'd think a kid wouldn't put a parent through that. All the anxiety."

"Can't argue with you there. But families are complicated. You never know what's going on behind closed doors."

"You mean the girl might've had a reason for running away?"

"Everybody's got a reason for running away. Or thinks they do."

He put his hands on top of the big wheels, moving the chair back and forth a quarter inch or so in each direction. It was a nervous habit. "Dixie Sue Folsom is an adult. Maybe she just got tired of living at home. Wants to spread her wings."

"Fine. But she could at least let her mom know. So she won't worry."

"Well, sometimes people get carried away. Apparently there's a boyfriend involved."

Molly flashed him a grin. Before they'd gotten together, back when they were still just colleagues, she never smiled. Or at least Jake didn't remember seeing her smile. Now, though, she smiled a lot. He liked to think that he was responsible.

"I know a little bit about that," she said.

"About what?"

"Getting carried away." She put a hand on his chest and leaned in, kissing his cheek this time. And he felt the miracle of his present life all over again, spreading through the parts of his body that could still feel. It *was* a miracle, to be sure, especially when compared to what he'd thought his life was going to be, the empty place he'd staked out for himself, the pointlessness, the dreariness.

After all, he was nobody's idea of a bargain.

There was the wheelchair, which wasn't going away. And there was the fact that he had to be meticulously careful about the most mundane aspects of life; he had to worry about bedsores and urinary tract infections and muscle atrophy. He was prone to fits of depression. Who wouldn't be? He was, to say the least, a handful.

But a year ago, after he and Molly had spent several months in a not-unpleasant-yet-not-totally-satisfying-either limbo, during which time she and Malik began spending weekends here, and some weeknights, too, and after Jake and Molly had made love many times, with increasing degrees of pleasure for both of them, Molly came to him one day and said:

I'm in.

That was it. No romantic speeches. Molly Drucker didn't do romantic speeches.

I'm in.

He knew a great deal about her by that point, from her history to her habits, and he knew that an *I'm in* from Molly Drucker was the equivalent of *I'm in love with you and I want us to be together for the rest of our lives* from anybody else. She could be brusque, and even a little harsh, but when she made up her mind, you could count on her. She was a rock. In a world of change and chaos—Lord, he knew about change, he knew too well how life could knock you down with a swipe of its big, nasty paw—Molly was stable and solid. Permanent.

I'm in.

She was committed. She had attached her life—and Malik's life, too, because it had to be a package deal—to Jake's life, and they were slowly creating a new world out of what they had known before, each of them, in their old, separate worlds, and this new world was a family.

But was this really enough for her?

When Jake allowed himself to think past the satisfactions of the present, a slow foreboding crept into his thoughts. What if Molly ultimately wanted things he couldn't give her?

The idea of losing her, of her not being a daily part of his life, filled him with anxiety. And unlike his other fears, he couldn't share that one with her.

What if she stopped loving him? Or simply decided that loving him was too much trouble, that it involved too many sacrifices and compromises?

What if she decided one day that he just wasn't worth it?

He willed his thoughts to settle down. She was here now, wasn't she? And there was nothing better than that.

He was just about to tell her about something Malik had said that morning—Molly's head was tucked against his shoulder by now, and she still had a hand on his chest—when his cell rang.

Jake answered, listened, and frowned.

"Damn," he murmured, after he'd clicked off the call. The word wasn't said in anger, but in sadness, in perplexity.

"What is it?"

"That was Nick. He just heard from Bell. She found her—Dixie Sue Folsom, I mean. Out at Wellwood."

Molly sat up straight. "Is she—?"

Jake shook his head. "She's dead. Definitely a homicide. Crime scene unit's coming from Charleston."

Chapter Eight

On her way back to the clearing, Bell startled two fawns under a massive black oak tree off to her left. There was no doe in sight. Chances were, the mother had been shot by a hunter or killed on the highway—the two fates most likely to befall wildlife in these parts—and the fawns would wander, confused and vulnerable, until they figured out how to survive on their own.

Or not, whereupon they'd perish. It could go either way. Nature was unsentimental; it was never swayed by cuteness, as humans were.

She stopped. The fawns stared at her, dipping their heads in unison, twitching their fuzzy ears. Their legs were as thin as stilts. Bell was close enough to count the spots on their tawny backs. And then, with a movement as awkward and clownish as it was abrupt, they gamboled away.

She kept going. She had recovered her emotional equilibrium by now, her poise, and she wanted to get back to the clearing ahead of the crime scene unit, ahead of Sheriff Harrison, and ahead of Nick, too. He was coming, despite the pain that the long hike would kindle in his back, that pinch and sear caused by bruised tissue and over-stretched ligaments as he crossed the uneven terrain.

To procure a cell signal, she'd had to return to the main road. Once there, she had called, in order, Pam Harrison and Nick. Her communication with the sheriff was clipped and calm: "Hey, Pam. It's Bell

Elkins. I'm in the woods behind Briney Hollow. At the old hospital. Found a body." She added a few more details about why she'd been searching for Dixie Sue Folsom.

And about how, unfortunately, she had found her.

Harrison's response was brusque: "On my way. I'll notify the state crime lab. They can meet us there."

Because this was Bell, and because they'd worked together for so many years on so many cases, the sheriff didn't have to add what she would've added, if this had been a call from anybody else: *Don't touch the body. Don't touch anything, matter of fact. Stay back. Might be footprints and other evidence in the area for the experts to look at.* The sheriff, knowing that the average citizen might wonder why they had to wait for a team to get there all the way from Charleston to start analyzing the scene, would have added an explanation: *We don't have our own forensics unit. Gotta rely on the state lab. They're usually pretty quick about getting here when we call 'em.*

Bell, of course, didn't need to hear any of that. She knew.

"Understood," she replied. But Harrison had already hung up.

Then she'd called Nick. Two sentences into her description of what she'd found, he'd interrupted her.

"I'm coming," he said. "I'll let Jake know."

"Wait—should we notify Maggie Folsom?"

"Not our job."

He was right. That happened sometimes; she slipped back into her old role, forgetting that it wasn't her responsibility anymore to notify the next of kin—even if the next of kin was a client. She wondered when she'd reach the point where her first impulse wasn't to be a prosecutor.

"See you soon," Nick said.

"What about your back?"

"Hell with my back." The change of subject came quickly. "Good thing it was you that came across the scene and not that hunter friend of Maggie's. You knew enough not to contaminate any evidence." She heard a grunt on the line, which probably meant Nick had wedged the cell between his chin and an upraised shoulder as he stood and gathered his gear. "Any sign of the boyfriend?"

"No."

"On my way. I know so many of those crime scene folks—it'll feel like a class reunion."

"Hey, Nick—be careful, okay? Some tricky spots in these woods. Rough terrain. Don't forget about your back."

Another grunt. "Not likely to forget."

Fifteen minutes after scaring the fawns Bell was back at the clearing again. She had only a short period of time before the place would be dominated by the forensics unit and all that went with it: hastily erected white plastic tents and sagging yellow ropes of crime scene tape and portable fold-out tables and picnic coolers for storage of perishable elements and fingerprint kits and snapped-together scaffolding for halogen lights—in case sundown came before they finished their exacting work—and cardboard boxes packed with gloves and gowns and shoe covers and evidence bags.

Plus the noise. Always, the noise.

The examination of crime scenes—especially outdoor ones—was not a quiet business. Hit-skip scenes, pileups on the interstate, recovery efforts after building collapses, arson fires: As a prosecutor, she'd been called to dozens of places suddenly rendered significant by unnatural death. The racket was always outlandish. Stress, she knew, tended to make people shout, even when shouting wasn't necessary. Radios added to the mess, spreading their crackling static. If vehicles were present—and that wouldn't be the case today because, given the landscape, the team would have to leave its van out by the road and come on foot, just as she had—the cacophony would include the running grumble of powerful engines, left to idle in total disregard of environmental etiquette.

Bell had a theory about the noise, a theory honed over a long career. Maybe all the yelling and bluster was a way to push back against the permanent hush of death. Most people grew quieter on the rare occasions when they were in the presence of a dead body; they whispered and shook their heads. But the voices of law enforcement personnel who saw death every day—EMTs, sheriffs, deputies, forensics specialists—invariably got louder. Their humor, coarser.

Their attitudes, even more brittle and cynical. Bell chalked it up to false bravado: *Lost count of the dead bodies I've seen. Doesn't rattle me one bit. Dead's dead.*

Was she correct in her drive-by psychoanalysis? Hell if she knew. But she did know this: The moment this space was invaded by the crew from Charleston, meditation would be impossible.

So she needed to do it now, or not at all.

Her explorations would all have to be visual this time. She couldn't move beyond the edge of the clearing. Her footprints would have to be eliminated, first thing, once the forensics unit got down to business, and the less she tromped around, the better. Every move she made, from here on out, would create more work for them, would instigate entire networks of data that would have to be meticulously excluded after they were procured. So she stayed where she was.

She was keen to go forward. She was, in fact, *desperate* to go forward. She wanted another look at the body beneath the hastily made blanket of leaves and branches and soil—after which she'd comb the area for any clues, anything left behind by Dixie Sue's assailant in a panicked rush to escape. But she knew better. Leaving a crime scene intact was a sacred tenet of law enforcement. It was second nature to her.

She was aware, all at once, of the sound of voices growing closer, rising from the woods behind her. They were on their way.

In her last minute of solitude, her eyes stayed fixed on the broken stone wall. Her mind stayed fixed on what was behind it.

The voices were louder now. The volume and variety meant that this was the team from Charleston. It also meant that Bell's questions would soon be answered, courtesy of the experts who were just about to reach the clearing and start their work.

And then Bell did something she had never done as a prosecutor, because it would have seemed unprofessional, as well as beside the point:

She uttered a swift, silent prayer for the soul of the young woman who had been so cavalierly discarded here in this remote and rugged place, thrown away like just another piece of trash.

Chapter Nine

"Let me guess," Bell said. "They flipped a coin to see who had to drive to Raythune County and you picked heads. Came up tails."

Barbara Masters uttered a small chuckle. "Bell. How are you?"

"Hanging in there."

Masters was chief of one of the forensics units. Bell had known her for years, although "known" was a bit of a stretch; she had called Masters as an expert witness in about half a dozen criminal trials. They'd had a cup of coffee once, at the end of a daylong seminar Masters had conducted for the Raythune County Sheriff's Department on ways to avoid contaminating a crime scene. That was six, maybe seven years ago now.

"Good to see you," Masters said.

She was a square-built, heavy-breasted woman with a yellowish complexion, wide shoulders, thick thighs, and no discernable waist. She wore her frizzy gray hair pulled back into a single braid that bisected her back like a weary pendulum that had lost the will to swing. Her silver-framed glasses constantly slipped down her nose, causing her to jab at them with a chubby thumb to restore them to their perch.

Masters pulled off her quilted coat. It had been a long, cumbersome march from road to crime scene. Despite the cold, sweat darkened the armpits of her gray sweatshirt. The cuffs of her chinos were stained with the same mud that covered her hiking boots. Behind her, two other forensics specialists, an older man and a youngish woman, had already begun unpacking gear.

Masters put out a hand. Bell shook it.

"Just like old times, right?" Masters said.

"Sure is."

It wasn't, not even close. But Masters, she knew, was trying to be cordial, despite the entirely predictable awkwardness that clung to the moment. Bell wasn't a prosecutor anymore. And yet here they were, in a venue that was familiar to both: a crime scene. Had their reunion occurred somewhere else—a restaurant, say, or a store or a street corner—they might have been more comfortable. But this was a replication of past encounters, with the odd asterisk that Bell was now a civilian, while Masters was still on the job.

Bell released Masters's hand and nodded to Sheriff Harrison, who had come up behind her. "Hey, Pam."

Harrison nodded. She doffed her sheriff's hat and wiped her forehead. The hat was a large, flat-brimmed brown one, big as a radial tire, with a loop of gold braid around the crown. Harrison was a petite woman in her early thirties, with a heart-shaped face and short brown hair that was one shade darker than her hat. She had a strawberry birthmark that wrapped around the left side of her neck, splashing up on her face. As long as Bell had known her, she'd been preternaturally fit. You might not be able to see the muscles bunching and flexing under the skin with every gesture the sheriff made, but you sensed them. There was a quality of firm reserve to Pam Harrison, a sense of absolute self-containment. Nothing got in or came out.

"You didn't see any murder weapon, I take it?" she asked.

Bell shook her head. "But I didn't do a thorough search. I backed off the moment I found the body."

"Good call." Harrison examined the dirt on the knees of her trousers. She didn't bother wiping it off. Bell wondered if she'd tripped and fallen in one of the same gullies that had taken her down. These woods could surprise you, even when you knew them well. "I didn't see any cars other than yours parked along the road," the sheriff noted. "No sign of the victim's vehicle."

Masters rejoined them. She'd been making notes on an iPad. She looked around at the ruins of the stone walls. "So what the hell *is* this place? Or was, I guess, is the better question."

"Wellwood." Bell said the word as if it settled the matter.

"What's a Wellwood?"

Harrison answered before Bell could. "State mental hospital. Burned down in the early 1960s."

"A hospital?" Masters asked. "Way out here?"

"Yeah," the sheriff replied. "The land was cheap. Donated by some Richie Rich who didn't have any other use for it and wanted the tax write-off. They made it a state mental hospital for the poor."

Masters looked around again, frowning this time. "I don't see a road."

"Long gone. Wasn't much of one to begin with." The sheriff's voice was flat. "Wellwood was where they stuck people that nobody cared about. The kind of people who didn't get a lot of visitors, in other words. So the quality of the road didn't matter."

Masters turned to Bell. Enough small talk. Time to work. "I understand you have a preliminary ID for us."

"Right. Dixie Sue Folsom. Nineteen years old. Missing for three days. My colleagues and I were hired by her mother to find her."

Masters winced. "Well, I guess you did. Not the way her mother was hoping for, though. Never easy when it's a young one. Okay, let's get started. I want this body out of here as soon as possible." Raising her voice, she addressed her team. "Time to suit up, guys. Lesley, seal off the perimeter. Mark, start your evidence sweeps. I want pictures of everything. I've already recorded the time and temperature." The forensics techs were ready to go; they'd tugged on pale blue gowns and gloves and snapped on shoe covers while their boss chatted.

To the sheriff, Masters said, "I'd appreciate some help turning her over, when the time comes."

Masters put on her own gear and approached the body. Each step was so slow and careful and premeditated that she looked as if she were moving underwater. Once there, she squatted and examined the wound.

Bell and Harrison watched her from a distance.

"I knew Maggie Folsom had hired you to look for her daughter," the sheriff said. "But what brought you way out here?"

"Maggie got a tip from a neighbor. A hunter thought he might have spotted the girl and her boyfriend in the woods."

"Any sign of the boyfriend?"

"No."

"Probably long gone, especially if he's responsible." Harrison's eyes swept the clearing. "Came out here a time or two myself as a kid. Used to stop at the Monster Tree first and use it as an observation post."

Surprised, Bell said, "You called it the Monster Tree, too? You mean the one by the creek with those weird branches that curl at the end?"

"Sure. Everybody called it that."

"I thought my sister made up the name."

"Nope. It's been that forever. My grandfather's the one who told me about it. He didn't like me playing in the woods, though. Whipped my butt a time or two when he heard I'd been out here. Claimed the whole area was still full of what he called 'retards'—even though the hospital had closed down a long time before I was born." She used two hands to readjust the big hat on her head. "Forgive my use of that word. It was before the age of political correctness. Not that Pops would've cared about that. He pissed people off for sport. Enjoyed making them mad or watching them squirm."

Masters was back. "Getting ready to turn her faceup. Sheriff, I could use that hand now. Gloves are right over there. And Bell—once we've finished with the initial examination, I'll send Mark over to get a formal statement from you about your actions from the time you entered the woods until you contacted us."

Bell nodded.

Sheriff Harrison and Masters moved forward. Bell instinctively began walking alongside them, but felt a hand clamped on her forearm.

"Right," Bell said. She got it. She didn't need Masters to say anything out loud.

I'm a bystander. I'm somebody who just happened upon a crime scene. I have no power here, no duties.

She wasn't a part of the official investigation. Not anymore.

From the woods that bordered the clearing there came a heavy swell of thrashing and crackling sounds, accompanied by a muttered chant of mild obscenities. Masters and the sheriff paused. They'd just stepped over the low part of the wall, preparing to bend down and flip the body.

Nick Fogelsong lumbered out of the dense underbrush. He batted at a branch that snapped back at him, prompting another *Damnation*. He shook a foot to dislodge a vine that had gotten tangled in his shoelaces. Didn't work. So he reached down, ripping it away from his boot and flinging it aside, adding one more *Hell's bells* just for continuity's sake.

"Sorry it—took me—so long—to get here," he said. His words came in splutters and bunches, and the bunches were separated by gasps as he tried to catch his breath. He looked disheveled, and shaky with exhaustion. He bent over again, this time to grab at the knees of his mud-streaked jeans. "Jogged most of the way. It's hell getting old. Not much of a news flash there, I guess."

"Nick Fogelsong," Masters said. There was a *Long time no see* lilt to her voice.

"Barb. How are you?"

"Fair to middlin'. I heard you were back in West Virginia. Nice to see you. But don't take another step. This is a crime scene."

He didn't like that, but nobody cared if he liked it or not. The area behind the stone wall was cordoned off with yellow tape. A technician continued to move around it in a wide circle, taking multiple photos of the body and the context.

"So," Nick said. "Any idea how long she's been out here?"

Masters shrugged. "Based on the amount of rigor, can't have been more than five or six hours. Nasty head wound. Administered at close range. She never had a chance. Would've been quick." She checked her gloves, making sure the fit was snug. "Pam and I were just about to turn her over to check for additional injuries. Here we go."

There was a soft *whump* as the body landed on its back.

Something was wrong. Bell could tell by the frown that had invaded the sheriff's face. Masters's expression was one of puzzlement.

"How old did you say your runaway was?" Masters asked.

"Nineteen," Bell and Nick replied in unison.

"Then we've got a problem." Masters took a step back.

"Yeah," the sheriff agreed. "You could say that."

Masters offered Nick and Bell a two-fingered wave, giving them permission to approach. "We've already swept for footprints. Come take a look," she said.

This was not the body of a young woman. The face was deeply lined. The chin had receded some years ago into a pale white pudding of excess flesh. A pair of thick-lensed glasses had smashed against the eyes. The victim, when struck in the back of the head, had clearly toppled straight forward onto the hard ground.

"That," Nick said with somber certitude, "is not Dixie Sue Folsom."

"So who is it?" Bell asked. "I don't think I've ever seen her before. Anybody recognize her?"

Even the trees that surrounded the clearing seemed to lean in a little closer, as if they too were keen to hear what would be coming next.

"Yeah," Nick replied. "I do."

Chapter Ten

The hunk of apple pie was so high and wide and delectably hefty that it sagged over the edges of the big white plate, trailing a kibble of crust on the tabletop. Bell reached for her fork. Yet instead of digging in—apple was her favorite, and the rich aroma proved that the slice was ineluctably fresh—she merely lifted a flake of the lattice top.

Then she set down her fork.

Why the hell had she ordered *pie,* of all things? Tonight of all nights?

She knew why. She'd done it because she wanted to pretend, by doing something ordinary such as having a slice of pie at JP's diner, that it hadn't happened. Wanted to pretend that she and Nick hadn't just made the long drive from Briney Hollow into Acker's Gap, after having stared down at a dead body that was not, as she had originally thought, Dixie Sue Folsom.

"Something wrong with your pie?" Nick asked. He'd ordered coffee, but hadn't touched it.

"Tell me about Darla Gilley."

That, according to Nick, was the name of the woman whose body she had found facedown at Wellwood.

Bell didn't bother answering his question about the pie. He knew the pie was good. He knew that *she* knew the pie was good, without either of them having tasted it tonight. The pie here was always good.

More than good—it was perfect. Pie was a JP's specialty. The owner, Jackie LeFevre, didn't make the pies herself—she was honest about that, honest about everything, sometimes to the point of rudeness. Jackie hired Ruthie Comstock to come over from Beaverton every other day to whip them up on the premises. Ruthie Comstock was a wizard with flour and sugar and lard.

Shortly after Nick had made the corrected ID at the crime scene, he and Bell departed in their respective vehicles. There was nothing more for them to do. The sheriff had only let them stay as long as she did out of courtesy, and out of a respect for the jobs they'd formerly held, and out of deference to the fact that Bell was the one who'd called them in the first place.

It was Nick's idea to reconvene at JP's. Fine with her, Bell had said; she wanted to know more about Darla, and more about what might have lured her into the woods behind Briney Hollow.

Because whatever it was, it had gotten her killed.

"What do you want to know?" he asked.

"Anything you got." Bell pushed the plate and its oversized cargo to one side. "It just feels—out of balance. All wrong."

He knew what she meant. He knew because they'd discussed it before, years ago, when he was sheriff and she was prosecutor. They had been in the presence of death many times, the two of them, and they often acknowledged the fact that the dead were on their own, and intensely vulnerable—more vulnerable, in some ways, than the living. The dead weren't able to protect themselves. A dead body was helpless. It couldn't hide. It couldn't tell you to go away and mind your own damned business.

And when the body was that of a stranger—as Darla Gilley was to Bell—then things were even more askew. Bell had seen her with all of her defenses down. She had seen her dead. The only way to make it right was to know more about her, so that the sum total of the information she had about Darla Gilley didn't begin and end with how she looked as a corpse.

"Like I told you when we first sat down," Nick said. "Darla's brother, Joe, was my best friend in high school. I knew Darla as Joe's little sister. She was quite a bit younger."

"Right. But I mean her personality."

He sampled his coffee while he pondered the question. "I knew her pretty well when I was eighteen, nineteen years old, but—" His expression turned rueful. "—that was a long time ago. Once we all got to be adults, I only saw her two or three times a year. At Joe's house, mostly, when Brenda—that's Joe's wife—threw parties for his birthday or when we got together to watch the Super Bowl. Things like that. Darla wasn't around Acker's Gap much. She and her husband—ex-husband now—lived over in Bretherton County. In Beverly, I think."

Bell nodded impatiently. "Okay. But what was she *like*? I mean— shy or outgoing? Funny? Not funny? Depressed? Cheerful?" She looked around. Her gaze finally came back to the plate at her elbow. She gestured toward it. "Hell—what kind of pie did she like? Come on, Nick—I'll take anything. Any little detail."

Nick, trying to buy more time to come up with an answer, also checked out the handful of customers in the diner. The place was less than half filled. It was shortly after six P.M., which meant this should have been the dinner rush; the word "rush," however, no longer had any relevance here. JP's, like too many businesses in Acker's Gap, was barely hanging on. No one was quite sure, in fact, how Jackie *did* manage to keep the diner going. She'd opened it eight years ago, close to the location of a now-gone restaurant owned by her late mother, Joyce. That's where the name came from: JP's was short for "Joyce's Place."

He set down his mug. "I'll tell you what she was. Feisty. That's the word Joe always used—'Darla's feisty as all get-out,' he'd say. That's my recollection, too. She speaks her mind. Does just as she pleases. Pins all that hair up on top of her head and faces forward and plunges right in. Joe's kind of quiet, he likes to hang back and bide his time, but Darla—she's a firecracker."

He'd slipped naturally back into the present tense. That would happen for a while, Bell knew, until the reality of her death settled in.

"Tell you this much," Nick went on. "This is gonna hit Joe real hard. I know the protocol says I can't call him until the sheriff's done the formal notification—but my God, I wish I could. Just to let him know I'm here for him. This is gonna tear the man apart. It's gonna be rough. Especially in his condition."

"His condition?"

"Pancreatic cancer. He's fading fast. Just a matter of time now. A month or two, maybe. Or weeks."

"Jesus Christ. How much sorrow can one person take?"

"'Bout as much as they're given, I reckon. No more and no less."

Now it was Bell's turn to glance around the diner, to cover up the fact that she didn't know what to say to that. There were six other people present at the moment, a group of four at a booth by the wood-stove and two people sitting by themselves at the counter, shoulders hunched over their plates of food. Mac-and-cheese casserole was the Friday night special. From time to time Bell heard the melancholy scrape of fork across plate as somebody gathered up a bite.

She decided to get back to practicalities. "Masters was about as forthcoming as usual—not much, that is—but she did say the weapon had to be an ax or a hatchet. Something with a very sharp blade."

That drew a grim nod from Nick. "Yeah. Good thing you found her when you did. Woods as remote as that—I think we both know what happens when a hungry animal comes along and finds fresh kill." With his thumb and middle finger he turned the white mug around on the tabletop, around and around, staring into its murky depths.

Bell caught Jackie's eye and signaled to her. She was in a far corner of the room, leaning over to arrange a few short pieces of wood in the stove. She dusted off her hands, stood up straight, and walked over to their booth.

"Never thought I'd have to crank that thing up in October," Jackie said. "Usually it's November before I need the extra heat in here. But it's been damned cold lately." She looked at Bell's plate. "You change your mind about the pie?"

"Thought I'd take it home and enjoy it later. I'd appreciate a take-out box."

"No problem." Jackie switched her attention to Nick. "How about you? Can I put a slice in a box for you, too? There's cherry and pe-can, if apple doesn't float your boat."

Nick shook his head. "I'm good."

Jackie peered at him. "You look about as miserable as Bell does. What's going on with you two, anyway?"

Bell waited to see if he chose to let Jackie know what had happened, as well as the victim's identity. Jackie might very well have known Darla.

In the old days, when they were on the job, there was no question about it; they never talked about a case to civilians. Here in the diner, they would take pains to lower their voices or speak in a terse private code. It was a matter of professional ethics.

But now, they were bound by no such strictures. They were civilians themselves.

"Nothing," Nick replied. He took a quick swallow of his coffee, as if he was mad at it. "Could use a refill next time you're over in this direction."

Jackie shrugged. *Fine,* her shrug said. *Be that way.* She eyed Bell's cup.

"Me, too."

Bell watched as Jackie headed toward the big gray urn on the long counter that ran the length of the room, sectioning off the area where the griddle, coolers, and food prep area lived. The woman moved with uncommon grace. Bell wasn't sure how old Jackie was, but she had to be at least forty-five and maybe closer to fifty. She was limber and fit, her age belied by that grace. Her long legs were encased in snug black jeans, into which she'd tucked a red plaid flannel shirt. Wavy dark hair trailed down her back, almost reaching her waist.

Bell had always been curious about Jackie; her personal life was as much of a mystery as were her finances—the magic trick by which she kept the diner open when business had dwindled so dramatically. All anyone knew for sure was that her devotion to her mother's memory was absolute. Speak a word against Joyce LeFevre—or any member of her clan, including long-dead grandparents and great-uncles and third cousins once removed—and Jackie's dark eyes would blaze with fury. Rivers of LeFevres and Brownings, her grandmother's family, branched through these valleys just as seams of coal did in the mountains themselves.

Jackie was single, and she didn't have any children, and that reality, Bell believed, might explain the fierceness with which she protected her family name. She couldn't count on much emotional sustenance from the living. So she relied on the dead. The dead never let you down.

Bell surmised all that because it was true of herself as well, and she'd recognized the signs. Yes, Bell had a daughter, and an ex-husband, and that made her different from Jackie; for both of them, though, the past could seem more real than the present.

"The sheriff'll be notifying Joe and Brenda right about now," Nick said, checking his watch. He spoke so quietly that Bell had to work to hear him. "They'll have to go over to the coroner's office to make it official, but there's no question about it. It was Darla." He winced. "Who'd want to kill a harmless old lady like that? And why do it so— so *savagely*? Why just leave her out there? God. What a nightmare."

And then the two of them were silent for a time, as if they had agreed in advance to that very strategy at this very minute, letting the sounds of the diner—unexceptional conversations, familiar voices rising and falling, the consolations of the ordinary—cushion them against the grisly bleakness of what they knew and the others didn't, but soon would.

Chapter Eleven

Jackie was back.

"Here you go," she said.

She'd brought a small Styrofoam container for the pie. She refilled Bell's coffee, and started to refill Nick's, but didn't. His cup was still too full. She kept her eyes on that cup, which struck Bell as a bit odd; Jackie was known for looking people straight in the face when she dealt with them. Her forthrightness was not always appreciated in a community where women who owned businesses were regarded with incredulity and a touch of suspicion, and who could only redeem themselves by being sweetly obliging.

"Thanks," Bell said.

The moment Jackie was out of earshot, Nick started talking. He was all business. "I've been thinking about potential suspects. I bet Pam Harrison's already tracked down Darla's ex-husband. Thad Connell's his name. He's a drunk."

"Violent?"

"Not back in the day, when I knew him. But people change."

The bell attached to the front door was roused into its tinny jingle. New customers had arrived. It was an elderly couple in matching blue vinyl windbreakers and white hair. They nodded at Bell and Nick, and settled into a booth across the way.

"Won't be long," Bell murmured.

Nick didn't need to ask what she meant. He already knew: In short order everyone in Acker's Gap—including the elderly couple who had just accepted a pair of laminated menus from Jackie—would know about the discovery of Darla Gilley's body out at Wellwood. As Bell often noted, bad news traveled at the speed of light in a small town. Or maybe—Einstein be damned—three or four times faster.

"In the meantime," Bell said, "we've got our own case to worry about."

"Dixie Sue."

"Dixie Sue," she agreed glumly. She was a little chagrined at how quickly the young woman had slipped out of her thoughts. Murder had a way of doing that: it rendered every other fate anticlimactic.

She wasn't eager to switch from discussing a homicide case to the search for a runaway teenager, and neither, she assumed, was Nick. But they had no choice. The murder victim wasn't their responsibility. The runaway was.

"Jake should be checking in soon," Nick said. "Maybe he's come up with something." He had called Jake on their way to the diner to give him the update: The dead body wasn't Dixie Sue. Jake had agreed to resume his inquiries to other sheriffs' departments to see if the young woman had gotten into trouble in any adjacent counties. "I know he's a little frustrated sometimes, just making calls," Nick added.

"He never says so."

"And he never will. That's Jake. He does his job. He's no belly-acher. But I know he'd rather be out in the field with you and me. Not sitting in a goddamned chair with a phone in his hand. He misses being where the action is." A wintry smile broke over Nick's face. "Sometimes I can sense it—that restlessness. That hunger to move. There's no quit in him. But there's a darkness."

"Because of his injury?"

"Not just that. He had to fight for a long time before that, too. So as not to get bitter or depressed, based on the hard things he witnessed in these hills. The fight, the not giving in to the blackness—it's what made him a great deputy." He shook his head. "Injury or not, he is what he is. That chair might have his body, but it can't hold his spirit. That's for damned sure."

"Sometimes," Bell declared, after a pause during which she let the unexpected beauty of Nick's words warm her soul, "you surprise the hell out of me, Nick Fogelsong. You're a poet."

"Hey—no insults." As was his custom, he'd turned aside a compliment with a joke.

The bell over the door jingled again. A red-bearded man in tan Carhartt duck bib overalls, a gray hoodie, and mud-slimed work boots trooped in. With a swipe of his hand he took off his ball cap—it was black, with a Pittsburgh Steelers logo—before he'd stepped too far in the room, uncorking a headful of kinky red hair the same rusty shade as the beard.

Jackie waved at him. He waved back, selecting a seat at a small table against the far wall, close to the woodstove. He pulled at his beard and then planted his elbows on the tabletop as if he were in his own home, waiting for supper to be served.

When Bell looked back at Nick, she was surprised to see a crease of annoyance on his face. Before she could ask him about it, his cell chirped.

"Yeah," he said into the black lozenge, around which his big hand curved like a bear's paw gripping a tiny pine cone. "Yeah. Yeah. I understand. Yeah, okay. No problem." He paused, listening. "Forty minutes. Forty-five, tops."

He hung up and reached into his jeans pocket, bringing out his brown leather wallet. "Your pie and coffee's on me. I gotta go."

To Bell's questioning expression, he replied, "That was the sheriff. She's at Joe Gilley's house. When she told him about Darla, he damn near collapsed. He's asking for me. Pam thinks I might be able to help settle him down—at least long enough for her to get some information. Wants me to get over there ASAP."

He slid out of the booth. By the time he stood up, Bell was standing, too.

"Let me come," she said.

"Why?"

She didn't have a good answer. Or at least not a simple one. Part of it, certainly, was the fact that she didn't like being left out of a big event. There had not been a major homicide in Raythune County in over a year. Not since the death of Brett Topping, a prominent banker shot to death in his driveway, a case Bell had helped to solve. There had been deaths from unnatural causes, yes, but they were open-and-shut, with obvious culprits: drug deals gone wrong, domestic disputes, longtime feuds that suddenly veered into violence.

But not the unlikely and seemingly unprovoked murder of a non-troublemaker by an unknown assailant.

This was the first significant and truly mysterious crime since she, Nick, and Jake had begun working together. And even though they weren't investigating it—not officially, anyway—and even though Bell hadn't known Darla Gilley, she felt the hard pull of it, the dark allure of a complicated death.

She couldn't fool Nick with some lame, made-up answer concocted on the fly, so she took a chance on the truth.

"I don't know."

"Okay," he said. "But let's ask Jackie for a to-go cup for your coffee. Long drive out to Joe's place. You get real grumpy when you run low."

He had questioned her motive out of habit, but her answer didn't really matter. He already had it. The answer was locked inside the larger, more abstract truth that linked them. They had known each other so long that he automatically understood the fierceness of her curiosity, of her hunger to find out what had happened to this victim, and why. Because he felt it, too.

They both loved this town. They both believed that any death diminished it.

Chapter Twelve

She knew the look.

Bell had seen it in her sister's eyes, too, shortly before Shirley's death from lung cancer. It was a sort of reverse nostalgia, a steady, quiet yearning not for the past, but for the future—a future that would never be. And now she saw it in Joe Gilley's eyes.

It was more than just grief for his sister, sudden and momentous as that was. This was something else. This was another kind of grief, a preexisting condition: Joe was dying, and his eyes told Bell that he understood it in a way that went beyond the dire words of the doctors, beyond their solemn prognostications and tidy percentages.

But they were here tonight because of his sister, and not the larger arc of tragedy that shadowed him.

"Nick—oh, Nick," Joe said, in a faltering voice. "My God. Darla. Who would—" He shook his head. The effort seemed to leave him depleted.

He had opened the door of the big-boned, two-story farmhouse in response to Nick's knock. Despite the chill of this cold night, Joe stood in the doorway, keeping his hand on the knob to support himself. He repeated Nick's name another time, as if trying to convince himself that his friend was really here, in the flesh.

By now it was after 9 P.M. The porch light was needed, but too bright. Bell, standing to Nick's right, squinted against the glare.

The man she saw was emaciated; his pleated trousers hung on him and the yellow plaid flannel shirt was too big for his neck. Wispy bits of white hair furred his scalp. The eyes in his sunken face were wide, unblinking, and their washed-out blue color had a haunting opacity. Bell instantly remembered where she'd last seen eyes like that: Shirley.

Joe coughed, swayed, caught himself. Nick started to reach out to help him, but Joe shook his head: *No.* He was okay.

Bell and Nick followed him into the living room. It was packed with heavy, dark furniture that looked as if it had taken root a few centuries ago. The thick draperies, closed tight against the cold, dragged on the ground. The house had the ponderous air of a place where time had slowed down and might never catch back up to itself again.

There was—incongruously, Bell thought—a small, fully decorated Christmas tree perched on a table in the corner, its lights blinking merrily. *A Christmas tree in October?* she wondered.

The answer came to her: They'd be celebrating the holiday early this year. Because chances were, Joe wasn't going to live until December 24.

Across the room, Sheriff Harrison sat stiffly on a wing chair, back straight, boots together, hands flat on her narrow thighs. She didn't get up when she saw them. Instead she nodded to Bell and mouthed *Thanks.* Bell nodded back. She and Nick didn't have to be here, and Harrison knew it. This was not their responsibility anymore. And it wasn't a place anybody would willingly come; sadness was weighing down the contents of this house like an extra helping of gravity. They were here because Joe Gilley was Nick's friend. Harrison acknowledged all of that with her nod of silent gratitude.

"Joe," Nick said. Somehow he packed a world of sympathy into his friend's name. He waited for a few seconds before adding, "I'm so sorry for your loss."

Joe nodded. His chin quivered. He and Nick shook hands. The handshake went on longer than it needed to. They didn't hug— although this moment was perhaps the closest they'd ever come to it, Bell speculated. Men of their generation didn't hug; hugs were not in their repertoire. Instead of hugging, they helped each other out in practical ways, across all the long years of their lives. They loaned wrenches and clamps and jumper cables back and forth. They joined forces to build decks and porches and patios. They watched Mountaineers games together on Saturdays and Steelers games on Sundays.

And when there was a death in the family, they showed up, even when there was nothing to say except *I'm so sorry for your loss.*

But they didn't hug.

Brenda Gilley was crossing the room. She arrived at Joe's side just in time, propping him up when he started to tilt sideways. He would accept her help, but not Nick's.

She was a sturdy, heavyset woman with a cap of short gray hair and a neat shingle of gray bangs. From behind a large pair of glasses, olive-green eyes assessed the world. She wore a denim skirt, brown leggings, and an XXL navy blue sweatshirt that bunched around her waist. The red turtleneck under her sweatshirt featured a pattern of tiny green Christmas trees. Her white tennis shoes had thick Velcro strips instead of laces.

Brenda guided her husband to the big maroon recliner in the middle of the room and covered him with a fleece throw, tucking it in around the sides. Breathing hard, Joe leaned back and closed his eyes. He'd seen enough for the time being.

Nick and Bell took seats on the couch, sinking down into the dark brown corduroy that was shiny from many years of wear. Nick and the sheriff exchanged a glance that passed for a greeting.

"Heard you knock but I was in the kitchen making coffee," Brenda said. "I hollered at Joe to just hold off. Keep his seat. Let me get the door. But he wanted to do it himself. He's just as stubborn as he ever was." This was said with a mixture of affection and exasperation.

"Yep. Same old Joe." Nick added a small, fake chuckle, as if this were a normal visit, and Joe's peccadillos were all they had to discuss. "Good to see you, Brenda. Damned shame you all have to go through this—on top of everything else." He waved toward Bell. "This is Belfa Elkins. She and I work together."

"Sure," Brenda replied, peering hard at Bell. "Nick has mentioned you from time to time." The truth was, Bell's story—her confession to a crime committed in childhood, her subsequent resignation as prosecutor—was local legend. Everyone knew about her, whether they knew her or not. "I don't get into Acker's Gap much anymore," Brenda added, "but I'm sure we've seen each other."

Bell nodded. "Yes. You look a little familiar to me, too." It wasn't true. Or maybe it was: By this time, everybody looked a little familiar to her; that was the consequence of living in a small town. You didn't know everyone, but you thought you did, and maybe, after a while, that made it true. "I'm very sorry for what you and your husband are going through."

"Appreciate that."

"And I hope you don't mind that Nick brought me along." Bell looked toward the Christmas tree. "That's such a pretty tree. Really brightens the room."

"Came from that big hill out back," Brenda stated proudly. "Behind the old barn. You can't see it in the dark, but there's about twenty acres out there, right along the ridge, that's been in Joe's family for more'n a hundred years. Used to be a small farm but now it's all grown over. They didn't have a pot to piss in, but they held on to the land, isn't that right, Joe? I went out last week and picked out that tree myself. I wanted Joe to have a—" She gulped hard. Changed direction. "We just decided we'd do the whole shebang a little early this year. But now—well, I don't know. Not feeling so festive anymore."

Joe started to add something, but was overtaken by a long, all-consuming cough. He shook his head at Brenda's proffer of a glass of water.

Keeping her eye on Joe, Brenda said, "It's like a bad dream, isn't that right, honey? We think we're going to wake up and it'll all be over and Darla'll be right here. When the sheriff knocked on the door tonight and came in and told us—" She swept a meaty hand toward Harrison. "—I swear I thought it was some kind of joke. It couldn't really be true. Not Darla. Not our Darla." With what seemed to be an effort, she regained her poise. "I'm just so glad you stopped by, Nick. And you too, ma'am," she added, turning to Bell. "I was afraid I'd have to ask the sheriff to help me take Joe to the hospital. He just couldn't handle it. Too much. Way too much to deal with."

Her husband's face had turned red from the coughing. He flailed his arms, causing Brenda to jump up and hurry to his side.

"Come on, now," she said. She held a tissue under his mouth, letting him clear his throat, catching the phlegm, wiping his chin. Not caring that people were watching. "Settle down, honey." Brenda wadded up the tissue and tucked it demurely in the pocket of her skirt. Bell remembered doing that for Shirley: helping her deal with the body's betrayals, small and large. If you loved the person, it wasn't gross, and it wasn't a burden. It was what you did.

Joe's voice was a hushed wheeze. "I just—I just can't believe Darla's gone." He turned a desperate face to Nick. "What was she doing out there, anyway? Way out in the woods? Doesn't make any sense."

Quietly, Sheriff Harrison had risen from her chair. Bell knew she'd been waiting for Nick to arrive so that she could get back to questioning Joe and Brenda. If she upset him again, Nick would be there for emotional support. Pam Harrison didn't do emotional support.

All at once Bell was aware of just how fervently *she* wanted to be the one conducting this interview. As prosecutor, she'd often joined the sheriff and her deputies in the field, interrogating witnesses, building the case. It wasn't the norm—most busy prosecutors left investigations to law enforcement, and the current prosecutor, Rhonda Lovejoy, did just that—but Bell had loved being out in the field. She relished the methodical compilation of facts, getting it right from the ground up.

It was all she could do at this moment to sit still and keep her mouth shut as Harrison began.

"When was the last time you saw your sister, sir?" the sheriff asked. She kept a respectful distance from Joe's recliner.

Brenda answered before he could. "We saw her all the time. She'd been living here for the last three months or so. Ever since she and Thad decided to separate for good. She couldn't afford her own place."

"I didn't know she'd moved in with you all," Nick said.

Joe sat up straighter in the recliner. "Family," he said. The word had the ring of iron finality to it, as if it explained everything. "I don't have to tell you about family, Nick. Darla knew she was welcome here.

Always. No questions asked. And you know what? Even though she and Thad had split up about a hundred times before—this time felt different. I was hoping, anyway." He took a deep breath. His voice shook a little. "She grew up in this house, same as me. She's entitled to be here."

"Made her a place in the attic," Brenda put in. "Fixed it up real nice."

The attic, Bell thought. *Doesn't sound too hospitable. Wonder what Darla thought about being relegated there by her sister-in law—when it's the family home? Couldn't have been as comfortable as a regular bedroom.* Moreover, Darla was in her fifties. The extra flight of stairs would surely cause a twinge or two in arthritic knees.

The sheriff was impatient now. "So when was the *last* time you saw her?"

"Yesterday afternoon," Joe replied. "At lunch."

Brenda nodded. "Darla always tried to help out in the kitchen. I'd made the turkey sandwiches and put 'em on plates and she started to cut Joe's for him—but she did it all wrong, bless her heart. Joe likes his cut on the diagonal."

"She left the house right after lunch," Joe said. "Asked Brenda to give her a ride into Acker's Gap."

"What time?" Harrison's voice was sharper now. She had a long night ahead of her and lots to accomplish.

Brenda and Joe looked at each other. "When was it, honey?" Brenda asked him. "Two, three o'clock?"

Joe shook his head. "I don't know. Don't pay much attention to time anymore. It seems to move along pretty well without me keeping an eye on it."

Brenda reflected for another few seconds and then said, "Best I can recollect, Darla and I left the house about two thirty. Meaning I dropped her off in town about three fifteen. I had to get right back to pick up Joe and take him to his appointment with Dr. Mann over in Blythesburg."

"Where was Darla going?"

"Don't know," Brenda replied. "We gave Darla her privacy. We didn't pry. She just asked me to drop her off at the corner of Main and Thornberry." She touched her temple with two pudgy fingers. "Wait. Hold on. Now I remember. She said she had some errands to run. Post office, that kind of thing. Plus something about stopping in at JP's. Meeting somebody there."

"She didn't say who or why?"

Brenda shook her head. "Sorry, no."

The sheriff was disappointed—Bell knew her well enough to tell—but she had to let it go and move on. "Okay, just a few more questions. Any idea who might have wanted to harm Darla? Did she have any enemies?"

"Enemies?" Brenda repeated the word as if it were a snake someone had dropped in her palm when she was expecting a cookie. She planted a hand on her chest, fingers splayed. *"Darla Gilley?* Heavens, no. Everybody loved Darla. Anyway—she was a grown woman, for pity's sake. Old ladies don't have enemies."

Bell wondered how much Darla would have appreciated being identified as an old lady. Bell knew how much *she* would appreciate it: not at all.

"How about her ex-husband?" the sheriff inquired.

"Thad's had his problems over the years," Brenda said, "but they still cared for each other. They'd just drifted apart." She mimed the upending of a bottle into her mouth. "And when I say 'problems'— that's what I mean. He's a drinker. Stops for a while, but always goes back. Darla'd finally had enough."

"Did she say that?"

"Not in so many words, no." Brenda, in a huff, fluffed out her skirt; apparently she was a bit offended that the sheriff didn't appreciate her informed speculations. "Like I said, they stayed in touch. She'd take him to his AA meetings when he lost his license on account of too many DUIs. That kinda thing."

So much for the anonymity part, Bell thought.

"So Darla had a car?" Harrison asked.

Brenda shook her head. "Used to. Sold it a few weeks ago. She was running low on cash and got a real nice price for it. I've been driving her when she needs to go somewhere—job interviews and such. No trouble at all. She's been looking real hard for work, but no nibbles so far."

"How about a cell? We didn't find one at the scene, but I thought maybe she'd left it at home."

"Gave that up last month," Brenda replied. "Canceled her contract. Said it was too pricey."

"Where is Connell now?"

"No clue."

"We'll locate him and let him know what happened," Harrison said. "Just one more thing. Any idea why Darla would've been out in those woods?"

Brenda shrugged. The sheriff looked at Joe. Eyes closed, he had sunk back into the recliner while his wife and the sheriff spoke. He still hadn't recovered from the trip to the door and back.

"If you think of anything," Harrison concluded, "please call my office. And we'll let you know when we're ready for you at the coroner's office."

She folded shut the front flap of her small notebook and slipped it into her coat pocket, followed by the short yellow pencil. She touched the front brim of her hat to the Gilleys and then to Bell and Nick, a shorthand for good-bye. She let herself out the front door.

There was, Bell thought admiringly, no fuss or folderol about Pam Harrison.

"Sorry, folks—forgot all about that coffee," Brenda declared. She'd followed the sheriff to the door, double-checking the handle to make sure it had shut tightly behind her. The chill that Harrison's exit had introduced into the room validated her action. "Can I get a cup for anybody?"

"I'm good," Bell said. It was a sacrifice, but this wasn't a social call.

"No, thanks" was Nick's response. His eyes traveled to the fireplace mantel, across which a dozen framed portraits were arranged. Most were of Joe and Brenda, and appeared to be vacation shots. One showed the two of them in matching Hawaiian shirts, with a white-sand beach spreading out behind them. Another had been taken at an amusement park; someone inhabiting a large cartoon dog suit stood between them, his arms slung merrily around their shoulders. A Ferris wheel sprouted in the background.

Nick spotted the single photo that included Darla. He rose from the couch—Bell saw him flinch a bit, and she knew his back was acting up again—and walked over to pick it up.

It was a picture of Joe and Darla standing on the front steps of Acker's Gap High School. She was in a cap and gown, he was in street clothes. Her long dark hair flowed out from under the mortarboard in a lively wave that looked almost electric, as if she possessed a secret internal energy that might be tapped as a natural resource. They both looked very young, which made sense; it had been taken more than forty years ago. Joe had graduated in 1970, in the same class as Nick, and Darla a decade later. Nick had given Bell the basic chronology on their way over here.

"That was the day before her graduation," Joe said softly. "I came to the school to take her home from the rehearsal. She was on cloud nine. She had all kinds of plans. Big dreams." He couldn't talk for a moment. Then he seemed to gather himself. "Can't hardly believe this. I mean—Darla was just getting herself back together after finally ditching Thad. Really making progress. And now—" He shook his head. "Times like these—you need your friends. The people you've known forever. The ones who know you best."

"You got that right," Nick concurred. He didn't look at Bell, but she knew what he was thinking, because they'd talked about that, too, during the drive: He had not kept in touch with Joe Gilley the way he should have, especially after Joe's diagnosis, and he felt guilty about it. Nick had let go of a lot of things over the past few years, as he'd tried to start a new life with Mary Sue in Florida.

But now he was back. With a chance to make up for it, a chance to renew his friendship with Joe Gilley.

Assuming, of course, that Joe was not involved in his sister's death, a possibility that would have to be explored. He couldn't have done it himself, but someone else could have done it at his request. Bell's mantra as a prosecutor had been simple: Anybody was capable of anything.

Joe was talking again, a low murmur that was shot through with grief. "My sister was a good person. Didn't have a mean bone in her body. I mean, sure—she could rub people the wrong way. She was stubborn. Prideful, too, especially about our family. The fact that we've lived right here on Roberts Ridge for so long. All the generations—that *means* something, she'd say to me. She'd get kinda wrought up about it. I had to settle her down sometimes. But you know what? She had a big heart and she always tried to do right by people." He uttered a small sob. "Why would somebody up and kill her like that, Nick? I don't understand. I just don't."

"Can't blame you," Nick answered in a solemn voice. "So many things about it just don't make any sense. Why would she have gone out to Wellwood in the first place?"

Joe's head twitched against the back of the recliner. In a startled voice, he asked:

"What did you say?"

"I just wondered why she'd go to the woods like that. It was cold and—"

"No. That's not what you said. You said 'Wellwood.'"

Perplexed, Nick conceded, "Well, yeah. That's where they found her. In the ruins of the old hospital. Out in the woods."

Joe was getting agitated. Brenda tried to reach over and take his hand to soothe him, but this time he pushed her away. "The sheriff didn't tell us that," he declared hotly. "She just said they'd found her in the woods behind Briney Hollow."

"Right." Nick wasn't sure what was going on. "Same difference. Sheriff Harrison probably just didn't want to give a lot of specifics that would only make it worse for you. Too many details—and people tend to picture things. Does it matter?"

"Hell *yes* it matters!" Joe's voice had a strangled quality to it as he cried out. "Our grandmother worked at Wellwood starting in the 1930s—all the way through to the 1950s. She was our mother's mother. Elizabeth Dresser. Bessie, they called her. She married a Gilley."

Nick nodded, still trying to settle him down. "That's an odd coincidence, Joe, no question, but I still don't see why you're so upset about—"

"In 1959," Joe said, interrupting him with a passion that by all rights should have been beyond his meager, dwindling strength, "Bessie was murdered on the hospital grounds. They never found her killer."

Chapter Thirteen

In the muted white glow of moonlight the object looked like an alien spacecraft of boringly benign intent. More like an exploratory probe, perhaps, than a weaponized craft with sealed instructions to destroy the planet and its moronic, sitting-duck inhabitants.

When Jake looked closer, he verified that it was a trailer. It was short and fat and gray, tapering off at either end. A rusty propane tank squatted on the ground nearby. Ten yards away, a firepit had been created by a single ring of bricks turned on their sides. Lawn chairs dragged close to the pit were empty but still aggrieved-looking, the bows and sharp creases in their aluminum legs attesting to the heft of some of the backsides that patronized these seats night after night.

Jake rolled down the window of the van. He thrust out his left arm and swept the beam of his flashlight across the dead ashes of the firepit, being careful to keep it aimed away from the trailer's tiny windows. In the powdery drifts and soft peaks, he spotted the tips of long-ago-smoked cigarettes; the whitish bits glowed in the artificial light like a scattering of alabaster gems. Only when you got closer, he knew, would the truth come out: Not gems. Just cigarette butts.

Story of my life, he thought, amusement putting a curl in his lip. *You fool yourself into thinking you've found beauty around here—but it's just the same old crap.* He pulled in his arm and raised the window.

He had driven the last quarter mile to this location with the van lights off. Malik, sitting beside him, was very excited; Jake had to keep tapping the boy's knee to settle him down. Malik had a tendency to squeal when his emotions were engaged.

Jake, using moonlight in lieu of headlights, had slowly edged the van down the double set of sunken ruts. It was a ghost road. When heavy rains and copious snow roared into the picture, it would vanish. Wouldn't reappear again until the weather improved.

When he saw what he was looking for, right where he'd been told he would find it, Jake switched off the engine and let the van roll to a gradual stop. The runty, turd-shaped trailer was mired on a chunk of swampy-looking ground off to the right, barely visible in the pale pink wash of moonglow.

No lights, inside or outside the trailer.

"Okay," Jake whispered to Malik. He didn't need to whisper yet; they were still in the van with the windows shut. But he wanted to get Malik used to it. He needed to hammer home the point that they had to be stealthy. Not that Malik knew what the word "stealthy" meant. He worshipped Jake, though, and wanted to please him, and if Jake let him know that he wanted him to be absolutely quiet, Malik would comply. Or at least try to comply. Malik didn't always have control of himself. But he'd give it his best. And that was all Jake ever asked of him: his best effort.

"I want you to get my chair out of the back and meet me over here at my door and help me get into it," Jake murmured. "And then I need you to get back in the van and wait for my signal. And be very, *very* quiet. Can you do that, Malik?"

Malik's head bobbed up and down excitedly.

Too excitedly. Jake put a hand on his knee. "Easy," he whispered. "We're moving real slow tonight, buddy. Being real calm. Okay?"

This time Malik's nod was subdued, under control.

Jake looked at the boy's face. The same moonlight that encased the trailer in a kind of dreamy cocoon of gentle illumination made Malik's broad brown face look firm and strong, resolute with his determination to help. His black eyes glittered.

God bless this boy, Jake thought, as an unexpected surge of tenderness overtook him. It was only unexpected because it was out of place just now: They were working. But Malik tried very hard to do what was asked of him, against the ferocious odds imposed by the stark incapacities visited upon him at birth, and sometimes his determination moved Jake. It could come at inconvenient times, this gush of feeling. Malik had the purest soul that Jake had ever encountered. Which didn't mean, of course, that the boy didn't occasionally piss him off, when Malik's playfulness or frustration got the better of him.

Back to business.

"Okay," Jake said softly. "It's go time. Remember—be very quiet." Truth was, Jake could accomplish the transfer from the van to the chair by himself. He had a nifty vehicle that operated with hand controls and featured access to the stowed chair from the driver's seat. But Malik liked helping him, and so Jake usually let him fetch the chair and place it just so.

"Okey-dokey," Malik whispered back. He opened the truck door in slow motion, sliding out with exaggerated caution and pinching his eyes shut with concern when he clicked the door shut.

Funny, Jake thought. Malik needed to feel useful, just as he needed to feel useful. Maybe everybody did.

Which made him cut himself a little slack about having brought the boy along tonight. He didn't really have a choice; he couldn't leave him home alone. And Molly had been called in to work the overnight shift again, even though she was scheduled to be off.

But would she approve of him including Malik in what might turn out to be a dangerous assignment?

Probably not.

Okay: Hell, no.

Well, he'd made his decision. He could have called Molly or texted her to ask for her permission, but he didn't, because he was fairly sure her response would be *Are you freakin' KIDDING me?* and then he couldn't have followed up on the tip he'd received from his informant. He'd be sitting on the couch with Malik, both of them bored and antsy. Letting a good chance of finding Dixie Sue Folsom slip away. Now that Jake had been informed that the body at Wellwood wasn't Dixie Sue, finding her was back on his radar.

And so for better or worse, here they were.

Time to move.

Jake had gotten the tip the old-fashioned way, the way he'd always done it when he was a deputy sheriff: One person told another person, and that person told another person, and that person told two other people, and one of those two happened to mention it to somebody else who knew that Jake Oakes was looking for a young woman named Dixie Sue Folsom.

No complex searches on fancy computers, digging through giant swaths of data. No algorithms. Just a basic, tried-and-true investigatory technique: working the phones. Asking questions of the right people. Calling in markers. Promising anonymity.

The source was positive: Jake could find Dixie Sue in a trailer off Bucktown Road. Travis Matson and his cousins and various other hangers-on lived there. Seven people in a trailer meant to house three people, tops.

Jake knew that Bell and Nick were busy with the body found in the woods. He would handle this on his own.

The air felt cold on his face when he lowered his body out of the van into the chair. But it was a good cold, the bracing, *here-we-go* kind. He motioned to Malik. "Climb back in the van," he whispered. "Wait for my signal. Then do what I told you to do. After that, keep your head down. Okay?"

"Okay," Malik whispered back.

The terrain was too rough for proper reconnaissance. The wheels of his chair wouldn't make it all the way around the trailer. He felt the old familiar self-pity starting up in his head—*If I wasn't in this stupid-ass chair I could do this right, get the lay of the land before I took on these guys*—but he batted it away and kept on going. He could still do the job, even in the chair.

He rolled himself toward the front door. The weeds had been flattened in a short winding path by the boots of the occupants as they came and went. There was no mailbox. No porch. The trailer looked as if it had been abandoned here by accident, stalled out amid the thigh-high weeds and broken-off branches and overgrown grass and piles of trash. He reached over the side of his chair and scooped up one of the crooked branches, the longest and thickest one he could find.

He moved his chair to the side of the trailer, close to the door but not in the line of sight of anybody who flung it open.

The trick, Jake knew, was to utilize a force multiplier—or in this case, to make Travis Matson and his buddies believe that he actually had a force multiplier. Or any force, period. They had to be persuaded to give up without a fight. Because if there *was* a fight, Jake would lose, and they would win—and that was knowledge he had to keep from them at all costs.

He took a quick glance back at the van. In the glint of moonlight, he could just make out the contours of Malik's face at the passenger-side window. The boy was watching him intently. He was ready.

Would he remember what to do?

Damned if I know. The thought made Jake smile. It was all part of the adventure.

There were two elements to the success of Part One of his plan: surprise and speed. He gripped the branch tightly in his right fist and leaned forward in his chair as far as he could go, and he slammed it swiftly and repeatedly against the flimsy metal door. It made, just as he'd hoped, a satisfyingly obnoxious noise, precisely the kind of brusque hello offered by a SWAT unit whose commander was in a nasty mood:

BAM BAM BAM BAM BAM

He took a second's break, and then resumed the assault:

BAM BAM BAM BAM BAM BAM

The trailer rocked back and forth on its narrow base as, he imagined, multiple pairs of feet smacked the floor; Jake could visualize the startled people inside jumping off couches and tumbling out of recliners. He heard, through the trailer's thin metal skin, a tangled chorus of angry shouts, followed by a snarled morass of *What the fuck* and *Jesus Christ* and *Goddammit* and *Get off me, you asshole* and *Hell* and a frantic sizzle of assorted other curse words.

The door popped open.

The instant it did, Jake waved at Malik, and at the same time, he uttered a small, fervent prayer that the boy remembered what they'd gone over—and over and over and over—on the way here:

Pull the knob, Malik. Here, like this. No, like this. *Great. You got it. Now, when I give the signal—that's what you do.*

The van's headlights suddenly sprang to life, smashing into the doorway in a fusillade of brightness. There were at least three people jammed into that doorway, Jake surmised from his sideways view, and their forearms flew up to their faces to block out the bright lights. He heard smacks and groans and a circus of surprised cries.

"What the *hell,*" one them yelped, but before any of the others tried adding their own epithets, Jake initiated Part Two of his plan.

As a deputy, he had learned the cardinal rule about disorienting an opponent who outnumbered you—and who might very well be armed, too: Hit loud, hit fast, and don't stop.

"COME OUT NOW! NOW NOW NOW!" Jake yelled. He waved at Malik, who mashed the van's horn with one palm and then pressed on that palm with his other one, straightening out his arms for even more pressure, creating a massive barrage of searing sound. "NOW NOW NOW NOW!" Jake continued, vying with the horn to be the biggest pain-in-the-ass irritant in the universe right now. "DO NOT STOP—REPEAT DO NOT STOP! COME OUT NOW!"

The trailer's occupants stumbled out onto the grass, barefoot and confused as they blinked, cursed, and turned in clumsy circles, searching for the row of armed cops in riot gear that currently surrounded their location—or so they would've bet every dollar they had. Jake counted six men: five young and one old, and all of them barefoot and wearing crusty yellow BVDs and raggedy T-shirts. Plus a single chubby young woman with long black hair that floated down her back, her body wrapped up in a man's oversized shirt that hung below her knees.

Well, hi there, Dixie Sue, Jake thought.

He signaled Malik. The van's lights cut off. It took the boy another second to release pressure on the horn. Malik, Jake knew, would be talking about that horn for weeks, months, to come. He'd be begging for permission to do it again, to let her rip and keep her going.

"The *hell,*" one of the young men called out, peering angrily into the sudden darkness, not sure where to direct his wrath. "What's going on? Whoever you are—we ain't done nothin'. This here's private property."

Jake pushed his chair out of the shadow at the side of the trailer.

"Hey, fellas," he said amiably. "Glad you felt like a little midnight stroll. Now that you're out here, I have a message for your visitor." He smiled at the young woman, who clutched the collar of her shirt, as if struck by a sudden attack of modesty. "Dixie Sue," he continued, "your mother's worried sick about you. She wants you to come home. So go get your clothes and I'll take you there."

It was one of the young men, not Dixie Sue, who spoke next.

"Guy's in a fuckin' *wheelchair*," he muttered. "And we was jumpin' around like it was the fucking *army* come to get us. Fuck this shit. I don't think he's even got a gun."

"I don't," Jake said.

Two of the young men started toward him. The old man grabbed them by their collars before they'd traveled more than three feet. He might have been old, but he was strong; he flung one to the ground. The other managed to break free, but he veered off to the left and stopped there.

The family hierarchy was instantly clear: Grandpa ruled the roost.

"Don't lay a hand on him," the old man growled. "You assholes need to grow a brain. You want to go to jail or what?" He spat a large wad on the grass. Jake couldn't see the expectorant—it was too dark—but he could hear the *phwott* as it landed.

"You," the old man added, jabbing a crooked finger at Dixie Sue, "get the hell out of here. We don't want no trouble with nobody." When Dixie Sue didn't move, the old man turned to the young man who stood next to her. The man had long, stringy hair that had been dyed such a bright shade of white that it seemed to glow in the dark. "Travis, put her in the van."

"But Lloyd, she don't wanna—"

"Shut your fucking mouth and do it," the old man interrupted him. His voice had gotten softer, not louder, which made it sound more, not less, menacing. "Told you she was nothin' but trouble."

"I wanna be on the TV show!" Dixie Sue called out, her petulant voice rising to a whiny crescendo. Each time Travis tried to take her hand to escort her to the van, she pulled it out of his reach and smacked his forearm. "You said you'd get me on the TV show. That's what you *said*. You said you'd talk to some people and get me on that show. That's why I came here with you. Because you *promised*."

Jake was tempted to make an observation about the relative likelihood of Travis Matson of Raythune County, West Virginia, possessing a vast network of contacts in Hollywood that he could tap at will on behalf of his girlfriend's nascent career, but decided to forgo the pleasure.

Besides, he needed to wind this up and get Malik home.

The friend who had tipped him off about Dixie Sue's whereabouts had been spot-on about the circumstances: She'd come here voluntarily, lured by Travis's promises of fame based on her ability to lip-sync Beyoncé songs while dancing in a lascivious fashion. But if Jake had approached in a straightforward way—by knocking on the door in daylight and asking politely if the young woman was inside—Travis and his relatives, Jake's snitch had warned him, would fight back out of habit. The best strategy was to get them outside the trailer, away from their firearms.

And to make them believe that the adversary was a crack paramilitary force—and not just a guy in a wheelchair, with his sidekick waiting in a van.

"So am I gonna be on the TV show *or not*?" demanded a miffed Dixie Sue. She stared hard at Travis, who twisted his mouth to one side and rubbed the back of his neck. "Answer me." He tried to turn away. She wouldn't let him; when he moved, she moved. "Answer me!"

"Nope."

Dixie Sue seemed to go through some five different emotional stages in about a second and a half: incredulity, outrage, repulsion, despair, and finally, resignation. She lifted her arms and let them flop back down again at her sides.

"Well, then—screw you, Travis Matson."

She turned around and walked to the passenger side of the van. Malik opened the door, and scooted over to make room for her. She didn't ask who he was or what he was doing here, and he didn't ask her anything, either, not even the obvious question about whether or not she was cold because, after all, she was wearing only a long-sleeved shirt and presumably underwear—but no pants. They both seemed perfectly content to sit and wait until Jake, after bidding Lloyd and the boys a pleasant evening, rolled around to the driver's side and transferred himself and then his chair up into the van.

Shortly before they reached the outskirts of Swanville, Jake pulled over to text the good news to Bell: Dixie Sue Folsom was on her way home to her mother.

Bell texted him back with news of her own. She and Nick were returning from Roberts Ridge. The woman in the woods had been identified as someone named Darla Gilley. They'd joined the sheriff at the home of her next of kin. Still no idea who had murdered her, or why.

Chapter Fourteen

He finally got Malik tucked into bed. It wasn't easy; the boy was so excited by the night's activities, by the fact that he'd helped Jake on a real job, that at first he couldn't stop bouncing and laughing.

"Listen, my man," Jake said, "if you're still awake when your sister gets home, we're both in big trouble, okay?"

Jake hadn't turned off the overhead light just yet, so he was able to watch Malik absorb this information. The expression on his face went from playful to serious—and then the playfulness returned, delivered with a giggle that carried no hint of sleepiness in it. Malik had agreed to lie down in his bed but still twitched with excitement. He kept flipping off the sheets and the comforter, kicking his legs and hitting the mattress with his fists.

Jake, angling his chair next to the bed, put a hand on Malik's ankle. "Hey, you," he said, keeping his voice light, because he'd learned long ago that unless you made it a game, any attempt to subdue Malik would only result in a ratcheting up of the young man's exuberance. "Tell you what. You can play with your cards for ten minutes. And after that, I'll come back in here and you'll try your best to go to sleep. Do we have a deal?"

Malik laughed and nodded. The nod went on and on; it was a new receptacle for his restlessness. He was pleased. Playing cards were the most important thing in his life. No other objects entertained him as they did. He reached over and opened the drawer of the nightstand, a small wooden one that Molly had found at the Goodwill and then painted red with black trim. Red and black were Malik's favorite colors, because they were the colors of the numbers and figures on playing cards.

He showed the deck to Jake, waving it over his head. Jake gave him a thumbs-up. Malik opened the cardboard container and dumped the cards all over the bed, watching eagerly as they fluttered in their fall. The game consisted of collecting them again.

"Ten minutes," Jake said, backing his chair out of the room. "Then it's lights out, buddy."

Malik was too involved with his cards to answer, but Jake knew he'd honor the agreement. That was how Jake had realized, a year ago, that he'd broken through with Malik; he and Malik made a pact that the cards were special, and that Malik could only play with them when Jake said it was okay. Malik was allowed to keep the pack in his bedside table—but he couldn't play with the cards whenever he wanted to. They were a privilege.

At first, it didn't work at all. Malik reached for the cards in the drawer nine or ten times a day, and screamed and flailed when Jake said *No, not now, buddy, you've got to wait for my say-so*. Gradually, though, as Jake spent more time with him, as he let Malik hang out with him while he sat at the kitchen table making calls or writing reports on his laptop, and as they did chores together, washing dishes and sweeping floors, Malik's attitude changed. He began to respect the boundary with the cards.

Jake wheeled himself into the kitchen. He needed to record the evening's events on his laptop while they were still fresh in his mind. The agency would provide Maggie Folsom with a detailed report about the case, even though it had turned out to be nothing at all, really, just a misguided young woman and her ludicrous would-be suitor and talent agent.

Damn. Now he remembered. He'd left the laptop not on the kitchen table, but in the bedroom he shared with Molly.

Jake backed his chair out of the kitchen. The house was so small that it only took him seconds to get to the bedroom. The first thing

he saw when he switched on the light was the large bed that dominated the room. It was covered with Molly's bedspread, thick and dark
green, her favorite color, and it constituted a major upgrade from his,
a lumpy brown embarrassment that she'd wadded up and thrown out
the day she moved in. He paused, letting himself feel what he always
felt when he stopped even briefly in this place they shared, night after
night—or, if Molly was working the overnight shift, day after day: a
wave of profound joy and contentment that had been completely unknown to him before she settled in for good.

Now, where had he left the laptop?

There it was, on top of the dresser. His battery was low and so
he'd plugged it in here after dinner, using the power cord that Molly
kept in the bedroom for her radio.

And that was when he saw it.

She had left him a note, propped up against the base of the lamp
on the dresser. He saw JAKE on the outside of the pale yellow envelope, written in Molly's careful hand. She had the best penmanship
he had ever seen. *That's because I take my time,* she had replied, the
first time he complimented her on the beauty of her handwriting.
No trick to it, really—just patience. He didn't agree, but he let it go.
There was more to it than just going slow. She had a grace about her
that extended to everything she did, from writing to fitting an oxygen
mask over somebody's face—he'd seen her do that multiple times at
accident scenes, back when he was a deputy—or unrolling a blood
pressure cuff or handling the wide wheel of the EMT truck as she
maneuvered it into a tight spot.

She sometimes left him short notes like this, tucking them around
the house for him to find when she was out working. Love letters, he
supposed he'd have to call them, although that description seemed
altogether too mushy. Molly Drucker wasn't mushy. The notes were
sterner than that, more straightforward, even matter-of-fact: *You have
changed my life and Malik's life in so many ways. We are grateful.
Just wanted you to know that. M.*

He didn't need her to be mushy. He just needed her to love him.

When had she left the note here? Molly had departed to start
her shift long before he and Malik had packed up and headed out

on tonight's mission to rescue—*Ha,* he thought—Dixie Sue Folsom. Jake's tipster had not called him with the information until after 8 P.M. And then Jake had spent another twenty minutes on the phone, verifying the data about Lloyd Matson and the Matson cousins: any outstanding warrants, firearms purchases, wage garnishments. Anything that would give him an edge in a confrontation, if the situation escalated. From what he'd learned, he felt good about his plan. They were dirtball deadbeats, but they weren't complete idiots—expect, maybe, for Travis. The patriarch, Lloyd Matson, had a prison record, but that was good news, not bad. It meant he was savvy. Savvy enough to know better than to risk his freedom on a trifle.

It didn't matter when Molly had left the note, not really, but still Jake wondered about the timing as he opened the envelope, because she had believed he'd be home all night. Which meant she thought he had already read it. Depending on how busy her night had turned out to be, that is.

He opened the note. He read it quickly. Its contents were not at all what he had expected.

He read it again.

A third time.

He wasn't sure, frankly, how he was going to take his next breath. He was too stunned. How would he do it? That breathing thing—how did it work, exactly? The bottom had officially dropped out of his world. He felt the heat rising in his cheeks. He was so stricken, his head so emptied out with surprise and dismay, that he forgot all about Malik and the playing cards and the ten-minute limit, so that, an hour later, when he finally *did* remember, he rolled his chair into the young man's room and found him asleep with the light still on, lying diagonally amid the crumpled comforter and twisted sheets, covered with playing cards, a smile on his face.

Chapter Fifteen

"He's a licker."

"Yeah," Bell said, turning her head so that she could wipe her chin on an upraised shoulder without using her hands. "I got that."

She couldn't use her hands because they were currently full. In fact, they were overfull; the dog was medium-sized but wide, and he spilled out over the edges of her cupped arms. He seemed comprised of equal parts hair, tongue, and joy.

Bell risked another glimpse at the squirming ball of butter-colored fur that Rhonda Lovejoy had just deposited, tummy side up, in her arms. The dog's first order of business had been to swipe his tongue across her mouth.

"He likes you," Rhonda declared.

"He likes anything he can lick," Bell corrected her.

They were standing on Bell's wide front porch in the cold night air, an odd tableau consisting of two women, one man, and one dog of indeterminate breed but easy-to-determine attitude: happiness and gratitude. The animal had been dumped in Bell's arms with a little *Ta-da!* from Rhonda, while her husband, Mack Gettinger, clapped and whooped.

Bell had been here for less than ten minutes. Nick had driven them back from Joe Gilley's house and left her at her car, parked in front of a now-closed JP's. She drove home. And that, in turn, had enabled her to embark upon what she had imagined would be another solitary evening in the large stone house on Shelton Avenue, the one she had bought when she first came back to Acker's Gap a dozen years ago with her very reluctant, and in fact downright enraged, fourteen-year-old daughter, Carla, in tow. Many things had changed since then—Carla was an adult now, Bell was no longer the county prosecutor—but the house had not changed. It was still solid, venerable, rooted. It still needed a new furnace and a new roof.

And it was still home.

She'd just fired up a pot of coffee in the kitchen when she heard it: the heavy *clunk-clunk* of the brass knocker on the front door. She was puzzled; as a rule, people in Acker's Gap did not make unannounced visits, especially not at night. Among the chief reasons thereof was the knowledge that a majority of homeowners had shotguns propped next to their beds and were prone to skittishness.

But there was no mistaking the sound.

Standing in the circle of porch light when she opened the big oak door were Rhonda and Mack.

They hadn't come alone.

Before Bell had a chance to say a word, Rhonda had handed her a dog, just the way she would've handed her a toddler. The animal's stomach was daisy yellow, drum taut. Four paws churned in the air. The shaggy head rolled from side to side and the pink, slobber-rich tongue rolled right along with it, searching for something—anything—to lick.

Before Bell could get her face out of range, she'd been slimed.

That caused a great scallop of laughter to pop out of Mack. He was a notoriously loud laugher. Rhonda had confided to Bell shortly after their marriage that of all the things she'd had to get used to about life with Mack—such as sharing a bedroom and a bathroom and a checking account—the biggest hurdle by far was bracing herself each time he uncorked his legendary laugh. *I swear it's loud enough to re-arrange the furniture,* Rhonda noted. *And if you think* that's *bad, you oughta hear his sneezes.*

"Yep—you two are going to get along just fine," Mack declared. "We saw your kitchen light was on. Knew you were still up."

"You'll get used to the licking," Rhonda added. "Pretty soon, it'll be the high point of your day."

Bell tried to hand the dog back to her, but Rhonda's arms remained crossed. "Nope," she said. "He's all yours."

"Yeah," Mack concurred. "Give him a kiss. Right on the muzzle. That'll help with the bonding process."

Before Bell could inquire as to what on earth had gotten into the two of them, she realized how cold it was on her front porch. "Let's go inside before we all freeze to death," she said. Taking note of the dog's thick coat, she added, "Not a fate this guy has to worry about." She set him down and he walked serenely past her into the house, as if he'd done it thousands of times before. She wondered at his provenance: He had the round head of a golden retriever, but was no bigger than a medium-sized terrier, with the wide chest of a pit bull and the flop-over ears of a Labrador.

Once they were settled in the living room—although "settled" was not a word to be used in conjunction with a dog, even a mature one like this, Bell thought ruefully—Rhonda explained the circumstances behind the surprise visit and the even more surprising gift. While she talked, the dog trotted round the room, sniffing every corner, occasionally flopping on his back and twisting back and forth, as if his rump was in desperate need of a good scratch.

Watching him, Rhonda said, "He's an old soul. Makes him perfect for you, Bell. The two of you can sit around of an evening and think deep thoughts." She giggled at the notion.

Rhonda was a heavy woman, with a whipped-up froth of bright blond curls that bounced across her shoulders. Her husband was tall, bald, and lanky. His iron gray eyebrows and large hooked nose gave his face a hawk-like severity. It was an illusion, Bell knew; Mack Gettinger was the gentlest of men, and he loved Rhonda Lovejoy with a passion that had almost restored Bell's faith in romance—a faith that had been severely tested during her years as prosecutor, when the savage domestic assaults and hostage-takings by heavily armed ex-spouses were depressingly frequent.

"So after our conversation last night," Rhonda began, realizing that it was time to explain herself, "I knew I had to do something.

I was getting really, really low. And no matter what I tried, I just couldn't cheer myself up. I mean, lately it's been all bad news, all the time. And then I got the report a few hours ago about Darla Gilley. I mean—my God, such a brutal murder. No suspects. I didn't know Darla all that well, but I know the Gilley family. Brenda used to sing in the choir at my church. Nowadays it's too long of a drive for her, all the way from Roberts Ridge, being as how Joe's so sick and all, but . . ." Rhonda let her sentence trail off. She'd been trying to cure herself lately of the habit of digression. The backsliding was frequent.

"Anyway," she went on, "I have no earthly idea how they'll get over this. It's a lot of grief to bear all at once. Sorrow on top of sorrow." She fetched two deep breaths before she continued. "And then there's the baby in the Burger Boss. I was talking to Mack—" Her husband, seated beside her on the couch, took her hand. "—and I told him I was ready to give up. I just wanted to go to bed and pull the covers up over my head and never come out again. And so he looked at me and he said one word: dogs. Isn't that right, Mack?"

"That's right." He grinned. "That's what I said."

"I asked him what he meant," Rhonda continued, "and instead of answering, he pointed out the kitchen window to his truck in the driveway and I followed him outside and we drove over to the county animal shelter and it just so happened that somebody had dumped a couple of dogs by the side door not two hours before—this little guy and his sister. So I said I'd take one. And Mack said, 'No, we'll take 'em *both*.' I gave him a funny look because, as you well know, Bell, our house is on the small side and we already have four dogs, and guess what Mack said then? He said, 'One for us. One for Bell.'"

"That's what I said, all right," Mack repeated, still grinning.

"Next thing I know," Rhonda resumed, "we're filling out the paperwork and driving home. We got them settled on some nice blankets in the living room. Then I had to go back to work and Mack had to go back to work, too, to supervise a delivery at the warehouse, and so it wasn't until about an hour ago that we had the chance to come by here. I temporarily named him Arthur. His sister's name is Marlene. Marlene's doing fine with my other dogs. They all get along great."

Rhonda squinted at Bell. "You can change his name if you like. I just started using 'Arthur' to have something to call him. Because he looks like an Arthur. He does to me, anyway."

She waited for Bell's response.

As interested as she was in Rhonda's narrative, Bell's attention had been diverted. The dog was entirely too enthralled with one particular spot on the rug. He pawed at it, smelled it, and then pawed some more. His ears flopped forward as he stared at it, twisting his head first one way and then the other. A few seconds before, he'd been rooting around the fireplace, peering up into the flue and scratching at the tiles, but now he was totally entranced by that corner of the rug.

Bell had had a dog once before, and she knew what such behavior might very well signify.

So did Mack. "That's my cue," he said, getting up. "I'll take him outside and let him do his business. You two gals can have your chat."

Bell had never warmed to the word "gals," but she knew that it was a habit with Mack—and with virtually every other man in Acker's Gap over forty. She was used to it by now, having filed her irritation under the heading "Pick your battles."

Mack was already at the door, a wiggly Arthur under his arm, when Rhonda called out, "You could take him for a little walk, too, while you're out there. Get him used to the neighborhood."

Rhonda waited for the door to close before she resumed speaking. Her voice was different from before, when Mack was present. It had lost its singsong quality, the storyteller's cadence that invested an ordinary anecdote with the magic of a fairy tale shared at bedtime.

"I don't like to discuss work in front of Mack," she said. "But there's something else. I mean—yes, I think a dog is just what you need right about now, and I hope you'll keep Arthur, but that's not the only reason I'm barging in on you like this, so late at night."

"Not a problem. You know that."

Rhonda nodded. "I do."

Their relationship had changed immeasurably since the days when Bell Elkins was the stern-faced, taciturn prosecutor and Rhonda Lovejoy the garrulous and flighty assistant prosecutor, a woman known more for her extravagantly colorful outfits than for her legal mind and courtroom finesse. Bell was now a private citizen. Rhonda was a serious and effective prosecutor who managed to walk a fine line between her dense and sprawling family connections in the area—and a rigorous enforcement of the law, even when it involved some of those very relations.

Through it all, she and Bell had maintained a friendship and a satisfactory off-the-books professional tie when she hired Bell's agency.

"The thing is," Rhonda said, "I need your help. More than ever. Here's how I see it. Darla Gilley's murder is going to rile up this town something awful. I hate to put it this way, but people around here have gotten pretty casual about drug crime. Dead dealers, overdoses—they shake their heads and go on about their business. But this is different. This is a decent woman with no history of any trouble with the law. And no known enemies. And somebody attacks and kills her. Viciously." Rhonda shook her head. "And we have no idea who did it. Or why anybody *would* do it."

"How can I help?"

"I'd like you to come with me tomorrow when I go talk to Thad Connell, Darla's ex-husband."

"So you found him."

"Wasn't hard. He's in the Bretherton County Jail. Felonious assault charge stemming from a bar fight the other night."

"What a prince."

Rhonda frowned. "I know you're being sarcastic, and it's understandable given what I just told you, but I've always kind of liked Thad."

"So you know him."

"I do. A little bit. He went to high school with my father. Daddy always said Thad Connell didn't have a mean bone in his body—unless he was drinking. Then he turned into the devil himself." Rhonda's face darkened. "But if he had anything to do with Darla's murder—drunk or sober—I'll go after him hard." She gave Bell a beseeching look. "So you'll help? After we talk to Connell, there'll be other things, I'm sure, once the case gets cranked up. I can use Nick and Jake, too." She made a face. "The county's flat broke, as you know.

But I'll find something in the budget. It won't be much—maybe just your expenses."

"Expenses would be fine."

Rhonda looked relieved. "I was sure you'd say yes, but I don't ever take it for granted."

"The usual rules, right?"

"Absolutely."

They had come to an understanding over the past year about how they would work together. Rhonda didn't have the time—and Bell didn't have the inclination—to report in on a regular basis. If there was information to impart, Bell would provide it; otherwise, Rhonda trusted Bell and her colleagues to follow their own lights.

In some ways, Bell felt constricted by her new role. She had no power over any other citizen, no authority. She couldn't request a warrant or make an arrest. But in another way, she had *more* power than she'd had while serving in public office—because she didn't have specific rules to follow, ethical bright lines to watch out for. She could talk to suspects without Miranda warnings. She could open bags and eavesdrop on conversations—as long as she wasn't caught.

Bell looked toward the big front window. "I guess Mack took you up on that suggestion of a walk."

"I told him I needed some time to make my pitch."

"Good man. By the way—Nick and I went over to Joe and Brenda Gilley's house tonight. Sheriff thought Nick might be a help to Joe, given how long they've known each other. As we were leaving, Joe got pretty upset. He said their grandmother was *also* killed at Wellwood, back in 1959. Case was never solved."

"I know."

"You know?"

"I remember my great-aunt Stella telling me about it when I was a little girl. Bessie Gilley was fairly young when she died—thirty-seven or thirty-eight, Stella said. Bessie worked at Wellwood—it was still in operation back then. No one was ever arrested for the crime."

"Do you think there's any connection? Or is it just a hell of a coincidence?"

Rhonda gave her a look. "As much as I'd love to dig into a cold case, I've got about a hundred red-hot ones to deal with. Right here, right now. And Darla's murder is at the top of the list. After we talk to Thad tomorrow I'll be taking a look at Darla's finances and then tracing her movements on her last day and then—"

The door opened. Arthur meandered in ahead of Mack. He went straight to Bell and climbed up into her lap, as if it were their nightly ritual.

"Told him to do that," Mack said. "In sales we call it the assumptive close."

Rhonda laughed. "How'd things go out there?"

"He peed and he pooped," Mack reported. "The double whammy. He's good for the rest of the night. Oh, and Bell—do you have a plastic grocery sack handy?"

"Don't worry about it," she answered. "I'll clean it up first thing in the morning."

"Southeastern corner of the yard. You can't miss it." He sat back down next to his wife. He smacked his lap, trying to entice the dog to come to him and leave Bell alone. She still looked a little stunned at the physical fact of Arthur, sitting on her lap, his tongue hanging roguishly from the side of his mouth.

The dog stayed put.

"It's okay," Bell said.

Rhonda sounded apologetic but hopeful. "Like I said, you don't have to keep him. I told Mack that it was a long shot—and that we'd probably have to take him ourselves. But I really do think a dog can help. Just when you're so depressed you can barely move—he'll do something funny and you feel better. And dogs don't gossip."

"I still have the bowl and dog bed from when I had Goldie," Bell said, ruminating aloud. Goldie was a dog she'd kept for a man named Royce Dillard several years ago, while he stood trial for murder. After the true culprit was found and Dillard was released, Bell had returned the golden retriever to him.

She'd never told anyone—not Carla, not Rhonda, not Nick or Jake—how long she had cried that night, missing the dog. She had grown so accustomed to having Goldie around the house that his absence cut deep.

She wasn't at all certain that she could ever love another dog the way she had loved Goldie. Arthur was very different from Goldie; despite the sprightliness he'd shown on the porch he seemed to have a somber, almost philosophical mien, as if he were half canine, half Kierkegaard, whereas Goldie was full-on rambunctious. All dog.

"We have some dog chow in the truck to get you started," Mack said. He winked at Rhonda, in full view of Bell. "And a collar and leash. Just in case."

Bell's attention was fixed on the dog, not on Mack's attempts at sweetening the deal. "Any idea what he is?" she asked. "The breed mix, I mean?"

"I think you'll have more luck figuring out what breeds he *isn't*—instead of the ones he *is,*" Rhonda answered. "That was my first comment when I saw the both of them—'Hey, Mack. They're mutts, just like us.'"

"Just like all of us." Bell had discovered the special area behind Arthur's ear, the one that, when she scratched it, caused him to lift his head in simple, dreamy ecstasy. Even philosophers had their soft spots.

"So do we have a deal?" Mack asked.

"Give her a minute," Rhonda chastised him.

The dog had settled down. He was very tired; this had been an eventful day and the fatigue had just caught up with him. He arranged himself lengthwise across Bell's lap, front and back legs stretched out in their respective directions.

Bell leaned her head back against the armchair. She stroked Arthur's round head while she debated the pros and cons with herself, quickly and silently, knowing that Rhonda and Mack would grant her the time.

This armchair was her favorite seat in the house, a dilapidated, patched-over, coffee-stained brown lump that would probably be rejected by Goodwill, should she ever care to donate it—which would never happen. The chair was a part of her history. She'd carted it from her college apartment to the first small apartment she'd shared with Sam Elkins in D.C. and then right back here to Acker's Gap, to this house she'd bought for herself and Carla after the divorce.

Many, many changes had occurred over the years, some sorrowful, some joyous. People and problems came and went. The only forever thing was this chair.

Maybe it was time to add one more forever thing.

Whoa, she cautioned herself. Dogs were messy and destructive and expensive, right? Dogs chewed your favorite shoes and peed on the rug and threw up for no particular reason and barked when you didn't want them to. Dogs were a nuisance. Dogs were an annoyance. Dogs were nothing but trouble.

Arthur raised his head and peered at her, as if he, too, were awaiting the verdict. He would not beg. He had his dignity, after all. It was up to her.

"Sold," she declared.

Rhonda and Mack had just left. Now she was alone again.

Well, no. She had the dog. There he sat by the front door, head tilted, rump tucked, front paws symmetrical. He appeared to be contented but also slightly aloof, formal, unsure of her intentions. Was this just another way station, a temporary refuge?

He might have been rethinking the unsolicited sprawl on her lap a few minutes ago, not to mention the spontaneous lick on the porch when he'd first arrived. Perhaps he'd overstepped.

She looked down at the dog. He looked up at her.

Arthur, Bell thought. *Your name is Arthur. I can't keep calling you "the dog." You need to learn your name, right?*

And then she realized that the chances of Arthur reading her mind were rather remote. If she wanted him to get used to his name, she'd have to use it out loud. Which meant talking to him.

"Arthur," she said. His tail swished against the hardwood floor.

Clearly he required another bit of time outside to conclude his evening ablutions. No matter what Jake said, you had to offer dogs plenty of chances.

The night air was much colder now. The stars were bright nail heads punched into the archway of sky stretched between the tops of the mountains. She let Arthur root around in the yard while she re-read Jake's text about Dixie Sue Folsom. He had taken the young woman home, staying long enough to witness the reunion. Bell could imagine the scene, having already decided what kind of mother Maggie was: the kind who did her best. There would have been an embrace, an expression of love for her daughter, and then a long look in the young woman's face and an earnest declaration: *But if you ever pull that kind of stunt again, young lady, you'll be grounded for six months. I mean it. My trailer, my rules.* And Dixie Sue, Bell surmised, would be pleased at being home, and might just do as she was told . . . for a while.

At least there was one happy ending tonight.

She watched Arthur probe the ground and turn around in circles until he finally located a suitable spot for a long, luxurious peeing session, the stream of his urine arcing high and adding a pungent aroma to the frigid night air. He seemed perfectly at home.

Maybe *two* happy endings.

Anyway, the Folsom case was closed, as far as the agency was concerned. Now they had just one case—and it had only become theirs ten minutes ago, when Rhonda Lovejoy made it official: Finding Darla Gilley's killer. And along the way, perhaps, even though no one had asked them to, and only if it didn't divert them from their main duty, finding out who had killed Darla's grandmother in roughly the same place, in roughly the same way, sixty years ago.

Sixty years, Bell thought. *Long time.*

No, she corrected herself, her mind on the mountains. *A drop in the bucket.*

As was always the case in Acker's Gap, the past wouldn't stay put. It seeped inexorably into the present, like a dark garment mistakenly washed in the same load with a light one, turning both garments an identical shade of gray.

Chapter Sixteen

It wasn't much of a place, but it was a place. That was about the best that could be said for it, Nick had decided a year and a half ago, the day he moved into this runty, three-room apartment with the freckled linoleum floors and the leaky windows. The walls were so flimsy that he could hear his neighbor blow his nose.

He had just arrived at the four-unit building after dropping off Bell at her car in Acker's Gap. Their conversation on the way back from Roberts Ridge had been restricted to logistics: next moves, best practices.

He closed the door behind him. He didn't turn on any lights.

Each time he came back, he remembered that first day here. Then as now, he didn't much care about its shortcomings. This was a way station, a convenience. A temporary residence. Not a home.

Although Randy Truscott, who was married to his cousin Lulu and who had helped him haul his stuff from the public storage facility, had risked a contrary opinion on moving day: "Anywhere's a home, Nick. If you hang your hat there, it's a home. You gotta come to terms with that." The two of them were standing in the tiny living room, having just set down the lime-green-and-orange plaid couch that Nick had purchased at the Goodwill store a week ago, before he even had a place to put it. The couch was the last of Nick's possessions. He had tossed Randy a beer to mark the moment.

"Keep on lecturing me that way," Nick had replied testily, "and I swear I'll take back the beer."

Randy grunted and, with thumb and index finger, made a sliding motion across his mouth.

Originally Nick had only signed a six-month lease with the Lesage Realty Company, the owner of record of the two-story, brown-stucco-sided apartment building on the outskirts of Blythesburg. He intended to go somewhere else once he'd found his feet again. Yet when the first lease expired, he signed another one, and then another. Six-month increments seemed about right. He didn't want to think any further ahead than that.

His apartment was on the upper right-hand side. "You *would* have to get an upstairs apartment," Randy had muttered on that sweltering June day, as they huffed and stumbled their way up the metal stairway on the outside of the building, each hoisting an end of the couch. Last month, Nick had returned the favor, helping him move a piano into the spare room on the second floor of Randy and Lulu's house over in Lawton Falls. Their ten-year-old daughter, Eloise, was taking lessons. Nick was happy to help, but halfway up the stairs he had felt something go *pop!* in his back, a fact he didn't share with Randy and Lulu, because he knew it would make them feel bad. He'd only shared it with Bell and Jake. He had no choice. They were his partners. They had to know about any physical limitations.

Tonight, Nick stood in roughly the same spot he'd occupied when Randy Truscott had uttered his silly platitude about home. Randy was a good man and he meant well, but he overstepped sometimes. Stuck his nose in places where it didn't belong. It figured: He was an academic advisor at the community college over in Muth County. He was specifically authorized to interfere in people's lives.

You're full of it, Randy. This isn't my home, Nick told himself, frowning at the bare walls. *Never will be, either.* Fact was, he didn't have a home. Not anymore. Not since Mary Sue had surprised him one day with the news that she didn't want to be married to him anymore. Just like that, after forty-one years, he was homeless. He might have a roof over his head and a door to close at night—but he didn't have a home. Not really.

He didn't take off his coat. Still didn't turn on any lights, either. He wanted to think for a minute, and he did that best in the dark, standing up, without the distraction of scenery.

He couldn't figure it out. Who would want to kill Darla Gilley, and why? She wasn't an addict and had nothing to do with the drug trade; by all accounts she wasn't involved romantically with anyone; she didn't have any income to speak of. That eliminated the top three motives, in order, for murder in Raythune County: drugs, sex, and money.

As he stood and pondered, he realized just how cold the living room actually was. The cold, in fact, was gradually working its way under the layers he wore: coat, sweater, T-shirt. Time to turn on the lights and check the thermostat.

Damn. Just as he'd suspected: The thermostat was fine. The furnace simply wasn't cranking out any heat. That cheap-ass landlord of his—Pete Lesage was a notorious skinflint—had resisted putting in a new furnace at the end of last winter even though the noisy contraption was showing definite signs of distress. Nick and the other tenants had complained, but Pete put them off. *It'll be fine. Got two, three more years before a new one's called for.* The result was predictable: The apartment was freezing. And it was still only October.

Nick wondered why the other residents put up with the shoddy maintenance. Then he remembered: They didn't. Only one other apartment was still occupied. The tenants in the other two, a couple named Bill and Trudy Something-or-Other and a woman named Taylor Something-or-Other—or was it Something-or-Other Taylor?—had moved out a few months ago in rapid succession, citing Pete's chronic fibs and general unreliability. Nick and the tenant across the hall in 2-A were the only ones left in the building. And 2-A, a gray, stooped-over man even older than Nick who sported the world's silliest-looking comb-over, spent most of his time at his daughter's home in Crosslanes. Nick hadn't seen him in weeks.

So why the hell do I stay here? Nick let the question take a few laps in his head. It had replaced the question about Darla Gilley and her destiny. He'd be returning soon enough to Darla.

He knew the answer: *I don't have the gumption to find somewhere else to go.*

Which was only part of the reason.

The other part was standing on the other side of his front door. He knew she had arrived because he'd heard her knock just seconds ago, using the signal that was so familiar to him that it made his heart quiver with anticipation: three quick raps, a pause, and then another two, followed by a low-voiced, "Nick?" He could plainly hear her say his name, which meant she was holding her lips close to the narrow place between the door and the frame, a fact that inflamed him.

Chapter Seventeen

She didn't wait for him to invite her in. They had dispensed with such niceties months ago, when this first began. She fit perfectly in his arms. She wrapped herself around him, closing the door shut behind her with a backward kick.

Her hair smelled cold, with an undertone of some mysterious spice that was always there, and that he assumed came from whatever shampoo she used. She never smelled like the diner—the twining odors of hot grease, coffee, baking bread. Not even at the end of the day, which was a neat trick. How did she do that?

"I took a chance," she whispered. "Wasn't sure you'd be back yet."

"I'm back." It was all he could think of to say. When Jackie was close to him like this, words flew out of his head; ordinary conversation was impossible. He sounded like a damned fool. She didn't seem to mind.

"As I recall," she said softly, "we were interrupted last night."

"Yeah."

"So I thought we could pick up where we left off."

"Yeah."

Her lips brushed his ear. "Terrible news tonight," she murmured. She was running her hands up and down the sides of his coat. Now she was unbuttoning it, sliding her hands inside, and in another few seconds she had lifted the bottom of his sweater, her hands nimble and practiced. "That poor woman."

"So you've heard?"

"Everybody's heard." She was untucking the T-shirt he always wore under his sweater. "I knew Darla. She came in the diner from time to time. Came in this afternoon, in fact, for a cup of coffee. Nice lady. Is that why you and Bell took off tonight? Something to do with Darla?"

"Yeah."

The moment her hands touched the skin on his chest, he drew in his breath sharply.

"It's a tragedy," he murmured, because it was, and because that's what you were supposed to say, and because he couldn't think of anything else *to* say—in fact, he couldn't think, period. She was kissing his chest.

He let her do that for a few seconds and then he put his hands on both sides of her head—her long hair was thick, a little coarse, and it fell forward when she dipped her head that way, to kiss his chest and his belly—and raised it up. He needed her mouth, her lips. He kissed her. Her mouth was hot. Burning. But even as they kissed, her hands never stopped; they were busy, industrious, they knew their business. She unbuckled his belt, and he wasn't sure how he was still able to breathe.

"That guy," he murmured.

She paused what she was doing. He wished she hadn't. "Guy?" she asked.

"Came in the diner tonight. Overalls."

She laughed softly. "Why, Nick Fogelsong. I do believe you're jealous."

She was right, of course. "You're wrong," he said.

She laughed again. "He's an old friend. Nothing for you to worry about. But I kind of like the fact that it bothers you." To his delight, she resumed her ministrations.

Somehow—he didn't know how—they made it into the bedroom, where she pushed him down on the bed and then straddled him. She knew just how to do it so as not to hurt his back. His back felt fine right now. So did the rest of him.

He watched her fling off her own coat, lift her flannel shirt off over her head without undoing the buttons, unhook her bra with a deft, one-handed maneuver. Her hair rushed over her bare shoulders. Seeing her fully dressed at the diner, day after day, he'd had no idea how round and full those breasts were, how goddamned beautiful.

"Cold in here," he muttered, because he felt he ought to say something.

"Not for long."

Chapter Eighteen

He wasn't sure how it had started. As crazy as it sounded, he really wasn't. Not specifically, anyway.

A glance. Just a glance from her one day at the diner, when he'd come in alone a few months ago. Conversation. Casual at first, then more intense. She checked on the other customers. She came back. Asked him to return that night after closing time to help her with the cooler. The compressor was shot; she was nursing it along until she could afford a new one. He'd mentioned, during that oh-so-casual conversation, that as a young man in his early twenties, a deputy sheriff, he'd thought about switching careers. He'd ordered a home-study kit on repairing HVAC systems. Heating, cooling. The way it all worked.

But then the old sheriff had passed away unexpectedly, and Nick Fogelsong was named interim sheriff. His doubts went away. The election came. He ran and won. The rest? Destiny—if by "destiny" people meant: *This is what happened.*

Still, he did know a little something about refrigeration. Remembered the basics, from all those years ago. Sure, he'd swing by and take a look. No problem.

That night was the first time. They left the diner and went to her place. He wasn't comfortable there—she lived right on Main Street, for God's sake—and so thereafter she came to his apartment, far enough away for privacy. Or so he hoped. Acker's Gap was a small town. Eventually, everybody knew everything.

And how did it develop into something more, a steady, regular thing? He didn't know. It was like the situation with his lease: He took it in small increments. Inching forward. No goal in sight. He lived in the now. Unlike the apartment, though, which stretched on because of his laziness and complacency, the situation with her was something else.

He had always admired her, found her attractive. But this was different. It was . . . *blissful,* he supposed he'd call it, but only to himself, and never out loud, because "blissful" was a sissy word, even though it fit. There was a reserve to Jackie LeFevre, a deep well of withholding, and the fact that she let all of that go when they were together just thrilled him. He knew she'd had a hard life. He didn't know the particulars, but he knew that. And he relished the idea that he brought her the same kind of pleasure that she brought him.

So what kept it from being ideal?

He wasn't officially divorced yet. That was the problem. There were people in town who wouldn't approve. *To hell with them,* Jackie said, when he gave voice to his worries. But he didn't share her attitude. He couldn't. He'd lived here a long time. Always tried to respect other people's beliefs and opinions. And to a fair number of people, what he and Jackie LeFevre were doing was sinful. Plain and simple. Because he was, technically, a married man.

He was especially sensitive about it with people who knew Mary Sue. People like Maggie Folsom.

Maggie had seen them together once, just after it started. He and Jackie had driven to Beaverton on a Saturday night. There was a restaurant in the town that Jackie liked, an Italian place. Low lighting, checkered tablecloths, cloth napkins, a wine list. The works. Nick had figured it was far enough away from Acker's Gap. They'd be safe. And so, on their way out the door after a fine meal that included, between courses, many flirtatious innuendos, with his belly full of lasagna and red wine, his mind woozy not from the wine—or not only from the wine—but also from the anticipation of heading back to his apartment with Jackie, he had seen, across the parking lot, Maggie Folsom.

She was standing with a group of friends, ready to go into the restaurant. He didn't know any of the others—but he knew her, and she knew him.

Wouldn't you just know it: Seconds before he spotted Maggie, he had paused and given Jackie a long, lingering kiss. He let her go and then leaned over to open the car door for her. When he rounded the back end of the vehicle to get to the driver's side, he glanced around and . . .

Holy shit. It's Maggie Folsom.

She looked away quickly. But she'd seen them. Seen the kiss. No question about it. And he had felt, in the instant before Maggie turned her head, her disapproval. Disgust, even.

Maggie didn't tell anyone. He was sure of it. He would've heard the gossip. But he didn't know how long her discretion would last.

Seeing Maggie again the night before, at the office, had made him exceedingly nervous. He had asked himself, at the time, why he didn't just come clean and tell everybody—Bell, Jake, Randy and Lulu, the rest of his friends—what was going on. They wanted him to be happy, right? Of course they did. And there was nothing wrong with what he and Jackie were doing. Nothing at all. His divorce was all but done.

It made sense. And yet, when it came down to saying the words, he couldn't do it. He was an old-fashioned man. He argued with himself—hell, Mary Sue hadn't shown any loyalty to their vows when she started screwing that good-for-nothing, suntanned jackass she'd met down in Florida; Mary Sue had explained haughtily to Nick that Russell Meeks didn't try to take care of her, didn't ask about how she was doing every other second, didn't check the pill bottles to make sure she'd taken her meds, and furthermore—

Didn't matter. It didn't matter what Mary Sue did or didn't do. He was what he was. And he was, for now, a guilty man.

So they sneaked around, he and Jackie. He'd gotten a prescription from a doctor in Charleston and filled it at a pharmacy there—it was a ways to go, but you can't be too careful, he told himself—and his nights with Jackie LeFevre were spectacular.

Once the divorce was final, he would come clean. With everybody.

Absolutely. The first person he would tell, in fact, was the person he was most afraid of finding out until the official documentation had been signed and filed with the court: Bell Elkins.

She respected him immensely, just as he did her. She'd known him since she was ten years old, and she looked up to him, and the affection between them was very much the bond of a daughter and a father. The idea of disappointing her was troubling.

But still. When Jackie LeFevre touched him, things happened inside him that he hadn't felt in years. *Or maybe ever,* he thought, when he was in the throes of it. *Not like this.*

Hence, the night before, when Bell had asked him to come back in to work, he was grumpy and out of sorts. Because at the time of Bell's call, Jackie was in his bed. Reluctantly—*very* reluctantly—he had sent her home, knowing that, soon, another night, they'd take up exactly where they left off.

A night like tonight.

Chapter Nineteen

Jackie almost never spent the whole night with him. She didn't on this night, either. She had to open JP's at 6:00 on Saturday mornings—her best day, by far, businesswise—and that meant getting to the diner at 4:30, and so it didn't make sense. The drive from Blythesburg to Acker's Gap took a good twenty-five, thirty minutes, as opposed to her usual commute, which consisted of walking down Main Street from her apartment above the post office.

Typically, she'd slip out of his bed while he slept. He never understood how she pulled that off. He had always been a light sleeper; it was the consequence, he assumed, of having been awakened hundreds of times by phone calls in the middle of the night from his deputies, to inform him about the latest catastrophe in the county he'd been charged with keeping safe for so many years. But not anymore.

In the morning there would be no sign that Jackie had even been here at all—beyond the hazy, luscious memory of what they'd shared, and the deep contentment it left in him.

And so it was this morning, too. Nick blinked awake, wondering what time it was. The sun was up; that's all he knew for sure. He swung his legs over the side of the bed, rubbed his eyes, and looked around the room.

It had a threadbare look: bed, nightstand, a folding chair in the corner. He didn't have a chest of drawers. He kept his clean clothes in piles on the floor. Neat piles, yes—but piles, all the same.

His cell chimed. It was still in his pants pocket; his pants were on the floor beside the bed, where he'd left them in last night's fumbled rush.

The caller was Brenda Gilley.

"Hi, Nick. Hope it's not too early to call."

It was, but he wouldn't tell her that. "I was up." With his free hand he pulled the covers around his bare shoulders. The room was freezing. He silently cursed Pete Lesage and the on-the-fritz furnace.

"Oh, good. Me, too. Matter of fact, I didn't really sleep at all last night. Too upset, too keyed up, what with the news about Darla. But I put the time to good use. Went up to the attic and started bagging up her things."

Jesus, he thought. *You're sure in a hurry. The body's still at the coroner's and you've already got her stuff ready for Goodwill.*

Maybe that was unfair, though. Brenda liked to keep things neat. The world made sense to her when it was orderly. Back in high school, her locker was always clean, and it smelled fresh. Everybody else's— his and Joe's, for sure—smelled like dirty tennis shoes and sweaty T-shirts and mummified sandwiches.

Out loud, he said, "Tell you the truth, Brenda, you oughta hold off on that. Best to leave the attic just as Darla did—at least until the sheriff says it's okay. It'll be part of the investigation."

"She already went up there last night and had a look around. So I thought it was okay." Defensively.

"Well, just stop where you are. And wait until Pam officially clears you to start moving things around."

"I will."

Would she? He couldn't tell. Her voice still reflected a prickly umbrage. Truth was, Brenda and Nick had never been close. "Never" might be an exaggeration, he corrected himself; they'd been fairly good friends as teenagers, joking around in the hall before the homeroom bell, because her maiden name was Fossett and that put her in the same homeroom with Nick Fogelsong.

But the friendship cooled when Brenda started dating—seriously dating—Nick's best friend, Joe Gilley. After that, she was jealous of anybody who was close to Joe, from Joe's best buddy, Nick, to Joe's sister, Darla. So many years had gone by, but there was still an edge to Brenda, still a sharpness, that defied the passage of time. Her body might have softened and spread over the decades, but the sharpness in her personality, the coolness, the suspicion, remained. And maybe even intensified.

"Anyway," she was saying, "that's not why I called."

Swiftly, Nick responded, "Is it Joe? Did something happen to—"

"No, no. He's fine. Well—no, not fine. You know that. But okay. For now. I mean, I think it's kind of sinking in—what happened to Darla."

"Right." Nick was feeling impatient now. He wished she'd get to the point.

"We had a visitor this morning. That's what I wanted to tell you about. A man named Roger Briscoe knocked on the door real early. Good thing I was already up, or it woulda scared the bejesus out of me. He was looking for Darla. He didn't know what had happened. When I told him, he was shocked."

"Who is he? What did he want?"

"He's a truck driver. Turns out Darla got a ride with him on Thursday afternoon from Acker's Gap out to Briney Hollow. He picked her up and dropped her off right where those woods get started."

"How did he find you?" Nick tried to keep his voice calm. This was a major clue; it answered the question of how Darla had gotten to the woods without her own vehicle.

"Turns out he found her purse yesterday when he was cleaning out his cab," she replied. "Darla must've dropped it when she was climbing down. He apologized for not coming by sooner, but said he was hauling a load to Charleston and didn't get back to Acker's Gap until this morning. He found her driver's license in her billfold and got here as soon as he could. Figured she'd need it. And then to find out—" She paused. "Well."

"Did Darla tell him why she wanted to go out there?" Nick's mind was in high gear. The truck driver's account could tell them approximately when Darla had arrived at Briney Hollow and begun the hike to Wellwood.

"Not really. She just flagged him down and asked for the lift. He thought it was a little strange, he told me. Somebody that old, out hitchhiking. And a woman, to boot. But no, she didn't tell him why she wanted to go. He just said . . ." She hesitated.

"What? This is important, Brenda. To finding Darla's killer. What did he say?"

"Well, this part was hard for Joe to hear. Made me wish I'd spoken to Mr. Briscoe alone, but Joe was right there. That truck driver said Darla was real upset—and Joe hated to think of her that way, on her last day on this earth. Something was bothering her real, real bad. And Mr. Briscoe said it seemed to him like she was scared. Scared so bad that her hands were shaking. Scared out of her mind."

Chapter Twenty

The man sat on the hard metal chair in the interrogation room of the Bretherton County Jail. It was a sunny Saturday morning in Beverly, West Virginia, the county seat and, at 7,646 residents, the largest town in the county. By far.

His big hands lay on the gray metal tabletop in front of him, palms down, one right next to the other, thumbs touching, as if he were showing off a manicure. But that couldn't be the case, because the nails were ragged and yellow. Two of the nails, both on his right hand, had been ripped off at the quick and still hadn't grown back. From the look of them, they might never do so. The exposed nail bed was a spongy red mess, either infected or getting there.

The knuckles on both hands were crosshatched with cuts.

His feet were flat on the concrete floor. One ankle was chained to the leg of the chair. He wore a baggy orange jumpsuit with BRETHERTON CO WV stamped on the back.

His hair was a light frizzle of gray. The skin on his face was so jaundiced and sallow that it looked slimy beneath the room's harsh lighting. The pores were craters with dabs of grease in their centers. Bristly white eyebrows overhung a pair of watery, bloodshot eyes. His nose, broken many times, looked like a gray blob of plumber's putty. The lax flesh of his cheeks draped both sides of his mouth, a mouth from which spidery wrinkles crept out in all directions. *Mark of a smoker,* Bell thought, because she'd seen the same cracks in the same place on the face of every smoker she knew.

But it was the color of his skin that she kept coming back to, when she looked at Thad Connell. Bell had reviewed his file while she and Rhonda waited for them to bring him in, but she really didn't need to. His skin told the story.

He was an alcoholic, and that fact was responsible for most of the bad things that had happened to him in the sixty-one years of his life. None of the dozens of arresting officers who had dealt with him over those years considered Thad Connell to be a cruel man or an incorrigibly dangerous felon—Bell had read the particulars of his arrests—but when he was drunk, or when, prior to that, he needed to become drunk and lacked sufficient funds to bring that about, he had caused himself untold sorrows. The items on his sheet, starting when he was a teenager, ranged from infractions such as shoplifting and burglary to aggravated assault and home invasion. He alternated periods of extreme and aggressive criminal behavior with periods of sobriety and a diligent record of work as a carpet installer.

It was during one of the latter periods that he had met and married Darla Gilley. He was forty at the time; she, thirty-six. They had moved in and out of each other's lives for the next two decades, chained to the cycle of his addiction: When he was "behaving himself," as Darla was quoted as saying in the transcript of one of Connell's numerous sentencing hearings, they lived together as husband and wife. When he "started acting like a damned fool on account of the booze," as Darla put it, they didn't.

And now the chain had been snapped for good, because Darla was dead.

That morning, Bretherton County Sheriff Bob Reed had informed Thad Connell of the murder of his ex-wife. According to Reed's penciled comments in the file of the most recent incident, the prisoner had not reacted overtly, nor did he ask any questions.

Bell sat in one of the two seats on the opposite side of the table. The seat beside her was occupied by Rhonda Lovejoy.

"Is this right, Thad?" Rhonda said. She looked up from the paper-clipped sheaf of about a dozen pages on the table in front of her.

"There's a report here from Sheriff Reed. It says you're charged with assaulting a bartender. The man wouldn't give you another drink until you demonstrated your ability to pay—and so you reached over the bar, grabbed him by the collar, and pulled him forward. And then you put your other hand on the back of his head and rammed him face-first down on the bar—hard—at least four times. Skull fracture and concussion. And a broken nose."

Connell didn't reply. He had yet to make eye contact with Rhonda or Bell beyond a brief initial glance.

He coughed. He led the tip of his gristly yellow tongue around his top and bottom lip, and then he closed his mouth again.

Placing one hand flat on the papers, Rhonda said, "But that's not why I'm here. I'm here to talk about Darla. First off—I'm very sorry for your loss. I want you to know that. I also want you to know that what Sheriff Reed said to you before still goes. You don't have to talk to us. If you do, we're free to use anything you say against you. You can have a lawyer here if you want."

"Can't afford no lawyer." His voice was low and soft. He had a slight lisp.

"If you want one, they'll try to find you one."

"Been through that," Connell murmured. "You wait and wait. Nobody shows up. Meantime, you stay in jail."

He was right. Bell knew it as well as Rhonda did. There weren't any public defenders in small rural counties, and not enough private-practice attorneys who volunteered to work pro bono for poor clients.

"So do you want to talk to us?" Rhonda asked. "Without an attorney present?"

He shrugged. "Might as well. Don't make much difference neverhow."

"Good." Rhonda nodded approvingly. "That's the right decision. Okay, Thad—here's the deal. If you had anything to do with Darla's death, I'm hoping you'll tell us. Right now. You can save yourself a lot of trouble if you do. Think of it as the last good thing you can do for Darla."

Connell swallowed hard several times.

"You don't know what you're talking about," he said. The way

Rhonda had put it—about him doing a last good thing for Darla—shook something loose in him. Now the words flowed. "I loved her. I wouldn't never hurt her. Never raised my hand to her. Twenty years—not once."

"Frankly, you don't seem too broken up about her passing." That came from Bell. She wanted to speed this up, and the best way to do that was to provoke him. She'd received permission from Rhonda to jump in when she wanted to.

Connell's face changed. He pulled in his mouth even tighter. One eye twitched. The hands on the tabletop were drawn up into fists. But there was no menace in the gestures, Bell believed. It was sadness he was trying to keep locked up inside himself, not anger.

"You don't know what you're talking about," he repeated.

Bell decided to switch topics. She'd found that to be an effective interrogation tool: keep the conversation herky-jerky, off-kilter; break up the rhythm of the suspect's denials. Otherwise they could be here for hours while Connell repeated his it-wasn't-me mantra.

"Okay," she said. "Let's back up a bit. When was the last time you talked to her?"

Connell blinked as he remoistened his lips. He appeared to be thinking about it. "Tuesday," he said.

"Tuesday as in four days ago?"

"Yeah."

That was a surprise. Bell had assumed that Connell and Darla weren't in close touch, despite what Brenda Gilley had said. They'd been divorced for over a year.

"In person? On the phone?" she pressed him. "And what did you talk about?"

Out came the tongue-tip again, and again it traced the contours of his thin lips.

"Best not say." His tone was respectful, not belligerent.

Rhonda smacked the tabletop, causing Connell—and Bell, too—to flinch.

"Come on, Thad," Rhonda said, raising her voice. "Enough of this crap. If you're going to talk to us, then *talk* to us. Otherwise we'll assume you have something to hide."

He turned his watery-eyed gaze her way. "I do."

"You do *what*?"

"Have something to hide." Passive now, he unmade the fists. His yellow hands were flat on the tabletop once more. His brief moment of looking directly at Rhonda was over. Instead he studied the backs of his hands, as if trying to recall the precise origin of every cut, scrape, bruise, and scar.

Those hands, Bell thought as she watched him, constituted a sort of wordless transcript of all that he'd endured throughout his adult life: the fights, the rages, the lashing out, the self-destructiveness. It was hard to reconcile the violent story told by those hands with the calm, soft-voiced man who sat across from them. But that gap—the space between visible reality and the hidden kind of reality, the distance between superficial appearance and deep, abiding truth—was, Bell believed, the very thing that made human beings more than just the sum total of their appetites and their compulsions, more than just animals that preyed on other animals. *We care what other people think about us,* she thought. *And sometimes that's the only thing that saves us.*

"So then tell us what you're hiding," Rhonda snapped at him. Unlike Bell, she wasn't looking at his hands. She was trying to catch his eyes again, for the purpose of intimidation.

"If I did that," he replied, in the same infuriatingly unruffled tone that had irked Rhonda in the first place, "it wouldn't be hidden no more, now, would it?"

Rhonda was ready to pounce. Bell put a hand on her sleeve. Her meaning was clear: *Let me try.*

"Okay, Thad," she said. "Maybe we need to start somewhere else. Tell us about Darla. Once somebody's gone, it's hard to know who they really were. All we get is age and hair color and social security number. All we get are numbers and facts. What was she like?"

He nodded. He liked the question. "Well, she knew her own mind. That's for damned sure. When we got married, she wouldn't change her name. Wouldn't even consider it. 'Already got a name,' she told me. 'Don't need another.'"

He stopped. Prodding him gently, Bell said, "Independent, sounds like."

"You bet." He said it with affection.

"So if Darla was sitting here with us right now, what would she be saying to you?"

He smiled. The smile came before he had time to stop it, because he wasn't expecting the question, and it broke over his face, transforming it. He answered without hesitation:

"She'd say, 'Thad Connell, you rascal, I can't believe you got yourself in trouble *again*. I'm gonna kick you in the rear end, you hear me?'"

The tone in which he delivered Darla's dialogue was gentle, bemused. "And I'd tell her what happened and the shameful thing I did," he went on, "and she'd say, 'Oh, brother,' and I'd say, 'I tried to stay out of trouble, honey,' and she'd say—she'd say—" Connell swallowed hard, and the affectionate singsong voice in which he'd been relating his imaginary exchange with his ex-wife changed, and suddenly it wasn't playful anymore, it was serious and somber, and there were tears sliding down his ruined cheeks as he continued:

"She'd say, 'Thad, I know you tried, I know you did, and God knows, too, and He's looking out for you, and no matter what you did, He'll forgive you and I will, too. You hear me?' And then she'd say, 'We both know what it's like for you, Thad. It's been that way since the first time you ever tasted alcohol. You told me about it, remember? You think you can have a drink like other people have a drink and that will be the end of it. But that's never the end of it, is it, Thad? Never.'

"And then she'd say, 'I can't be married to you, Thad Connell, and you know why that's so—we've talked about it over and over again, for so many years, and we always come back to the same place. I can't love you like I do and watch you destroy yourself. I have to keep some distance. But my love won't go away, whether we're married or not. I'll always be here for you, and on the day you finally get this thing licked—I know you will, I *know* you will—I'll be right here.'"

He lifted his hands, turning them over to make a nest of them, and then he thrust his face into that nest. His shoulders heaved along with his muffled sobs.

Bell waited. Rhonda started to ask him another question, but Bell shook her head.

They waited.

Finally, Connell took some deep breaths and lifted his head. He'd found his equilibrium again.

"Darla moved into her brother's attic about three months ago," he said. "Finally decided—for good, after a lot of back-and-forth—that she couldn't live with me." Ruefully, he added, "Wish I coulda done the same thing—decided not to live with me. But I'm stuck, looks like." He'd made a joke, albeit a grim one, which let Bell know it was okay to press harder now.

"How often were you two in touch after she moved out?" she asked.

"All the time. I got sober for a good long spell and I wanted her to know. So we talked a lot."

"How long a spell?"

"Two weeks. Well—twelve days. Longest I'd gone without a drink in twenty years. I called Darla—this was on Monday, five days ago— and we talked about what was different. I was working, for one thing. Got a carpet job over in Blythesburg. New senior center over there. Buddy of mine bid the job and needed an extra hand. Really felt good, you know? Showing up on time in the morning, without a headache or having to check for puke stains on my jacket. Feeling tired at the end of the day. A good tired. A hard-work kind of tired."

"So you two had a nice chat on Monday."

"No," he replied flatly. "We didn't."

Bell and Rhonda waited for him to explain.

"I was all proud of myself," he said. "Busting-out proud. I wanted to tell her all about it. And I did. Guess I even bragged a little bit— which is why, now that I look back on it, it didn't stick. But during our talk that day, I just kept bragging about the fresh air and having a clear head in the morning—even though, after a while, I could tell that she wasn't really listening."

"What do you mean?" Bell asked.

"I mean I could tell she was distracted. Had something else on her mind. I'd say something, and she'd go, 'Uh-huh. Uh-huh.' Finally I just said, 'What the hell's going on with you, Darla?' And she told me." He shifted his feet. The ankle chain rattled. "She'd found something in the attic."

"What?"

"Some kind of book." He rubbed his chin. "That attic's where Joe and Brenda store a lot of family stuff. In fact, there wasn't much room for Darla's stuff. She told me that, the day she moved in. Brenda agreed to let her come there—which, if you ask me, shouldn't've even been her decision, because Darla and Joe *grew up* in that house, for Christ's sake, same as their daddy did, and same as their grandmother Bessie did. Brenda has a lot of gall. A lot of *damned* gall."

"A book," Bell said, hoping to get him back on track. She risked a glimpse at Rhonda, to see if she'd noticed that Connell shared her propensity to turn any story into a Russian novel with 147 chapters and 934 characters. Impossible to tell.

"Don't know much more about it," he said, "except that she'd found some kind of book in an old steamer trunk that'd belonged to her grandmother. It was pushed way, way down in there, Darla said, and she only came across it because she was looking for an extra blanket last week when the cold set in early. She could see her breath in that attic, she told me. Mice've eaten away the insulation."

"Did she tell Joe and Brenda about what she'd found?" Rhonda asked him.

"No. She'd never tell Brenda nothing personal—in fact she called her 'Brenda the Bitch' behind her back—and she didn't want to bother Joe, given how sick he is. But we talked again the next day and by then she'd read what was in that book. She was real agitated about it."

"She didn't give you any more details?" Rhonda sounded skeptical. "If she was that upset, surely she'd tell you what had gotten her so riled up."

Connell shook his head. In a mournful voice, he said, "I didn't let her. Didn't give her the goddamned chance. It was all about me, remember? All I wanted to talk about was how great I was doing. I wanted her to praise me. So I yakked and yakked. Never let her get a word in edgewise."

"When we first came in here," Bell said, "you told us you were hiding something."

He nodded. "Yeah. I'm required to."

"Required?"

"Yeah. See, I go to AA off and on. One thing Darla did have a chance to say to me on the phone was—'Go back, Thad. Go back.' So I did." He closed his eyes, opened them again. Bell wondered what memories were working their way through this man's conscience. She knew what lay behind the gaggle of words he was providing: torment. The words were his attempt to put something between himself and the searing memories. "I lasted two days," Connell said. "According to what the sheriff told me, Darla was killed on Thursday night or early Friday morning."

"And?"

"And I was with my sponsor then. I got to his house on Wednesday and I didn't leave until Friday afternoon."

"We'll check on that," Rhonda said.

"'Spect you will."

"Who's your sponsor?"

"Reverend Trace McFall. Broken Tree Baptist Church over in Lewiston. We prayed for forty-eight hours straight, which is what we both needed at the time, because we'd both been feelin' a powerful thirst. Rules say I'm not supposed to tell anybody who's a member and who's not—but if it's to prove I didn't kill Darla, I guess they'll let me slide."

Damn, Bell thought. The Reverend part always went over well with juries.

She and Rhonda stood up. They had obtained his alibi. If it didn't check out, they'd be back.

"One more thing," Bell said. Rhonda was gathering up the papers on the table. "When you left the pastor's house, where'd you go?"

A flush of shame gave the side of his face a sudden ruddy glow.

"Straight to the bar," he muttered. "All I'd been able to think about, the whole damned time I was down on my knees praying to the Lord, was getting drunk again, quick as I could. You know what? Darla was right to leave me. Best move she ever made. God rest her soul."

Chapter Twenty-one

Sheriff Reed met them outside the thick metal door of the interrogation room. He was a short, fat man who knew very well that he was short and fat, and didn't try to hide that fact. He didn't use the old man's trick—not a trick at all, really, because it was ineffective—of belting his pants down below the overhang of his pendulous belly, in hopes of sustaining the illusion that his belly was the only part of him that had swollen over its banks, and instead situated it honestly around his actual middle. The truth was, he was fat all over, head to toe, and his fingers looked like jolly slugs just exiting a now-stripped garden.

Watching Sheriff Reed as he and Rhonda talked, Bell reflected, not for the first time, that people in the region tended to be either terribly fat or terribly thin. No in-between. And when outsiders muttered mean, sarcastic remarks to the effect that, with all the poverty supposedly lurking in the area, a goodly number of West Virginians were puffed up with obesity, Bell would angrily inform them that the foods that packed on weight—chips and crackers and bread and potatoes—were cheap, whereas fresh vegetables and quality meats were expensive. *You do the math,* she wanted to add with a snarl, *and until you do, shut your damned mouth.*

"Thanks again for letting us have a crack at him," Rhonda said. "Hope nothing we talked about in there complicates your case."

"Not likely." Reed pushed back the brim of his sheriff's hat, revealing a shiny forehead as pink as a baby's. The hat sat on the back of his head like a sunbonnet. "He's in trouble this time, ole Thad. We've arrested him so often that you start thinkin' he'll always get out soon just so's he can come back in again. But that bartender's got permanent brain damage. They had to airlift him to a hospital in Charleston. Thad's gonna be locked up a good long time for this one." He scratched behind his right ear. "'Course maybe that's for the best. Seems like Thad don't do too well with handlin' his freedom. Just squanders it, again and again. Don't treat it precious-like."

A lot of us do the same thing, Bell thought. *A hell of a lot.*

The sheriff added, "You all think he was involved in his ex-wife's death?"

Rhonda shrugged. "We'll have a better idea about that as soon as we verify his alibi. And if we ever find the murder weapon—we'll check for fingerprints. But my instinct is no. What's the motive? They got along. No financial incentive."

The sheriff's eyes swiveled to Bell. "And you?"

"Rhonda makes a good point."

He shook their hands and escorted them to the main door. By the time they'd descended the gray front steps and begun the two-block walk to where Bell had parked her Explorer, Rhonda had already placed a call to Reverend McFall. After a brief chat, she ended it.

They were in the car now. Bell started the engine. "What'd he say?"

"Confirmed Connell's account. The two of them were together from Wednesday night through late Friday afternoon."

"You didn't tell him about Connell and the bartender," Bell noted. She directed the Explorer away from the curb. "The fact that he's in jail again. That was deliberate, I assume."

Rhonda stared out the window, chin in hand, as the SUV slowly rolled through the drab streets of downtown Beverly, which bore a distinct resemblance to the equally drab streets of downtown Acker's Gap.

Her reply surprised Bell, because Rhonda was among the most sincerely religious people Bell had ever known; Rhonda's faith was the lighthouse in her life.

"No, I didn't tell him," she confirmed, her eyes still on the bare streets, the empty storefronts. "He'll find out soon enough. Let him live a little longer with the illusion that all that praying made one damned bit of difference. Just a few more hours. Least I can do."

Chapter Twenty-two

Molly had gotten home a little after 9 A.M. Jake wasn't in the kitchen waiting for her, as he'd been the morning before. He didn't want to talk to her right away. He still didn't know what to say. He'd thought about her note all night, and in fact he'd read it at least ten more times, but he still didn't know what to say.

Malik had been picked up at 7 A.M. by the church bus. On Saturday mornings he went to a youth group at the Rising Souls Baptist Church; a counselor there had made a special point of reaching out to Molly and Jake last fall, asking if Malik could come be part of things. Playing Bingo and Go Fish, making birdhouses out of wood and glue, singing "Head, Shoulders, Knees, and Toes"—Malik loved the group, and always came home calmer.

Jake heard the front door open. He was in the bedroom, where he'd gone after watching from the front window to make sure Malik got on the bus. His elbows were on the armrests of his chair. His hands were in his lap. He had put the note back in the envelope—he'd run a finger across JAKE, which she'd written on the front, as if he expected it to have a texture somehow, like the letters chiseled into marble on the base of a statue—and put it back where he'd found it. For a few minutes before she arrived home, he had tricked himself, pretending that he had yet to read the note. He pretended that things were just as they'd been before. The things she'd written were still sealed up in the envelope, and because he had not read them, they had no power over him.

"Jake?"

Molly was looking for him. She'd started in the kitchen, of course, because that's where he usually was. Now she was moving through the hall. In seconds she was in the doorway of the bedroom.

"Jake? Are you okay?"

"Fine." He wasn't, which was always the case when someone said *Fine* the way he'd said it: flatly, dully.

She waited. She had probably worried about this moment throughout her shift, Jake speculated. And now she was confused by his placidity. She knew she had shocked him with her note. She'd expected drama, the second he saw her.

Not this quiet man sitting in his wheelchair in their bedroom, hands in his lap.

Finally, she asked, "Did you find the—"

"Yeah." He didn't look at her. He looked at his hands.

"We don't have to talk about it right now," she said. "I'm tired as hell, for one thing. We had thirty-three calls in the first four hours. Jesus. It was impossible. Let me get a shower, maybe grab a quick nap, and then we can—"

"Okay."

She waited. When he didn't offer anything else, she said, "Hope Malik did a good job this morning. Dressing himself, I mean. You know how he is. He gets out of the habit and he expects us to take over, when he's perfectly capable of—"

"He did fine. Bus was right on time."

Again, she waited. When it was clear that he had nothing more to say, she moved past him into their bedroom. He watched her as she emptied her pockets on the dresser: cell, wallet, tattered yellow pack of Juicy Fruit, spare change. A dime rolled off the edge of the dresser. She didn't pick it up. She stripped off her shirt and bra. She sat down on the bed to take off her socks and boots and then her trousers and panties. She left everything in a heap on the floor.

He could sense her exhaustion; it lifted off her skin and wafted away, a little at a time, as if all the sorrows and troubles of the people she'd helped overnight somehow clung to her, like an odor, and could only dissipate on their own timetable, not all at once. It was impossible to do the job she did and not have it stick to you, he thought; there was the shock and the physical agony you witnessed and tried to alleviate, the fear and panic. She had to deal not only with the person undergoing the medical emergency—overdose, heart attack, stroke, gunshot wound, abdominal aneurysm—but also with the loved one often standing nearby, helpless, terrified, as every known and familiar thing in the world, and the future itself, seemed to be shifting, up for grabs.

He looked at her naked body as she swept past him on the way to the bathroom for her shower. She was one of those rare people who moved exactly the same way whether naked or fully clothed; she didn't slink or try to cover certain parts with her hands or hunch over in that sort of half-cringe that he'd observed in other women with whom he'd been involved, when they were nude.

Molly was a beautiful woman, strong, substantial-looking, legs and arms corded with muscles, and the fact that she was his lover, his partner, seemed impossible. It had started out as a dream and then it had become reality, but now, in light of what he'd read in her note, he was afraid that it might be receding, flying away from him, becoming a dream once more.

He heard the shower start up, heard the fizzy, frothy sound of the water being throttled through the tiny holes in the showerhead.

What had ever made him think he would be enough for her? What madness had possessed him, believing that she'd be satisfied with just *him*—Jake Oakes, a man in a freakin' *wheelchair*? Half a man, really. A cripple. A pathetic fraud.

Self-pity gripped him. He had promised himself, when he was finishing up his rehab at the center in Pittsburgh, that he would never give in to self-pity. Self-pity was a trap, and he knew it. Self-pity was the real handicap—not whatever the injury was. Once he'd made the decision that he wanted to live—and that was by no means a foregone conclusion, in fact he'd contemplated suicide frequently in those days, calmly weighing the pros and cons, thinking about it from a practical standpoint and not an emotional one—his next decision was to banish the self-pity from his life. You had to get rid of every trace of it. It was like mold. It bred too quickly and easily, multiplying itself like crazy, to be allowed any access at all, the smallest foothold.

But here it was again: self-pity. The old enemy, slippery and coy. He'd let down his guard. No—that wasn't it. He hadn't let down anything. The truth was, she'd blindsided him with the letter she'd left him. She'd done it with no warning, no hint that anything would ever have to change about their lives.

The self-pity had roared right back, settling in, making itself at home. *What the hell made me think all of this was possible for me— Molly, Malik, this life?*

While he waited for her to finish her shower, he opened the envelope and took out the note and read it again. For the eleventh time. Her handwriting was clear and precise, just like her. It wasn't fancy, and there were no flourishes. Just even rows of well-formed letters.

Dear Jake,

I think you know how much I love you. I don't say it out loud, because that's not my way, but by now, I've made it very clear.

We haven't had an easy road. I think back on the night you first asked me out, there in the street outside my house, and how scared I was.

Please understand: I wasn't scared of YOU. You made me feel safe. Safer than I'd ever felt before. And not the kind of safe where one person takes care of another person. No. I mean the kind of safe where both people take care of each other, separately and together. The kind that makes it so different from what I do with Malik: I have to take care of him, because he can't take care of himself. And I did not want to be your Malik, nor make you mine. Because I can take care of myself—just as you can take of yourself.

We were great together, weren't we?

He was only halfway through the letter, but he paused his reading. The "were," the past tense, struck him like a blow. The note had been written on notepaper that was very light, a mere trifle, but now it felt heavy in his hands. He remembered reading it for the first time last night—*We were great together, weren't we?*—and wondering how he was going to live through the next ten minutes, and then the next ten minutes after that. The rest of his life felt like a death sentence.

But then he forced himself to go on reading. And even though he'd read the rest of the note before—ten times, for God's sake—what she wrote managed to surprise him all over again. It still rocked him back in his chair, making him question everything he believed about the world and himself.

And I think we can be great again, Jake. But I need more.

The job I do makes me feel hopeless, and sad. It's down, down, down, and sometimes I can't climb back out of that hole at the end of my shift. I can climb halfway out, but not all the way.

I see life at its darkest. I see people at their worst. I see drunks who have run their cars off the road, or fallen down stairs, with their brains leaking out. I see people whose veins are so clogged from smoking and drinking and everything else people do to wall themselves off from the sadness of their lives that Ernie and I can't start an IV when they're having a heart attack. They're dying and we can't save them because their bodies are too filled with the residue of how they lived.

I see addicts who have overdosed. Those addicts might be fourteen or they might be sixty. I see both. And all ages in between.

I have to do this job. I want to do this job. But I can't do it this way anymore.

That's why I need more, sweetheart.

Sweetheart. That created a flutter in his heart, a hope. She had called him sweetheart. She still loved him. Maybe it meant that nothing had to change. Even though he'd read this letter over and over again last night—so many times!—it was as if he were reading it for the first time, right now. He half expected the words to change, to dissolve and rearrange themselves, as he was reading them. Why should the letters of the alphabet be stable, when nothing else in the world was? He kept reading. He was almost finished. There were only a few more lines.

> *I need hope. And there is only one real hope in the world, Jake. A baby. A child. A new life.*
>
> *I know that when we first moved in together I said I didn't want to have any children, because I will be taking care of Malik for the rest of his life. But I've changed my mind. Malik is my brother—not my child. I will always take care of him. But I want to have a baby. My own. And if you don't want that, then we should say good-bye now.*
>
> *I don't want to live without you, Jake—but I know for sure that I can't live without hope.*
>
> *Molly*

He reread the note one more time, giving it a final chance to say something else, shift its meaning. That did not happen.

Chapter Twenty-three

He hadn't noticed that the shower was off. When he looked up, she was back in the bedroom, towel around her torso, the edges tucked in between her breasts. Another towel was wound around her hair.

"So can we talk now?" she asked.

"I thought you wanted a nap."

"Changed my mind." Her eyes were bright. "What do you think, Jake?"

Never before had she made any demands on him. But the truth was, he would have given her anything he had the power to give. Anything.

This wasn't that. This was something he *couldn't* give—because he didn't have it himself.

Out of the blue, she had asked him for the one thing he no longer possessed and knew he would never regain—not after what had befallen him: the capacity for hope. His bargain with himself, the one he'd made back in the rehab hospital on a night when the stars were visible from the window of his room, had been simple: He'd stick around in this life and he would get through the days, and he would work hard at whatever job he could get. Later, he added this to the list: He would love Molly and Malik. He would keep everything neat and manageable. He would believe in the things he could see and touch—but that was all.

He would honor the exact dimensions of his life as it was. No more.

And with that, once he'd made his bargain, he had turned away from the window of his hospital room. When the nurse came in the next morning, he told her to shut the blinds at night, and keep them that way.

"Jake?" Molly repeated.

"I don't like ultimatums," he said. He was afraid his voice might break, and so he fortified it by making it surly, brusque.

"It's not an ultimatum."

"Sure sounds like one. We don't discuss it—you just lay down the law."

"We're discussing it now, aren't we?"

He put his hands on the tops of the wheels. Palms against rubber. "You've made up your mind about what you want."

"Yeah." Softly, not belligerently: "I have."

"So it's not really a discussion at all."

She sounded defeated. "No. I guess not."

"Okay, then." He rolled forward and backward in his chair. Part of him could not believe this was happening; he waited for her to back down, to say she didn't mean it, to say that she wanted what they had—and *only* what they had, nothing more.

But she didn't.

"We have this terrific life—you, me, and Malik," she said. "So why can't we expand it? Widen the circle?"

She didn't understand. She didn't get how careful he had to be, every day, every *minute* of every day, rationing his hope. Measuring it out, bit by bit.

The person that the world saw—amiable, cheerful Jake Oakes, the guy who'd survived a gunshot wound and whose life was now confined to a wheelchair, although you weren't supposed to use the word "confined" anymore, or so he'd read, even though it was true—that guy, that Jake, was someone he'd created, made up. It took every ounce of his hope to keep up the projection.

There was no hope left over for anything else. Nothing extra.

He had never told her these things, never let on how meticulously he had to weigh and measure, all the livelong day. It wasn't her fault that she didn't know.

"Jake?"

He waited, spooning up what he needed right now in order to be Affable Jake, Well-Adjusted Jake.

"Can I make you something to eat?" he asked.

She turned away from him. Her disappointment was obvious. "No. Just want to sleep." By now she'd rustled up a T-shirt and sweats, and she was pulling back the comforter. "Can you give me a holler in a couple of hours? I need to be up. Got a ton of things to do today because tomorrow's spoken for." She paused. "I made a doctor's appointment for tomorrow morning. Just to make sure everything's okay." She didn't add, *And by "okay," I mean—okay to start trying to get pregnant.* But she might as well have said it, because it was in the air, anyway.

Just as she had blindsided him with her request, Jake realized, he had blindsided her with his response. But no matter what he decided about his own participation, she was going on with her life.

He couldn't blame her. That was who she was: forthright, determined. She couldn't be any other way. It was one of the reasons he'd fallen in love with her.

"Sure."

He backed his chair out of the bedroom. He had work to do. Bell had texted him earlier that morning and, lost in the fact of his life's unraveling, he hadn't yet replied. They had a case, it seemed. The prosecutor wanted them to help find Darla Gilley's killer. And he was wildly eager to work, desperate to focus on something other than his own crushing sadness.

"Sweet dreams," he said as he closed the bedroom door behind him. Only later did it dawn on him that Molly might have thought he was being sarcastic. He wasn't. He really did want her dreams to be sweet and golden, because he loved her, even though she had broken his heart.

Chapter Twenty-four

"Want some company? It's a long drive."

"Thanks, but I'd better go by myself," Bell replied. She sipped her coffee. Jackie's coffee was always good, but this batch was superlative.

It was a few minutes after 6 P.M. She and Nick had just finished up their suppers at the diner. Why did coffee always taste better when you drank it out of a white ceramic mug, the only vessel available at JP's? Bell didn't know, but it did.

Nick nodded. "Probably a good idea. I can't be objective. I've known Joe my whole life. I could make excuses the first time around— the sheriff needed me to help settle him down—but from here on out, I'd better recuse myself when it comes to Joe and Brenda." He cleared his throat. "So what exactly are you going to be looking for out there?"

Bell heard the note of I'm-Trying-to-Be-Casual-Here in Nick's voice. She knew how worried he was about his friend. Facing a terminal illness, and now dealing with the death of his sister—it seemed an intolerable burden of grief. The idea that Joe or his wife might somehow have been involved—a possibility that they had to consider—was bothering him, too.

"Don't know," she answered. "Just want to track down what might have frightened Darla. I'm trying to figure out what she found in that attic."

Their attention was diverted by a gust of laughter from a nearby booth. Three young men were whooping it up.

Sunday nights were surprisingly busy at the diner, even rainy ones like this, which is why Jackie kept the place open late. Several churches in the area featured a second service on Sunday nights. Jackie took note of that fact and began to offer special items exclusively after 5 P.M., so that people would develop the habit of stopping by on their way home from worship. Beef stew served over scratch-made biscuits did the trick; she almost always ran out and was scraping the bottom of the kettle by 6:30. And she only charged half price for kids' meals—chicken nuggets or grilled cheese or fish sticks, take your pick—on Sunday nights, another lure.

Thus when Bell and Nick arrived, they'd had to wait a few minutes for a booth to open up. They took a seat at the long counter until Jackie waved them over. Once they had settled into the crinkly red Naugahyde that was torn in several places and mended with silver duct tape, she'd filled their mugs and taken their orders: beef stew for Nick, a BLT for Bell. She returned with a new pot in five minutes, having a good idea of how quickly Bell would get through the first round.

Before Jackie could utter even the briefest and most cursory of greetings, a customer hailed her from across the room and she was gone.

"That woman works harder than anybody I know," Bell said.

Nick turned his head in the same direction, watching Jackie as she bantered with a tableful of elderly women on her way to the booth in the opposite corner.

"She looks tired," he muttered. "I keep telling her she needs to hire more help. She's got Karen back in the kitchen and Karen's boy, Greg, to do the cleanup. But they're both just part time."

Bell took another drink of her coffee. She needed a few seconds to think.

Was this the secret he'd been keeping from her?

She reviewed the evidence. It was definitely out of character for Nick Fogelsong to comment on how other people ran their businesses or their lives. Moreover, Bell had picked up something oddly intense in the tone of his voice—a protectiveness that ran deeper than mere concern for a friend. The fact that he remembered the names of Jackie's cook and bus boy was the clincher. And so in that moment, Bell made two decisions:

The first was that Nick's feelings for Jackie were more personal than she'd realized before now, or that Nick was prepared to admit to her.

The second was that she wouldn't say a word to him about it. If he wanted to share anything with her, fine. She'd listen. But she didn't pry. She had been disappointed at the news of his breakup with Mary Sue; their union had given her a faint hope that human relationships didn't have to be the noxious, ongoing tire fire that most of them—including a hefty number of hers—turned out to be. But when Nick returned from Florida he hadn't discussed it with her, beyond a bland notification that divorce was imminent. She had said, "That's a shame," and he'd replied, "Yeah," and that was it. Which was a good thing, all told, because it meant he would continue to withhold comment on *her* romantic life.

Or the lack thereof.

"So you don't think," Nick asked, "that Thad Connell had anything to do with her death?"

"Unlikely. Rhonda did a little more digging and found some parishioners who could back up his claim about that marathon prayer session. Turns out there was some kind of revival going on. Folks—reliable types—were in and out of the sanctuary over those two days. Line up their Thad Connell sightings, back to back, and he's covered. Looks like he was telling the truth. He and Reverend McFall were there the whole time."

"So now we're back to wondering what Darla found in that attic."

"Yep. And whatever it was," Bell said, "it shocked her. Apparently she didn't tell Joe or Brenda about it, though. Maybe she meant to—but she ran out of time. She was killed before she got the chance."

The diner's front door popped open. Another big family barreled in. Bell counted five kids, two parents, and an elderly man she assumed was Grandpa. The kids made a crazy racket as they stampeded across the floor to claim a booth. Dad and Mom hung back with the old man, each taking a frail arm as they guided him across the checkerboard linoleum at a torturously slow pace.

"Did they have any theories about what Darla might've found?" Nick asked.

Bell was distracted. "Who?"

"Joe and Brenda."

She hadn't told them about Connell's recollection. But they were Nick's friends. It was a delicate situation.

"Seems to me," she said carefully, "we ought to play prosecutor and sheriff again with this one. Not tell one source about anything we get from another. Rhonda might want to use a particular piece of information as leverage later on. During an interrogation, I mean."

"Good point." He drank his coffee. "Still can't figure why Darla was heading out to Wellwood that day. And why she was so upset— upset enough for a stranger to remark upon it."

"The truck driver."

"Yeah. Briscoe. I'll get us more details on Darla's demeanor when I talk to him. Pam Harrison tracked him down through the state police. They've got a relationship with all the trucking companies that go through here. He's headed back to Charleston tomorrow. Pam checked out his alibi and cleared him, but I still have some questions. We're supposed to get together for a chat."

"Keep me posted."

Nick nodded. "I will." There was more on his mind. "Listen, Bell, just for the record—Brenda's a good gal. I know how much Joe loves her. She's taking real good care of him, too. Sick as he is, he'd be in a lot worse shape without her. I'm only saying this because I get the impression that you don't much like her, and if that's based on anything I might have said or—"

"I like her fine."

"Okay. Good."

But in truth, there *was* something about Brenda Gilley that rubbed Bell the wrong way. This wasn't the first time she'd had a problem with a woman who had made different choices in her life from the ones Bell had made; Brenda had never had a job outside her home, and her marriage to Joe was, to Bell's mind, so traditional as to be suffocating. Bell often felt judged by such women, even if they never said a word about it.

She'd felt the same way many years ago, back in Acker's Gap High School, when the girls who joined clubs and had nice clothes and sighed over boyfriends would watch her slouch through the halls in her jeans and her ratty sweater, her nose stuck in a battered paperback copy of *Zen and the Art of Motorcycle Maintenance*. She'd almost been able to channel their thoughts: *That Belfa Dolan is just plain weird.* If she'd had the nerve, she would have whirled right around to face them and declared, *Yeah. Damned right I'm weird. I don't fit in with you losers. That's why I'm going to be getting the hell out of here and I'm never EVER coming back.*

Which was not exactly how things had turned out.

Bell knew her resentment toward Brenda Gilley was, on the whole, irrational. Brenda, after all, belonged to a different generation. And she didn't really know Bell, beyond what Nick Fogelsong had shared with her. But Bell still didn't trust her. She'd only tell Brenda what she had to. No more.

"Been meaning to ask," Nick said, breaking into her thoughts. "How's the new roommate?"

Bell grinned. "Arthur's great. We had a few tense moments this morning when he tried to turn a corner of the couch into a chew toy—but that's all behind us now. Rookie mistake."

"You're keeping him, then. Rhonda said she wasn't sure you would."

"So far, so good."

Bell was about to tell another story about Arthur, but Jackie was back.

"Either of you two still hungry? Got a little bit of stew left. Not much, though—Grandma Opie's recipe was a hit, just like always." Jackie attributed the provenance of her most popular dishes to a long-deceased grandmother who went by the nickname "Opie."

"No time," Bell replied. "Nick here's a man of leisure, but I've got work to do. Maybe he'll want to stick around for a little something extra." She slid out of her seat, reaching for the coat she'd taken off and flung on the seat beside her.

Had her comment been too obvious? Apparently not. Nick's attention was elsewhere as she swung on her coat. If he'd detected even a hint of a double entendre in her valedictory remark, he would've let her know with an irritated frown. He didn't appreciate subtle digs any more than she did.

She'd have to watch herself from now on. Secrets were hard work.

Chapter Twenty-five

Rain made the night a dreary, chilly mess. Wet leaves were doing their part, too, to induce a sodden misery; the roads were dark, slick tunnels where skidding after a quick stop or a sudden turn was a given. The windows of Bell's Explorer misted up as she drove. She had to keep the defroster on high during the entire trip out to Roberts Ridge.

On the way, she called Sheriff Harrison and asked if she was cleared to poke around the attic. "Suit yourself," Harrison replied.

The sheriff added that Barbara Masters and the coroner had filed their reports: Not surprisingly, cause of death was exsanguination from blunt force trauma to the head. No weapon had been found, but it had to have been something with a sharp blade such as a machete, ax, or hatchet. "Something with a handle, that is," the sheriff added, "instead of a knife, because of the shape of the wound and the required force of the blow. The killer would've needed considerable leverage to drive the blade in so deep." Very little usable evidence had been retrieved at the scene; there were too many footprints in the ruins of Wellwood. And too much crap to sort through, Bell knew.

"Any defensive wounds?" she asked.

"No. Looks as if she had her back turned. Never saw it coming."

We can only hope, Bell thought with a shudder.

The big farmhouse loomed large in her headlights, rearing up out of the slimy darkness. It was the only house for many miles. The porch circled it like a lariat. At some point in the past the sides of this old, proud house had been sheathed in vinyl siding, and the choice of the color white was a grave mistake; it looked irretrievably gray and grimy now, like something the ground was constantly trying to reclaim, and soon would. White was a hard color to maintain, Bell thought. It was lost as quickly as the innocence it signified.

Getting out of the Explorer, lifting her head even though it exposed her face to the rain, she found the small window at the very top; that had to be the attic. It was a dark oval. She imagined Darla Gilley up there on a night like this one, looking out, having just settled back into the family home, her marriage over and her life in limbo. What would she have seen? Waves of wet darkness, perhaps, the kind that seemed to spiral back into her family's long history on the ridge.

Brenda was not especially welcoming. Bell had called first, but that didn't matter.

"I hope you don't expect me to stay up here with you," Brenda said, crisp dismissal in her tone. "I've got a lot of work to do." She had just led Bell up the narrow staircase into the attic. The ceiling joists and rafters made the space feel close and constricted. A good four-fifths of it was stuffed full of boxes, plastic storage bins, and brooding, old-fashioned furniture such as armoires and chifforobes. This, Brenda told her, was the clutter left behind by six generations of the Dresser family, with additions along the way from in-laws. Set off in the corner was a single bed with a wooden headboard adorned with a small carving of a bird perched on a tree branch, plus a simple wooden nightstand and a lamp with a pull chain.

Darla's "room."

"I'm fine," Bell replied.

Something seemed to shake loose inside Brenda. A knot unwound. She relaxed, and her words had the gush of confession, as if Bell's visit was just what she'd been waiting for, even though she hadn't known it until now. "I don't mean to be rude," she said. "I've just had a lot to deal with today. Joe won't eat. Stayed in bed all day. He's still so broken up over Darla that he can't speak about it. And a couple of TV stations in Charleston keep calling. They want to send over a camera crew. I tried to be polite when I said no, but they won't stop pestering us. You'd think the death of somebody like Darla—somebody who's not famous, I mean—wouldn't be something folks'd care about."

They don't, Bell thought. *The only reason Darla Gilley's murder caught their eye is because it was violent and brutal. And because we don't know who did it. Otherwise, the death of a middle-aged woman from Beverly, West Virginia, wouldn't merit a single sentence in any news roundup.*

"You can just refer them to the prosecutor's office," Bell advised her.

"Really?"

"Rhonda's used to dealing with the press."

"You think that'll get 'em to back off and leave us alone?"

"All they want is a quote. Doesn't matter who it's from."

"Then I'll try it." Brenda smoothed down the front of her denim skirt with two hands. It might have been the same skirt she'd been wearing the day before, or she might've bought them in multiples. Hard to say, Bell thought.

Brenda glanced around the attic, as if realizing for the first time how it must look to other eyes. She uttered a long sigh. "I know what you're thinking—how could I put Darla way up here? Off by herself, when Joe and me have got this big old farmhouse all to ourselves? Joe wasn't too happy about it. But you know what? It was Darla's idea."

"I'm surprised to hear that."

"Well, she made me promise not to tell Joe. But it's what she wanted." Brenda walked over to the small bed. It was covered by a busy-looking quilt. Bell spotted reds, golds, purples, and ivories in the interlocking pattern. Brenda reached down and touched the quilt, running her fingertips slowly across it as if she might be deriving sustenance from the texture alone. Bell expected her to follow up the gesture by sitting down on the bed; clearly Brenda had had a long, grueling day, and a desire to get off her feet would have been understandable.

But she didn't. She smoothed the quilt, and then she stood upright again and turned to face Bell.

"Their great-grandmother made this quilt," she said. "Bessie's mother. Her name was Theresa Dresser. That was Bessie's maiden name—Bessie Dresser. The way I heard it from Joe, Theresa was an unusual woman. She made all kinds of things—quilts, clothes, even a lot of the furniture that's stacked up over there. Designed everything herself and then put it together. Real creative. But then something happened."

"What do you mean?"

"Her life just kind of . . . kind of *stopped,* I guess you'd call it. Joe didn't have a word for it. Darla didn't, either. Theresa had two children—Bessie and her brother, Donnie. And they weren't around when Joe and Darla were growing up, so there was nobody to give them much information. Their dad, Nelson, was Bessie's only son. And Nelson only remembered a few of Bessie's stories about Theresa. He was twenty-two when Bessie died, but I get the idea he didn't pay much attention. You know how men are." Brenda touched the quilt one more time, just a quick brush this time, and then moved away from the bed. "Thing is, when Darla called and said she wanted to move in here so's she could get back on her feet after the divorce, I said, 'Sure. You know the layout here. We've got three extra rooms just down the hall from where Joe and I sleep. You can have your pick.' And she said, 'No, I'd rather just stay in the attic. Bed's still up there, right?' And it was. Because Bessie used to sleep up here, first as a little girl, then later after she was married. Bessie and her husband—well, it wasn't a love match. Let's put it like that.

"When Darla asked me if she could make this her room, I didn't know what to say. Especially not when she told me to keep it from Joe. I said, 'Why on earth?' And she said . . ." Brenda swallowed hard. "She said she couldn't stand to be that close to Joe's room. She knew he was slipping away. She could see it, plain as day. Same as we all can. She was afraid of watching. Of being there when he . . ." Another swallow. "Staying in the attic gave her a little distance, she said. Which I guess made sense to me—there's nights lately when I sleep on the couch down in the living room, because I can't bear to hear Joe breathe. All I can think of is the moment when that breathing is gonna stop. I can't get it out of my head."

Bell nodded. If she had been a different kind of person, she would have reached out and touched Brenda's arm. But that wasn't her way. "You love your husband," she said quietly, "and Darla loved her brother."

The words seemed to help Brenda recover herself. "And after a few weeks, I think there was something else that kept Darla up here."

"What was that?"

"This." Brenda swept her hand around the room, indicating the vast trove of boxes, plus the old sewing machine and the dressmaker's dummy and the rolltop desk and the whatnot stand and the long case clock and the rolled-up rugs and the mismatched chairs, all jammed together under the rugged beams. "All of it. The whole history of the family. Darla got so's that's all she wanted to talk about. I think she liked being up here, next to these things. Rubbing up against the past. Lord knows the present hadn't been too kind to her—she'd gone back and forth with Thad Connell so many times she must've gotten dizzy. But here . . ." Brenda's eyes climbed the piles. "Here, it's all boxed up and waiting for somebody to care. It's been years since anybody went through it all. I moved into this house with Joe a year after we were married, and this attic was already stacked up to the rafters. All we've ever done since then is add, not subtract."

"And Darla was interested in family history."

"*Interested?* More like obsessed. Matter of fact, I was reflecting on that right before you got here. The night you and Nick came over, you asked me to remember whatever I could about the last time we saw Darla. That lunch on Thursday."

"Right."

"Well, she talked and talked about family. How it's a part of you, wherever you go and whatever you do. She was kinda riled up. I couldn't make out what had gotten under her skin like that—but *something* had, that's for sure. And then she said she just *had* to go into Acker's Gap. Errands, she said. She had errands. That's all she told me. The whole ride there, all she wanted to talk about was her grandma Bessie."

Bell let her eyes sweep over the vast cornucopia of stuff that surrounded them. She'd spotted the enormous steamer trunk slotted next to a coat rack and a tall cherry dresser.

"I better get back to Joe," Brenda said. "If you need anything, just give a holler."

Once she was alone, Bell headed straight for the trunk. It was easy to pull it free from the morass of stuff in which it was mired; someone had already done the hard part and loosened it. It slid out as if it were on casters.

She needed two hands to hoist the heavy hinged lid. The perverse perfume of age—the smell of mothballs and lavender sachets—bloomed from the depths of the old trunk. Quilts, blankets, hand-knitted sweaters, and blouses with pearl buttons spread out before her, in rows that had once been neat but now were comingled after what looked to have been a frantic jostling.

Bell searched the trunk thoroughly. She found only clothes, quilts, and blankets.

Just as she was about to close the lid, however, she spotted a small translucent ball of crinkled tissue paper jammed into a corner, smushed up against the red cloth lining. She smoothed out the square piece.

The missing book—whatever it was—might very well have been wrapped in this paper. Darla had found it, removed it from the paper, and taken it . . . where? And what was in it? Why did its contents so disturb her?

Too many questions.

Only one thing was known for sure: Shortly after finding it Darla had been murdered, her body left facedown on the ground at Well-wood, a crude and terrible wound in the back of her head.

Chapter Twenty-six

Bell had one more stop to make on this chilly, rain-fringed night. It didn't have anything to do with death. It had to do with life.

A small white light illuminated each crib in the row. The cribs were made of clear acrylic, so that the tiny bodies inside would be visible from any angle. A gentle, rhythmic swishing sound permeated the room, produced by the machinery that was monitoring the vital functions of each infant, from heartbeat to respiratory rate to body temperature.

"When I let my cynicism drop for a second," Bell said, "I sometimes think this place is heaven. And the babies are waiting to be assigned a soul so that they can be sent down to earth."

Glenna Stavros laughed softly. "And I thought *I* was the sentimental softie," she said. "Never figured I'd hear that kind of Hallmark-card stuff from you, Bell."

"I have my moments."

"Well, truth be told—and I know you know this—it's a far cry from heaven. Little bit closer to the other place, frankly, when you think of what these kids are facing."

Glenna was the night nursing supervisor at Evening Street, the clinic that took care of babies born to drug-addicted mothers. It was located in a former tobacco warehouse on a slanting side street of Acker's Gap, a street that gave the place its name. Business, sadly, was booming.

Bell had once worked here for several months to fulfill the community service portion of her prison sentence. It was not fancy work; she mopped floors, scrubbed toilets, emptied tall bins of medical waste into the special locked containers in the alley. She had become friends with Glenna, a tall, wide-faced woman with frizzy red hair and the kind of steady, reliable competence that Bell admired more, perhaps, than any other trait.

Evening Street was the kind of place that chewed through personnel, using up nurses and aides and volunteers at a frantic pace. People stayed as long as they could, but sometimes that was not very long. It was not a hopeful place. A great many of the infants died, after a few hours or a few days of agony, and those who survived faced lives filled with daunting physical and cognitive and psychiatric challenges. Often the parents—or parent, as was usually the case—were unable to care for children with such dire and endless needs, because the parent herself was struggling with her own addiction, her own grievous burdens.

Glenna had been in charge of Evening Street for three-and-a-half years now. It was a record. But when Bell stopped by on her way home from Roberts Ridge, the first thing she thought upon seeing Glenna was: *It's getting to her. She can't do this job much longer.* The lines around her eyes cut deeper. The stoop in her back was more pronounced. Batting away the daily swarm of depressing circumstances was aging her at an abnormal rate.

"So what can I do for you, Bell? I get the feeling this isn't a social call." Glenna checked her watch. "Not at almost midnight on a Sunday night."

They stood side by side in front of the two rows of cribs. The other nurses walked by from time to time, checking on the babies and the monitors ranged around their cribs, but there was little conversation. Time seemed suspended here.

"You're right," Bell answered. "Just wanted to see the baby from Thursday night. The one born at the Burger Boss."

"Ah. Casey."

"You named him?"

Glenna shook her head. "Not us. His mom."

"I didn't know she was involved."

"She wasn't. Not until yesterday afternoon."

Glenna inclined her head toward an area just to the left of the cribs, where she kept her desk and a couple of chairs. It wasn't much of an office; the only thing that separated it from the rest of the floor was a waist-high wall on two sides. There was a small window above the desk.

They sat.

"She showed up and demanded to see him," Glenna said. "Andrea Krieger's her name."

"How was she?"

"You're asking me if she was high. I don't think so. She seemed okay. Bossy and unpleasant—but okay. After she'd looked at him for a while, she said she was taking him home with her."

"What did you do?"

"It was easy this time. He's not anywhere near ready to leave here. When he is—well, I won't have a choice. She's his mother."

"But she's facing child endangerment charges," Bell said.

"Yes. And she has a court date. Frankly, though, if she proves she's sober and is following a plan to stay that way—well, I've not met the judge yet who will take a child away from his mother, if the mother shows even a faint glimmer of an intention to stay on the straight and narrow." Glenna spoke in a deadpan way, as if she felt no emotion about what she was saying. Bell knew better. "Deputy Brinksneader has come by every day to check up on the little guy. He's a favorite of the nurses." She smiled. "Casey, I mean, not Deputy Brinksneader. Although Steve's pretty special, too." The smile lingered. "Sometimes I think it's the force of all that caring that is helping Casey heal. Holding him up, so that he doesn't sink under the weight of all the problems he has. I know, I know—I'm a nurse, and that's a very unscientific thing to say. Don't care."

"No need to apologize. You caught me talking about heaven, for crying out loud."

Bell's attention moved back to the row of cribs; a monitor's beeping had changed. It was louder now, and the beeps came closer together. Glenna started to rise, but another nurse was already hurrying over to the crib.

"Got it," the nurse said, waving.

"Thanks, Tammy." Before Glenna could get back to her conversation with Bell, her cell rang. "Stavros," she said. She listened. "Okay. Right. Right." A pause. "Understood. Thanks." She hung up. "That was Linda McComas. She's the case worker for Andrea's baby. She's still at her desk, even at this hour. Turns out Andrea has changed her mind now. She doesn't want him after all. She told Linda to find him a good home. She'll agree to give up parental rights."

"She called her at midnight?"

Glenna smiled. It was a grim smile. "So how many addicts do you know who keep regular hours? Anyway, Linda will notify the judge about Andrea's change of heart. Casey will go into the system."

"Just like that."

"Just like that. For now, that is." Glenna sighed. It was the kind of deep sigh that seemed to take an eternity to finish. "Happens all the time. You and I both know how this'll go, Bell. Back and forth, depending on how Andrea's feeling from day to day—or from minute to minute. If she wants to get high, she'll say she's giving him up. If she stays clean for two days in a row—she'll want him back. Swear she'll raise him right."

"Rinse and repeat," Bell said.

"Rinse and repeat." Glenna rose. "Follow me."

She led Bell over to the second crib from the end of the first row.

"Meet Casey Krieger," she said. "Casey, this is Bell Elkins."

He was impossibly, unbelievably small. Bell had seen babies born to addicts before, but the first sight was always a shock: His head was small enough to fit in a coffee cup. His fist would go through a wedding ring. He had wires attached to tiny round patches on his torso. His skin was gray. He twitched constantly. His mouth opened and closed, opened and closed. His discomfort was clear.

They were doing what they could for him, Bell knew, but the mother's addiction had been passed on to the child. He was going through withdrawal—a painful, prolonged ordeal—and there were no shortcuts.

"Born in a damned toilet," Glenna murmured. "When I think about it, I just—I just get so angry. A toilet. Something this precious— coming into the world that way. He could've drowned. So, so easily. Thank God for Steve. And the EMTs. If they hadn't been there . . ."

"But they were."

"Sometimes," Glenna went on, as if Bell hadn't spoken, "I fanta- size about just grabbing a kid like this and making a run for it."

Bell didn't answer.

"Don't you?" Glenna added. Challenge in her tone. It was a real question, not a rhetorical one.

"Sure."

"Of course you do. We all do." Glenna's mood seemed to plum- met. Bell had the sudden image of an elevator in free fall, cords snap- ping, brakes frayed and smoking, nothing to stop the relentless dive. "What does he have to look forward to? A mother who's going to ig- nore him, neglect him, or—worst-case scenario—abuse him, because she's strung out and pissed off at his crying. Or her next boyfriend is. Or maybe she'll pass him along to some relative, and then that rela- tive will pass him along to somebody else. Who cares? He's just a nuisance. By the time he's two, three years old, it's done. Casey here is done. He'll never be held, never be cuddled. All he'll ever know is pain and emptiness and despair. And that'll be it. End of story."

Bell, surprising herself, said, "Hold on. Maybe his mother will do what's best for him and let him go." She was always the Most Cynical Person in the Room. She wore it like a badge. But here she was, arguing the opposite. What the hell was going on?

"Or maybe," Bell went on, "Casey will end up in a decent home. A loving home. We have to hope for that, don't we?"

"You can hope if you want to." Glenna's voice was flat and bitter and cold. "I'm tired of hoping. I'm just so goddamned tired of hoping."

But then, just when Bell was afraid that Glenna might up and storm out of the clinic, having left her resignation on the hospital CEO's voice mail, the nurse changed. She shuddered, as if she were emerging from a bad dream.

"Okay," Glenna said. "Okay." Deep breath. "That happens to me sometimes. But it's over. I'm back. I'm fine." She gave a small laugh. "Don't worry—you won't have to report me for kidnapping."

"I wasn't worried," Bell responded, even though she had been. A little bit. "I can't imagine having to deal with this all the time. It must be incredibly hard. Seeing what you see, day after day."

"Yeah. It is."

They stood for a few more minutes without talking, letting the ambience of the room—a stillness that fell like an early snow, dropping softly and spreading in all directions—soak in. They watched the boy in the crib. Casey whimpered, moved his fist, did a series of frog-kicks with his right leg. Then he seemed to sleep.

Yet despite the sadness and the sickness all around her, Bell was aware of a peace here, too. The infants in these cribs were being tended to by strangers. Somebody cared. Somebody gave a damn. And maybe that was why, with Glenna just now, Bell had been so uncharacteristically optimistic.

Out of the muck and rubble and ruin of the lives of drug addicts, these fragile creatures had somehow emerged, venturing forth like tender green shoots in the corner of a landfill. Some would survive, and some would not, and all would suffer, but all would know—for whatever length of time they were here at Evening Street—what it felt like to be cherished.

Chapter Twenty-seven

The line at the Acker's Gap post office on a Monday morning was almost always long, but it tended to move quickly. This was the only post office for many miles, thus its popularity was assured.

Bell took her place at the end. A little girl and her mother were just ahead; when Bell looked down and smiled at the girl, she scrambled to hide under the long maroon flap of her mother's coat.

The mother looked down. "Sissy, leave that lady alone." She turned back around to face front as the line inched forward.

Bell winked at the girl, who giggled as she darted back under her mother's coat. She had frizzy pigtails and a scattering of freckles. Four years old, Bell guessed. Maybe five.

"Sissy." The mother's voice had a warning note in it now. This time she didn't turn around.

Bell made a face, sticking out her tongue. The girl's giggle expanded into a full-bodied laugh.

"Sissy, I'm gonna whip your butt if you don't stop."

Bell didn't want to get Sissy in any more trouble, so she looked away. The line inched forward a little more.

This was an old post office, and one constantly on the verge of being closed. When a list had been released a few years back of the post offices in small communities that would be shut down, Acker's Gap was there. But Raythune County Commissioner Sammy Burdette had called a state official who then called another state official, and the request for a stay of execution worked its way up the political food chain until finally a person with real clout was contacted, and the post office was spared—for the time being. Among the compelling arguments for the reprieve was the fact that the elderly residents of Acker's Gap, few of whom had cars, would've had to drive forty miles to the Blythesburg post office to buy a stamp or mail their Christmas cards.

Bell loved the old building, with its stamped tin ceiling, its deep oak wainscoting, and its high wooden counter, behind which presided Burt Dittmer, the ancient postmaster. Rumor had it that Burt harbored a recollection of the days when the mail was delivered by Pony Express, and that when filling out a requisition form for supplies, he had once absentmindedly included a request for a dozen bales of hay.

She never minded starting her day with a brief conversation with Burt. He was a wise and cheerful old man with a flaky forehead, cloudy spectacles, and, wrapped around his thick torso, the same brown cardigan he wore winter, summer, spring, and fall.

"Belfa Elkins," he declared. Her turn had finally come, and she stepped up to the counter. "What can I do for you?"

"Morning, Burt." She handed him the small lime green card that had been in the morning mail at the office. "Somebody sent us a package, looks like." The mail slot in the door was too small for anything beyond a standard letter.

"Kinda early for a Christmas gift," Burt opined, "but you can always hope." He peered at the card's particulars over the top of his glasses. "Be right back."

The package he handed her was the size of a small pizza box. The sender had used a black Sharpie to print on the front:

INVESTIGATIONS
34 Main St.
Acker's Gap WV

There was no return address.

"Thanks," Bell said.

"Anything else? Stamps, maybe? We got some pretty Christmas ones."

"I'm good."

"We got Madonna and Child. The mother of Jesus, I mean—not the singer. Come on. You know you need some."

"They give you a cut on those things? I'm getting suspicious."

He chuckled. "Just don't want you to run out. They go fast."

"Appreciate you looking out for me, Burt."

She started to move away when he added, "How's that girl of yours? Any chance she'll come to her senses and move back? We need the young folks to stick around."

"I agree. But she loves Charleston. I miss her, too. Made the same suggestion that she get herself back here. And to tell you the truth, I've only met one person in my life who's more stubborn than I am."

"Lemme guess. Carla Elkins."

"Bingo."

Another chuckle. "Well, give her my best, willya? Always enjoy talking to her. Good head on her shoulders."

A muted chorus of impatient throat-clearings and deliberate boot-shufflings reminded Bell of the other people in line behind her. She waved at Burt and stuck the box under her arm. Grasping the big door-knob to depart the old building, she relished the feel of the chilly brass.

Main Street was marginally busy this time of the morning—by Acker's Gap standards, that is, meaning that she passed three people on her way back to the office. Last night's hard, driving rain had rinsed off the sidewalks and the fronts of the buildings. The town gleamed in the cold air as if somebody had polished it. They hadn't done a very good job, but they'd tried.

The office was still cold. No surprise there. Bell sat down at the wooden table. Next to her laptop was the cup of take-out coffee she'd purchased at JP's on her way in this morning. She'd only finished half before leaving for the post office.

She took two sips. Any colder in here, she groused to herself, and she would've been forced to break the ice on the top before she could drink it.

She opened the box. A small notebook with a thin leather cover: That is what she found inside. It had a musty odor, and there were spots of mildew on the cover.

When she lifted the notebook, she saw a single piece of paper lodged beneath it.

Her pulse quickening, Bell read the words on the paper. The handwriting had been done hastily, but it was legible:

> *Dear Nick,*
>
> *I don't know your address anymore. I used to know, but that was a long time ago, when you and Mary Sue lived in the big house by Smithson's Rock. I'm in a hurry. I don't have time to call you and ask. Or track you down and hand this to you in person.*
>
> *But I saw the address of your office on the window, and so I decided to mail it to you there.*
>
> *I found this notebook in my grandma Bessie's trunk in the attic. The story it tells—well, you can read it for yourself. I wasn't going to show it to you, or to anybody, but I think I have to now. I need your advice. Part of me wants to make sure the world knows about what happened at Wellwood. But part of me is worried about what it'll do to people who are still living. I don't want to cause any pain to good people. But the truth matters, doesn't it?*
>
> *I know you work with Bell Elkins and Jake Oakes. You can share this with them if you want to.*
>
> *Thank you, Nick. I need somebody to trust, and you are Joe's best friend. That's good enough for me.*
>
> *Darla*

Bell hesitated only a second. Then she opened the notebook, folding back the cover to reveal the title page with its careful cursive handwriting.

DIARY OF ELIZABETH ANN ~~DRESSER~~ GILLEY

Guilt made her pause again. Shouldn't she let Nick read this first? Darla, after all, had sent her grandmother's diary to him, not to her.

She started to punch his number in her cell. She stopped. Nick had a meeting scheduled this morning with the attorney in Charleston who was handling his divorce. He always turned off his phone. *With what I'm paying her per hour,* Nick had grumbled the last time he and Bell discussed it, *I'm not going to waste time by taking any damned personal calls. Gonna be in debt for the next ten years as it is.*

After that, he would still be busy; he had set up an interview with the trucker who'd given Darla a ride out to Briney Hollow.

It took her only an instant to decide. She was motivated by more than just curiosity, although her curiosity was certainly intense. The fact was, they were trying to find a killer. Time mattered. And if something in this diary had disturbed Darla so profoundly, then it might be related to her death.

Back to the diary.

She examined the title page again. Bessie had yet to marry at the time she had undertaken it, Bell realized, and when she did, she had crossed out her maiden name and added "Gilley." In Acker's Gap in those days—hell, it was still true—it was outlandish for a woman to keep her own last name. Almost unthinkable.

Except for Darla Gilley. What was the word Nick has used? Oh, yeah: feisty. *Here's to feisty women,* Bell thought, and she raised her coffee cup.

She flipped through the pages to see how the diary was organized. It covered the years 1935 to 1959, but there were entire years—many of them—with no entries at all. The earliest entries were the longest.

She read a few entries at random, and quickly, to get a sense of the whole. She could see that the diary was conversational, as if addressed to an unnamed person. Most young diary-writers did that, she reflected. Part of it was grandiosity—*someone will care about my life, enough to read about what happened to me*—but part of it was loneliness, too. The diary was Bessie Dresser Gilley's message to the world.

And if Bell's instincts were right, finding it had somehow gotten her granddaughter killed.

She started from the beginning.

August 15, 1935

I do not want to go. I try to hide how I feel about it, but Daddy knows. I can fool Mama but I can never fool Daddy.

A lot of people say it is the other way around. They say they can tell any kind of story and their daddies will believe it, but their mamas can sniff out a lie right away.

My best friend Penelope Reardon says her mama knows when she is lying about something before she has even finished her sentence. She is three words into the fib and her mama interrupts her. Mrs. Reardon has this way of talking that lets you know you do not have a chance. "No lies from you, girlie," is how her mama says it. Penelope says that is why she just gives up and tells the truth from the start.

My mama is not like that. She is too sick to be watching over us that way, and she does not listen too well, either. She mostly stays in her bed, and so when you tell her something, you have to go up the stairs to her room and see if she is sleeping or not. Usually she is sleeping.

It used to be Daddy's room, too, but about a year ago he started sleeping in the barn. Daddy says he is plenty warm out there. But I do not know how it could be comfortable. Because there are rats. I have seen them. So has my brother, Donnie. He caught one once. Daddy made him let it go. First he let Donnie name the rat, because Donnie wanted to so bad, but Daddy still made Donnie let it go. Morris was the rat's name. If you do not live around here you will not get the joke. Morris DePugh is the name of the principal of Acker's Gap High School. Donnie hates him, hates school. Hates everything.

If mama is not sleeping you can tell her something but she will not know if you are lying. I do not think she even tries to know. She is liable to say, "Okay, then. That sounds alright." You can tell her you are going to burn down the house and she will say, "Okay, then. That sounds alright." Her eyes do not focus right. Once Donnie called her crazy and Daddy whipped him. But the whipping does not mean Donnie was wrong. It only means he should not have said what he did.

Because I told about the barn you might have got the idea that we live on a farm. We do not. Maybe it used to be a farm but it is not anymore. The woods have grown up over the fields. The fences are all gone except for a post here and there, sticking up out of the ground and broken off at the top. The barn is just a little ways away from the house, and it is big and the boards are coming off the sides. It has a dirt floor. There is a hole in the roof, getting bigger all the time. Daddy used to park the truck in there but he does not do that now, because the barn is falling apart, he says, and he is afraid the pieces will drop down and hurt the truck, which Daddy says we are lucky to have. And lucky to have Donnie to fix up when it stops running.

I can guess what you are thinking: If the barn is falling down like that, how can Daddy sleep out there? I cannot answer that question. I just know that is where he goes at night. Sometimes I think he just wants to get away from Mama, but I cannot say that out loud or I will get a whipping, too. There is a kind of upstairs in the barn. You have to climb a ladder to get there. Well, it is not a ladder, really. It is a post going up to the roof, and there are slats nailed to it crosswise. It is a hard climb and you have to be real careful. Me and Donnie used to play up there but we do not anymore. Not since Daddy started sleeping there.

Daddy is not the only one who changed his sleeping place. Last month I moved my bed up to the attic. There is plenty of room in the house but I did that. Sometimes Mama makes noises at night. I like to be far away so I cannot hear them.

Last Wednesday, two days after my 14th birthday, Daddy told me I have to go to work at Wellwood. He asked me if I minded.

I said no. I could tell he did not believe me, but that did not change things. I wonder why he even asked me in the first place. It does not matter what I think. It has to be done. Donnie is already working. He has been working since he was 14, too. He has a job at Larry Kinnamin's car repair shop in Acker's Gap. Like I said, Donnie is real good with engines and he is a highly prized employee. That is what Larry Kinnamin said when he dropped off my brother one day after work. "Your boy is a highly prized employee," Larry Kinnamin said to Daddy. I am not sure why the man gives Donnie rides to and from work. Daddy is not working and so Donnie could drive the truck. Nobody around here cares how old you are when you drive. But Larry Kinnamin does that. Sometimes they get back real late. I know for a fact the shop closes up at 5 so it is a puzzle. I asked Donnie about it once and he got real mad. He told me to shut up and mind my own g—d— business. Then he got nice again and started chasing me around like he used to do. Chasing and laughing. We both like that.

I went up to Mama's room this morning, my first day of work at Wellwood, to tell her about it. She was asleep but I thought it would be okay to wake her up. Daddy got me the job. He said I will be washing people who cannot wash themselves and helping them into and out of their beds. Which seems kind of funny in a way because that is what I do for Mama. I do not know who will do it for her while I am working at Wellwood.

I put a hand on her shoulder. It was sticking out of the top of the blanket while the rest of her body was covered up. She was wearing an old orange sweater and old pants because it is cold now. There is a bad smell coming off her. Well, not bad, really, but not fresh, neither. Like a room that has been closed up too long. Her skin is rough and kind of dry. White flakes come off her sometimes. I touched her shoulder and before I knew it, she started screaming.

"Mama, no," is what I said. "I am Elizabeth." Everybody

else calls me Bessie but Mama still calls me Elizabeth. I like Elizabeth better but you cannot stop a nickname once it has taken hold. That is what Daddy says.

"Mama," I kept on saying, until she settled down. "Mama, mama, mama." I had startled her. That was the problem. Scared the bejeebers out of her. But I know how to settle her down. I rubbed her shoulder.

She stopped screaming and she looked at me like I was a stranger and not her daughter.

"I am starting a job today," I said. "At Wellwood. I will not be back home till real late tonight on account of the long walk home through the woods."

She stared at me. I do not think she understood me but she said, "Are you happy, Elizabeth?" Her eyes, right then, were almost normal. There was no gray film on them.

I said yes. Yes, I am.

"Good," she said. "That sounds alright." And her eyes sort of went all funny again, kind of misty, like she was through with me, through with everything, and especially through with trying to focus or even stay awake.

I waited another minute or so, hoping she would know I was not telling the truth, the way Penelope Reardon's mama knows when she is not telling the truth, hoping she would know I did not want to go work at that place. Another place would be alright, maybe, but not that place. But she turned away from me to sleep.

I do not recall my mama ever being any other way. She has been like this since I was born. Girlie, you were the straw that broke the camel's back: That is what Daddy says to me. First a baby that died and then two more babies, boom boom, one right after the other. Donnie and then me. Too close. Too much. That was what did it. That was what people told Daddy, anyway, according to him. And so that was what Daddy told me and Donnie, when we were old enough to wonder why Mama is like this.

August 16

I started crying last night in front of Mama, when I brought her supper up to her. She never eats it but I bring it anyway. Even with my tears, Mama did not catch on to the fact that I do not want to go to Wellwood. I am scared of going there, scared of the whole place. It is way back in the woods, miles from here.

I have to work there. I know that. There is no way out of it. Most other places do not want a 14-year-old girl working for them, especially one who is small for her age, like me. Aunt Tillie tells me all the time that I do not look any more than 9 or 10. But the people at Wellwood do not mind, Daddy says.

The job means I cannot go to school anymore. Daddy told me not to say anything. That is how you do it. You just stop going. That is what he did when he was my age. He told me about it.

One day he did not go, and then the next and then the next. Nobody said anything. Nobody came by the house. Everybody knows that children have to work and help the family. The teachers at the school know that, but even if they do not know it, Daddy says, they do not care, anyway. Why would they care? Those teachers get paid even if nobody shows up for school. So Daddy's teachers did not care and he did not care, either. And that is the best way to live, he says. Because if you do not care, then nobody and nothing can truly hurt you.

No matter. I do not like school, anyway. There will be no missing it.

Donnie, if you are reading this, you better stop. You are a big snoop.

August 20

The work is real easy. The woman who showed me what I am supposed to do is named Judy Souther.

Two days ago, on my first day, I walked up to the big front

door at Wellwood and I just stood there. It is a real pretty door. It has a rising sun on it, carved right into the wood. The sun is made from these pieces of copper that somebody stuck in the wood in just the right way so it really does look like rays of sun. I started to touch it but then I did not. It did not seem right. It was too pretty to let my hand spoil it.

I did not mind just standing there because I was tired from the long walk through the woods. You have to go up and down hills and jump across a lot of creeks. I just breathed.

I wonder how I am going to make that walk in the winter, when the snow gets real deep. It will be okay in the morning but at night the woods get real scary. I have tried to put that out of my mind but I cannot. I keep thinking about how dark the woods get. And cold. You do not know cold until you have been in the woods around Briney Hollow in the winter, when the wind gets to going real hard and there is ice hanging from the trees.

I was thinking about one tree—Donnie calls it the Monster Tree, so I call it that, too—and how it looks in the winter, with all the leaves long gone and the bark all iced up so bad that you cannot climb it or even think about climbing it. The Monster Tree is over by the creek. The creek gets iced over, too, real early in winter. If you cross it and you do not jump far enough and your foot lands in the water, breaking the ice on top—oh, my, my, it is so cold.

I stood there at the front door of Wellwood. It opened up and there was Judy Souther.

She is a big fat woman and she is not nice. She looked at me. She had one side of her upper lip lifted, like she had seen something disgusting or maybe smelled something bad, and then she said, "What are you standing there for? What is the matter with you? Are you simple?"

That is what they call it when somebody cannot take care of themselves. It is called simple. Penelope asked me once if my mama was simple. I said no, she is not simple, she is just tired.

"Get on in here," Judy Souther said.

There is a real big room when you first go into Wellwood. The floor looks like the board you play checkers on. Red squares and black squares. When you walk on it with hard shoes, you can hear the clicks.

But I had nowhere to walk right then. I stood where I was. Judy Souther was looking at me. She still had that lip of hers raised up. It made me wonder what I was doing wrong. I could not fix it if I did not know what I was doing wrong.

Later I found out that her lip was something she could not help. She had been attacked by a dog when she was a little girl. The dog's name was King. He chewed her face before they could pull him off of her. They did not take her to the doctor because her family lived in the country, like we do, and they were poor, even poorer than we are. Her mama sewed up her lip. It did not heal right. So her lip is twisted. It will always be twisted.

Donnie told me the story about Judy Souther and King. How he found out, I do not know. Donnie hears things. He picks up stories about people and then he uses them like sticks or rocks, to make them do what he wants. He is my brother but I need to say this: Donnie Dresser is sneaky. I have to watch myself around him if I want to keep any secrets.

"This is where they drop off the patients," Judy Souther said to me. She grabbed my shoulders and turned me around in a circle so I could see it all: There are big shut doors in the wall to the right. Double doors. At the back of the room is a big staircase.

"When they bring them in," she said, "somebody will call for you. You or one of the other girls. If it is you, you come and take the patient up those stairs over there." She was still turning me by my shoulders, in fact I had been going in a circle two or three times by now, and she pointed to the staircase as my eyes went past it. "And you make sure you take the patient's suitcase, too, if they have one. You DO NOT say anything to the patient. You DO NOT say anything to the people who bring the patient in. Is that clear?"

She said the DO NOT real loud and slow, like I was simple and would not understand it otherwise. That is why I am writing it in all capital letters, to show how she said it.

I said, yes that is clear. I wanted to say, YES THAT IS CLEAR, but I thought Judy Souther might not be the kind to joke with.

She repeated the part about not talking to the people who bring the patients here. I said, "You mean their families, right?"

"Sometimes it is their families and sometimes it is not," Judy Souther said. "And sometimes it is nobody at all. Sometimes they bring themselves here."

I said again that it was clear. She had stopped turning me by now, which was a good thing, because I thought I might throw up.

"Do I take them to their room?" I asked her.

Judy Souther frowned at me. With that twist in her lip, she cannot frown like a regular person. Her mouth bunches up real bad, like the top of a drawstring feed bag and somebody is pulling that string real tight. Her frowns look like they hurt her. Which you think would make her not want to frown. But no. Judy Souther frowns all the time.

"You DO NOT take them to their room," she said. "You take them to Dr. Trexler's office on the second floor. They have to be checked in."

I said, that is clear. And then I said, "Do I take them to their room after they have been checked in?"

I could tell she was not happy with me. I was asking too many questions. I was getting ahead of her. I think that was the problem. But I wanted to do things right. And she was going pretty slow. The only thing she had done fast was holding my shoulders and turning me in that circle.

"No," she said. "They must get a bath first."

I noticed that she did not say TAKE a bath. She said GET

a bath. I knew what that meant. I would be giving them their bath. That would be okay. I give Mama a bath sometimes, when she has been in bed a long time and Daddy tells me to.

It turned out that I did not see any patients that first day. Only one patient came and they had Loretta Snavely take her and her suitcase. Loretta is another girl who works here. She told me about it at the end of the day.

The patient's name was Evelyn. She had funny eyes, Loretta said. They looked like they were moving around in her head. You couldn't look at them too long. She was young, like me and Loretta. She did not want to be at Wellwood.

When she was taking her upstairs, Loretta said, Evelyn stopped and wrapped her hands around the railing. She leaned over and she spit. Right over the side, like she was a man on the street and not a young girl on a staircase.

The spit landed on a red square down in the lobby. You could hear it land, Loretta told me. It made a sound. But the lobby was clear by that time, so nobody else heard it or saw it. Evelyn wiped her mouth and went back to climbing the stairs like nothing at all had happened.

When Loretta told me the story, she said that all she could think about was what if Judy Souther had been standing down there? And what if the spit had hit her on the top of her head? That made us laugh, that picture of Judy Souther with spit in her hair, and her looking up real mad, wondering where it came from.

I like Loretta. I think we are going to be good friends.

I still have not seen Dr. Trexler.

August 22

Yesterday I took my first patient from the lobby up to Dr. Trexler's office.

I got the call when I was rinsing out the tubs where we give the baths. By that time I had given five baths. One was to a young girl—not Evelyn, another one—and the others were to four old ladies. They had sagging skin and gray hair on their heads and in their personal areas, too, long and gray. My mama's personal area does not have hair as long and gray as that. But the funny thing is that after you give one or two baths to old ladies you do not look at their personal areas anymore. Or maybe you look but you don't really see. They are all the same, anyway, the old ladies, their personal areas, all of it. Everything about them is the same. I am not sure I could tell them apart if somebody asked me to.

I was rinsing out the tubs and thinking that might be all that I would ever do at Wellwood, give baths or rinse out tubs. But then I heard the bell ring. And Mary, another girl who works here, came in from another room. It is her job to check the bells when they ring.

"They want you in the lobby," she said. "There is a new patient."

I do not know how to describe Mary. She is heavyset, with big red hands and a red face that looks like it was rubbed hard by the wind and never got back to normal. She wears her hair in little curls pinned around her head. There must be two dozen bobby pins in her hair.

That part is easy to describe—the part on the outside. The part that I can't tell you about is on the inside of Mary. She can smile one time and then the next time she will slap you. Loretta warned me but I did not listen and on my second day at Wellwood I got too close to Mary and before I knew it she had slapped me.

Now, I have been slapped before but only by people I know, like Daddy or Uncle Ken. With family, you get to know their moods and so you know when it is coming and you can protect yourself, stiffen up to take the blow. It is different when it is somebody you do not know. My face felt hot and it commenced to stinging. I put my hand on the stinging part of my face where Mary had slapped me and then I took my hand off, and I looked at my hand, like I thought I might see something there, like a clue, a clue about why she had done it.

I looked at Mary and she looked back at me. Her face was empty. It was like she was wondering, too, who had slapped me and why.

I was nervous about having my first call to meet a patient in the lobby. But I was excited, too. I nodded when Mary told me that I had been called, but I gave her a wide berth when I walked around her to get to the staircase. The bath area is on the third floor.

"Bessie."

I heard Judy Souther's voice when I was almost down to the lobby. She stood on two squares of the lobby checkerboard, her big feet spread out that wide. She was wearing the lumpy gray sweater she always wears. Saying "Bessie" like that was Judy Souther's way of telling me to hurry up but I was going pretty fast down the steps already.

There was a man standing in the lobby next to a woman who looked a lot like my own mama. Or at least the pictures of my mama before she got sick. Daddy never showed us the pictures but Donnie found them when he was sneaking around, and he and I looked at them for a long time. If Mama's name was not written on the back of the pictures you would not know it was her. The woman in the lobby had on a flowered dress and she had a flower in her hair. Her hair was long and sort of golden. She was beautiful.

"This here's Claudette," the man said. He was very skinny and he was wearing a blue suit. He held a gray hat between his two hands and I could not help but look at his knuckles. They stuck way out like there were little balls sewn under the skin of his fingers. The little balls jumped when he moved his fingers, running those fingers around the stiff front of his gray hat. He was plainly nervous.

"Hello, Claudette," Judy Souther said. "Welcome to Wellwood. I am Judy Souther." She did not introduce me. "This girl here will take you to Dr. Trexler's office. We are going to make you feel better."

"I feel fine," Claudette said. She sounded like she was

mad at somebody. Well, truly, she sounded like she was mad at everybody.

"Claudette," the man said. He did not say it in a friendly way. "You go along with these nice folks. You behave."

"Welcome to Wellwood," Judy Souther said. I do not know if she forgot that she had already said it, or if she repeated it on purpose to make sure Claudette felt welcome.

I stood there until Judy Souther poked me in the back with her fist. It did not feel too good but I was quiet. Then I picked up Claudette's suitcase. I started walking to the staircase. I was NOT supposed to say Come This Way or Follow Me. I was just supposed to start going and the new patient would get the idea.

But Claudette did not get the idea. Or maybe she got the idea and did not want to do it.

I turned when I got to the staircase. It was then that I saw that Claudette was not behind me. She was still standing in the lobby next to the man, with Judy Souther a few feet away from them.

"Now, Claudette," the man said. "We talked about this."

Claudette flipped her golden hair off her shoulders. "You talked about it. I did not. I have a headache. Take me home." I think the man was her husband but nobody ever told me so I do not know for sure.

"This is for the best," the man said. "It is all decided." Before she could do anything to stop him he reached up and grabbed the flower out of her hair. She shrieked. That is the word: shrieked. It was not a scream. It was sharper than that. "There," the man said. "If you do not behave, then you get no flower."

The shrieks did not seem to bother him. Or Judy Souther, either. I got the idea that Judy Souther had been through this kind of thing many times before, with other people.

They waited. Finally Claudette stopped shrieking. She was breathing very hard. "You see?" the man said to her. "That is why you are here. That kind of behavior." Claudette nodded, tucking in her lower lip like a little girl does. She let Judy Souther take her arm and lead her over to the staircase, where I was waiting.

Claudette went up the steps. She did not say a word to me. I looked down at the lobby one time, just before we reached the first landing. The man was signing some papers and handing them back, one by one, to Judy Souther.

September 4, 1935

I still have not met Dr. Trexler. Loretta has met him. She says it was an accident that she met him. Most of the girls on the staff do not see him. He works in a part of Wellwood where we are not supposed to go unless we are told that we may.

Loretta was delivering some medicine to the other side of Wellwood. Judy Souther had called and asked her to bring some needles and gauze from the supply cabinet. The girl who usually brings it was sick. So Loretta got what was needed from the head nurse, Sally Tarver, and put it on a tray and carried it over to that part of Wellwood I have never seen.

At first it looked the same as the rest of the hospital, Loretta told me. There are rooms with a lot of beds in them, all in a row. But at the end of the hall, there is something different. They call it The Room.

Loretta's voice got real funny when she talked about it. It was not like any other room she had ever seen, she said. Loretta is the only girl on the staff who goes to The Room to work. Dr. Trexler goes, of course, and Ophelia Browning and Judy Souther, and the nurses, and Carl Winton, a big, strong man who does odd jobs at Wellwood. But not the girls like me, girls who only give the baths. Loretta is special because she gets to go to The Room but she does not brag about it.

September 10, 1935

Yesterday was the day I finally met Dr. Trexler.

The funny thing is, he came looking for me. He walked into the room where I give baths to the girls. I had finished rinsing out the tubs and was getting ready to fold the dry towels and put them on the shelf, which is part of my job, too.

I knew who he was, of course. He wears a white coat and everybody steps aside when he goes by.

"Hello," he said, and I said it back. "I understand your mother is Theresa Dresser. Is that right?" I said, yes, it is. He had my file in his hand. That is how he knew Mama's name.

He nodded and he smiled. He looked at me like he was trying to check on something, like maybe I had dirt on my chin or my blouse was on crooked. I said, "Thank you," because sometimes that is what people want you to say. They wait until you say it.

He said, "You know, Elizabeth, sometimes we are not able to help people the way we hope to do. We try our best but we cannot." I said, "Well, I am sure that it is true." I did not say anything else. I think he wanted me to talk about Mama but I would not do that. Daddy never talks about Mama outside the house and I will not do that, either. That is a private family matter. Dr. Trexler did not mention it again, which I was glad about.

February 4, 1937

Craig Gilley comes by the house sometimes. I can tell he wants to court me but to tell you the truth I do not want to be courted by anybody. He hums that song "Cheek to Cheek," which does not please me. Donnie teases me about Craig but I told Donnie to hush up. Like it or not, Craig shows up some mornings and asks to walk me to Wellwood. It is nice to have company but there is not a whole lot to talk about.

He came to Wellwood at the end of the day yesterday to walk me home through the woods but I can tell Dr. Trexler was not happy about that. He said, "Elizabeth, I would prefer that you not have your friends come here to pick you up. Perhaps your young gentleman could wait for you at the edge of the grounds." The words made it sound like it was a question but it was not really a question.

I told Dr. Trexler that of course Craig Gilley will not come into the lobby of Wellwood anymore and wait for me to be finished with work. That WILL NOT happen.

I do not know if Dr. Trexler understood my joke. I was talking the way Judy Souther talks when she is trying to make a point.

"Good," is what he said back to me. "I am glad to hear that, Elizabeth."

Craig is not happy about waiting in the woods, especially when it is raining. But it cannot be helped. That is how Dr. Trexler wants it.

August 17, 1937

Craig Gilley and I were married this morning. He is going to come live in the farmhouse with Daddy and Donnie and Mama and me.

My baby will be here soon. I have nothing more to say about that.

Well, I do. Ophelia Browning asked me if I was having a baby. The other girls knew by looking at me but they did not ask, because that is something you do not ask about. But Ophelia Browning saw me in The Room the other day and she said, "Elizabeth, I do believe you are in the family way."

She is the supervisor of everybody and everything at Wellwood except for Dr. Trexler. Judy Souther told me that if Ophelia Browning asks you to jump, you say, "How high?" So I did the only thing I could do and that is to say, "Yes." She said, "That is unfortunate." I did not know what to say to that and so I was quiet, and she said, "Please understand. That is a compliment, Elizabeth, it means that you are an important member of the team, and Dr. Trexler and I will hate to lose you." I said, "Lose me?" Ophelia Browning said, "Yes, after the baby comes, because you may not want to work here at Wellwood anymore." I said, "Oh, no, no, I will be right back. That is no problem." She said, "Good."

November 12, 1937

We have decided to name him Nelson, in honor of Craig's uncle, who mostly raised Craig. Well, Craig decided. And if you ever met his uncle, then you would understand why Craig is the way he is, having been raised by such a man.

I love my little boy but sometimes I look at him and I think, "It is too soon. I am only sixteen years old." I have taken to sleeping in the attic again. It is the only way to keep Craig away from me, if you see what I mean. He wants another baby but I do not. I also do not want to fight about it every night, night after night, because I have to get up so early in the morning to walk to Wellwood. So the attic is where I sleep now. It is better this way. Poor Craig cannot control himself sometimes in his sleep. That is what he says.

NOTE TO DONNIE: I know you are reading this diary, you rascal. You stop it. Or I am going to stop writing in it.

NOTE NO. 2 TO DONNIE: Okay, so I can tell you are still reading this. You have engine grease on your fingers, Donnie, and do you see that spot right there? I will draw an arrow to it so that you can see the mark you left on the page. There. Right there.

I am going to stop writing, then. Because you will not stop. Or maybe I have another plan up my sleeve, Donnie Dresser. I will not do it right away but someday, I will.

January 9, 1949

I have to write this down. If Donnie reads it, I do not care. I want to have a record of it.

Yesterday was the most exciting day ever at Wellwood. Judy Souther called us down to the lobby and she clapped her hands and said, "Girls, this is a day you will remember forever." We looked at each other and wondered what it could possibly be.

The front door opened and a man walked in. He smiled at all of us. Especially the pretty ones like Colleen Herbert and Trudy Fitzsimmons. He looked a lot like Dr. Trexler, because he had a mustache, too, only he was shorter. We looked at each other and we thought, "This is the exciting thing?"

Well, it turned out that the man was Dr. Walter Freeman. He is a great, great man, Judy Souther says. He is a doctor, too, and he is the one who taught Dr. Trexler how to be a doctor.

Dr. Trexler came down the stairs and he and Dr. Freeman shook hands. It is clear they are old friends. Dr. Trexler asked Trudy Fitzsimmons to take Dr. Freeman's bag up to his office. I could see that Dr. Trexler was very proud of Wellwood. I can remember so well what he said to Dr. Freeman: "We do more with less than anyplace else you will ever visit, Walter," and Dr. Freeman said, "Good for you, Emmett."

Judy Souther told us that we would be glad we met Dr. Freeman. "Mark what I say, girls," she said. "Dr. Freeman is a great man. You can tell your children and your grandchildren that you met him."

January 17, 1949

Dr. Freeman left this morning. We are all sorry to see him go. He is polite to everybody, especially to Trudy and Colleen. There was a time when I was jealous of girls like those two, because I am an old married woman, and a mother, and they are young and pretty, and men like Dr. Freeman are always giving them little pats on the bottom. Trudy giggled when he did that to her. Colleen pretended like it wasn't happening. She would just hum a tune and smile. She likes the song "Buttons and Bows" and that is what she hums. Now that he is gone, though, it does not matter. They are regular girls like the rest of us and we all do the same work: We give baths and clean the toilets and mop the halls. There is always plenty to do at Wellwood.

Dr. Trexler's mood seemed to dip a little bit after Dr. Freeman left us this morning. I could see right away that he is missing Dr. Freeman.

The good thing is that when Dr. Trexler is blue he has Ophelia Browning to cheer him up. She and Dr. Trexler spend a lot of time in his office with the door closed. I asked Judy Souther about it once and she said, "You do not understand. They have patient records to go over. Do you think it is easy to run a hospital like this? Well, it is not."

I do not know what they do in The Room, but Loretta says that sometimes it does not go so well. A girl died yesterday. Dr. Trexler told us that she was already real sick when she came here and what happened to her in The Room had nothing to do with it. Her name was Sunny Bauer. She would scream when I was giving her a bath. Once she said she was going to jump out of the window and they called Carl Winton to stop her. By the time he got there she had climbed down from the sill and was standing in the room brushing her hair. She looked at him and asked him what he was doing there.

Loretta told me that they did not know right away that something was wrong. The operation was going along fine. Dr. Freeman had turned the dial for the last time and Sunny flopped and shook all over, and then she was still. Dr. Trexler saw what was happening. He looked over at Ophelia Browning, who was standing there like she always does, and he said, "Something is not right."

Too much current, is what Loretta told me later. Sunny Bauer's heart had stopped. She was dead, just like that. Dr. Freeman did not say anything at all, not even, "That is too bad. I am sorry that happened."

I wondered what her family was going to say but then I remembered that most of the girls who come here do not have families, or at least not families who ask questions about what happens to them.

February 21, 1951

Judy Souther did not come to work today. Ophelia Browning came into the room where we gather in the morning to get our duties for the day, and she said, "Judy Souther is not feeling well." We all looked at each other. Judy Souther is what my daddy calls a tough old bird, meaning that she is not the kind to get sick or to let on to anybody when she is sick. We could not feature how she could be sick.

Ophelia Browning told us what to do. Some of us would give baths, some of us would sweep and mop, some would help the cooks in the kitchen. She did not know the usual jobs that Judy Souther gives to each girl, but when somebody said, "That is not what Judy Souther has me do," well, that did not sit right with Ophelia Browning. She said, "So what? Get to work." And that was that.

Ophelia Browning is what I would call elegant. One of the girls said that she started out just like one of us, sweeping and the like, but that Dr. Trexler took a shine to her. Now she works in the office.

I used to want to go into The Room, just to see what it was like, but not anymore. I will leave all that to Loretta.

February 24

Judy Souther died. Her husband came today and told Dr. Trexler. We were all surprised. We were surprised that she died, yes, but mostly surprised that she had a husband. Nobody knew. She never talked about him. She had a child, too, a little girl. Her husband cried when he showed us the picture. She looks a lot like Judy Souther. I did not tell him that, though, because it is not much of a compliment.

I guess what surprises me most is how you can work with somebody for so many years and not really know them at all.

She died of the cancer. It turns out that Judy Souther had a big tumor inside her for the past few years. She knew about it, but she never told us. I was kind of mad about that at first, because I was not able to say good-bye, and she had ended up being a good person and not as mean as I thought on that first day, but then I let it go. It was Judy Souther's business how she lived and died, and nobody else's.

April 14, 1952

Nelson's wife, Sandra, gave birth today to a little boy. They named him Joseph. Sandra is a good girl and she works hard, but there was a moment when she moved into the farmhouse to be with Nelson that she realized I sleep in the attic. First she laughed and then she said, "Well, to each his own, I guess." I did not care for that comment at all. I did not care for the laugh, either.

May 4, 1952

I have been working at Wellwood a long time now. They trust me. I can go most anywhere I want to go around there, except for The Room, of course. Nobody bothers me or asks me any questions. When the new girls come to work I am the one who shows them what to do. I guess you could say I am the new Judy Souther.

The girls tell stories about what happens in The Room, even though they do not know. They try to scare the new girls. If Ophelia Browning catches them telling stories like that they get in big trouble. She says that everything Dr. Trexler does is for the best.

I need to watch what I say about Ophelia Browning because I have to have this job. Wellwood is the only place to work around here. Craig is laid off now with his back. My boy Nelson is laid off, too, not because of his back but because there are no jobs. Nelson and Sandra and little Joe all stay in one room in the house and there are unsaid things in the air, hard and hurtful things, because the three of them live here and do not pay for anything. My husband wishes they would get their own place but he will not say that to their faces. And how could that happen, anyway? They have no money. Last Sunday at the supper table Donnie said, "Maybe we should talk about some things, everybody," but Craig just stared at him and said, "Pass the mashed potatoes." So Donnie said, "Is that all you got to say?" And Craig said, "Okay, pass the butter, too." That is Craig's way. He makes a joke and that is that.

July 19, 1958

I know for sure now that somebody is reading this diary again. (Hello, Donnie, I know it is YOU.) I still keep it in the trunk in the attic. I am very careful about how I hide it each time I put it back after I write in it. I wrap it in tissue paper and mash it down at the very bottom, next to the side, where you cannot see it unless you are looking for it.

The other day, when I went up there and opened the trunk, I saw that some of the sweaters were in different places. They had been messed up. Just a little bit, but that was enough. Somebody tried to put things back the same way I do, every time, but they did not do it right.

If this is you again, Donnie Dresser, I want you to stop it.

I know I should just not write anymore and throw this away. But I have worked too hard to make a record. Not just the things I have done but what I think about and my impressions of things. If I tear up this diary now, it would be a waste.

You just keep on reading, Donnie, if this is you doing it. I do not care. And I will keep on writing.

October 10, 1959

Today is Sunday. I do not have time to write a lot today. I have so many things to do. When the work week starts I never have time to do all my chores.

Oh, I hear Joe crying. He is seven now but he does cry a lot. This house is big but the sounds go right through it, like there are no walls at all. When Craig is mad because of Joe's crying he will say to me, "So now I know why you moved up to the attic all those years ago. You were just planning ahead. You knew you'd want to get away from the g—d—noise one day." Well, if that is what Craig wants to think, then that is fine with me. But that is not the reason.

Chapter Twenty-eight

Nick Fogelsong did not care for fast-food restaurants. He found them sterile and bland, and it seemed to him that they turned what ought to be a comforting ritual of fellowship with friends into a dreary experience about as romantic as filling a slop bucket and flinging it out the back door. The food in such places filled a hole. Then it was eliminated. That was all.

The names ran together in his mind, creating one monstrous, sprawling, impossible word that was roughly the size, he thought with distaste, of one of the sandwiches available on the premium menu, the kind whose contents oozed out over the sides of the soggy bun, shortly before causing flesh to ooze out over the tops of waistbands:

Tacobellmcdonaldsarbysburgerkingsteakadnshakewendyshardees

His dislike of them had intensified in recent months. He knew the reason: Fast-food joints were the principal reason why JP's had fallen on hard times, imperiling Jackie's livelihood. The garish huts strung out along the interstate were like siren songs to truckers, the same men—and it was mostly men, although Nick had known a few female truck drivers, and admired their moxie—who formerly had signaled a turn to take the exit for Acker's Gap on a regular basis, not minding the short detour for a good meal.

Dangle a greasy burger and a carton of fries in front of those same truckers, though, and Jackie's home-cooked food—fried chicken, meatloaf, liver and onions—flew out of their memories like an eighteen-wheeler hitting one of those runaway truck ramps after a steep descent down the mountainside.

Well, times changed. Nick understood that. But he didn't have to like it.

The fact was, however, that the choice of location for today's meeting had been up to Roger Briscoe, not him. And Briscoe had picked the McDonald's midway between Charleston and Blythesburg because he had deliveries in the area that morning.

Fine: Nick would finish up with his attorney and meet Briscoe there on the way home.

He pulled his Chevy Tahoe into the McDonald's lot just after 11 A.M. He looked around. No sign of Briscoe's big rig. The trucker had only been able to give Nick an approximate time for his arrival; he didn't know what kind of traffic he would hit.

Despite his distaste for the place, Nick decided to wait for Briscoe inside.

"Large black coffee," Nick said when it was his turn to step up to the counter.

"That it?"

"Yep."

"Credit or debit?"

"Huh?"

"Are you using a credit card or a debit card?"

"For a cup of coffee? You gotta be kidding me." He pulled out his wallet while the clerk grinned nervously. The skinny young man in the black shirt and matching black trousers appeared to be about twelve years old. An expanse of pink pimples made his face look like a glazed ham. Braces caged his fulsome teeth.

Clutching the tall brown cup of coffee, still muttering about what kind of dope wouldn't have a dollar in cash for a cup of joe, Nick found a table as far away from the kids' play area as possible. The play area was stuck on the front of the restaurant and accessed through a bright yellow archway. To Nick it resembled a miniature version of hell. Under a see-through dome was a twisting snarl of colorful tubes across which kids were expected to shimmy and dangle, plus a plastic statue of a clown with floppy red shoes and a serial-killer grin. Kids, he imagined, were supposed to climb all over this creature while sugars and starches ping-ponged ominously in their small bellies.

He realized that he was seeing everything through the gray haze of his resentment of the competition on Jackie's behalf. Truth was, if he'd been nine, ten years old himself, he would've gone crazy in the play area, bouncing and climbing. He would've loved Happy Meals, delighting in the toy and the cut-up apple slices. Nobody had ever cut up apples for him when he was a kid; an apple was something tossed your way when you headed out the door to do chores. If you were lucky.

And besides—people could eat where they damned well pleased. If they preferred this to a decent meal at JP's, then so be it. And—

"Nick Fogelsong?"

The man loomed over Nick's table. He was broad and tall, with a slab of wheat-colored hair that flopped over on his forehead. His hair was shaved down to the nub on either side but allowed to stay thick on top. His face included a large nose and flabby, too-red lips. He wore a flannel shirt and jeans, and he smelled like cigarettes and diesel fuel.

Nick stuck out a hand, which the man grasped and shook.

"Have a seat," Nick said.

"Gimme a sec. Just wanted to make sure it was you first. Wanna grab some food. Been on the road since four this mornin'."

Oh, brother, Nick thought. Now he'd be forced to smell whatever greasy, oniony crap this guy bought and spread out across the table.

To his surprise, though, Briscoe brought back a salad in a plastic bowl with a snap-on lid.

"Gotta watch the carbs," Briscoe said.

Truck drivers watching their carbs?

Wonders, Nick thought, *never cease.*

"So how can I help you?" Briscoe went on. He'd pried off the lid, pulled the wrapper off his plastic fork, stirred up the lettuce, carrots, and croutons, and dug in. "I sure was sorry to hear that gal got herself killed. It was a shock."

"Yeah," Nick said. "And it looks like you were the last person to see her alive. Except for the murderer, of course." He waited to see if that had any impact on Briscoe. It didn't. The man stirred his salad again, and proceeded to indulge in several hefty bites in a row, spearing the lettuce with gusto. "I was hoping you might have a few more details about her mood at the time you picked her up."

"Well, like I told her sister-in-law when I brought her purse back, she had her mind stuck on something. Something that was upsetting her. Big time."

"And she didn't say what it was."

Briscoe waited until he'd chewed and swallowed a mouthful of greenery. "No. Not really."

Quickly, Nick said, "Is that a 'No' or a 'Not really'? Because they're two different things."

"Hey—whoa, there," Briscoe said. "Whoa, whoa, whoa." He set down his fork. "What the hell *is* this? Am I a suspect or something? I went over all this already with your sheriff. Her name's . . . Harrison, right? Yeah, Harrison. She checked out my story. I was at a strip club Thursday night. That big one just off the interstate." Moving his eyebrows up and down, he added with a lascivious growl, "And speaking of *big ones,* lemme tell you . . ." He waited for Nick to react. When that didn't happen, he shrugged and went back to his tale. "Your sheriff talked to the buddies I was there with. And checked the time stamp on my credit cards—the works. No *way* I coulda gotten back to those woods to kill that lady."

"You just seem a little murky about what you and Darla talked about."

"So you want me to remember every damned second of a ride with a stranger? A ride that lasted all of about twenty minutes? Jesus Christ, mister."

Nick relented. "Okay. Sorry. But we don't have many leads. That's why we're bearing down so hard on the few we've got."

Briscoe sulked for a few seconds. He decided his salad was too dry. He had trouble opening the plastic packet of ranch that had come with it, trying and failing to pull the tiny tab across the top with his callused fingers. He finally reverted to the use of his incisors. When he ripped open the package the dressing squirted out. "Feisty little bugger," he said. And then: "Yeah, I get it. Still hard to believe. Nice lady like that. And yeah—something was definitely bothering her. But I didn't ask her to tell me what it was. None of my business, right?"

"So you're not the type to get involved in other people's problems."

"Good way to put it." He drizzled the dressing over what remained of his salad, pumping the plastic sack until it was empty. "Got problems of my own. Try two ex-wives and four kids between 'em. And the oldest one takes karate classes that cost me an arm and a leg." He laughed. "The oldest kid, that is, not the oldest ex-wife. Although if she could get 'em to make me pay for it, I swear she'd give it a whirl. Just to take my money."

Briscoe bugged Nick. Bugged him royally. He couldn't put his finger on it—but there was something about his story that didn't add up. Had Darla told him more than he was willing to say? Or was it darker than that—had he harmed her? Molested her? Could Briscoe even be the killer? Well, hold on: Pam Harrison was satisfied with his alibi, and she was no pushover.

Moreover, if Briscoe *was* involved in some way—why had he brought Darla's purse back to Joe and Brenda's house? Most likely they would never have found him if he had stayed anonymous, if he had never come forward.

Maybe he was one of those bad guys who got off on toying with investigators, trying to outfox them. Paying people to say he was somewhere at the time of the murder when he wasn't. Maybe, that is, he *was* the murderer, and he was playing a game with them, matching wits with law enforcement, Hannibal Lecter stuff. The game wouldn't be fun unless they knew who he was, and questioned him, as Sheriff Harrison had already done, as Nick was doing now. For sport, he'd give them a few tantalizing details, and then sit back and watch them try to ensnare him, cackling into his Chianti . . .

Nick stopped his thoughts. He took a hard look at Briscoe. He had a dab of ranch dressing on his chin. And no trace of a Hannibal Lecter–style intelligence behind the bovine eyes.

"I'm gonna get me some of them hot apple pies to go," Briscoe announced. He stood, gathering up the empty salad bowl, the plastic dressing container, the crinkled napkin, and looked around for the trash bin. "Want me to grab you a couple?"

"What about the carbs?"

Briscoe grinned. "Gonna treat myself. Talking about my ex-wives put me in a bad mood. Gotta bounce back."

Nick indicated his coffee cup. "I'm good. Thanks."

"Okay. But you can't beat them little apple pies. I can eat three of 'em without comin' up for air."

Chapter Twenty-nine

"Mind if I take a look at your rig?"

"Be my guest. She's a beaut."

Nick had walked out to the parking lot with Briscoe. His truck—massive and silver-sided, with a cab so high that it made Nick's back hurt just imagining the climb up into it—was parked sideways across a long row of spaces in the far corner of the lot, so as not to block the regular traffic.

"How long've you been driving?"

"Seventeen years," Briscoe declared. "And I got the hemorrhoids and sciatica and big belly to prove it." He guffawed at his own joke. "Worked for five carriers. Not a dime's worth of difference between 'em. Offer you a lot when you sign up—not so much later."

"My general understanding is that companies have a rule prohibiting you from picking up hitchhikers. Isn't that right?"

An irritated Briscoe eyed him. "Here we go again. There a reason why you're busting my balls, old man, or is this just a way to pass the time?"

The "old man" hit Nick like a hard slap.

"A woman died," he snapped.

"I know she did. And I'm real sorry. But I had nothing to do with that. Which I've told you in plain English. More than once. Either go get that sheriff of yours and tell her to bring the cuffs—or get outta my face. I'm done listenin' to this shit." His face now tight with a scowl, he swung himself up into the driver's seat.

"Hey, hold on," Nick said. He didn't want to end his talk with Briscoe like this. Hostility was a hard material to work with, and Nick had a strong instinct that their business with Briscoe wasn't finished. He needed something more malleable. "Sorry if I've insulted you. You didn't have to talk to me today and I appreciate it. Darla was my friend. That's the bottom line. So I'm a little out of sorts."

Briscoe glared down at him, right elbow cocked on the steering wheel, booted foot propping open the big door. Nick looked up. *I would've needed an extension ladder to reach that damned seat,* he thought ruefully. Briscoe had managed it in a single nimble hop.

"Okay," the trucker said. No warmth in his tone. "Apology accepted."

"So we're good?"

Briscoe shrugged. He reached for the inside handle of the door, so that he could yank it shut and crank up the engine and be on his way.

Nick stepped back.

Just before the door closed he spotted it: Jammed behind the driver's seat was a hatchet.

"Hey—wait a sec."

Briscoe dropped his arm. He made a sigh-heavy show of his disgruntlement. "What is it now, mister?"

"I see you've got a hatchet back there."

"Don't know a trucker who doesn't."

"What do you use it for?"

"Lots." He sounded belligerent. Then he softened a bit. "For me, it's on account of Curtis Kane. Buddy of mine. Went right through a bridge railing back in '08. His rig submerged. Electrical system shorted out. He couldn't open the door." Briscoe rubbed his chin. "His widow made me promise I'd always keep a hatchet in the cab. To break out the glass if I needed to."

Nick let the story live uncontested for a few seconds.

"You know that Darla was killed with a sharp-bladed weapon, right? Blow to the head."

Briscoe's face changed. He looked truly shocked. "No. I didn't. *Damn,*" he said, shaking his head. "*Damn,* that's a hard way to go."

"So you wouldn't mind if the sheriff asked to take a look at that hatchet of yours? Check it for evidence? If you're not involved in the murder, you've got nothing to worry about."

"Sure." Briscoe's voice was hard again. "Absolutely. You've got my number. In fact—you want the hatchet right now? You want to take it with you, cowboy? Be my guest. I told you and told you. *I didn't do it.* All I did was give a nice old lady a ride. And then when she asked me to—" He cut off his sentence abruptly.

"Asked you to do what?"

"Nothin.' I gotta go. So what'll it be—you want to take the damned hatchet right now? Or send somebody to get it later? I don't give a rat's ass which way you want to go. I'll be at the Holiday Inn at exit 47 tonight. Need to treat myself—more'n just the apple pies—after going through all this third-degree crap with you. Jesus Christ."

Truth was, Nick had no authority to confiscate the hatchet. And even if he did, possessing one was not a crime.

"Hope you get a good night's sleep," he told Briscoe. "If Sheriff Harrison wants to test your hatchet, you'll be hearing from her. And if you're harboring any thoughts of getting rid of it between now and then—well, don't."

Nick put a hand on the truck door, intending to push it closed. Before he had a chance to do so Briscoe ripped it away, pulling it shut under his own power.

Through the closed window, Nick could plainly read the word on the man's lips: *Asshole.*

Nick didn't turn his cell back on until he'd reached the city limits of Acker's Gap. He needed to think about his conversation with Briscoe, and figure out what it was about the man that needled him. He was holding something back. But what?

The hatchet was a jarring find. Jarring—and way too easy, if it was the murder weapon. Briscoe hadn't hidden it. Nor did he seem rattled when Nick spotted it in his cab.

Was that just an extension of the game Briscoe was playing with them?

Nick would give the information to Sheriff Harrison. She'd get the hatchet from Briscoe for forensic testing. If he refused, she'd get a warrant.

There was just something peculiar about the man. *And it's more than that damned salad,* Nick groused to himself, although that was still a head-scratcher. Next thing he knew, his hunting buddies would announce they were all going vegan. And then he'd know for sure that the world was heading straight to hell in a—

His cell chirped.

"Hey, Bell," he said, recognizing the ringtone.

Before he could utter his standard "What's up?" she told him, quickly and succinctly, about the diary and its contents. She had spent her afternoon reading it. The story was interesting but nothing jumped out, Bell said, about why Darla was so determined to get it to them.

"The thing is," she went on, "I just naturally assumed that the diary had to be related to Darla's murder. But maybe it's not. Maybe the two things—her finding and mailing you the diary and her death at Wellwood—just happened to occur in the same general time frame."

"Hell of a coincidence," he muttered. "Sort of like two murders happening sixty years apart, in the same general area, to a grandmother and a granddaughter."

He filled her in on his interview with Roger Briscoe, and his misgivings about the man. He saved the best for last: the discovery of the hatchet wedged behind the driver's seat.

"Wow," she said. "But you know what? Seems way too convenient."

"You got that right. Anyway, the crime lab'll have the last word on that. Out of our hands. I assume we'll keep the existence of the diary and the nature of its contents to ourselves for the time being."

"No question about it," Bell declared. "We don't know where it fits in yet—or who might react to the fact that it's been found."

"So where do we go from here?"

"I know where *I'm* going—home to my dog. Hope he'll still be speaking to me after being left alone so long. I paid a kid in the neighborhood to come by and take him out every few hours, but that's not the same. Just ask Arthur. And first thing tomorrow, I'll go where I always go when the questions are piling up so fast that they're blocking my view."

"Where's that?"

"An investigator's favorite hangout."

The names of a tavern or two strung out along Route 12 came to him, but he'd never known Bell to frequent them, and so he asked, "Which is . . . ?"

"The public library. And I'm taking Jake with me."

Chapter Thirty

When Carla Elkins had first bumped into the microfilm reader in the Acker's Gap Public Library five years ago, she didn't even wait for her lunch break—she had a part-time job at the library back then—to tell her mother about it. Beneath a quickly snapped cell photo of the clunky, dusty, weird thing with the milky-white screen that vaguely resembled a picture she'd seen of a TV set from the 1950s, Carla texted:

?????

Carla knew what it *was*; she just couldn't figure out why anyone would still *have* one. Hadn't the whole world gone digital by now?

The world, yes. Acker's Gap, no.

Bell remembered that text as she watched Jake fumble with the same microfilm reader that had so amused Carla. Back issues of the *Acker's Gap Weekly Gazette* had never been deemed important enough to digitize—and even if they had been so deemed, who was going to pay for it?—and thus if you wanted to see an old copy of the paper, you had to indulge in a tediously elaborate ritual:

You had to haul the machine out of the storage closet; paw through the nearby drawers filled with small, tattered cardboard containers with the faded white labels—1927, 1928, 1929, say, and on up through the flat pageant of years—until you found the date you desired; pull out the metal sprocket with the rolled-up film that looked so brittle and venerable that you wouldn't have been shocked if it ended up containing George Washington's home movies—*Hey, look! There's the cherry tree!*; thread the film onto the little wheel; and scroll past a trudging army of black-and-white newspaper pages of yore until you found the one you were looking for.

"You're kidding, right?" Jake asked. He'd wrangled his wheelchair up under a table in the back of the library and had been fiddling with the machine for several minutes. "I can't just go online and click on the link to bring up all the issues in the second half of 1959?"

"Sure you can," Bell replied cheerfully. "Just as soon as you digitize all the back issues and upload them to the library's Web site. The *Gazette* started publication about 1866, I think, and until 1950 or so it used to publish seven days a week, so that should take you—" She looked at her watch. "Hmmm. Maybe ten years, give or take, assuming an eight-hour day and a five-day workweek, and a week's vacation per year. If you don't mind, I'll wait over at JP's. Just text me when you're done."

"Hilarious." He sounded more discouraged than sarcastic. The bleak mood of unknown origin that caught him a few days ago had, instead of relaxing its hold as Bell had expected, driven its hooks in deeper. And the prospect of employing a technology that struck Jake as something out of *The Flintstones* clearly wasn't helping.

"Thing is, Jake, you're the best researcher among the three of us. Not only will you find the story about Bessie Dresser's murder—but you'll see other stories from back then, too, while you're at it, and if something is relevant, you're the man to spot it."

"That flattery thing—does it always work?"

"Usually." She grinned and gave him a light punch in the shoulder. "Seriously—we need to see if there's any link between the two murders."

"Got it." He pulled a pair of reading glasses out of the breast pocket of his flannel shirt. He angled his elbows against the armrests of his chair, and then he leaned forward until his nose was just inches from the cloudy screen.

"I'll be up front with Libby," Bell said.

Libby Royster, the one and only employee and a trained reference librarian to boot, waited for her at the rectangular table near the circulation desk. She'd amassed an impressive haul of books and printouts. She stood alongside them, jaw set, arms crossed, like a warrior returned from a siege, laden with spoils.

Bell settled herself in one of the slat-back armchairs that matched the table. The wood was blond and old, the seat rubbed smooth and shiny by the innumerable butts of library patrons gone by. That thought used to be rather off-putting—it was Carla who had pointed out the link between the indentation in the buttery soft wood and the shifting-around of multiple backsides as people made themselves comfortable to read—but now it didn't bother her. These days, it was new furniture that caused Bell to become slightly ill at ease; new wood hadn't been broken in yet. A chair's history grounded it. Lacking a long memory of the derrieres that had docked themselves there, the chair might just go flying right off the face of the earth.

"That was quick," Bell said, waving at the stack.

"You called an hour and a half ago and told me what you needed. And we're not exactly swamped." Libby frowned. The library's single room featured, at the moment, a population of three: herself, Bell, and Jake.

The shelves were neat and straight and full. Everything was in proper order. But the library was in trouble, and no amount of careful organization could save it. The Raythune County commissioners had cut the budget to the proverbial bone—and then kept right on cutting, until the saw poked through on the other side.

Operating hours were squeezed back. Maintenance was deferred. Most grievously of all, the fund for new books and periodicals was eliminated. Libby did the best she could; she worked many hours with no pay, and used her own money to buy what new books she could afford. Her efforts, though, were for naught: The library was dying a chunk at a time, year by year, like a coastal area amid rising sea levels.

Libby was a young woman, just twenty-seven, but she looked like an old woman. That's what Bell always thought when she saw her again after any interval. Libby wore her curly chestnut-colored hair in a thick braid that she pulled over her left shoulder and parked there. Thick-lensed glasses prevented easy access to her face. If you looked closely at that face—and few people did, Bell surmised, because Libby held herself apart from the world and its unwanted scrutiny, rarely looking anyone in the eye—you would see that it was attractive, with creamy skin, an expressive mouth, and thoughtful eyes. She was recently divorced, and it was as if Libby didn't want to bother with the fact that she was pretty. It would only mean trouble.

Once she had provided a great deal of help to Bell, back when Bell was digging up every data point she could find about Utley Pharmaceuticals. The company made billions of dollars from the opioids it patented and distributed—the chemicals that were relentlessly destroying Acker's Gap and the rest of Appalachia, the same way the emerald ash borer was killing ash trees: from the inside out.

Bell had hoped to go after company executives with a strategic zeal. She'd be armed with the best weapon of all: information. But the executives ignored her letters and e-mails, refused to take her phone calls. She never got past the lobby of the corporate headquarters in Connecticut. Nobody in the West Virginia state legislature—or in the West Virginia delegation in Congress or the U.S. Senate—was willing to take on a powerful corporation and its massive political influence, beyond making bland statements of faux concern about addicts and their families. She couldn't make enough people care.

Drug dealers on the streets were easy to demonize. They were low-life scum and they looked it. But drug dealers who wore nice suits and drove fancy cars—that was harder. And yet it was the latter who had created massive amounts of new business for the former. When physicians overprescribed opioids, people became addicted; when the prescriptions ran out, they were forced to go to the dealers.

Libby had been angry with Bell for giving up. So angry that she didn't speak to her for weeks. Bell would come in the library, say hello, and receive silence as her reply. It was awkward, and strange, and Bell had tried repeatedly to explain to Libby that she hadn't capitulated, not really. She'd only changed her method of attack. Picked her battles—winnable ones. But as she tried to craft the sentences to convey that, she realized that in a broad sense, Libby was right. When it came to going toe-to-toe with a behemoth such as Utley, she *had* given up.

She wasn't going to give up on finding Darla Gilley's killer.

Chapter Thirty-one

"Looks like a lot to get through," Bell said. She eyed the intimidating piles of documents Libby had assembled. "Was there really that much stuff on Wellwood?"

"There were a lot of Wellwoods."

"Come again?"

Libby twisted her braid. It was a nervous habit. It reminded Bell of the way Jake would roll his chair forward and backward, forward and backward, an inch at a time. All the smart people she knew in Acker's Gap found their own ways to channel their restlessness.

"Wellwood," Libby said, "was just one of dozens of state-run mental hospitals that used patients as guinea pigs in the middle of the last century. I skimmed a lot of this material while I was waiting for you. Want a summary?"

"I'd be much obliged."

"Walter Freeman."

"Who's Walter Freeman?"

"He's the reason that hospitals like Wellwood became what they did in the 1940s and '50s—places where men deposited the rebellious, unruly women in their lives, trying to get them under control. I'm simplifying, and yes, there were some male patients who were victimized, too, but that's the bottom line. Freeman created his own variation of a surgical technique first done in the 1930s that was known as a leucotomy. It's from the Greek word for white—'leukos.' So the term means 'cutting white matter.'"

Libby, like every good reference librarian Bell had ever known, including the fabulous staff of the law library at Georgetown, where she'd received her law degree, always gave you more information than you wanted—or thought you wanted. But you never interrupted them or requested that they speed it up: Facts were sacred things to reference librarians, information a sort of Holy Grail, and so you listened with gratitude.

"In a leucotomy, a surgeon would drill burr holes in the area of the skull above a patient's frontal lobe and pull out cores of brain matter," Libby continued, wielding her voice as precisely and unemotionally as one of those surgeons would a cutting tool. "The patients had debilitating mental illnesses such as schizophrenia and what we now call PTSD and obsessive-compulsive disorder and clinical depression. The idea wasn't to cure the disease—but to eliminate the patient's emotional response to the symptoms. Freeman came along and dreamed up another way of doing it. A quicker, handier way. He'd slip a small scalpel-like instrument through the eye socket—right up under the eyelid—and sever the neural connections in the frontal lobe."

"Lobotomy," Bell said. The word sounded ugly on her tongue.

"Right. It made patients less agitated, less violent. More malleable." Libby's chin twitched. She was trying to stay professional about material that she clearly found disturbing. "Basically, less of a pain in the ass for the men who had to deal with them."

"So Freeman performed lobotomies in West Virginia?"

"West Virginia was the answer to his prayers."

"How so?"

Libby took a few seconds to compose herself before she continued. "Public hospitals in this state had a very large patient population. And zero medical oversight. Small budgets. Indifferent staff. In the 1940s and '50s, Freeman would roll in, set up shop, do a bunch of lobotomies, and then move on to the next hospital. Per capita, the number of lobotomies done in West Virginia was the highest in the nation."

"Jesus." Bell was shaken. "I had no idea."

"Not many people do." Libby put a hand on the top of one of the stacks. "It was well documented at the time, but the trouble was— and I'm going to be blunt here—nobody gave a damn. The patients in state hospitals in West Virginia were poor, and mostly female, and their mental illnesses weren't pretty.

"Here's an example," she went on, her voice gaining energy and momentum from what sounded to Bell like barely-tamped-down outrage. "Anesthesia was expensive—so guess how they sedated those poor West Virginians for surgery? Electroshock. Three quick jolts. Knocked 'em right out, and they didn't remember a thing."

Bell shuddered. "I used to play out at Wellwood when I was a kid. Never gave any thought to what was done in there."

"The medical director at Wellwood," Libby rolled on, ignoring Bell's remark, "was a doctor named Emmett Trexler. Freeman was his mentor at George Washington University Medical School. He'd demonstrated lobotomies to the class—it was the coming thing. The future of medicine. Once Trexler got the job running Wellwood, he invited Freeman to come and help him refine his technique. Trexler worshipped him. And Freeman put on a helluva show. He'd line 'em up, whip out his custom-made ice pick, and then dive in and destroy healthy brain tissue.

"Freeman's normal fee for doing a lobotomy was twenty-five hundred dollars—that's what he charged the families of his rich patients back in D.C. Here in West Virginia, though, he only charged twenty bucks a head. Such a deal!" She gritted her teeth with distaste before she could go on. "Hell—Freeman should've paid *them*. Look at all the great practice he got. And if a patient died—which happened from time to time, because Freeman worked fast and got pretty sloppy—well, *Oops*. Who gave a rat's ass? These were forgotten people. Throwaway people. People nobody cared about. The dregs."

She paused to take a few deep breaths. Bell had seen this before in Libby, back when they had discussed Utley Pharmaceuticals—a tendency to work herself up into a storm of controlled but still slightly scary rage. The world needed people like Libby Royster, Bell believed; they reminded others of the injustices, of the inequities, of what needed to change. They served as the world's conscience. But the price Libby paid for taking that role was high. Bell knew a bit about her personal life. Libby's divorce had come because, after a while, her husband had backed away from that intensity, that unremitting fierceness, as if it were a hot stove he'd touched with his bare hand once too often. He wanted a normal life. They still loved each other, but they had parted.

There was a time when Bell had considered herself to be that as well: a hard-charging, single-minded, self-appointed crusader. The noble warrior who was going to save Acker's Gap, save West Virginia. But Shirley's death had changed her. She couldn't save anybody. She could barely take care of herself.

Bell let the information sink in. "So were they monsters—Freeman and Trexler?"

Libby pondered her reply. "Monsters," she said, repeating the word as if she needed to consider it from a variety of angles before taking a position. "In one sense—yes, because what they did was horrific. Freeman wasn't even trained as a neurosurgeon. He overstepped his medical knowledge and lost his moral compass—because no one stopped him. But there's evidence that he and Trexler really did believe they were helping the patients they operated on. Mental illness brings terrible suffering. That was especially true back then, before the rise of psychotropic medicines. There's no doubt about that. So—monsters? No. Fatally misguided and damned arrogant and pretty slipshod with lives they didn't consider important? Yes.

"According to some accounts," she added, "Trexler had begun to change his mind about lobotomies by the late 1950s. But a staff member persuaded him to keep going. Keep operating. And so he did."

Libby pushed a stack of printouts across the table at Bell. "Take these home with you. I know you don't have much time, but you can just skim them. They'll give you context. They're from articles about the treatment of psychiatric patients in the 1940s and '50s. Lots of outrageous incidents from all over the country."

"Trexler, then, wasn't the only doctor who took Freeman's method and ran with it."

"Not at all. He was just the most prolific. The champ, you might say." Libby added a bitter coda: "And why not? His victims were West Virginians. So nobody cared."

Chapter Thirty-two

"Hey." Jake Oakes wheeled his chair up next to the crowded table. "I've been following your conversation from back there, but now it's my turn. Come and take a look at this."

"You found the article about Joe's grandmother?" Bell asked. She was glad to hear excitement in his voice. This was the old Jake.

"Yep. Took longer than it should have because I got a little distracted," he admitted sheepishly. "You'd be amazed at what happened around here in 1957 and '58. A few mysterious drownings, a couple of mine disasters, a kidnapping, a plane crash in Charm Lake—this place was *hopping*. And I had to check the papers for the next several years after Bessie Gilley's murder, too. Nobody was ever charged for the crime. Of course, they didn't have the services of Elkins, Oakes, and Fogelsong, now, did they?"

The three of them gathered around the microfilm reader. On the screen was a copy of the *Acker's Gap Weekly Gazette* dated Sunday, October 18, 1959. The lead story spread across the black-and-white page, the stiff black letters of its headline looking somewhat alarmed at the news they had been commandeered to impart:

LOCAL WOMAN FOUND DEAD AT WELLWOOD

Elizabeth Dresser Gilley, known as "Bessie" to her friends, 38, of Roberts Ridge, was found dead last Wednesday morning on the grounds of Wellwood Hospital. Foul play is suspected, said Sheriff Paul McCabe. He would provide no further details, but a source tells the *Gazette* that the deceased woman's skull was crushed by a heavy instrument. She was found by Ophelia Browning, administrative director of Wellwood. Miss Browning, upon making the gruesome discovery in a pile of leaves, immediately notified authorities. "We are all stunned and saddened by the loss of our dear colleague," Miss Browning tells the *Gazette*. "Our thoughts and prayers are with Mrs. Gilley's husband and son. We will miss our friend and colleague, and the entire Wellwood family joins me in wishing the Raythune County Sheriff's Department well as they try to solve this heinous crime. Let me add the condolences of Dr. Emmett Trexler, medical director of Wellwood, who did not know Mrs. Gilley personally, on account of the size of our staff, but who is nonetheless saddened at her untimely passing."

The deceased woman's purse was found at the scene, leading the sheriff to conclude that robbery was not the motive for the crime. He had no explanation for pen markings found on the palm of the deceased woman's left hand, which appeared to be names of unknown persons. There is some speculation that the indecipherable names might have been men with whom Mrs. Gilley had been having illicit carnal relations, although friends of hers denounced that theory.

She is survived by her husband, Craig Gilley, and her son, Nelson Gilley, 21. Services will be held at 10 A.M. next Tuesday at Lone Tree Church of the Nazarene, Black Bear Run, with the Rev. Levi Mayhew presiding.

There was a small photo of Bessie Gilley in the upper right-hand corner of the page. Bell searched it for a resemblance to Darla. Bessie had the same long, straight, dark hair, the same dark eyes, although black-and-white photographs, Bell reflected, always looked smudged and abstract. They tended to make everyone look like everyone else.

"Lots of unsolved crimes back then," Libby pointed out. "Primitive forensics. It's amazing, really, that they ever caught anybody for doing anything."

"Might be helpful to track down some of the people on the scene back then," Jake said. "How about this Sheriff McCabe? Is he still around?"

Bell shook her head. Sometimes she forgot that Jake wasn't born and raised in Acker's Gap, that he'd only arrived in his mid-twenties to take the deputy's job.

"Nope," she replied. "His name is notorious in these parts. Crooked as a dog's hind leg, as the saying goes. McCabe killed himself in 1961. Turns out he'd been helping himself to the departmental budget for years, to the tune of about twenty thousand dollars. That would've been a fortune back then."

"Sounds like a fortune right now," Libby murmured.

"Anybody else?" Jake asked.

"Well, let's see," Bell said, ruminating. "I know from going through the courthouse records for another case that McCabe only had one deputy throughout the 1950s. Leroy Sohovich."

"Where's he?"

"Thornapple Terrace," she answered, naming an Alzheimer's care facility in an adjacent county.

"Damn." Jake, frustrated, smacked the armrest of his wheelchair.

"How about some of Bessie's colleagues?" Libby suggested. "When I was researching Wellwood this morning, I found a company directory that covered the '40s, '50s, and early '60s. Right up to the fire in 1963."

They returned to the front of the library. Libby pulled a big leather-bound ledger from the middle of the stack she'd compiled for Bell.

"Here it is," she said, tapping a spot on a page with her index finger. "A staff roster from Wellwood. Emmett Trexler's right at the top, of course. I Googled him. He died in 1976 in Berkeley, California.

Ophelia Browning—she's dead, too. Died in a nursing home down in Georgia in the '80s."

Names from the diary came to Bell. "Bessie had a friend named Loretta Snavely. Maybe we can locate her."

Libby's eyes went up and down the rows on the page, and then the next page.

"There's no Loretta Snavely here."

"That's odd. Maybe I've got the last name wrong."

Libby checked again. "Nope. No Lorettas at all."

Bell switched tactics. "Okay, let's get back to Bessie's family. Is her brother Donnie still around?"

"I got that one," Jake said. "Searched the *Gazette* obits for Bessie's relatives." He tapped his notepad. "Donald Lawrence Dresser. Died in 1960, a year after his sister."

"Cause?" Bell asked.

"Suicide. Gunshot wound to the head."

"Was he ever a suspect in Bessie's murder?"

"Not that I·could tell from the follow-up articles. Sounds like a weird dude. Kept to himself. No friends, no wife, no kids, plus a reputation as a drinker. The suicide wasn't a shock."

Bell started to lecture him for sounding as childish as a Trump tweet: "Weird dude" could easily be a euphemism for gay. As a homosexual man in West Virginia in the late 1950s, Donnie Dresser would not have had an easy life. Maybe his sister's death gave him the final, fatal push over the edge.

But she held back. Jake wasn't here for lectures. "And her parents?" she asked.

"That one's mine," Libby said, as if she and Jake were a doubles tennis team and the other side had just served. "I checked the county death records. They both died in the '50s. Natural causes. Cancer and cancer. A matched set."

"Bessie's husband?"

"Died in 1971."

"Let me guess," Bell said. "Cancer."

"No. Craig Gilley had ALS. Lived the last decade of his life in a nursing home over in Banleigh County."

"So none of Bessie's friends or family members were ever serious suspects," Bell said. "Which means that, like everything else in this case—it all comes back to Wellwood."

"Speaking of Wellwood." Jake picked up a photocopied article on the top of the stack. It was from a regional history magazine, and the headline referred to the massive fire that had consumed the facility. "When it burned down in 1963, was there any suspicion of arson?"

"No," Libby answered. "The electrical system had never been updated—this was a state hospital, remember, and the budget was, like, nothing. A lightning strike turned the whole thing into an inferno. By then, the patients had all been transferred to other facilities. Lobotomy was reviled. New drugs were helping people with severe psychiatric illnesses. Trexler and Browning were long gone. And that was that.

"Wellwood was just a shell after the fire—a bunch of caved-in stone walls and a lot of bad memories. Nobody had any appetite to restore it. Vandals picked it clean. Time and weather did the rest. The woods closed over the road. It was a remote spot to begin with."

"Still think it was a mighty funny place to put a hospital," Jake muttered. "Out in the middle of nowhere."

"That was the whole idea." Libby snapped the reply. Her anger, Bell saw, had returned—directed not at Jake, but at hearts that were blacker than any soot-stained walls. "They didn't want prying eyes. Didn't want any witnesses to the awful business going on out there." She laughed a short, grim laugh, apparently to drive home the point she'd been making all morning. It was the same point she'd been making for years—the fact that Appalachians were endlessly exploited—and it might, Bell worried, end up consuming her one day, like the fire did Wellwood. "They didn't really have to bother, though. Nobody gave a damn, anyway."

Chapter Thirty-three

Shirley was dead. But that did not keep her from showing up just about everywhere Bell went—especially places such as the woods behind Briney Hollow, where Bell headed the next morning, with Arthur on a leash. It was cold but sunny. The sky was a curve of translucent blue, like the inside of a seashell.

She wasn't sure why she was here. She just knew that this was where she needed to be, in a place where other sounds fell away and she could sometimes hear her sister's voice. The stories that Libby had dug up about Wellwood haunted her.

Bell and Arthur walked at a brisk pace for twenty minutes or so. Arthur smelled everything; that was the chief challenge for Bell, pulling him away from the scintillating scents that called to him from the right, the left, ahead, and behind. She'd read once that a dog's nose was thousands of times more sensitive than a human's. She tried to imagine what woods like these—filled with the richly layered, dizzyingly complicated odors of animals and animal excrement and dead things and living things, too—would do to a dog's nose, overwhelming it with a bubbling fountain of smells, a smorgasbord of smells. Arthur, normally a rather reserved and sedate dog, was transformed out here; it was as if his nose was attached magnetically to the ground and the seal could not be broken. He didn't lift his nose for long minutes at a time, plowing ahead, his tail moving in crazy exuberant circles. Bell tugged on the leash when she needed to change direction, and Arthur would reluctantly change direction, too, having no choice, but otherwise he ignored her, this dog who never left her alone at home, who followed her from room to room— out here, she did not exist for him, other than as a slight occasional pressure tugging him this way or that. All he cared about were the divine, intoxicating scents, and getting to the bottom of them, which was impossible. But he had to try.

She passed the Monster Tree, which looked even more ghoulish now that its leaves had abandoned it, and she stepped across a small stream. The stream was so clear that she could see the dime-sized stones that lined its bed, rusty red and yellow striped and deep gray and bone white, polished by the water to a glossiness that she found breathtaking. Darla Gilley had played in these woods, too, as a girl; she would've known this stream, she might've plunged her hands in the icy water and pulled up stones just like these, and dried them against her jacket, and taken them home and arranged them in a se- cret box that she kept under the couch, because that was what Bell had done. One day Bell's father found the box; he laughed and opened the front door of the trailer and threw them out into the yard, box and all. *Rocks,* he'd muttered. *Keepin' a goddamned box of rocks.*

It didn't matter.

Arthur looked at her quizzically because they had stopped. He didn't know why. He wanted to go on. And he had a point: There were a lot more woods ahead, a dense scribble of pure possibility, ripe for exploring. Plus it was cold if you stood too long in one place. So on they went, Arthur's nose returning joyously to the ground.

Shirley had watched their father toss out the stones. She didn't say a word.

But that night, while Bell slept, Shirley crept out into the front yard and picked them up, one by one, by the faint light of the new moon. Next morning she waited until their father was preoc- cupied—it was easy, he was always sick in the mornings, and he raged and he moaned until he'd sloshed the liquor in his glass—and she put the beautiful stones into Bell's hand and made her close her fingers around them, and Shirley whispered, *Find a better hiding place.*

Arthur barked and insisted they go to the left, toward a giant log that had fallen and now—or so his nose told him—promised olfactory fireworks: the scintillating odors of decay and putrefaction.

She veered to the left. Arthur leapt merrily at the log.

She could remember the feel of Shirley's arm slung across her shoulders as they bounced along through these very same woods. She remembered the sound of Shirley's voice as she laughed or whispered or told funny stories. Shirley was ten years older and a lot taller, and so they didn't fit together terribly well when they walked side by side; there was an off-balance, hip-bumping clunkiness to their tandem stride, Shirley tilting slightly to accommodate Bell's smaller stature, keeping her little sister's shoulders cinched tight in her sideways embrace.

If Bell tried to break free—if she'd spot, say, a climbable tree just ahead and was wildly, passionately impatient to scale it—Shirley would playfully tighten her grip on her shoulders, murmuring, "Oh, no you don't. I've *got* you, little sister. You're mine, all mine! Never gonna let you go." Bell would squirm and twist, but Shirley was so much stronger, and it was only when Shirley laughed and said, "Oh, fine—go on!" and unhooked her long arm from Bell's shoulders that Bell could scoot away.

Don't do it, Shirley. Please don't let go of me. Ever. I don't really care about some stupid old tree. Just don't let go.

She really did believe sometimes that she could speak to Shirley. And that Shirley could hear. It was as if there was something inside one sister that would beckon to the other sister. As if nothing— especially not something as small and insignificant as death—could keep them apart.

Blood calls to blood. That was something their father said. It was one of the few things about him Bell could remember clearly, not fractured or distorted through a haze of fear: him saying that. He meant that family is destiny. Only he hadn't meant it in a sweet, wholesome, who's-bringing-the-cranberry-sauce-to-Thanksgiving way. He meant it, Bell now understood, in a dark, twisted, obsessive way: *Blood calls to blood.* You can't escape the taint of who you are, who you were born to. Don't even try. Blood will find you.

But she and Shirley had changed all of that. They'd changed the meaning. The bond they'd had was not dark or twisted. It was strong and bright. At the beginning it was that, certainly, and at the end. Maybe not in the long middle part, when Shirley was in prison, and wouldn't talk to Bell, and not in those first bad years after she was released, when her anger and resentment toward Bell reached a bitter crescendo. But in the end—yes. When it really mattered—yes.

Sometimes she missed Shirley so much she was afraid she'd burst into flame. Or start screaming and not be able to stop. In the first terrifying months after Shirley's death, Bell had felt as if she was living inside a kind of fog, and there was nothing solid, no edges to the world. Carla had given her the precious gift of not insisting that she "get over it." There was no getting over Shirley's absence. There was learning to live with it—but that was not the same as getting over it. Not the same at all.

She had not screamed, however. And her fears of bursting into flame had gradually gone away.

But what if they hadn't? What if she had fallen deeper and deeper into a trance of despair? So many of the women hauled off to Wellwood were, Bell surmised, simply less fortunate than she was, unable to control the compulsions that arose in the wake of some vast, spiraling grief, or some incorrect ratio of chemicals in the brain. Something that was not their fault. And so a husband or a father or a brother or a son had taken them to Wellwood to be "fixed." Improved. Quieted down.

It could've been me.

It could've been any woman.

She walked deeper and deeper into the woods, drawn by the invisible thread of memory and intuition. Arthur's tail grew even busier; it was indexed to the level of his excitement as he rooted around in the crackling piles of leaves, circled the trees and looked up searchingly into the branches. Something was up there. He could smell it. He could smell everything.

Soon they reached the clearing. Before them lay the ruins of Wellwood. All at once, Bell understood why she was here, the day after Libby's urgent and outraged history lesson, and why there was nowhere else she *could* be, in light of what she'd learned.

Chapter Thirty-four

She stood in the imaginary shadow of what had once been towering stone walls. Arthur had settled down; momentarily separated from the dazzling smells that ran wild in the woods, he was content to sit and pant. She reached down and patted the top of his head. When she finished, he licked her hand.

She thought about Darla Gilley. She thought about all the women who lived before Darla, too, the women brought to Wellwood because they would not behave. The women who were escorted up the stairs, one by one, and shown to their beds. The women who did not fit neatly in the world, and so had to be made to fit. The women who eventually were deemed well enough to go home. And the women who weren't.

Discovering what had been done in this place—in the name of science, in the name of healing—had drawn Bell back here today.

Back to the smoke-blackened walls that had encapsulated such anguish.

Back to a world dominated by a misguided, all-powerful doctor who dealt with human misery by creating another kind of misery, swapping out one wound for another.

But what did any of that have to do with Darla Gilley's death? Or Bessie's?

She waited.

Sometimes, when she was a prosecutor, Bell would go to a crime scene long after the experts had left, long after the yellow tape had been taken down and rolled up. She would stand in the place where a heinous act had been committed and she would try to see it in her mind's eye; she would watch it unfold, like pixels spreading across a page, image by image, forming the terrible picture.

Spaces had specific energies, she believed. They quivered with the endless vibration of everything that had occurred in their midst. If it *had* happened, it was still happening.

Rarely did she experience an epiphany while standing in the same spot where violence had ignited, where a life had ended. The epiphany would come later. It was as if she needed to soak up some essential knowledge, and take it home with her and live with it awhile, turning it over and over in her mind, before its true significance would emerge.

Arthur gave out a short yappy bark. He pawed the ground. He was right, Bell decided; it was time to go. Time to hike back to the road.

As they rambled across the familiar landscape, Bell had the same experience she'd had on her way in: She felt she could hear Shirley's voice and see her tall, agile figure just ahead, ducking under branches, jumping across streams. If Bell focused on the vivid particulars—her sister's laugh as it threaded through the woods, or the times when Shirley would stop and stare at the gray slate of mountains in the distance and then raise both arms, as if she wanted either to embrace them or tear them down, hug them or destroy them, Bell never knew which it was—then Shirley was here, right here. Always.

And maybe that was why she stayed in Acker's Gap.

Because blood calls to blood.

The moment she broke into the open, with the road just ahead, her cell cheeped. She had a message.

It was Nick. Sheriff Harrison, he told her, had found Briscoe at the motel, just where the trucker had promised he would be. Briscoe had surrendered the hatchet without incident. With gloved hands, Harrison had put it in an evidence bag and instructed Deputy Previtt to drive it over to the state crime lab in Charleston. He would deliver it in person to Barbara Masters, who was waiting for it.

In the meantime, the sheriff had suggested to Briscoe that he not leave the area. With a snicker and a jerk of his thumb toward the cocktail lounge next to the Holiday Inn—the sheriff's reports were always richly detailed, recording every nuance of an interview subject's behavior—he had said, *Sure thing.* And then he'd added another word under his breath: *bitch.*

Chapter Thirty-five

"Hey."

She knew the voice on the phone very well.

"Jake?" she said. "Is everything okay?"

She had already donned her nighttime outfit—winter edition—of baggy plaid sweats, even baggier gray sweatshirt, and thick wool socks, and had tucked herself into her favorite chair in the living room. The new *Atlantic* was in her lap and a cup of decaf was on the coffee table.

"Yeah. Well—no. Sort of. Just needed to talk for a minute."

So it wasn't an emergency. At least not the kind that would require her to abandon the gloriously mushy armchair.

Arthur had lifted his head at the sound of the phone. Bell leaned over and patted him. He had taken to settling in right next to her chair on evenings such as this, when the day's work was done and it was just the two of them, alone in this too-big house, her reading and him dozing. Their resemblance to an old married couple was not lost on Bell. She didn't share that with anyone, however, because it was a little pathetic, wasn't it? An old lady and her dog. Jesus.

Well, at least it's not a cat.

"Hope I'm not interrupting anything," Jake said.

"No." She closed the magazine.

Satisfied that all was well, or at least that his services weren't required at the moment, Arthur dropped his head back down again between his paws. The light snoring recommenced immediately.

"This isn't the kind of thing I can bring up at the office," Jake said. "I need to—wait. Hold on. I think I hear Malik. Put him to bed an hour ago but he's been pretty restless lately. Let me listen." Thirty seconds passed. "False alarm. He's still asleep. Here's the thing, Bell." Another pause. This one had nothing to do with Malik. "It's hard. Talking about certain subjects."

She waited. He would get to the point or he wouldn't; there was no use prodding Jake Oakes.

"I need your advice," he said.

"My advice." She repeated the word back to him and put a twist of amusement in her tone, hoping he'd see the joke: Advice from *her*? She was a convicted felon who probably couldn't get a fast-food job if they did a thorough background check. She was divorced and disbarred. She hadn't had a significant romantic relationship since— well, never mind. A long time. Put it that way.

"Yeah," he said.

"Why me?"

"You're a mom."

That threw her. "What's this about, Jake?" She pictured his face in the library. The information they'd unearthed had made his eyes light up, had made him lean forward expectantly in his chair, the way he usually did when the tantalizing elements of a case began to co-alesce. By the time he left the library, however, his enthusiasm had begun to wane. He had returned to the somberness that seemed to own him of late.

"Molly wants a child."

"Oh," Bell said. "Oh, my."

"It's a deal-breaker for her."

"Really? Molly said that? Doesn't sound like her."

"Well, no—not in so many words. But she implied it. And you know what, Bell? When she told me what she wanted, I realized that it's all wrong for me. I *don't* want a kid. I just don't. I love Molly, but I can't do that. I like our life the way it is."

"Jake, you really need to be talking to Molly about this. I'm not good at this kind of—"

"Wait. I'm not finished." He took a deep breath. "What I said—about me not wanting to have a child with Molly—well, that's how I felt at first. But then I thought about it. And I changed my mind. I told Molly that I was all in."

Bell was relieved, but still a bit confused. "So why did you call me, Jake? Sounds like a happily-ever-after if ever I've heard one. Here's a tip, though—if it's a girl, don't name her Belfa. She'll be correcting people her whole damned life. They never get it right."

He didn't laugh.

"Molly got a call this afternoon," he said. He waited, and then he rushed forward. "From her doctor. She can't have kids. There's practically no chance she'll ever conceive naturally." He made a snorting sound, a sound of disdain. "Hell of a thing, right? Just when I make up my mind to do it, to put aside all my doubts and my fears—this. *This.* It feels like a joke, you know? Like a big, sick, sad joke. Like a punch in the damned face."

"I'm sorry." She couldn't think of anything else to say. "I'm so sorry, Jake." She still didn't understand why he'd called her. They had never shared details of their personal lives. Not like this. Only what was necessary for their working relationship.

"So how do you do it?" he asked.

"What do you mean?"

"How do you let yourself be—be open and vulnerable, the way you have to be to think about having a kid, right?—when it hurts like this? God, Bell, I just—I've never felt so raw. I'm afraid I'm losing my edge."

"Your edge." She knew what he meant, but she wanted him to make the effort to explain it. That way, he'd realize that he already knew the answer. The answer was inside him. Answers to the real questions always were.

"Yeah," he said. "That edge. The thing that makes us able to do our jobs. Being tough enough to see what you saw as a prosecutor and what I saw as a deputy—all the death and pain and the sad crap that people go through, every day—without getting torn apart. We still need the edge, even though we're not doing those jobs anymore. Because of where we live. And what we do. I mean—you love your daughter, right?"

"Sure."

"Okay," he said. "So when she was a little girl—weren't you scared? All the damned time? Scared that the part of you that loves her would get too big and too soft and just—just take over your life? So that you couldn't do your job anymore because you were weak? Weren't you scared that loving her so much would put *both* of you at risk?"

"Yeah. I was."

"So what did you do?"

"I loved her anyway."

Through the phone line she could hear his breathing, steady and regular, with a slight trace of huskiness to it. Normally he kept himself under tight control. It was an effort, she knew, to be as breezy as Jake Oakes pretended to be. It cost him.

He had let himself go for these few seconds he had spoken to her like this, and it must have been terrifying for him.

"You loved her anyway," he said. "Pretty simple, huh?"

"Not simple at all. Hardest thing I've ever had to do."

"But it got easier, right?"

She chuckled. "Nope. Sorry. Only gets harder. Carla's an adult now and I don't see her every day—but when I think about her, I feel like I'm walking around without any skin." Another soft laugh. "I'm tormented, pretty much all the time."

"Jesus. So who in their right mind would ever fall in love or have a kid?"

"Damned if I know, Jake. Damned if I know."

Chapter Thirty-six

The first serious snow of the season came two days later, shortly after 4 P.M. At first it was just fluttery bits of white, but the flakes became steadily bigger, wetter, and heavier, with a ponderousness to their fall. The color of the sky changed from gauzy blue to stark white. It was a sky that promised more snow was on the way, and more after that, too.

By the time Bell walked from her car to the office on Main Street, her coat was soaked from melting snow. Her hair looked as if she'd just stepped out of the shower.

Jake and Nick sat at the round table, a sheet of much-written-on paper in front of them.

"Looks like you've already started," Bell said. "What do we have so far?" She kept her coat on. The space heater in the corner gamely whirred and hummed, but it was no match for the cold coming through the front window and the walls.

Nick, ever the daredevil, had taken off his coat and slung it across the back of his chair. "Pulled out our list of suspects again. Even if none of these people killed Darla, some of them are not telling us everything they know. They're holding back. We have to find out why." He put his coat back on. "No use being a hero," he muttered. "Damned cold in here."

Bell looked at Jake. Nothing on his face gave away the fact that they'd had an extraordinarily personal phone conversation recently, during which he'd shared with her the intimate details of his life with Molly.

"Let's get to work," Jake said brusquely. "I've got to leave pretty soon. Have to run an errand."

It was what she'd expected from him, and it was a relief. That was then; this was now. And they had a case to solve.

"So the way I see it," Nick said, "we've got a couple of ways to go here. Following the theory that you're most likely to be killed by folks you know—happy thought, right?—first person we've got to consider is Thad Connell. The ex-husband."

"And Joe and Brenda," Bell said. "Brother and sister-in-law."

Nick winced. "Come on. Joe? He's dying. He can't lift a carton of milk. How the hell would he fling an ax?"

"He wouldn't be the first person to outsource a murder," Bell countered. "Agreed?"

He waited. "Agreed," he said. "Okay, so—in the category of relatives, we've got Thad, Brenda, and Joe. Thad has a decent alibi. Joe, I'd argue, is too weak. He can't drive. And there's no motive."

"How about Brenda?" Jake asked.

Nick tapped pencil tip against paper. He didn't like using a computer. He was an old-school note-maker. "Motive?"

"Maybe she was jealous of Darla's relationship with Joe. They were close," Jake answered. "She stuck Darla in the attic, right? Not too friendly, you ask me."

"To be fair, she explained that," Bell said. "Said it was Darla's request."

Jake made a snickering noise in the back of his throat to indicate his skepticism. "Yeah, right—she *explained* it. We can't exactly check out that story with Darla, now, can we? Brenda's got no real alibi. Says she was home with Joe that night, after they got back from his doctor's appointment. But he's a cancer patient. Sleeps most of the time. How hard would it be to sneak out while he was dead to the world? Not hard at all. He's already got a foot in the grave." He looked over at Nick. "Hey, sorry. He's your friend. I didn't mean to be—"

"Forget it." Nick tapped the paper again with his pencil tip.

"Anyway, you're right. Brenda doesn't have a solid alibi. Just her word. Okay, moving on to non-family." He looked down at the paper. "Briscoe. He's definitely hiding something. Is it a big something or a small something? We'll know soon enough, when the state crime lab tells us if that hatchet of his could've been the murder weapon. Okay—who else?"

Bell let out a frustrated sigh. "Face it. The 'what else' is what we're all dreading. What if it was just some random, unknown assailant who happened to be in the woods that day? Someone with no connection to Darla? Who then left the area? In that case—we're screwed. End of the line."

They sat in a gloomy silence.

Jake was the first one to break it.

"So what's next?"

"According to Brenda," Bell said, "Darla was meeting somebody at JP's that afternoon. Nick, did you talk to Jackie about that yet?"

He looked at her. Something moved in his face.

Does he know that I've got a hunch about him and Jackie? Bell wondered.

Didn't matter. They had work to do. Nick's private life was beside the point.

"Yeah," he said. "It's in my notes. She doesn't remember Darla sitting with anyone in particular. But says it's possible. It was a busy afternoon."

"How about the register receipts for that afternoon?" Bell pressed him. "That'll tell us who was there."

Nick spread out his hands, palms up. "Most everybody paid in cash. So very few credit card receipts. Jackie's checking with her staff, though—and with some regulars—to see if anybody can recall who Darla was talking to."

Another spell of silence.

Bell stood up abruptly. She paced for a minute, both to revive circulation in her very cold feet and to change the topic.

"There's something else that's bothering me," she said. "I'd appreciate hearing what you two think about it."

"Do tell," Nick said. Jake grunted, which was his way of echoing Nick's assent.

"All right. Here goes. I read Bessie's diary, right? Every word of it. She went to great lengths to get it to us. When I first read the cover letter, I thought, 'Wow, this is going to be a bombshell. Whatever's in here might very well have gotten Darla killed. Somebody didn't want it to be made public.' I was thinking, you know, illegitimate babies, payoffs to public officials. That kind of thing. But it *wasn't* a bombshell. I mean, yes, it was sad, and it told a lot about the sorry history of Wellwood. And yes, it sounds as if Bessie and her colleagues knew on some level that Trexler was doing lobotomies and it didn't sit right with her. But nobody at the time seems to have understood just how truly terrible the procedure really was. They were ignorant—not evil. So why is the diary so critical? It doesn't reveal a smoking gun."

"Or even a smoking ice pick," Jake cracked.

Nick groaned, then grew serious again. "Now that you mention it, Bell, I see what you mean. When I read it, I thought it was a little disappointing, too. Like she was holding back on some things. It wasn't exactly Watergate."

"Right," she agreed. "And Bessie was mostly an observer, not a participant. I can't think of anyone who would've gone to all the risk and trouble of killing Darla just to keep those details quiet."

"Unless," Nick said.

"Unless what?"

He had put his pencil down. He rolled it back and forth across the paper while he spoke. "Remember how many times in the diary Bessie scolds her brother for reading it? Actually addresses him, calls him out, in case he is?"

"Yeah. And then Bessie says she's going to outsmart him."

"She was driven to keep a diary—she said as much—but she also wanted to keep her privacy. Donnie was apparently a serial diary sneak. What would be the best way to get him off the trail? So that she could record her real thoughts but also have her privacy?"

Bell sat back in her chair. "A *second* diary. A true one. One that Donnie didn't know about."

"Exactly," Nick said. "Donnie might not have known—but maybe, all these years later, Darla *did* know. Somehow, she found out about it."

"Wouldn't she have told Joe?" Bell said.

Jake decided he'd been quiet long enough. He had to leave soon, but the next place he needed to be was close by: Evening Street Clinic. He could do his job first.

"I can answer that one—nope," he said. "Telling Joe meant telling Brenda. They're a married couple in their sixties—believe me, they tell each other everything. It's practically a law of physics. And Darla, let's remember, didn't much care for Brenda. That might turn out to be a real good call."

"What do you mean?" Bell asked.

"In your report about the night of Darla's death—when you and Nick went out to Joe Gilley's house—you mentioned the Christmas tree. The one they'd put up early this year because of Joe's condition."

She nodded.

"Well," Jake went on, "you said Brenda told you she'd gotten it right there on the property."

Bell and Nick realized his point simultaneously, but Jake still finished his thought:

"How do you cut down a Christmas tree? Most folks use an ax, am I right?"

Chapter Thirty-seven

Four months ago, Molly Drucker and her EMT squad partner, Ernie Edmonds, had answered a call for a possible cardiac arrest. The address was 612 Donnelly Lane, located in a relatively affluent neighborhood on the east side of Acker's Gap.

When they arrived at the brick Colonial with the detached two-car garage and the yard that included visible evidence of ongoing ministrations by a landscaping service, they entered and found thirty-two-year-old Malcolm McComas sitting on his couch, his left hand pushing a small pillow against his belly, a sour look on his face. His wife, Linda McComas, stood next to the couch, holding the cordless phone with which she'd called 911.

"He says he's fine now. In fact, he's mad at me for calling you," Linda said.

"We get that a lot." Hands on hips, Molly turned to Malcolm. She looked him square in the face. "Sir? I gather you're feeling better now?"

"It's acid reflux." Dismissal in his tone. "Look—my wife just panicked. There's nothing wrong with me."

Linda broke in. "He was moaning. Said his chest felt like some-body was stepping on it. And his father died of a heart attack at fifty. *Tell* them, Malc."

"I'm fine. I feel great. You want me to run around the block? Prove it to you?"

"Malc, I wish you'd just let these people do their—"

Molly held up a hand.

"Okay, Mr. McComas," she said, smoothly and calmly. "Here's the deal. I can't force you to let my partner and me examine you. And it's true—you look like you've recovered from whatever it was that gave your wife such a scare. But let me be honest here. I've seen men just as fit-looking as you are experience some mild chest pain, then come to the same conclusion: False alarm, I'm A-OK, I don't need anything, nosiree. So they go to bed. And then sometime in the night, the little valve in the heart that's narrowing—which is what gave you the pain—snaps shut altogether. By the time we get back here, it's too late."

The face he showed her was filled with doubt. The irritation was gone.

"So what should I do?" he asked.

"We'll look you over. And then we'll take you to the hospital."

"What if it's nothing?"

"Then we'll all have a good laugh. Ernie here will buy you a beer."

"I will," Ernie put in.

Malcolm let go of the pillow. He handed it to his wife. "Okay," he said.

Three hours later, he was being prepped for surgery at the Raythune County Medical Center. Multiple blockages had been discovered in the arteries of his heart.

Linda McComas was very grateful to Molly Drucker. "Not only did you do your job," she pointed out the first time they got together, at Linda's invitation, for coffee at the Chimney Corner restaurant in Blythesburg, "but you did it by virtue of superb negotiating skills. Malc doesn't listen to *anybody*. If you'd come in that night with guns blazing and insisted that he go to the hospital—he would've flat-out refused. But you didn't. And so he listened. And so he's alive."

Molly waved away both the thanks and the compliment. She wasn't sure why she'd agreed to have coffee with this woman. But during that initial conversation, she learned that Linda was a case worker for

Raythune County Child Protective Services, and that created an instant bond: Molly had seen the good work done by the agency. She'd had to contact them on some of her squad runs, when she and Ernie came across kids in unbelievably squalid circumstances.

That day at the Chimney Corner, she told Linda about Malik. Linda told her about some of the children that broke her heart.

They both knew the dire problems of Raythune County. They knew them from the inside, from stepping across syringe-littered kitchens to reach crying babies who had been neglected for days, from finding toddlers hiding in closets and clutching ratty stuffed animals to their ears to block out the sounds of gunshots. And yet they both maintained an optimism that sometimes felt incredibly fragile, gossamer-thin, but that was, when you considered the assaults of reality that it endured, amazingly tough and resilient.

Which was why they had become good friends.

Which was why, when Molly had received the news from her doctor that she was unlikely ever to conceive a child, the second person she had called—Jake was first, of course—was Linda McComas.

Linda had offered sympathy and understanding and love. And then she had offered something else: a plan.

Chapter Thirty-eight

"This friend of yours. Does she know I'm in a wheelchair?" Jake asked.

"I don't know."

"You don't know?" He jerked his head backward, to indicate disbelief.

"I told her you were handsome and funny and smart and honest and that you were really good with Malik. Not sure I mentioned the wheelchair part. We haven't been friends long enough to get to the nonessentials."

He sulked a bit. "Okay, now I feel like a big jerk."

Molly smiled. "My work here is done." She leaned over and kissed him.

It was closing in on 7 P.M. They sat next to each other in Glenna Stavros's office in Evening Street Clinic, Jake in his chair, Molly in one of the two matching metal ones that barely fit in the small space alongside the desk. This was the appointment that Jake had mentioned to his colleagues that afternoon.

He had an inkling of what this might be about, but he didn't let himself speculate. All he knew for sure was that he was finally going to meet the McComas person that Molly had mentioned several times. Molly had asked him to show up at Evening Street by 6 P.M.

So here he was.

He'd been here previously, back in his deputy days. Twice. Or maybe three times. He wasn't sure. He had brought ailing newborns here, kids born to drug-addicted moms, in emergency situations, when the EMTs had their hands full. One of the infants died. That, he remembered. A little girl. The nurses here assured him it wasn't his fault, that she'd had no chance. Her death did not occur because he hadn't moved fast enough.

Still, when he got home that night, he cried. He never cried. But he did that night.

The moment he arrived here today, it all came back to him in a gush of sensual familiarity, the sounds and the look and the feel, even the smell: something astringent and medicinal, plus baby powder, plus a faint underlayment of shit. Chronic diarrhea, he knew, was among the ailments these infants suffered from. He remembered the steady *whish-WHISH* of the machinery, the beeps. The nurses' murmured conversations. The fussing of the infants, the whines, sometimes a low moan that went right through you, like a miniature shock wave, to think of a child in such pain.

Molly's friend Linda was late, which annoyed him—hey, *we're* here on time, he thought, so it looks like she could be a little more considerate—but then Molly reminded him that Linda worked for Child Protective Services and she never knew what her day would bring. *Neither do you,* he'd pointed out. And Molly replied: *Yeah, but when I'm off duty, I'm off duty. Linda's never really off duty. If it's a kid she's responsible for—she goes.*

So they waited.

They could see Glenna Stavros, the nurse who had led them back to her office, across the room, in the middle of a circle of nurses, going over a chart.

He wished he were working. He wished he could've gone along with Bell and Nick tonight to Roberts Ridge, to have another talk with Brenda Gilley. But he had promised Molly he'd come.

A flurry of beeps erupted from one of the cribs across the room. Jake was startled. Molly reached for his hand. As they watched, two nurses hurried over to a crib in the middle of the second row. That was all Jake and Molly could see from where they were. In a few minutes, the beeps resumed their normal rhythm, and the nurses withdrew. Molly's hand slid out of his. He wished she had left it there; Molly rarely seemed to need anything from him, and it had felt good to be helping her in some small way, just as she was helping him, by holding hands in a tense moment.

"Linda will be here soon," Molly said.

He nodded.

A few minutes later McComas arrived. She was as small and bright as a new penny, and with her short, copper-colored hair she even *looked* like a penny, Jake thought, albeit one in a matching coral skirt and sweater and a beige wool winter coat. She moved with a brisk perkiness that put him slightly off-balance. Given her job, he had expected someone dour and heavy and depressed-seeming, but that was not what Linda McComas was like at all; she had a lightness about her, as if she had found a mysterious source of optimism that never ran out, a sort of cold fusion for the soul.

After the hellos she went away for a moment. She came back with Glenna Stavros. The nurse was holding a breathtakingly small baby in her arms, white cap on his head, white booties on his tiny feet, white diaper around his midsection.

"This is Casey Krieger," McComas said. "His mother missed her last court date. Which probably means she's using again. That's a tragedy—but *her* tragedy doesn't have to become *his* tragedy. I'd like you all to consider asking the court to award you permanent custody of Casey, after a period of foster care. I don't know what the judge will say. But in the meantime, I thought it couldn't hurt for you all to meet him."

Glenna started to hand the baby to Molly, but Molly shook her head and touched Jake's arm. The nurse took her meaning: him first.

Later Molly would admit to Jake that she had been here the day before, with Linda McComas. She had already held Casey.

Before Jake quite knew what was happening, the baby was placed against his chest. The nurse held him there until Jake could get his own hands into place to secure Casey, one hand on his head, another on his bottom. He could feel the heat emanating from the small body. At that point Glenna let go and backed away, and Jake was now totally responsible for the infant he held. He couldn't let go. If he did, Casey would slip out of his hands and onto the floor.

At first that idea filled him with fear and dread and a panic that clawed at his mind—*Oh my God, I can't let go*—but gradually he realized something else: He didn't want to let go. And that was a different feeling altogether.

Chapter Thirty-nine

"What about your recusal?" Bell asked.

"I'm still recused." Nick held the "u" sound a bit too long, his way of making fun of the excessively legalistic word that represented, nonetheless, a valid point. "I'll talk to Joe while you deal with Brenda."

They had almost reached the farmhouse. The night was dark, and the patches of unmelted snow on both sides of the road glittered at the moment they were hit with the headlights of Bell's Explorer. They were in an in-between season now, when the weather made wild swings in either direction; there might be five inches of snow one day, followed by a day so warm and glorious that it felt as if someone had put away a piece of summer for safekeeping long ago and now unpacked it in dank, surly November.

As Bell parked in the long gravel drive, her cell went off.

"Hey, Pam," she said, having checked the caller ID. She listened for a few seconds. "Okay. Thanks. Got it." She clicked off the call, turned to Nick. "Masters eliminated Briscoe's hatchet as a possible murder weapon. Took her all of about thirty seconds. Something about the dimensions of the blade."

"So he was telling the truth." Nick reached for the door handle. "About one thing, at least. Not about everything. Just because he didn't kill Darla doesn't mean he had nothing to do with her death."

Bell shoved his shoulder. Teasing Nick was a harmless pleasure. "You just don't like him because of that whole salad thing. Come on—at least it wasn't kale."

They hadn't called first this time, and Brenda's face when she opened the door went from pissed off—who'd come calling this late?—to hopeful, when she saw that it was them.

"You found out who did it?"

"No," Nick replied. "Nothing like that."

"I just need to see the attic again," Bell said quickly. "And ask you a few more questions, if that's okay."

Brenda brought them into the living room. Joe dozed in the recliner, his hollowed-out body easily pinned beneath the weight of two blankets. The lights of the Christmas tree gave the room a jaunty, festive air; it clashed with the reality of the dying man in its midst, the one who wheezed through an uneasy sleep that seemed too much a foretaste of the final one.

"Mind taking me up there?" Bell asked.

Brenda's worried eyes shifted toward Joe.

"I'll stay down here with him," Nick said. "It'll be fine."

That satisfied her. "There's coffee," she told him. "And plenty of food in the fridge, if you're hungry."

Brenda led Bell up the stairs to the second floor, and then on up to the attic.

"Here you go." She stood to one side. "I haven't been back up since the last time you were here. Once I'd thought about it, I guess it did seem a little . . . well, a little too soon. I don't know what was going on with me before. I was half out of my head with the shock. I do crazy things these days. Taking care of Joe, thinking about poor Darla—it's made me forget what I'm supposed to be doing. I found a gallon of milk in the cabinet the other day. I'd put it there instead of the fridge. Just absentminded as all get-out—that's me." She put a hand to the side of her head, smoothing down her hair. "You don't need to listen to me go on and on. Just tell me what you need."

Bell waited, and then she said, "After my sister died, I lost my car keys four times in a row. I wrote the wrong year on checks. And one night I took a walk in my own neighborhood—and couldn't remember how to get home. The streets were like a maze. Finally it came back to me, but while it lasted, it was . . . pretty terrifying."

"That's the word. Terrifying." There was relief in Brenda's voice. "So you get it. I'm not going crazy."

"I do get it. And you're not going crazy. Mind if I look around?"

Brenda stepped to one side. The massive wall of furniture and boxes looked just as steep and unyielding to Bell as it had before, the material version of a family's long history, packed tight to protect it against time and loss. The bed and nightstand were still in the corner, smaller and frailer than they would have seemed had they not been dwarfed by the towering piles.

"That bed—was it already up here when you moved in with Joe?"

"Oh, yes," Brenda answered. "It belonged to Joe and Darla's grandmother, Bessie. She used to sleep up here when she was growing up. The old bedframe and mattress are hers, too. Theresa Dresser carved that headboard—see the little bird? I think it's supposed to be a cardinal. The design's a little crooked, but at least somebody tried to make it pretty." She peered at the bed. "That's funny."

"What?"

"Oh, it's nothing. Just that there's a pillowcase missing. See? Two pillows, but only one has a pillowcase. I didn't notice it till now because the pillowcase is white, too, just like the pillows. Those pillowcases are over a hundred years old. They were sewn by Joe's great-great-*great*-grandmother, Gertrude."

She turned around to face Bell again. There was a change in her face. She didn't want to talk about pillowcases.

"I need to speak my mind here, Mrs. Elkins."

"Bell. Please."

"Okay. Bell it is." Brenda drew her lips in tight, making a straight line of her mouth, and she held it for a few seconds before releasing it so that she could continue. When she spoke, the words came quickly: "I know you."

"Pardon?"

"The things you were saying just a minute ago. About grief. About what it does to you. I know how you know that. I didn't want to say anything that night you and Nick came over—the night Darla died—

because it wasn't the time. There was already so much sadness in this house because of Darla. But I want you to know—Nick told me the story. A long time ago." Brenda clasped her hands in front of her corduroy skirt. She made the line with her mouth again. Swallowed hard, and then resumed: "You were ten years old and you killed your daddy. He was messing with you and your sister. That's what I heard. And so you protected yourself."

Brenda waited for Bell to respond. When she didn't, she went on, anyway, as if she didn't want to change direction even though the road had become treacherous.

"It's a terrible thing," Brenda said, her voice low and solemn, "when something happens to you when you're young and you can't defend yourself properly. Terrible." She shook her head. "Joe doesn't like to talk about it, you know, but it happened to somebody in his family. To his great-uncle Donnie."

"What?"

"Joe told me about it right after we got married. Donnie was Grandma Bessie's brother. He went to work at a car repair place in Acker's Gap when he was barely more than a boy. The owner was a man named Larry Kinnamin. Anyway, everybody knew why Larry hired young boys to work for him—and it wasn't about them being good with cars. But nobody in this house much cared what was going on. Not if Donnie brought home a paycheck. Families around here were bad off in those days. Heck—what am I saying? Families around here aren't much better off *these* days, either. But I pray to the good Lord that they don't use it as an excuse anymore to—to let their children suffer."

Bell's mind was moving rapidly. Bessie's diary had mentioned her brother Donnie and his job at Kinnamin's—but it said nothing about any allegations of sexual abuse. Just as it hadn't mentioned the fact that Bessie's mother had once been committed to Wellwood.

The diary had left out key information about the family. Key— and *negative* information. Bessie had censored herself. She was compelled to write her life story, but she was afraid to tell the truth—at least in the diary Bell had read.

"You sound as if you like children," Bell said. "And yet you and

Joe never had a family." When she'd first taken the prosecutor's job she had hated asking people personal questions. Now it came as naturally to her as breathing. People, she'd discovered, didn't mind talking about themselves and their troubles; in fact, they seemed almost grateful when you asked. It was as if, by taking the sad things in life—the clumsy accumulation of outsized sorrows and seething fears—and forming them into sentences, you robbed them of some of their power to wound you. Talking about them brought them down to a human scale.

It had been true for her, just now, when Brenda brought up her father's death and that long-ago night, the night everything changed for her and Shirley. Bell hadn't answered, but she was aware of a distinct feeling of relief, as if someone had opened a window in a stuffy room.

"Joe wanted children," Brenda said. "It was me. I was . . . *afraid.* Yes. I was afraid. His family—well, let's put it this way. I loved Joe, but I could tell that he and Darla had a shadow over them. A shadow they couldn't get out from under. I was afraid of inflicting that on a child. Afraid that any children of Joe's would have the same . . ." She was searching for a word. "The same sadness. Built-in sadness. Like a disease. I didn't want to pass that on."

Brenda looked around the overstuffed attic again before continuing. "I never wanted to move into this house. And at first we didn't—did you know that? Well, of course not. How could you? Anyway, we got married and we had a little apartment over in Chester. Oh, that was a time. My favorite time. But then Joe was laid off—he worked at the Raven shoe factory. Did a good job but they closed it down. Money got real tight and Joe's parents were gone and this big old house was just sitting here and so . . ." She gave Bell a rueful smile. "Thirty-eight years later, here we are."

"The Christmas tree."

"What?"

Bell didn't like knowing it, but she knew—from all those interviews she'd done as prosecutor, trying to get people to admit to things against their better judgment—that a quick change of topic worked better than waterboarding when it came to breaking through a facade. You surprised the truth out of them.

"The Christmas tree downstairs. You said you chopped it down. Where's the ax?"

Startled, Brenda blinked several times while an expression of bafflement spread across her broad face. Then she laughed.

"Oh—now I see! You think I killed Darla."

"No. I have no idea if you did or you didn't. Just need to know about the ax."

"Don't have one. Joe sold his tools right after his diagnosis. He knew he'd never use them again."

"Then how'd you chop down the tree?"

"I didn't." Her voice gathered momentum as she spoke, a snowball rolling downhill. "What I told you the first night you came over here is that I *picked out* the tree on our property. I didn't say I cut it down. That was the neighbor boy. Timmy Blevins. He's eleven years old. I paid him twenty dollars. Go ask him. I'd like to say he's saving that money for college, but I happen to know he bought a used fishing pole with it. I like Timmy. You know why? There's no shadow on him. No shadow at all."

Brenda was breathing heavily now. "I don't mind you asking me that," she continued. "I know you had to. You and Nick are trying to find out who killed Darla. But let me be real clear with you. It's true—I wasn't thrilled about the fact that Darla had moved back here. She and I were never close. Never. Barely cordial, really. Different personalities, I guess I'd say. But you know what? The reason I didn't want her back here had nothing to do with *me*. It had to do with *her*."

"I don't understand."

Brenda's voice had a strained, tentative quality to it. She was trying hard to make her point but wasn't sure she had the proper words to do it with.

"Darla had a lot of spirit to her. And she made it out. She'd broken away from her family. I don't mean the actual *people* in the family, because there was nobody left but Joe, and they were as close as can be. I mean the generations before her and Joe, going back and back. That shadow—*that's* what I mean. Their great-grandmother Theresa—she'd been a patient at Wellwood once, did you know that? From the sound of it, from the stories Joe heard from his father, who'd heard them from Bessie, she had postpartum depression. But in those days, they didn't have much patience for new mothers who stayed in bed and didn't eat and just sighed a lot. They told them to cheer up. Or they sent them to a mental hospital—like Wellwood. Joe remembers stories about cold baths and shock treatments and all kinds of awful things. This was the 1920s. Couldn't be worse for a poor woman with the baby blues—except it *did* get worse at Wellwood, later on. They came up with new ways to make 'em behave. That's what Joe heard, anyway, from his father. The whole family was just caught up in this—this darkness, this idea that nothing was ever going to get better."

"Except for Darla."

"Yes—except for Darla. She beat the shadow. She got out. Even when she was having all that trouble with Thad, she was living her own life. I admired that. But coming back here, it was like she was stepping right back into the dark place. I held out hope for a while that she might move on—on to a life somewhere else. Maybe this was just temporary. She never officially changed her address at the post office or on her driver's license. Hadn't gotten around to it yet, which made me think maybe she was waiting to do that until she'd settled somewhere permanently. But I don't know. I just don't know.

"Joe and I—we never had a choice," she went on. "We had to be here. Darla, though—she was *free*. And then she moved back in and . . . it grabbed her. Like it had been waiting for her all along. Waiting to spring."

With the back of her hand, Brenda wiped roughly at the tears that had spilled onto her cheeks while she talked. "You take your time up here. Do what you need to do. I'll be downstairs." She groped for a wadded tissue in the front pocket of her skirt, drew it out, blew her nose. "I've known Nick Fogelsong just about my whole life. Best judge of character I know—which is what made him a good sheriff, I'll wager. And he says you're a smart woman. Good at your job.

Well, I hope that's right. Because you've got to find out who did this to Darla. It's the only way to do it."

"The only way to do what?"

"The only way to get rid of that shadow, once and for all."

Chapter Forty

Alone in the attic, Bell checked her cell. Great: full bars.

She Googled the number of the Holiday Inn on the interstate and instructed her cell to make the call. She asked for Roger Briscoe's room. He answered on the first ring.

"Mr. Briscoe, my name's Belfa Elkins. You talked to two associates of mine, Nick Fogelsong and Sheriff Harrison."

"Yeah. What of it?"

"We're tying up some loose ends. First, your hatchet wasn't the murder weapon. We'll be returning it to you shortly."

"Screw you, lady." He belched. "Told you folks I had nothing to do with what happened to that lady."

"We had to be thorough. I'm sure you can understand that. I do have another question, though. How did you know where to return Darla's purse? How'd you know where she lived?"

"Already explained it. I looked at the address on her driver's license."

"That was her old address. She was getting a divorce. She wasn't living there anymore, but she hadn't yet changed the address on her license to the house on Roberts Ridge. So I'll ask you again, Mister Briscoe—how'd you know where Darla lived?"

He mumbled a few curses. "Shit, lady—I promised her I wouldn't say nothing. You're asking me to go back on a promise I made to a dead person."

"It's important."

More mumbled curses. "All right. All right. It's like this. I picked her up in Acker's Gap. She just looked so pitiful, standing there in front of that diner. We're not supposed to take any riders, but—well, it was so damned cold, and she kinda reminded me of my own mama, what with that long black hair and them eyes. Anyway, I did it. She got in and I asked her where she was headed. She said, 'Two places.' I laughed. I said, 'Lady, don't you know the rules of hitching? You get one place. Not two.' She was real upset though, and crying and all, and so I said, 'Hell, lady, I got some extra time. Gimme the first address.' Took her just where she said she wanted to go—out to Roberts Ridge. Big old farmhouse. I waited while she went inside. Didn't look like nobody was home. She came out a few minutes later. Holding something. Looked like an old pillowcase. I said, 'What's that?' She said, 'I can't tell you.' So I said, 'Well, as long as it ain't nothing illegal, I guess I don't care.' And then I took her to the second place she wanted to go."

"Where was that?"

"Briney Hollow. She asked me to let her out right where them woods start up. I was worried about her, what with the cold, but she said, 'I'll be okay. And thanks.' She was holding real tight to that pillowcase when she got down outta the cab. I think that's maybe how she forgot her purse. Last I saw of her, she was heading into the woods."

"And she never told you why she wanted to go there."

"Nope. Just got more and more agitated, the closer we got to them woods."

Chapter Forty-one

I am Darla Gilley.

Bell stood in the center of the attic, trying to channel the mind and heart of a woman she'd never met—not formally, that is. Over the years she had surely passed Darla on the streets of Acker's Gap, or in the courthouse or JP's or Lymon's Market; surely they had occupied the same general spaces at the same general times, for at least a few moments over the decades. Acker's Gap was not a large place.

She pictured Darla's long dark hair, her glasses, her earnest, curious expression. Her personality. Feisty, Nick said. She'd kept her maiden name. She'd loved Thad Connell, but when he didn't seem to love himself enough to change his self-destructive ways, she decided to divorce him. A difficult choice to make in this area, a place where few women kept their own names when they married, where divorce caused whispers and judgments—mostly against the woman, not the man.

Bell focused:

I am Darla Gilley.

If Bell's theory was correct, and Bessie had indeed started a second diary, then Darla had somehow found it and taken it with her—in the last hours of her life. Which meant that Bell was trying to prove a negative: She needed to ascertain the existence of something that wasn't here anymore.

But *had* Darla found it and removed it?

Bell tried to imagine the scene. She tried to put herself in Darla's shoes, tried to channel Darla's thoughts and feelings on the day that, unbeknownst to Darla, would be the last time she was ever to stand in this place:

I've figured it out. The diary I mailed to Nick is not the only secret kept by Bessie Gilley. Somehow—between the time I left this attic and rode with Brenda into Acker's Gap, and the moment I climbed up into that nice man's truck—it came to me:

Bessie kept another diary.

Was that how it went? Bell wondered. Yes. The lightning bolt of insight had struck Darla sometime *after* she left the attic that afternoon, bound for the post office and, following that, a meeting with somebody at JP's.

Who had she met at the diner? Bell recalled the stranger who'd come in that night in the Carhartt bibs, the man with the unruly red hair and the starburst beard. And the regular customers, the ones who sat at the counter, hunched over their plates of food. And the guy who dropped off the fresh produce each day from Lymon's Market. Could it have been—

No way to tell. So table that for the moment.

Leaving the diner, Darla was desperate. That was how Briscoe had described her: nervous, frantic, preoccupied. And Bell knew why: Darla *had* to find the second diary. For some reason, that was what she had to do. And she had to do it fast.

It was a lucky break for Darla that Brenda and Joe had left for Joe's appointment at the doctor. But they might be back any minute. And Briscoe—he would be getting antsy, waiting in his truck outside.

I am Darla Gilley.

Bell's eyes scoured the room, honing in on particulars. There were untidy Everests of boxes and bins and shopping bags and tables and broken chairs. There were shelves jammed with knickknacks and doodads. Old lamps and cracked flowerpots and umbrella stands. Framed portraits, stacked sideways in a tight row like playing cards in a deck. Three guitars, stringless and warped. An old accordion in a fancy black case with a sprung lid.

Would Darla have had time to go through any of this stuff? If she pulled out one item, the entire edifice might collapse.

So: no.

No, I won't look there. But where?

The steamer trunk. Bell returned to it, hauling open the heavy lid, rifling through the sweaters and scarves and blouses again. She came upon, once again, the tissue paper in which the first diary had been wrapped. She checked the trunk's four corners, in case Bessie had hidden the second one here, too, and Darla had found it. If so, Bell would somehow know. She'd sense it. She pushed her fingers in between the layers of clothing.

Nothing. No hint that the second diary had been hidden here.

Bell straightened up. The attic, Brenda said, had not changed much in generations; it was roughly the same space it had been when Bessie slept up here, first as a young girl who went to work at Wellwood, and then later as a married woman. It was a safe, familiar place. A refuge.

Bessie and Darla, sleeping in the same attic, all those years apart. Same bed, same headboard, same mattress, same pillows, same pillowcases . . .

Pillowcases.

Bell moved to the bed. Darla was carrying something in a pillowcase, Briscoe had said. And a pillowcase was missing. If she'd found the second diary somewhere in the vicinity of the bed, she naturally would have reached for something handy in which to wrap it, safeguarding it against Briscoe's eyes and then, inevitably, his questions.

She ran her hand across the top of the headboard. The wood was old and scarred but of high quality; it had weathered the years well. She wasn't sure she agreed with Brenda. The carving, she thought, looked nice. Simple but nice. Not crooked at all.

She sat down on the bed. She poked a flattened hand under the mattress, between the box spring and the frame. The tips of her fingers traveled the length of the mattress . . . until they grazed a round, soft-sided object. When she poked it, it made a crinkling sound.

Bell drew out a ball of wadded-up tissue paper. She smoothed it out flat against her knee, ironing it with her fist. It was roughly the same size as the first one she'd found in the trunk during her first visit to the attic. It was also roughly the same size as a leather notebook, the kind with ruled lines, the kind one might use as a diary.

I am Darla Gilley.

I'm skimming the diary—quickly, quickly—and I can't believe what I'm reading, I'm horrified, I have to take this and get rid of it, I have to hide it . . .

But where? Where would Darla go to hide the second diary?

Somewhere close to Wellwood. Yes. That much was obvious. That's where she had asked Briscoe to take her, once they left here.

But the woods around the ruins of the hospital went for dozens of miles in all directions. You could search for months, even years, and never find it.

Bell stood up. The view from Darla's perspective had winked out. She was herself again. And she had no idea where to start looking.

Time to go. It was late, and Joe Gilley needed his rest. Nick would be waiting for her in the living room, probably sitting on the couch across from Joe's recliner, glad to have had this chance to visit his friend—you never knew which visit might be the last one—but eager, too, to know what Bell had found in the attic.

Nothing.

That's how she would answer Nick on the ride home, and she would try to keep the discouragement out of her voice, but the truth was, she had no idea where Darla had hidden the second diary—or why its contents had made the hiding of it so necessary.

The only thing Bell knew for sure—and this was her intuition kicking in, based on all those years of prosecuting homicides—was that the second diary was somehow related to Darla's murder, and that if they found it, the killer would be close by.

Chapter Forty-two

The *plink-plink-plink-plink* sounds of dry dog food hitting the bottom of a ceramic bowl caused Arthur to erupt into spasms of pure ecstasy, including no small amount of drool-slinging. It was the next morning, and as soon as Bell began loading his bowl with successive scoopfuls from the big yellow-and-blue Pedigree bag, the dog bumped her leg repeatedly. He wanted to make sure she understood just what an excellent decision she had made, and how just one more scoopful would be an even better idea.

Only two things moved Arthur to such emotional heights: eating and taking a walk. Other times, he appeared to be preoccupied, even fairly indifferent. Mack Gettinger had taken to calling him "the canine Perry Como." He was that laid-back, that calm. He was an obedient dog, and a sweet-natured one, but sometimes Bell wished he had a little more . . . gumption, maybe. Initiative. Zest.

"I bet he'd eat the bag, too, if you left it within his reach," Rhonda said. She laughed, shaking her head at the sight of Arthur's little tap dance alongside his food bowl.

Rhonda had accepted Bell's last-minute, texted invitation to come to breakfast. The house on Shelton Avenue was a better meeting spot than Rhonda's office in the courthouse, where they'd surely be interrupted every two minutes. Bell knew that from her days as prosecutor, when her rule was: If you want to get anything done, get the hell out of the office.

"Good thing you invited me," Rhonda added. "I didn't have breakfast at home this morning, figuring I'd grab a bite at JP's. But there's a sign on the door. Closed today. Some kind of mechanical problem."

Bell had made waffles. The smell from the waffle iron was marvelous, a nutty, yeasty aroma that was so irresistible that it was either illegal or ought to be, Rhonda had noted, the moment she'd walked into the kitchen. The air was glazed as well with the ooey-gooey smell of homemade syrup. The syrup recipe came from Bell's ex-mother-in-law. It was the single good thing Bell had gotten out of knowing that cold, judgmental woman, who'd never hidden her conviction that her precious baby boy deserved far better than the likes of that strange, intense little orphan named Belfa Dolan.

"Carla sent me the waffle iron for my birthday last year," Bell explained. She had seated herself across from her friend. She pushed the butter dish her way. "I said, 'Sweetie, really? A waffle iron? I'll probably only use it once a year.' And Carla said, 'Totally worth it, though, right, Mom?'"

"Smart girl." Rhonda added a dollop of butter to the side of her plate. It instantly melted from the heat of the syrup, making a drowsy lake into which she dipped small forked-up chunks of waffle.

"I suspect it was also Carla's way of suggesting I ought to cook more. I mean—it's not really *cooking,* I guess, but it's also not another take-out order from JP's."

Rhonda savored several bites before resuming the conversation. "God, that's good. If I were by myself, I'd probably be dancing around on all fours like Arthur over there does." She set down her fork. "Okay. The Darla Gilley case. What do I need to know?"

Truth was, Bell didn't want to give Rhonda too many details. She didn't want to be cautioned about going slow and following protocol and all the rest of it. The beautiful part about working as a private investigator—and not answering to the county commission or to anybody else's rules—was the independence.

"Still plugging away," Bell said with deliberate vagueness.

"Haven't wanted to bother you. I know you have that big drug trial starting this week. I figured Nick and Jake and I can handle this. Drugs affect the whole region. Darla was just one person."

"Come on. You know better than that. You grew up around here. You know how we do things. Doesn't matter who you are—we look out for everybody."

You grew up around here.

The words touched off something in Bell's memory.

It was hardly a new thought—in fact, she'd expressed the same sentiment herself, many times. It was, rather, hearing Rhonda say it in the shadow of Bell's intense ruminations the day before about where Darla Gilley had hidden the second diary.

You grew up around here.

Yes.

And so did Darla.

There were things that people who had grown up in Acker's Gap knew that other people didn't know. Couldn't.

"And speaking of looking out for folks," Rhonda said. "Guess who stopped by my office yesterday? Okay, don't guess—I can't wait through all the wrong guesses. It was Dixie Sue Folsom."

"Really." Bell added more syrup to her waffle. Was there such a thing as too much syrup? No, there was not.

"Yeah. Just sashayed right in and told me how sorry she was that so many people had been inconvenienced by having to go out and look for her. And she had a question. Asked if she could do some volunteer work around the courthouse to make up for it."

"Whoa—you mean she expressed *remorse*? And offered to work for free? That doesn't sound like the Dixie Sue Folsom we've come to know."

"Well, hang on—you'll see in a sec what's going on." Rhonda laughed. "I got the story from Maggie Folsom, who called me right after Dixie Sue left. Maggie said, 'I told that girl not to bother you, but she just goes her own way.' Turns out Dixie Sue wants to enter a beauty pageant over in Clarksburg. Somebody told her it was a sure ticket to Hollywood. And there's a place on the entry form where they ask about volunteer work. So she had to scramble."

"Sounds like her show-business aspirations remain intact," Bell said. "What did you tell her?"

"I said we could definitely use some help keeping the ladies' room spic-and-span. The toilets get real dirty, what with it being a public facility and all."

"And?"

"And Dixie Sue suddenly remembered a previous engagement. Said she'll be in touch. Not holding my breath, if you know what I mean. Hey—is there any juice?"

A few minutes after Rhonda's departure, Bell called Nick.

He sounded sleepy, and she was afraid that she'd awakened him. But when she said she had news, he perked up: "Do tell."

"Think I know where Darla hid the second diary."

"Really? God, Bell, that's great. How did you—"

"Wellwood," she said. "Everything comes back to Wellwood."

"But we already knew that. Trouble is, Wellwood's smack-dab in the middle of about forty square miles of woods. You can't dig up the whole dadburned area."

"Don't have to." While she spoke, a chant was going through Bell's mind, a scrap of the past blown her way on a gentle but insistent bit of wind: *Monster! Monster! At the gate . . .*

Chapter Forty-three

Nick clicked off the call. He dropped his cell on the floor and rolled back over to embrace Jackie.

"That was Bell," he said.

"I heard." She kissed him. "You two just never stop, do you?"

"You go at things pretty hard yourself," he murmured, feeling himself respond to the deep kiss. Since when did he indulge in corny sexual innuendos more befitting a randy teenager than a senior citizen? Since now. "Kinda glad you closed the diner today."

"Had to. Freezer's still acting up."

He winced. "Guess I didn't fix it right, after all."

"I didn't fall in love with you for your mechanical skills, Nick Fogelsong." She was kissing his chest. Her warm tongue, flicking against his skin, was driving him crazy.

She stopped. With two fingers she touched a spot just below his left nipple, stroking the roughed-up skin where the hair didn't grow anymore. "So close," she said. "When I think about you being shot—oh, my God, Nick. Oh, my God."

A drug dealer had ambushed him at the Highway Haven. He had almost died. But that was years ago, and while it was a close call—a tenth of an inch to the right and he would've ended up in the cemetery over in Breckenridge, next to all the other Fogelsongs—he was still here, wasn't he? Still able to enjoy life.

And God knows he was enjoying it now.

"You're lucky," she said, her voice a shimmery whisper.

"What?" He wasn't sure he'd heard her right. What was lucky about almost dying next to a diesel pump?

"Yeah," she said. "Your scar—it's on the outside. It's the ones on the inside you have to worry about. The ones nobody can see."

That sounded, he thought, like something Bell Elkins would say: Mysterious. Murky. Deep. But he didn't want to think about Bell right now. She was like a daughter to him and he wasn't feeling fatherly. Jackie had started kissing him again, her mouth moving urgently across his chest. She climbed on top of him. Her long, hot, moist body fit perfectly. He moaned, feeling her shudder. *Oh, my Jesus.*

What she'd said just a few minutes ago—the part about loving him. He was dazed by it. He didn't say it back because he couldn't speak. Not now. Not while they were doing . . . *this.*

Later, he told himself. In the morning. That's when he would tell her. And so once they had finished and he felt himself drifting off, pulled irresistibly toward a heavy, delicious sleep, he thought, *I'll tell her later. When I wake up.*

He'd only said such a thing once before in his life. To Mary Sue. All those years ago. Never dreaming he'd ever, *ever* be saying it to another woman. It was time, though. The time had come. He knew how he felt. He was utterly, passionately happy. He would tell Jackie that he was in love with her, too.

But he couldn't do that. Not yet. He'd do it later. Because when he woke up, she was gone.

Chapter Forty-four

Arthur twitched a fuzzy ear. The sight of the leash intrigued him, but he was skeptical; a walk in the middle of the day was atypical, and so he didn't quite trust that it might be happening. Thus he held off on his usual dance of dog joy—four paws scratching madly across the tiled kitchen floor, his body quivering like a Jell-O mold in an earthquake—until he was positive.

Yes. Bell was taking him for a walk.

She snapped the leash onto his collar. Minutes later he jumped up into the passenger seat of the Explorer.

But before she'd backed out of the driveway, she reconsidered. If her theory was wrong, she might have a long day of searching ahead of her. Keeping track of Arthur in the woods, maintaining a good grip on the leash, would be too distracting.

"Sorry," Bell said as she led him back into the house. "I'll make it up to you, buddy. Promise."

His expression was noncommittal.

The day was milder than it should have been. November had been playing its usual trick, doling out snow and cold one day, clear skies and warmth the next. Yesterday's snow was melting so fast it made the streams run as if they were being chased. Moving through the mud-floored, tree-lined wilderness, Bell wondered if Arthur thought of her as just another specimen of weather: moody, changeable, un-reliable.

She made good time. Halfway to her destination, she shucked off her jacket and tied it around her waist. In another ten minutes she reached the spot in the woods that she remembered from so many excursions here as a kid.

Darla had remembered it, too. Bell was sure of it.

The Monster Tree.

Branches twisted and askew, bark so craggy and sharp that you could cut your skin just brushing past it, the tree presided over this section of the woods with menacing splendor. It wasn't especially tall but it spread out with fiendish enthusiasm, those claw-like branches stretching out in ugly kinked segments. At the other end, down on the ground, two of the tree's roots had heaved up on one side, like a pair of scaly, undulating serpents frozen in mid-strike, and the nar-row place between them created an indentation that could serve as a rough seat.

As a kid she'd spent a lot of lovely, aimless hours tucked in that very spot, transforming it into her own personal reading nook. And daring the Monster Tree to disturb her. Daring it to bother her at all.

I'm not afraid of you.

And then Shirley would call. Time to go home. Spell broken, Bell would scramble away, jamming the paperback copy of *The Martian Chronicles* or *The Hobbit* into her back pocket.

She scanned the ground around the tree, looking for evidence that someone else had been here recently. She widened the circumference of her search area. She kicked away the leaves that had fetched up in great unruly piles, moved crisscrossed clumps of branches. In one area, a square of earth looked slightly darker than the ground that sur-rounded it. She used her heel as a digging tool. The soil was easy to displace.

She knelt down, pulling away the dirt with her bare hands.

It didn't take long—Darla had been in a desperate hurry, and wouldn't have had the time to go deep—thus within a minute or two Bell had located what was buried here: a pillowcase. Inside it was a small leather volume identical, outwardly at least, to the one Darla had mailed to Nick.

Bell didn't want to wait. She couldn't wait. She had to read it *now,* not when she returned to civilization—or to the not-quite-reasonable facsimile of it constituted by Acker's Gap. She opened the diary and, as she had done with the first one, flicked through the pages quickly to get a preliminary sense of its organization, of the time period with which it dealt.

She saw right away that it only covered the last three days of Bessie's life. Bessie could not have known that, of course. Her body had been discovered on Wednesday morning, according to the newspaper story.

The handwriting was the same as in the first diary: It was the product of a practiced, deliberate hand. Bessie was older when she had written this, and much different from the fourteen-year-old who had begun a diary in 1935. But one thing was the same. She was still a girl determined to tell the world the story of her life, even if the world had shown no indication that it gave a damn about her or anything she had to say. And so once again she had taken considerable pride in the crafting of her letters. Because *she* gave a damn, even if the world didn't.

Bessie had thought she had plenty of time. She'd felt no inclination to rush, Bell realized. Her handwriting was so careful because she wanted her words to be legible. She wanted somebody to know. *She wanted what we all want,* Bell mused, willing to speculate because by now she'd been privy to some of this woman's deepest emotions. *To be understood. And, perhaps, forgiven. Forgiven for being the flawed, frightened creatures that we all are. Forgiven for making mistakes. Forgiven for being human.*

Bell needed to get comfortable so that she could concentrate on her reading. She looked around. She didn't need to look far.

Ah.

There in the makeshift seat created by the twisted roots of the Monster Tree, with her jacket serving as a so-so but better-than-nothing cushion, Bell sat and read the diary, and thereby discovered the secret that Darla had given her life to protect.

October 9, 1959

This is my real and true diary. I am going to write the truth here, and put this diary where it will not be found for a long time, especially not by Donnie, because nobody will be looking for it.

I have kept that other diary since I was 14. I am 38 now. So many years! Sometimes I cannot believe that so much time has gone by. But then I look around and see how things have changed. Mama is dead. So is Daddy. My boy, Nelson, is 21 now. His boy, Joe, is almost 7. I see all that and it seems to me that even more years should have gone by, for so many things to happen in them, so many changes.

I ask myself what really holds a family together. "Love" is what the Reverend Mayhew would say. But he only says that because he has to. That is what being a preacher means. You have to give simple answers to things that are not simple at all.

Love is not the right answer. What holds a family together are secrets. Which is another way of saying, lies. I never wanted to be a liar. But somehow I have turned out to be one.

I need to write this new diary because I need a place for the truth. The truth about my family. About Mama. About Donnie and Larry Kinnamin. About Craig Gilley and what he does to me when I won't let him lay with me like he wants to. About Wellwood.

There was a time when I would not have done this. I believed that family meant one thing and one thing only: keeping those secrets. Not just from other people but from yourself, too. But I do not believe that anymore. Now I believe that there has to be a place where I can hold the truth in my hands, hold it apart from everything else, and raise it up so that it catches the light. No matter how dirty my truth is, it is my only real treasure.

I am writing this in chunks, not day by day, the way a diary is supposed to be written. I have so many things I need to make right. My mind is full of those things. I cannot break them up into days. Diaries are supposed to be neat and in order but this one will not be. It cannot be. It may sound mixed-up but it is not. It is true and clear.

I did want to go. From the very beginning, I did want to go to work at Wellwood. I said in my other diary that I did not, that I was nervous and scared of going, but that is not true. I wanted to go. I wanted to get out of the house.

But I did miss not going to school. I know I said I did not like school but that was a lie. When Daddy told me to just stop going, there was a part of me that was grieving. I wonder still what my life could have been if I had gone to school more. Maybe even graduated high school.

I am writing down the names.

June McCrae and Bridie Willis and Sandra Toms and Annie Mae Worth.

Gina Plunkett and Sue Bonner and Marvel Jones and Mamie Bateman and Lula Beth Smollet.

Jeannie Binns and Amber Smith and Helga Sang and Patty Ann Findlay.

Those are just some of them, the ones I memorized because I remember those girls so well. Marvel was just 9. Patty Ann had a singing voice that was so clear and bright, it sounded like an angel singing. Some of them I don't remember. There are so many. That is why I am writing down the names. So that there will be a record. Because one day, somebody will care. They will care about what is being done here.

Judy Souther told me something I will never forget. She said that yes, the women who come to Wellwood do go home after Dr. Trexler operates on them. It is not like they are trapped here. They are not prisoners, except for a few who are very bad off and who cannot take care of themselves. Most of them do go home. But they take the cold way home. Because they are never the same.

What happened to Judy Souther, God rest her soul, is like

what happened to me. That is what I think now. At first she was alright with what we do at Wellwood, and then, after a while, she was not alright with it anymore. It came on her slowly, like it came on me, a little bit more every year. But nobody cares if we are alright with it or not. It is our job.

In some ways Judy Souther was lucky that she passed away when she did. She did not have to live a long time with what she knew, with the terrible knowledge of what she had done.

Pretty soon after I started working at Wellwood, Judy Souther figured out that I would be a good worker in The Room. She told me that I had quality eyes. She meant that I could see certain things, things that will bother other people, but that I will take them in stride. I do not make a fuss. Once you have seen hard things, you cannot ever not see them. They are in front of your eyes forever. Even when you close your eyes. But you have to go on.

Well, she was right, and not only in the ways she knew about.

When I was thirteen years old I saw Donnie in the barn with Larry Kinnamin. I was in the house, cooking supper for Daddy, and I saw a mouse running along the kitchen wall. So I went to the barn to get the bushwhacker. That is a tool with a long wooden stick and then, at the end, a sharp curved blade. You have to be careful with it because it is so sharp. Daddy had a friend once who was trying to kill a mouse with a bushwhacker, and him being so mad, well, it made him careless and he swung too low and too wild and he took off his own toes. Two of them. I know that sounds funny, Daddy said, but it is not, except for the part about the mouse, who got away. So the man made a story out of it. He would explain to everybody that he lost three things that day: big toe, second toe, and the mouse.

We keep the bushwhacker in the barn. So I walked over there and as soon as I was inside that cool, dark place I heard a funny sound, like a pig rooting in the mud. And then there was another sound. It sounded like somebody was in pain, terrible pain.

It was too dark to see at first but my eyes got used to it. Here is what I saw in the corner: Donnie was on his hands and knees, like a dog, and Larry Kinnamin was behind him, also on his hands and knees, like another dog. Larry Kinnamin was ramming his pecker inside my brother but he must have been doing it too hard because Donnie sounded like he was getting hurt. Larry Kinnamin was grunting but my brother was not. He sounded like he was crying.

Larry Kinnamin saw me and he yelled. It was a curse word. I will not write it down here. He pulled his pecker out of my brother and he jumped up and yanked up his pants. He did not stop to do up his belt buckle but just let it dangle while he ran away. Donnie fell back on the ground. I heard Larry Kinnamn's truck starting up. He had parked it behind the barn so I could not see it from the house. He got out of there as fast as he could. Donnie just sat on the floor of the barn. He did not put his pants back on right away. He was crying. I told him it was alright and that I had heard of such things and that if he loved Larry Kinnamin and Larry Kinnamin made him happy, I would have nothing more to say about it. He looked at me and he said, "Love him? Love Larry Kinnamin?" and then he said, "He pays me, Bessie. And I give the money to Daddy. How simple can you be? He pays me to let him do that."

Well, I thought, that explains it. I knew that Donnie and his best friend, Pete Collier, got along real good, and had talked about building a house together on the other side of the ridge. But I also knew that when Donnie started working for Larry Kinnamin, Pete did not come to the house anymore. I never saw him, ever again. That is too bad, because Pete is a good person. But we need money bad. Everybody does, everybody I know. That is why I work at Wellwood. It is a shame what money does around here and maybe everywhere. From what I see, it does not bring happiness. It gets in the way of happiness.

Donnie made me promise not to tell anybody about him and Larry Kinnamin. I never did tell and I never put it in the other diary. Maybe that is why Donnie will not stay out of that diary. He wants to see if I am keeping my promise.

I put it here because this is mine. Here, I tell the truth about everything. You have to have one place in this world where you can do that.

If I can tell that about my brother, then I can tell the rest.

When I first came to work at Wellwood I gave baths and I swept floors and I carried out the trash from the kitchen. But then Judy Souther saw my quality eyes. It turns out I knew how to settle the girls right down, the ones who were going to have the operation. I knew the words to say. I knew how to stroke their arms and get them to start breathing normal again, so we could strap them down and get them ready. And no matter what I saw, I did not ask any questions. There were other girls working at Wellwood who did not ask any questions, either, but they were simple. I was special, Judy Souther told me, because I did not ask any questions and I was not simple. That, she said, is a "rare combination." That is the phrase she used. It made me proud.

Do you hear that? It made me proud.

So real soon after I came to Wellwood, I had a new job, a job I have done ever since: I bring the girls to The Room. First Ophelia Browning tells me which girls to bring. She chooses. Every morning, you can hear her high heels click on the hard floor as she is walking fast down the hall. She is always in a hurry. She stops at the door of a room, and goes in, and marches across the floor, past the long rows of beds, until she finds the bed of the girl she is picking to go first today. Click, click, click.

I follow right behind her. She looks at a list she carries in her hand, a list of names. She nods and points to the girl, and that means: This one. Then she goes to another name on her list and another bed and she points to that girl: This one. And: This one. It is like she is not really seeing the girls, just the names on the list.

Then Ophelia Browning turns and leaves the long room. I stay, because it is my job to get them ready. It is my job to calm their fears, and tell them it will all be fine, and tell them Dr. Trexler is a good man, a caring man, a healer. A genius, even, because that is what Ophelia Browning calls him. "My genius," she says. I can hear them in his office sometimes, when I am working in the outer office. "Oh," she says, "my dear darling, my genius."

I have to talk about The Room. There are three tables that are raised up real high, with straps that have padding on them. I bring in the girls and Carl Winton helps me get them up on the tables. We lay them flat on their backs. Carl Winton has worked at Wellwood a long time. He is the one who pulls the straps around the girl so that she cannot move. He is a lot stronger than me and that is why he does it.

Then he takes a thick pad and puts it between her jaws. While he is doing that, I say to her, "It will all be fine. I promise," because the girl is nervous. I rub her arms. Sometimes I hum a hymn. I like to hum "In the Garden." That settles them right down.

There is a machine in the corner with lots of round dials on it. You know the plug-in cord like you see on a vacuum cleaner, well, there is a cord like that. It goes from the machine to the patient on that table.

Then Ophelia Browning comes in, and then Dr. Trexler. I have settled the girl down real good by now but sometimes a girl will backslide when she sees Dr. Trexler. She will say, "I want to go home." Or she will cry. But other times the girl will giggle and laugh. One time a girl said "I love you" to Dr. Trexler, and he laughed and said "I love you, too," and that made everybody around the table, Judy Souther and

Ophelia Browning and another nurse and me and Carl Winton, laugh, too.

Everybody knew he did not love her. He was making a joke.

The first time I saw what he did to the girls, I got sick to my stomach but nobody else was sick and so I pretended I was fine. I wanted to stay, and if I was sick I was afraid they would make me leave. Being in The Room was special. I wanted to be special.

It goes like this. Dr. Trexler says, "Ready?" Ophelia Browning says, "Yes." Once, I asked Judy Souther why Ophelia Browning answers the question instead of the girl. The girl, after all, is the one who is getting the operation done to her, not Ophelia Browning. Judy Souther said she did not know why.

Dr. Trexler turns the dial on the machine. Carl Winton is holding the girl's legs, which is a good thing because she starts shaking all over. The straps hold her but they need Carl Winton, too, to make sure she does not go right off the table. The shaking is very bad.

Dr. Trexler turns the dial up and down three times, waiting a minute between each time. When he turns the dial up the shaking starts again. The electrical shock makes it so the girl does not feel the operation. It is a kindness, Ophelia Browning says. When I saw it for the first time she thought I was going to be upset and that is why she told me that. But I was not really that upset. A little bit, like I said, but not much. You get used to it. You can get used to anything.

After the shaking, the girl is real quiet. She just lies there. A lot of times she soils herself and you can plainly smell it, but nobody points it out. I am in charge of cleaning her up and getting her new panties. But that will come later.

First there is the operation.

Dr. Trexler has what he calls a surgical instrument. It is very sharp and looks like an ice pick. He also has a tiny hammer that looks like a toy. He leans over and he lifts up the eyelid of the girl on the table and he puts the ice pick up under it, and then he taps the end with the hammer. Tap, tap. You can hear a little crack, like the ice cracking on the top of the creek when you step on it in the winter. And then Dr. Trexler moves the ice pick around a little bit and then he takes it out and that is that. Maybe five minutes goes by, maybe six minutes, but no more.

After a while the girl wakes up. She cannot walk by herself so I help her back to her room, holding her up or else she will fall to the floor. Her eyes are all swollen and they are getting black and blue, like somebody punched her in the eyes. I get her settled in her bed. I ask the girl if she is alright. Sometimes a girl is real confused and she says, "Why are you asking me that?" I say, "Well, you had an operation." The girl says, "I did not, you are trying to play a trick on me." And nothing I say makes any difference. The girl does not believe me. She is real quiet after that, even if she has been one of the loud ones, one of the screamers who tried to jump out the window. But after going to The Room, she is real nice. Nobody has any problems with her.

There is no Loretta. There never was a Loretta. I made her up. I do all the things that I said Loretta did. I bring the girls to The Room. I help Carl Winton put the thick piece of cloth between their jaws so they won't bite through their tongues when the electricity hits them. I speak softly to them, just before Dr. Trexler gets there, and I say, "Do not worry, it will be alright." They are simple, and so they believe me.

I say again: It never bothered me. Not until now. Not for all those years I helped Dr. Trexler and Ophelia Browning. I sometimes pretended it did. Every now and again I would frown and shake my head, and act like I was kind of upset, but the truth is, I liked it. I have power over those girls. They have to do what I tell them to do. If a girl disobeys me, if she talks back to me, I call Ophelia Browning and I point to the girl and say, "This one."

Ophelia Browning taught me how to do that, and she is real proud of me when I do it, too.

But then it started to change for me. That is why I am writing this. It has taken a very long time, too long, for me to change, and I do not know why it is changing now, but it is. I feel shame for helping in The Room like I do.

I think it may be changing for Dr. Trexler, too. I am not sure, but there are times in The Room when he stops and looks down at the girl. She looks like she is sleeping. The other day, he lifted the ice pick but he did not lean over her and put it in her eye right away. He stood there. Ophelia Browning said, "Emmett? What is it?" Then she caught herself and said, "Dr. Trexler, do you need something?" He said, "No, I am fine." He went on with the operation.

Sometimes, when I am trying to fall asleep at night, I swear that I can hear the clicking of Ophelia Browning's high heels. I wake up all sweaty and scared. I am breathing real hard. I look around. I see the high dark shapes of the boxes and the chairs and the old tables piled up all around me here in the attic, and it is like they are watching over me, taking care of me. Other times, they look like they are planning something, like they are waiting patiently till I fall asleep so they can come after me.

Oct. 12, 1959

I knew this time would come. I did not know when, but I knew it would come.

I have to leave soon. Ophelia Browning knows. She has figured out that I am writing down the names—the names of the girls that she and Dr. Trexler kill. They do not kill them all the way, of course. That would be a mercy. They only kill them halfway. They kill their spirits, their souls, not their bodies. So you could call it halfway murder. That is how I have started to think about it now. I wish Judy Souther were still alive so I could talk to her. She would know what I mean. And she would help me keep the names. I am sure of it.

I ask myself how Ophelia Browning found out. Well, she saw me on the front walking path two weeks ago. I spotted her up in one of the windows, looking down, watching me. I do not want to carry a notebook around because that would look suspicious to them. So I wait until I am by myself and I write on the inside of my hand. I know I can scrub it off later:

Josephine Carr

Mary Brundy

Helen Tucker

So many, many names. I write them down three at a time, when I take a walk for my break. I go home at night and I look at the names on my palm and then I write them in this diary. It is safe from Ophelia Browning. Someday, my diary will be found, here in the attic. First they will find the other diary, the one my brother has been reading, and then they will find the real one, the true one, the one with the list of names. Something will be done.

But now Ophelia Browning knows. And so I have to go away from here. It will mean leaving my home and my family, but I have no choice. I cannot stay, not with Ophelia Browning knowing what she knows. I will not miss the sound of the screams, the screams of the girls strapped to the table in The Room. They scream like that until I settle them down, speaking softly, humming to them. I tell them Jesus is looking after them.

In truth, there is something worse than the screams. And that is the sound of Ophelia Browning's high heels on the hard floor, the click click click, going to pick the girls.

Ophelia Browning is different now. Ever since she saw me writing on my palm that day, she treats me like someone she does not trust. Well, I do not trust her, either.

On Monday afternoon she came to me and said, "Mrs.

Gilley, please meet me in The Room in five minutes. There is something I would like to show you." So I walked up the stairs and down the hall, and I started to go in The Room. I did not go far before I stopped.

Carl Winton was there. Dr. Trexler was not there. But why would Carl Winton be there? I felt a chill going up my arms. Ophelia Browning has watched Dr. Trexler do the operation many, many times. Once he was sick with a bad cold and he stopped and told her to finish it. So she can do the operation.

I was nervous and so I turned around to leave. This did not feel right to me. But Ophelia Browning was standing in the doorway. She had come in behind me. She was smiling. "Mrs. Gilley," she said. "Why are you leaving? I told you to meet me here. Please stay."

The secret is in not hesitating. That is what Donnie taught me. I asked him once about how to get away from Craig Gilley when he is coming after me and Donnie said, "Never hesitate. Do what you do—but do not stop to think about it."

I ran past Ophelia Browning and I was out the door before she could do anything about it. She was very surprised, which is what Donnie said would happen. The one who moves fast always wins.

Was she going to do something to me? Was she going to ask Carl Winton to put me on the table and strap me down? Would I take the cold way home?

I do not know. I do not want to know.

I will go to work tomorrow because I have to pick up my paycheck. It will be my last one, but they will not know that. You need money in this world. There is no way around that fact. You can ask Donnie about that.

I will look out for Ophelia Browning and stay out of her way. Then I will come home here and get what I need. She knows where I live, and so I cannot stay here, either, even if I want to.

I will run through the woods like I always do—but this

time, I will not stop at the Monster Tree and make the turn for Wellwood. I will keep going until I reach the road. I can get a ride there.

I will never look back. And someday, when I am far away, I will be able to tell what I saw and what I know, and to prove it I will show this diary and the names. The souls of those who died at Wellwood will have their peace at last, a peace they never had in this life.

I must stop now and go to sleep. I must be ready for tomorrow, and all that it will bring.

Chapter Forty-five

The diary ended there. A good three-quarters of the pages were still blank. Bell flipped to the last one and there, in Bessie's careful, upright script, minus any flourishes, was a list of names: four long rows, the names having been added in groups of three at a time, with a small space between each group. The writing was tiny and the rows were crowded, to accommodate all the names, but the names were clear nonetheless.

Bell could imagine what happened next, the sights and colors and sounds:

Bessie goes to Wellwood in the morning to get her paycheck. She tucks it into her purse. Quietly, calmly, she slips out, pulling the fancy front door of the hospital shut behind her.

Deep in the woods, she senses that she is being followed.

She turns.

It is Ophelia Browning. *What do you think you are doing? I see you, writing the names, day after day. Who do you think you are?* Bessie is frightened—too frightened, at first, to move. *You answer me. Answer me now. Where are you taking those names? Who are you talking to? You have no right. You are NOBODY.*

Bessie is too scared to answer. All she can think is: *Run. Run.*

She runs. And her pursuer, enraged, lifts a bladed tool high over her head. Bessie has waited too long. She is not quick enough off the mark and the weapon comes down with a fierce and deadly force . . .

Sixty years later, it is Darla running through those same woods. Darla, clutching the second diary she has found in the attic and stuffed in a pillowcase. Darla, burying it under the Monster Tree. Darla, running toward Wellwood. Darla, confronted by someone who will go to any lengths to find and destroy the diary. Darla, refusing to disclose where she has hidden it. Darla, chased by that person, a person as obsessed as Ophelia Browning, a person who raises a bladed tool and hurls it toward the back of her head . . .

But who?

Bell knew that both visions—the deaths of Bessie and Darla— were pure conjecture. There was no way to prove that Ophelia Browning had murdered Bessie. What about the high heels? In the woods, they would've held her up. Perhaps she sent a surrogate—Carl Winton, say, or another willing employee, a fleet and strong young woman, a new Bessie—to do it. Carl Winton would have had access to tools.

Too much time had passed for Bell to be sure. All she had was informed speculation.

But Darla's murder was solvable. Bell just had to put the pieces together.

The identity of Darla's killer was somehow bound up with Bessie's passionate and guilt-soaked truth, a truth that had moved through the years in a cloud of righteous fury, traveling relentlessly toward the present, where it had brought about a terrible reckoning for Darla.

Abruptly, Bell looked up. She'd been gripping the edges of the diary with both hands, elbows propped on her knees, keeping it secure while she raced through the final pages.

In the near distance, she heard cracking sounds, rustlings. The sounds were too rhythmic, too deliberate, too relentless, to be an animal. Someone was coming, crunching across the fallen leaves and scattered branches, closing in fast.

Sheer instinct told Bell to hide the diary, to shove it back into the pillowcase. Yet she had to be careful; she didn't want to take a chance on ripping the brittle, fragile pages. The diary was sixty years old. It had survived a great deal. In the next few minutes, it might have to survive a great deal more.

"Hello, Bell."

Trying to keep the surprise out of her voice, Bell replied "Hi, Jackie."

Chapter Forty-six

"So you found it." Jackie pointed to the ledger on Bell's lap. "Good. I'll take it now."

"It's not yours."

"It's not yours either." Jackie stretched out her palm, wiggling her fingers as if she might be able to summon the object in question by some obscure sorcery, some magician's trick. Or maybe by the sheer magnetic force of her desire for it.

"Look, Bell," she said. She sounded calm, even marginally friendly. "I don't want to hurt you. But I will. I swear to you that I will. Give it to me."

They regarded each other across a distance of roughly fifteen feet, Jackie standing, Bell sitting. All around them, the woods of Briney Hollow simmered in the golden drift of this unseasonably warm day in late autumn.

"No."

"Can we not do this?" Jackie's voice was still calm but a slight annoyance had crept into it. She reminded Bell of a teacher who knows a pupil isn't putting forth her best effort. "Just hand it over. Then we'll be done. I'll let you walk out of here."

Until that moment, Bell had not realized there was any possibility she *wouldn't* walk out of here. But now it dawned on her: She had never seen Jackie like this before. A thread of menace twisted through the other woman's words, through her very presence. There was an odd zeal in Jackie's dark eyes.

And furthermore, Jackie was holding something in her other hand, the one Bell couldn't see because it was behind her back.

She could run. But she wouldn't get far. And the moment she ran, Bell knew, she would have upped the stakes of this encounter, defining it. Hunter and prey: Those would be their new roles.

"What's this all about?" Bell asked, affecting a mild bemusement. She was sticking to affability. She still hoped she could reason with her.

That drew a heavy sigh from Jackie. She lifted her shoulders and held her breath for a beat or so before letting it back out again.

"It didn't have to go this way," Jackie said. "I hoped it wouldn't."

"What do you mean?"

Jackie appeared to be studying Bell, making a calculation before she replied. "Okay. I guess it doesn't matter. You might as well know the whole story. It's lonely, you know. Being the only one who knows the whole story. That's what nobody gets about secrets. It's so damned lonely keeping them."

She peered around, at last locating a spot on the ground that was cushioned by enough thick leaves to make it a decent place to sit. She sat down cross-legged. "Nice to relax for a minute. Hard work, getting through these damned woods. Too many trees." Whatever she had been carrying in her left hand was now on the ground behind her, still out of sight. "One thing before I start. It's going to sound funny under the circumstances, but I like you. Always have. Wanted you to know that. I wish we could've been better friends. You know why?"

"No."

"We're the same. Tough as all get-out in business. But shy as hell when it comes to emotional connections. We keep ourselves closed up tight. It's a kind of prison, right? A prison that locks from the inside. But we can't help it. We can't change. It's too risky. We know the price of letting down our guard. And it's too high."

Bell took a chance. "You do okay with Nick."

Jackie smiled. It was genuine, Bell believed. Nick's name had relaxed her, loosened something inside her. She really did care for him.

"Yeah," Jackie said. "Me and Nick. He said you didn't know. But I figured you'd guessed. You don't approve, do you?"

"He's a grown man. I'm not his mom."

"But you don't approve."

Bell shrugged.

"I make him happy," Jackie said. "He deserves that, don't you think? He's a good man."

"No argument there."

"I didn't plan it. And it's got nothing to do with—with the reason I'm out here." A sharp birdcall startled her. She flinched. But she never took her eyes off Bell. "My relationship with Nick was this wonderful thing that just sort of *happened*. And if the timing had been different, if I didn't have this other shit to deal with—well, I don't know. Maybe it could've worked out. Long term, I mean."

"And it can't?"

"Nice try, Bell. I think we both know this is the end of the line. For both of us. After today, I'll have to leave town."

"What do you mean?"

Jackie made a face. "Please. I didn't waste my time following you through these damn woods just to play games." Her eyes dropped to the object in Bell's lap. "You read Bessie's second diary, right? The one that's not total bullshit?"

Bell didn't answer. She wasn't sure how much to reveal. Jackie might be fishing.

"Fine." Jackie picked up a stick and dug idly at the ground, still watching Bell. "Okay—clearly, you've read it. And so you read about Ophelia Browning. My grandmother."

Startled, Bell responded, "How can Ophelia Browning be your grandmother? I've heard you talk about your family, but the only grandmother you've ever mentioned is your mother's mother. You call her 'Grandma Opie.'"

"Right. 'Ophelia' was way too hard for a kid to pronounce. My mother never called her 'Mother.' She called her the same thing my grandmother's friends all called her—OB. Ophelia Browning. Her initials. When I was a toddler, I heard 'OB' as 'Opie.' So I called her 'Grandma Opie.'" Jackie dug harder with the stick. "She was a vile woman. Cruel and selfish and—" She stopped. "I'm getting ahead of myself. The point is, by 1963, when Wellwood burned down, Trexler was a broken man. Totally disgraced. Long gone from Acker's Gap. He'd kicked Opie to the curb a few years before. My mother heard that she'd died in some nursing home. Mom didn't even claim the body. They could drop Opie in a landfill for all she cared.

"But as bad as Opie was, she was family. The things she did, the crap she pulled—well, it reflected back on *us*. And so when I was all grown up and we'd reconciled, Mom asked me for one thing. Just one. She asked me to make sure nobody found out about our family's darkest secret—about Grandma Opie and what she did at Wellwood." Jackie dug even harder. The stick snapped in half. She flung the two halves aside and dusted off her hands. "There was a rumor—it floated around for years, Mom told me—that somebody had kept a diary. Some low-level worker at Wellwood had recorded the names of the patients that Trexler and Opie had operated on. It would personalize all the horrible things they'd done in the name of *science*." She practically spat the word. "Their families might not have cared about those women, but if the information got out, and if the lobotomies were attached to the names of actual *people*—well, somebody might go poking around the records of Wellwood. Mom was terrified that it might end up being true—that somebody *had* kept a diary, and that it might be found one day. And our family name would be trashed."

Bell had known Jackie's mother, Joyce LeFevre, very well. She was a stubborn, boisterous, hard-working woman. When she divorced her husband to live with a woman named Georgette Akers, the court awarded sole custody of three-year-old Jackie to Joyce's ex-husband. Jackie had been raised in Tennessee, not West Virginia.

Joyce and Georgette ran a diner together. They died years ago in an explosion in downtown Acker's Gap.

"You loved your mother, didn't you?"

"I *adored* my mother," Jackie corrected her. "I missed her every day while I was growing up. When I was finally old enough to tell my father to go to hell, I reunited with my mother. We only had a few years to get to know each other again before she died. But every day was precious. And I'm going to keep my promise to her." As Jackie continued speaking her voice changed, shedding the fond tone with which she'd talked about her mother. She recited facts blandly, methodically, as if she were reading bullet points:

"Darla Gilley told me about finding her grandmother's diary in that attic. She read it—read all about Wellwood. She did her homework. Found out who Ophelia Browning was. She traced Ophelia's daughter—my mother, Joyce—and then Joyce's daughter."

"You."

"Yeah. Me. She called me. We arranged to meet at the diner that Thursday to talk about it." A low laugh. "Darla thought she was very, very clever. Because she didn't come straight to the diner. Her first stop was the post office—she mailed the diary to Nick, for safekeeping." Another laugh. "In case I *snatched* it, I suppose. Right out of her grubby little hands. I only found out later that she'd mailed it to him. I thought she still had it."

"So you were the person she was meeting at JP's. Not a customer."

Jackie nodded. "Darla wanted to let me know why she had to go public. A lot of bullshit about justice for the victims. She was going to donate the diary to the library. Contact some historians. Even some TV stations in Charleston. So that somebody would tell the story of Wellwood." She snickered. "Would anybody have cared, after all these years? Cared about a bunch of crazy hillbillies who got their brains dumped in a blender? I don't know. It would've been embarrassing, I guess. To have it all brought up again. Whatever. Truth is, once I'd talked to Darla and realized what was in the diary, I didn't much care anymore.

"But that," Jackie said, "is when I made my mistake."

Chapter Forty-seven

"What do you mean?" Bell asked.

"I wasn't upset enough."

"Still in the dark here, Jackie."

"That day in the diner—I was too calm when Darla told me what she'd read. I didn't freak out enough. It was a far cry from how I'd been earlier. When she first told me over the phone that she had it, I was frantic. Desperate. I made all kinds of threats. I *had* to get that diary. So that I could destroy it. I was—I was out of my head with anger. I'd promised my mother. *Promised* her.

"And then, as Darla and I talked that day and she told me what she'd learned, it dawned on me. She didn't know the real story. It sounded like those idiots at Wellwood didn't really know what they were doing. And Opie? All the diary proved was that she was a mean bitch. So what? My mother *admired* Opie for that. Hell—Mom was no shrinking violet, either. *That* wasn't the part my mother wanted to keep hidden from the world. Whatever it was that Darla had stumbled across—it wasn't the story my mother was so afraid of."

Now Bell understood. "Darla saw the change in you. And she realized there must be another diary. One that you *were* afraid might get out."

"Right. If it exposed even a tenth of what Opie actually did at Wellwood, my mom would be rolling over in her grave to think that people would know. Mom was never fooled by Opie's fancy ways. Snooty as hell, my mom said. But a killer at heart. Dear old Granny was Trexler's right-hand woman—as handy in his operating room as she was in his bedroom. Opie wasn't confused at all. She knew *exactly* what was going on at Wellwood.

"She and Trexler were a team. She'd bring in those poor suffering women, one by one—and he'd do his thing with the ice pick. That was their foreplay. My mom told me the whole gross story." After a bitter laugh, Jackie added, "Bet it really turned them on, old Trex and Grandma Opie. One light tap of that ice pick with a hammer, one small cut and—presto! Instant zombies. Bet they stared adoringly at each other over those scrambled frontal lobes." She shuddered. "I knew there had to be a second diary. And now Darla did, too. But I didn't know where it was. Neither did she. Not then, anyway. I don't know where she found it."

In her prosecutor days, Bell had learned the simple technique of trading information. You gave up a little to garner a lot in return.

"Darla went back to the attic," she explained to Jackie. "Same place she'd found the first diary. Her grandmother's life was lived in a small orbit—home and Wellwood. Even after Bessie was married, she and her husband still lived in the farmhouse. So Darla found the second diary—because now she knew there *was* a second diary—and tried to hide it."

"That's what I don't get," Jackie said, a perplexed expression on her face. "Why'd she need to hide it? Once she had found it, she could have just released it—the same thing she threatened to do with the first one. Why'd she go to all the trouble of taking it from the attic and burying it way out here?"

"Because when she read it," Bell answered, with slow, sad certitude, "Darla discovered that she was in the same boat you were. Her grandma Bessie aided and abetted the horrors at Wellwood. She helped Trexler and your grandmother perform the lobotomies. Eventually Bessie changed her mind—it's all detailed in this second diary—but that was a long time coming. She was just as guilty as they were."

"Christ," Jackie said. "I had no idea."

"So now it's my turn. How did you know Darla was coming out here that Thursday?"

Jackie shrugged. "When she left the diner, I watched from the window. Saw her hitch a ride in the big rig. The direction they were going—it could only be Briney Hollow. But it was an hour or so before I could get away from the diner."

"How *did* you get away?"

"I always take a break in the late afternoon. Get the firewood for the stove. Karen runs the place while I'm gone."

The hatchet, Bell thought grimly. *She cuts the firewood with a hatchet.*

"Darla had the trucker make a detour to the farmhouse," Bell said. As long as she kept Jackie engaged in conversation, she was safe. "She found the real diary. Stuck it in this pillowcase. He dropped her off at the edge of the woods. She hid it before you got out here."

"I confronted her," Jackie said. She wanted to finish the story. "Asked her where it was. She wouldn't tell me. In fact, she ran. I chased her to Wellwood. And things . . . escalated."

"You mean you killed her."

"I *mean,*" Jackie said testily, "things got out of control. I mean that I had to have that diary. I mean that I loved my mother more than anything on this earth. And my mother loved her family name. I wasn't going to let Darla Gilley and some stupid damned diary destroy that name."

"How would you find out where she'd hidden the second diary, if Darla was dead?"

"I didn't need to find it. It could stay hidden forever, for all I cared. Only Darla knew what it said—and she wouldn't be telling anybody anything." Jackie gave Bell a crooked smile. "But then—*you* came along. Once you found out about the second diary, I knew I had to act. Because I knew you'd find it. You grew up here, just like Darla. You played in these woods. I didn't." She gestured toward the book in Bell's lap. "And you didn't disappoint me."

Jackie stood up. Bell was not surprised at the sight of what she gripped in her left hand: the hatchet.

"This really isn't like me," Jackie said. She examined the hatchet, its keen edge, the stubby stock of wood around which she'd wrapped her hand, as if she had just noticed it, simply found it in her possession. "It's really not. But when Darla refused me, I had to stop her. You get that, right? My mother was all I ever had. I couldn't let Darla hurt her. I had to hurt Darla first. And I had a way." She raised the hatchet. "With this." She lowered it. Her voice faltered. "I didn't think about it. I just *did* it. When I saw I'd hit the back of her head, I wanted to scream. It was—it was the worst moment of my life. But I had no choice."

Jackie stopped. She was breathing hard, her shoulders rising and falling. There were, Bell saw, tears on her cheeks in response to the searing memory of what she'd done, the horrific act that—as Jackie saw it—she had been forced into committing.

Then the moment passed. Wonderingly, her voice steadily regaining its strength, she went on: "But you know what, Bell? Once it was done, it was somehow . . . okay. Isn't that strange? Darla was lying there, and I had to go up and take out the hatchet, and there was all the blood—oh my God, so much blood—but I had the funniest feeling. It was like I could hear my mother telling me that I'd done a good thing, and that everything was going to be fine."

"Yeah, well—she lied." Bell's voice was flat and hard.

"What did you say?" Jackie's voice, too, was hard; it had lost its dreamy edge. She tightened her grip on the hatchet.

"I said that your mother's ghost—or whatever the hell you think it was—lied to you. Everything is *not* going to be fine. You're so lost, Jackie. So terribly lost. You haven't even realized the implications of what I just told you."

"Shut up."

"Darla's grandmother was there at Wellwood, too. She was right there with Trexler and your grandmother. She got the patients ready. She was as guilty as they were. That's what the second diary is all about." Bell held it up, clutching it with the same ferocity with which Jackie held the hatchet. "It's a confession. Bessie Gilley's confession. And Darla didn't want the world to hear that. Just like you, she didn't want her family name tainted. She wouldn't have released it. She didn't bury it to keep it from *you*—she buried it to keep it from the *world*.

Do you know what that means, Jackie? *You didn't have to kill her.*"
Bell's voice shook. "But you never gave her a chance to tell you that.
You killed her first. You ruined your life for nothing."

For a few seconds, Jackie didn't move. She seemed to be ponder-
ing Bell's words, letting them gradually seep their way into her con-
sciousness. The hand that held the hatchet was down at her side.

And then, abruptly, she raised it again.

"You're the only one who knows," Jackie said calmly. She started
walking toward her.

Chapter Forty-eight

"Jackie—wait." Bell spoke hurriedly.

"I didn't want this. But there's no other way."

Bell felt a steep wave of fear. The lack of emotion in Jackie's voice now alarmed her. Jackie wasn't listening to her anymore. She could tell by her eyes—dark, empty, her mind turned inward.

She was listening to her mother, long dead, always present.

"I'm sorry, Bell." Jackie had closed to within ten feet.

"No. Please."

"I'm really sorry." Five feet. She raised the hatchet over her head, both hands on the handle.

"Jackie, for God's sake—"

From somewhere off to Bell's left came the sound of dog's crisp bark, followed by the mad thrashing of branches and more barks, linked and rising.

Jackie turned her head. The moment she did, Bell flew at her, going for her wrists, trying to dislodge the hatchet. Jackie fought her off, twisting wildly, spinning, wrenching her arm out of Bell's grip. They toppled onto the ground, Bell grunting, Jackie snarling. Bell's hands fought desperately for the hatchet; she clawed at Jackie's hand while the other woman kicked and cursed, desperate for leverage so that she could use the weapon. One blow at such close range would be fatal.

Another voice, sharp and hard, rang out from some distance away: "Drop the weapon! Now!"

It was Nick Fogelsong.

Even as he shouted, Bell was aware that a third person had joined her struggle, much closer than Nick could have been. A solid body had crashed in between her and Jackie, sinking big teeth into the other woman's wrist until she screamed and released her grip on the hatchet.

The person wasn't a person at all, Bell realized with a rush of gratitude. It was Arthur. Behind him, moving as fast as he could—which was a great deal slower than the dog—was Nick Fogelsong. He was breathing heavily, the air tearing in and out of his lungs, sweat glistening on his face.

He kicked away the hatchet. He reached down to give Bell a hand, pulling her up, slinging her to one side so that she'd be well out of Jackie's reach. But there was no need. All the fight had gone out of Jackie LeFevre. She wasn't moving. She lay flat on her back, eyes open, breathing hard, staring at the sky.

"Get up," Nick commanded.

She didn't answer.

He grabbed her wrist and yanked her to her feet. Jackie wouldn't look at him. To keep their eyes from meeting accidentally, she dropped her head like a person in prayer. She wouldn't lift it.

With the length of twine that hung from the carabiner on his belt, Nick secured her wrists behind her back. He did it nimbly and surely; he hadn't lost his touch. He pushed her forward so violently that she almost fell to her knees; at the last minute he yanked her upright again by the back of her collar.

Bell tried to get a quick read on him. She couldn't imagine what he was feeling: shock, betrayal, a pain that cut a groove in his soul as quick and deep as any acid. But he'd never show it. Anybody watching him now, Bell thought, anybody who saw how rough he was being with Jackie, would assume he'd never met the woman before. She was his prisoner. Nothing more.

"Take it easy, Nick," Bell said.

"Pam Harrison's on her way," he muttered, as if Bell hadn't

spoken. "Let's head back to the road." He glanced at Arthur, who stood nearby, panting heavily, alert as a sentry. For the first time, Nick seemed to relax a bit. "Sure glad I stopped by your place and picked up Lassie over there."

The mildness didn't last. Nick began to march forward, shoving Jackie ahead of him, not caring if she stumbled. How, Bell wondered again, was he feeling? This was *Jackie,* for God's sake. His lover. How was he—

"I said let's go," he shouted, giving Jackie another hard push.

Whatever he was feeling, he would keep it to himself for the time being, Bell knew. Or maybe forever. Nick being Nick, he might never tell her. Everybody had their secrets.

Chapter Forty-nine

When they had finished giving their statements to Sheriff Harrison, Bell and Nick walked slowly out of the courthouse and down the wide, worn gray steps. They paused at the bottom. For once, Bell wished it were colder; she wished the wind and the sky hadn't delivered up this incongruously nice day. She wanted it to be cold and dreary, to match the numbness she felt inside, the aftermath of shock and deep sadness. She shook her head. She started to share that with Nick, but decided not to. Later, maybe. They were taking separate vehicles to the same destination: Bell's big stone house on Shelton Avenue, where they would indulge in the luxury of comfortable chairs, drink, and food.

The two of them had just settled down in her living room, Nick on the couch, Bell in her favorite chair, Arthur on the floor next to her, when the first call came. It was Jake, demanding details. Bell put him on speakerphone. Now that he knew they were safe, Jake declared, he fully intended to rip Nick the proverbial new one for leaving him out of the action. Bell reminded Jake that he'd done precisely the same thing: He'd gone rogue in his search for Dixie Sue Folsom, and left them in the dark. Reluctantly, he'd conceded the point.

The next call came from Rhonda Lovejoy. Paperwork filed, duty discharged, she wanted to stop by with Mack—not as a prosecutor, but as a friend. And she intended to bring Marlene, Arthur's sister, for emotional support, in case Arthur needed it after his ordeal in the woods. Bell had texted Carla with a brief sketch of the afternoon's events; Carla called and announced she was driving over from Charleston forthwith.

"Gonna be a full house," Nick said after Bell ended the call with her daughter. He looked around the living room. "I've always liked this place. I remember the day you bought it. You stopped by the courthouse and you marched into my office and you said, 'I think I just made the worst mistake of my life. Either that, or it's the best move I ever made.'"

Bell laughed. "Jury's still out."

Nick was exhausted. He stretched out his legs, and then he arched his back. That made him wince, so he stopped. When he looked over at Arthur, the dog's tail thumped four times.

"Your buddy there wouldn't come with me at first," Nick said. "When I used the spare key you'd given me and came charging in the front door, he barked at me for about five minutes. Then he just stared. Like he was waiting for the reference check to come through."

"Sounds like Arthur."

"Finally I told him the truth. 'I've got a bad feeling, pooch. Ten bucks says she's heading to Wellwood. Bet she's gotten herself into a hell of a mess. Let's go rescue her.' He got me the leash himself. Held it in his mouth until I took it and put it on him."

"He didn't."

"No. He didn't. But he *would* have, if he'd had any idea what the hell I was saying."

Bell laughed again.

"Once we got to the woods," Nick went on, "his nose took over. He tracked you like a hound with a fox. Headed straight to where you were. All I had to do was hang on and let him drag me."

"He's a determined dog."

"Brave, too. Didn't hesitate to go after an armed woman." Nick frowned. They had come back round to difficult territory again: Jackie LeFevre. He grew somber. "Before anybody else gets here, I need to say something about me and Jackie." His voice was low. His embarrassment, Bell knew, was acute. "Look, Bell, I had no idea she was capable of—"

"Good God, Nick, of course you didn't," she said, interrupting him. "*She* didn't know she was capable of that."

"When I think of her with that hatchet—and going after you—" He put a hand to his forehead. "I don't know how to think about this. With what she turned out to be."

"She'll be punished. The arraignment's tomorrow."

"Yeah." He paused. "I tried to talk to her before Pam took her away to lockup. Didn't work. She still wouldn't look at me. Not sure what I would've said, anyway."

"She might change her mind later. She's going to need a friend, Nick."

"She can look somewhere else." He grunted. The grunt was Nick's version of *No friggin' way.*

Bell knew how hard it was for him to talk about personal matters. She expected him to change the subject at any second.

Bingo, she thought, when he began speaking again.

"I called Brenda Gilley on the way over here," he said. "Filled her in on Jackie's arrest. She had some news, too." Bell waited. "Joe took a bad turn last night. She's decided that hospice care is the next step. He doesn't have very long."

There was nothing to say. Bell had known Nick for so many years, and they had weathered such a variety of crises and near-crises, from shootouts to stakeouts, from her divorce to his breakup with Mary Sue, from frustrations and disappointments to celebrations and simple good times, as well as an untold number of long talks over pie and coffee, that she knew he'd feel her compassion for him, her deep and plangent empathy for what he was going through as he contemplated his friend's imminent death. She didn't have to sully the moment with a canned platitude.

They sat in silence.

"When I think about Wellwood," Nick finally said, "I can't help but think about Mary Sue." His wife had been diagnosed with schizophrenia shortly after their marriage. She was doing much better now, but there had been times early on, Bell knew, when her struggles had been a challenge for Nick. Watching Mary Sue suffer had almost undone him. "If she'd lived back in those days," he added, "she would've been one of the ones they operated on. Thank the Lord we're more enlightened today."

Bell nodded. "Absolutely."

She thought he might go on, thought he might express some bitterness at the fact that he'd been loyal and devoted to Mary Sue throughout her long ordeal, until her doctors found the medications to stabilize her—and then she had turned around and rejected him.

But he didn't. When he spoke again, Nick changed the subject back to the new woman he'd lost his heart to.

"Can't help but wonder what Jackie really feels about me."

"You know the answer to that. Your relationship started before anybody knew anything about any hidden diaries. She was sincere."

"Sincere? Maybe. But did she love me? Or was it a fling? And am I just a damned idiot who likes feeling young again?" He repeated his question, with a small but crucial change in tense: "Does she love me?"

"I don't know."

In a soft voice, a voice she could not recall ever having come out of Nick Fogelsong before, he said, "I really did love her, Bell. And you know the worst part? I still do."

"That's not the worst part," she replied. "That's the best. Shows what you're capable of. After all you've been through, you can still love with your whole heart. Damned good thing to know in this cold old world of ours, don't you think?"

Chapter Fifty

Jake ended the call to Bell.

He was happy to hear that she and Nick weren't hurt, happy that the case seemed to be over. His call of inquiry had been necessary— they were his friends—but the truth was, he didn't really want to talk to anyone. Not now.

He was in the living room. He could hear Molly in their bedroom, hear her muffled crying.

Molly.

Crying.

The two words didn't go together. Not because she wasn't sensitive, not because she didn't feel things deeply—she did. She was the most empathetic person he'd ever known. But she had learned, early in her career as an EMT, the rugged truth that *feeling* emotion and *showing* emotion belonged to different universes. If you were going to be effective in your service to others, Molly believed—and had expressed to Jake many times, during the conversations that helped seal his love for her—you could feel, but you couldn't show. The showing didn't help anything. It only got in the way of helping.

But everything had changed now. The world was upside down. Molly was crying, and there was nothing he could do for her. Never, not even in the first days after his injury and the breadth of the catastrophe that had befallen him was just becoming clear, had he felt so helpless.

He'd only heard her cry one other time since he'd met her: on a night two years ago when Malik went missing, wandering out of the yard when Molly was taking a work call. Neighbors quickly organized a search. Hours later, they found Malik two miles away, curled up in the fetal position in a tool shed in a stranger's backyard, confused and cold and distraught. Once home, he was fine. Ravenously hungry—but fine. He ate four bowls of Honey Nut Cheerios in a row. Jake, refilling the bowl each time while Molly stroked the back of Malik's head, was amazed.

Molly had been crying ever since the phone call that afternoon from Linda McComas. It was a good thing Malik was taking a nap, Jake thought; it would be scary for him to see his big sister so upset. It wasn't normal. Malik needed normal.

Linda's message was brief. That morning, Andrea Krieger had showed up at Linda's office. She claimed she was clean. *I found the Lord,* she said. *I want Casey. I'm working the program. So I want my boy. You tell that judge I want my boy just as soon as he's fit to come home. I'm his mama. I know my rights.*

"Granted, the timing sucks," Linda had acknowledged at the end of her call. *You think?* Jake wanted to yell back at her, because he and Molly had informed Linda, just the day before, that they'd made up their minds. After long conversations with each other and much deliberation, putting aside their apprehensions, they had decided to ask the court if they could foster Casey Krieger, with the expectation of adopting him. They knew it would be challenging. They were ready for that. Commitment made, they had embraced. Jake had never thought he could feel happier than he'd felt on the day Molly moved in with him. He was wrong.

And now: this.

Well, he had warned Molly, hadn't he? Yes, he had. He had warned her about hope, about its treachery. She didn't listen.

Chapter Fifty-one

They could tell nothing from the face of Glenna Stavros. Jake wondered if this was a skill she had developed early in her career to help her do her job. A nurse, surely, could not let her expression reflect the prognosis for the patients in her care, could she? The patients' loved ones would be desperate to interpret everything they saw: a frown, a smile, a blink, a twitch, a scratch of the chin or a raise of an eyebrow. It would be intolerable. And so she'd developed a perfect deadpan to aid her life-sustaining work.

Either that or she was practicing for a poker tournament.

Three weeks had passed since Jackie LeFevre had been arrested and charged with the murder of Darla Gilley. She awaited trial in the Raythune County Jail. Her attorney had filed a motion for a change of venue, claiming that Jackie was too well known in Raythune County to receive a fair and impartial trial here; the jury pool would be irreparably tainted. The judge's decision was expected any day.

Glenna had called Jake and Molly an hour ago and asked them to come to Evening Street. She greeted them in the small lobby, where a blue-uniformed security guard sat behind a particleboard desk. When he saw Jake struggling to get the wheelchair over the metal strip of the threshold, he'd jumped up to help, but Molly had waved him back. *She understands me,* Jake thought, *right down to the bone. If*

I need help, I'll ask for it. And I have to ask too often as it is. Don't need any damned volunteers.

He knew he could handle the threshold at Evening Street. It just took him a little extra time. He had to back up and try again, making sure the wheels hit it at the right angle.

"Glad you could come," Glenna said. She looked very tired. That was the only thing Jake could discern from her face: fatigue. Not the nature of the news she was about to divulge.

"I can't stay long," Molly said. No apology in her tone; this was business, this was reality. She was herself again. No more tears. She and Jake had not discussed her lapse. The idea of raising a child to-gether, those hopes—that had not been discussed, either. They were living in limbo now. Not a bad limbo, and not an uncomfortable one, just a sort of holding pattern for their souls. They kept busy, which helped; Molly took extra shifts, Jake was rewriting security protocols for county offices, a side job to get him through the fallow periods when the agency had few cases.

They had not mentioned Casey Krieger's name since the day they found out he was lost to them forever.

"I'm working the overnight tonight," Molly added crisply, by way of explanation. "Been doing that for two solid weeks. We're swamped with calls. Really messes with the schedule."

Glenna nodded. "Same thing around here. Not sure how we're going to get through the holidays, frankly. I try to give people time off to be with their families, but we're a twenty-four/seven opera-tion. Makes it hard." A rueful smile. "Like I'm telling you something you don't know. An EMT squad can't just say, 'Sorry about your emergency—I'm drinking eggnog and decorating the tree.' Right?"

Molly laughed. "If I thought I could get by with that, I'd give it a try."

Jake was feeling impatient. He wanted to know why she'd called and asked them to come. He was ambivalent about the place; the last time he and Molly had visited Evening Street, they'd left with an armful of shattered dreams.

"Come on in," Glenna said.

The guard pushed the button under his desk that opened the heavy door. Inside, the clinic was bathed in the same blue-white glow that always suffused it, with the same sounds and rhythms. Monitors beeped softly. Nurses moved between the rows of cribs, bending over to check on the infants who fidgeted and whimpered.

Glenna led them over to the area she used as an office, the one with her desk positioned below the single window. As they approached, Bell rose from a chair alongside that desk.

"Hey," Jake said. "Didn't expect to see you here."

"Didn't expect to *be* here," Bell said. "Just stopped by on the spur of the moment. Glenna asked me to stick around for another few minutes." She nodded to Molly. "Hey, Molly."

"Bell. You don't have to get up."

"Actually, I do. I need to get home." Bell looked at Glenna. There had been no explanation about why she ought to stay; now, surely, she could leave. "Snow's expected and I've got a dog to walk."

Bell had not told anyone—not Nick, not Jake, not Rhonda, not even her daughter, Carla—that she'd resumed her visits to Evening Street. It wasn't a secret; it just wasn't anyone else's business. The ritual was the same. She would chat with Glenna, and then Glenna would pick out an infant who needed to be calmed by a few minutes of being held in a rocking chair. Casey Krieger was among the sickest of the children here. Bell had only touched him a few times—he was still far too frail to be rocked—but she had a small secret and completely unrealistic hope that many, many years from now, when Casey was an adult and looked back on his life, he might have a faint, barely there memory of a woman who had leaned over his crib and wished him well.

Tonight, in particular, she had come because she'd been thinking too hard about Darla Gilley and Jackie LeFevre, and about wasted lives and deaths in the woods.

But she didn't like to talk about why she came here. It smacked of self-aggrandizement: *Look at wonderful me, visiting babies born to drug-addict moms. Aren't I just so noble?* She hated the idea of anyone knowing other than the Evening Street staff.

"Glenna's a friend," Bell said. She hoped that would suffice as an explanation. It was true—but it wasn't the whole truth.

She started to move past Molly. Glenna touched her arm. "I'd like you to hang out for a few more minutes, Bell. If you can. Need your help with something."

Now all three of them—Bell, Molly, and Jake—were perplexed.

The nurse addressed herself to Jake and Molly. "Do you two mind if I let Bell know what's going on?"

They both shrugged. It didn't matter now, did it? No. It didn't.

"Okay. Good." Glenna turned to Bell. "Molly and Jake were all set to apply to adopt Casey Krieger. Linda McComas was putting through the paperwork."

"That's great," Bell said. This was new information to her, which was entirely appropriate; it was a private matter between Molly, Jake, and Child Protective Services. But why was Glenna telling her now?

"The mother changed her mind," Glenna continued. "First she wanted to keep her baby, and stayed clean long enough to persuade Linda that it was a real possibility. Then she relapsed. Then she showed up and said she was back in rehab. So she said—again—that she wanted to raise him herself." She closed her eyes and shook her head. When she opened them again, she said, "Thank God Casey doesn't know about any of this."

Jake's voice was brusque. "Okay, now Bell's up to speed. Why are we here?"

Molly put her hand on the back of his neck, first sweeping away his long hair so that she could touch skin. "Easy, Jake."

He let a moment go by. "Fine. Can we get to the point?"

"Sure," Glenna responded. "Look, there's no doubt that Andrea Krieger is unreliable. She's a drug addict. She says she wants to beat it, says she wants a different kind of life. Does she mean it? Sure. At the time. For the few seconds it takes to utter the homily—absolutely. And then she slides back into her same old habits with her same old friends. The affirmations and the promises are all forgotten. But she won't give up permanent custody for now—not as long as she thinks there's a chance of ever staying clean.

"In this case," Glenna continued, shrugging at the perversity of the situation, "Andrea's interest in Casey—as sporadic as it is—is bad news for us. And by 'us,' I mean the people standing here right now, the people who care about him. We're a club. A special club. Team Casey, I call us. The only members not present right now are Deputy Brinksneader and his wife, Holly. They've been coming by every few days to check on him."

"And?" Jake said. Restless, tired of hearing speeches, he rolled his chair back and forth.

"It's true that the court will always rule in favor of a birth parent," Glenna stated. "As long as there's even a shred of proof that the parent is trying to get sober, and as long as the parent says she wants the kid—that's it."

"Understood." Molly's voice was scraped absolutely clean of any emotion.

"However," Glenna said, "I saw how you two reacted to Casey when you held him. I saw a real bond there."

Molly's face changed slightly, like the surface of a lake stirred by the faintest breath of wind. She nodded, and once again, she stroked the back of Jake's neck.

"I know there are other babies here that might be available," Glenna went on, "but I don't think that would be the best idea. Not after I saw you with Casey. You'll never be able to forget him. Never be able to forget the feeling of holding him. Sometimes people tell me that these babies are basically all the same, because they all suffer from the same thing, but they're not. They have individual personalities, even though they're just days and weeks old. And you two and Casey—well, I saw it. I saw the connection."

"So where does that leave us?" Jake snapped. He was irritated and didn't mind showing it. "What are you saying? Just go home and grieve? His mother's not giving him up. She wants to keep him."

"Today she does." Glenna shrugged. "Tomorrow, maybe not. I've seen addicts like Andrea change their minds dozens of times. Sometimes in the same day. Sometimes in the same *hour*. And so my advice is—hang in there."

"Meaning what?" Jake pressed her.

"Meaning you should tell Linda McComas that you're all in. Don't withdraw your petition for adoption. Make it clear to her—and she'll make it clear to the court—that if the day comes when Andrea finally says 'I can't do this' and gives up her parental rights, you'll be there. I've seen that happen. I've seen it work out. Many times."

"When he's what—fifteen years old? Or sixteen?" Jake muttered.

"No." Glenna was firm. "A few days from now. Or weeks. I would be surprised if it was months. Bell?" She turned. "You've seen it too, right?"

"I have." Bell spoke with great care. She wanted to keep any sentiment out of her voice. She was stating a fact, not arguing on behalf of an action she believed that Jake and Molly ought to take. She wasn't an advocate for either side.

And that, Bell realized, was surely why Glenna had asked her to stay. Because Jake and Molly trusted her to tell them the truth, even if it was an unpalatable one. Bell's reputation as a hard-ass—blunt-speaking, tough as old boots when need be—was just what was needed.

"Andrea Krieger's life is a total disaster," Bell went on. "Casey is the one good thing that's ever come out of that life. Period. Would you two make amazing parents? God, yes. Might Andrea be a miserable failure as a parent, dragging Casey down with her until she finally realizes she can't do it? Right again. But she's his mom. That's the bottom line.

"I've seen it go both ways. I've seen wonderful couples like you who were forced to say good-bye to a child they instantly loved—and I've seen it go the other way, too. The mother realizes she'll never get it together enough to raise a kid and finally gives up custody. If you want odds, statistics, about which way it might turn out—I don't have any. No such thing as a smart bet."

Jake's voice was anguished as he looked up at his partner. He didn't care who was listening. "I don't think I can do it, Molly. I just *can't*. I can't wait and hope. It hurts too much. I don't want to hope anymore."

"We can't give up on hope," was Molly's quiet reply.

"Why not? Why the hell not? What's so special about hope?"

"Sweetheart," Molly said, and the word caught Bell by surprise, because she'd never heard Molly Drucker use any sort of endearment. "It's all we've got. It's all anybody's got."

Molly stroked Jake's hair. She swept it off his collar. Her hand stayed on his shoulder. The gesture, like the endearment, was a revelation to Bell. This was a new side to a woman she thought she knew.

"Stay as long as you like," Glenna said, but neither Jake nor Molly acknowledged the remark. They were looking out the small window above her desk. They were a single unit now, fused by Molly's hand on Jake's shoulder and by the decision they had to make, a decision that would affect the rest of their lives: to hope or not to hope.

Glenna signaled to Bell with her eyes, and the two of them left the office area. Glenna went back to work, checking the monitors on the rows of cribs, one by one. Bell walked over to the big oak rocker in the corner, and soon a nurse brought over an infant who was well enough to be rocked, and placed her in Bell's arms.

"Ernestine," the nurse murmured to Bell, telling her the baby's name, so that Bell could whisper it as she rocked, reminding the tiny being of her specialness, of her absolute uniqueness in the long history of the world. *Such an old-fashioned name,* Bell thought, and she wondered, as she held her and rocked back and forth, back and forth, if perhaps a grandmother or great-grandmother had named her, because the mother was too high, or too indifferent, or maybe even dead from an overdose, and the older relatives had taken over, naming her and—in a perfect world, which this one wasn't—loving her.

When Bell glanced toward Glenna's office a few minutes later, she saw that they were still there, Molly still standing next to Jake's chair, hand still on his shoulder.

And they were still looking out the small window above the desk.

Bell, cradling Ernestine on her chest, changed her position in the rocker just the slightest bit, so that she could see what they were looking at through that window.

The snow had started up again, each flake as soft and distinct as a separate prayer. Soon the street would be covered, and the sidewalks, and the cars and the roofs of the houses, and beyond and above the little town the mountains, too, would slowly vanish beneath the drapery folds of snow, the entirety transformed by the hush and the sweep and the density of it.

The snow would fall all through the night. In the morning the world would be white again. A light wind would tousle the top layer, rearranging the closely packed crystals. That wind would whisper of fresh starts and it would promise new dawns. It would murmur of clean slates and second chances. But the only people able to hear its voice were those who had been deeply wounded and thus, through the hard lesson of their pain, had learned how to listen.